DRAGON GOD

E E Montgomery

Copyright Information

Published by
E E MONTGOMERY
www.eemontgomery.com[1]

---

1. http://www.eemontgomery.com

Australian Publishers Online

EBOOK ISBN: 978-0-9876316-2-6
Print Book ISBN: 978-0-9876316-4-0

Also by E E Montgomery:

Published by Dreamspinner Press:
Between Love and Honor The Courage to Love
Ordinary People
The Planet Whisperer
Warrior Pledge
What About Him
JUST LIFE
Just His Type
Just Like a Date
Just in Time
Just the Way You Are

Independent Publications:
Shattered Lives
Tangled up in Blue (written with Fiona Greene and Danielle Birch)
Shattered Lives in Queermance Vol 2., an anthology published by
Clan Destine Press, 2015
The Overseer in Darkest Depths, an anthology published by Vision
Writers, Brisbane, 2017

ABOUT DRAGON GOD

Dragon God is the chronological sequel to Warrior Pledge (Dreamspinner Press). The story in Dragon God stands alone but your reading pleasure would be enhanced if you also read Warrior Pledge.
DRAGON GOD IS A FANTASY story of taking responsibility for your life and making right the mistakes of your past.

Fisher has lived a life of hardship and horror and made many decisions that harmed others. He now has an opportunity for a new life, a new beginning, where he can live in harmony with the world and the people in it. When he discovers an elixir he helped create is killing innocent people, he knows his only way to freedom is to destroy the sources of the elixir. He must confront the circumstances of his childhood and his banishment from the city of his birth in order to prevent more deaths.

Unfortunately, the destruction of his past lingers and everywhere Fisher goes fire and death follow. It takes an encounter with the Dragon King, who reveals Fisher's true nature, and the love of a dragon god for Fisher to embrace who he truly is and begin to move forward.

MAP OF THALAZAR

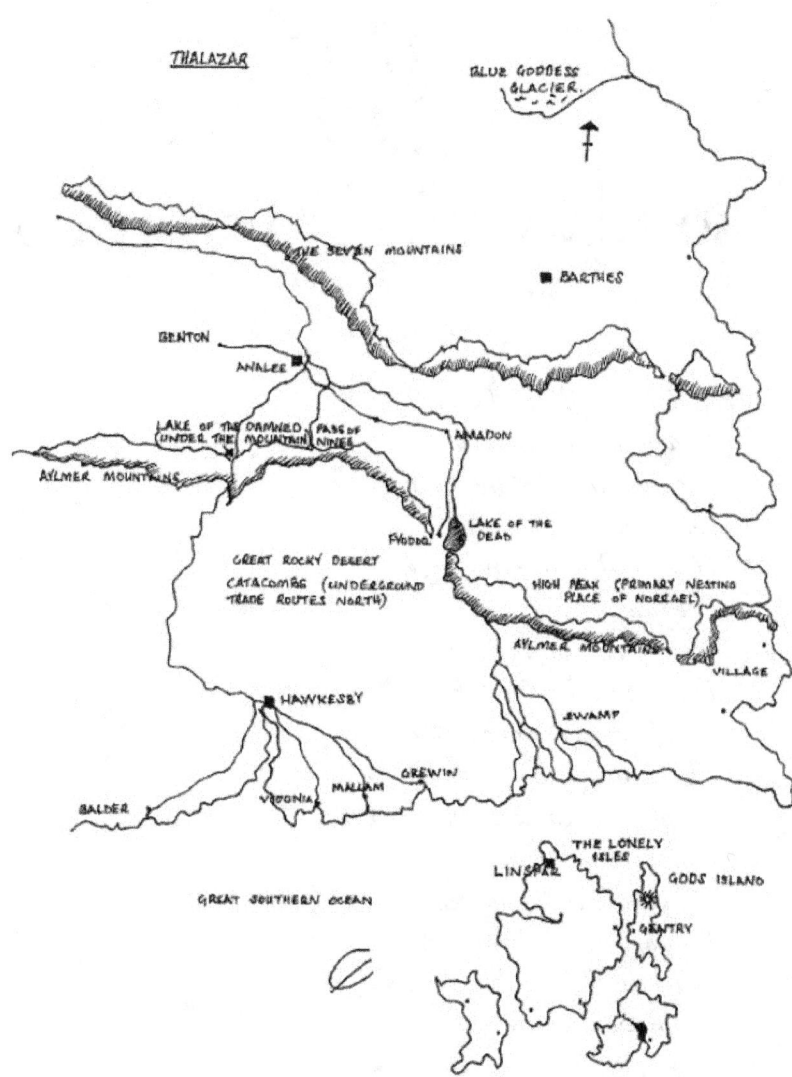

SONGS OF THE DRAGON GODS

Dragon Gods

WHEN THE WORLD WAS young
And people swam in the sea
The dragons ruled the land
Each one
Hard as the stone they bore.
The eldest, Diatera,
Carves a life for her people
Deep beneath the earth
And forgives not one transgression.
Far in the north where ice flows
Sapphirus, beautiful and determined,
Nurtures her wards
And becomes one of them.
Rubéo, fierce and protective,
Rides the plains
Reading the sky
Through tall grasses.
Laperoni, warm and beloved,
Guards the jungles
Walking amongst them
To protect the ones he loves.

6

Opalesa, pale as the
Sands that give her life,
Weeps for her people,
Abandoned in the dust.
Each dragon will find
Of the people
Their one Concubine
Blessed to live and serve,
A treasure above all.

Song of the Blue Goddess

BELOVED LOCKED IN FROZEN world
   Trapped by fear and hate
   Rising new freedom
   Back into being
   Everyone that sees
   Everything you need
   Never could be
   Swimming in the blue depths
   Falling sparkling
   Forever through the clouds
   Of the ancient river.
   The danger has passed
   The black has risen
   And so must you.

Concubine Mine

WHEN THE DRAGONS RETURN,
   So will the concubine.
   Indigo will tumble down mountains
   And burn in ice that releases
   Sapphire wonder.
   Past and future collide.
   Dragon king claims kin while
   Air is washed away and shared.
   The brown and cream comes home to
   Silence loud and darkness lightened.
   Heart-soul recognized, the Concubine
   Wanders into dragon land,
   Claimed.

The Song of Promise

THIS SONG IS FOR YOU
You know who you are
You are everything to me
Everything I was
Everything I am
Everything I will be
Is for you
Because of you
We'll meet in the water
And breathe each other in
We'll fly in the air
And float in the same breath
Your blood
Will be my blood
Your victories
My surrender
Our lives entwined
Together we'll
Merge and grow
Blue and gray
Under one sun
Two moons
Forever lovers

Dragon Pledge

WHEREVER YOU ARE, I will be
Wherever you go, I will follow

Until the end of my days.
You complete me
Always.

You're my chosen
Mine to protect and cherish
Mine to hold and love
If you leave me, I'll come with you
If you need to be alone,
I'll stay and you'll be safe
If you tell me to go away,
I'll go and I'll wait,
Watching for your return.
I'm yours.

CHAPTER ONE

GAELAN DRAPED HIMSELF over the crest of the volcano. His forelegs hung comfortably over the uppermost rock while his hindlegs rested sturdily on the jagged outcrop, propping him in exactly the right position. His tail swished slowly from side to side in the warm air rising from below and his wings twitched where they sat folded against the spines that ran down the center of his back. He rested his chin on the rock and stared at the sky.

The two moons, Makai and Nayeli, would come together that night in their never-ending fight for supremacy. He knew Nayeli would win. She was larger and brighter and closer to the isles than Makai could ever hope to be.

But Makai never gave up. Every thousand years he'd try once more to be the most powerful and for a few seconds, it would seem like he could win. Then Nayeli would move in front of him, swallow him whole and spit him out the other side.

Gaelan knew Makai would regain his strength but in those first seconds when Nayeli rejected him, he would seem ragged and dull, ready to concede defeat. He wouldn't, though. By the next night, he'd have moved farther from Nayeli and would be as bright and beautiful as he always was, his face a calming motley of cream and brown.

Shortly before the first time he'd witnessed the moons' fight, his mother told him Makai would bring love to him. Then she'd flown north, as was her destiny. He had waited, but his mother had never returned, and once the fight between Nayeli and Makai was over, no one came for him. Decades later, he'd decided it must have been because he'd been too young. The next battle would be the one.

The second time Makai and Nayeli battled, Gaelan had sat eager and watchful, sure it would happen then. He was an adult, with wards of his own to watch over and protect. But again, Makai limped away and left no one to watch over him as he watched over his wards.

This would be the third battle Gaelan witnessed. He had traveled far in the intervening years, returning a mere fifty years before. Deep in his soul, he knew there was no hope of him finding love. There were no others of his kind left in the land save his mother, who ruled the Icy Wastes far to the north, and would never return. His destiny was to live, adored and worshiped by his wards as much as he was feared by them, but alone.

Always alone.

Gaelan sighed as the moons moved inexorably closer. The light intensified, making every shadow in the valley, every village and every house, shimmer with gilded silver.

His wards left their homes and gathered in the village green, torches glimmering fitfully in the valley breeze. Softly, the chanting began and rolled across the land like a whistle in the dark. Almost imperceptibly, the shining rooftops dimmed like neglected jewels and the torches waved above dark heads.

The chanting grew faster and louder. Frantic undercurrents were held in check only by the soft drumbeats that, one by one, joined them.

Gaelan lifted his head and watched as Nayeli pushed in front of Makai, eventually covering the moon completely. His heartbeat thudded in time with the drums that beat across the valley and he waited for Makai to fight his way out.

Long after the time he thought the smaller moon should push through and emerge, there was still no sign of him. He dared not even blink. Makai would emerge soon, Nayeli releasing him, and he didn't want to miss a moment of his victory. It wouldn't be a victory of power; never that. But it would be a victory of survival.

A ruby red light shimmered and pulsed between Nayeli and The Lonely Isles, and across the waters in between. He jerked upright. In the valley, the drums ceased and the screams and wails of his wards intensified in their panic to escape. Below, dark shapes ran and tumbled in a blood-red landscape.

Gaelan froze, his heart pounding in time with the pulsing red light. His panting breath wafted smoke down the mountain. Was Makai going to win this time?

The red faded to pink and Makai emerged. He was just a sliver at first, tired and dull from his fight, but he kept pulling away until Nayeli had no option but to release him. As their connection severed, the last of the pink winked out, leaving the land once again awash with bright white light of the two moons in the full.

The valley echoed with the cries of his wards, but the tone of terror changed from one of fear of the unknown to one of pain.

Gaelan scrambled over the lip of the volcano. His wards needed his protection and, regardless of the portent of the moons, it was his duty to provide it. He ran, dislodging loose boulders and rocks, hearing them tumble and crash down the mountainside.

The tone of the screams changed. At least some of his wards had heard the rockslide and knew what it meant.

His wings unfurled as he reached the edge of the escarpment and he floated, weightless, on the air currents for a few seconds before pushing his wings down and turning toward the town. As he came closer, he trumpeted a warning.

As he flew over the town, the moons moved and the light grew stronger with each second. He watched his shadow flow over the buildings and streets, deepening from gray to black. Below him, people ran for their doors, the celebrations forgotten.

He continued flying throughout the night. When the moons finally separated, Makai was whole again, and he left the land and flew low and fast over the ocean. As the dawn sparked the water with multi-colored droplets, he dipped his wings and sprayed rainbows of color through the air.

Gaelan swooped over the village one last time before he began the ascent up his mountain. Linspar had seen the most violence during the night but Gentry, below, had generated the most fear. They were quiet now as the edge of the sun pushed the darkness over the top of his mountain. The stronger light would soon reach the rooftops and his wards would emerge to take stock and begin their day. After the fight between Makai and Nayeli, he needed to walk among them and soothe their fears.

He flew over the mouth of his volcano then raised his wings, tail and head to slow his descent and landed softly on the far side of the mountain where the lip of the volcano dipped lower and muddy brown rocks were scattered down the gentle slope. He picked up one of the crystals, his violet talons sharply contrasting with the yellow-brown stone.

He cupped his hands in front of his face, closed his eyes and breathed a thin stream of blue flame onto the stone. As it heated, his scales popped and sizzled, softening in equal degrees with the hardening of the stone.

A shiver ran through him as his scales sank into the soft human skin he'd learned to adopt in his second millennium. The deep violet shimmered and darkened as it softened and became a rich umber. His claws shrank into soft-pink fingernails and toenails and his sparse mane thickened into flowing curling locks of hair so black it shone blue in the light.

Beams of violet light shone from his eyes and he blinked until it faded. He knew his eyes had taken on a more human appearance—violet-blue with round black pupils. His skin was now the pale brown the stone had been.

In his hands, he still held the stone, changed to a brilliant violet-blue from the heat of his breath.

Gaelan picked up another stone and breathed fire on it, humming his clothing into being. When the stone turned blue, his clothing dropped into place around his solid frame—soft, worn jeans and an equally worn cotton button-down shirt, both in deep blue, faded to violet in places. His boots were black, creased in comfortable places, the soles soft and pliable.

On his back he wore a backpack the same brown as the stones scattered around him, and just large enough to hold a change of clothes, a jacket, a blanket and, when he got it, some food.

He took the backpack off and stuffed the two tanzanites in amongst his clothes. They'd provide him with enough money to travel through the Isles and check on his people before he headed north to search of his mother. She'd be able to tell him the portent of the red light during the eclipse.

Finally ready, he looked around and groaned. He was three thousand years old and he still couldn't remember to shift forms lower down the mountain where walking was easier. At this altitude, his change would have gone unnoticed, hidden behind the steam and fog that wreathed the mountaintop, and the ragged rises and falls of the landscape.

He settled his backpack on his shoulders and began the trek down the rocky slope. It would take him nearly two days to reach his wards' small village where he could catch the ferry across to Linspar.

CHAPTER TWO

THE BRINY SMELL OF the sea thickened the closer they came to shore, mixing with the nose-curling odor of dead fish, sweet fruit-bat feces and unwashed humanity.

Fisher shifted from foot to foot as the tenders were brought alongside the ship and cargo was unloaded. Finally, with the air still and the sun high and hot, passengers tottered down the gangplank and onto the last tender. Fisher sat where he was directed, his gaze never leaving the land they headed toward.

The broad, clipped tones of the Lonely Isles, so similar to those of the Grewin Peninsular, washed over him as the other passengers talked. As he listened, he silently practiced the tones, determined to sound like a local within a week.

His breathing quickened as, with one last wooden groan and bump, the boat settled against the jetty. He jostled forward, never allowing more than a few inches between him and the person in front.

His first few steps off the boat were stumbling ones as the boards on the jetty refused to move in time with the waves. Fisher's pack bumped against the upper curve of his buttocks as he overtook the other passengers and crew transporting the last of the cargo to the waiting warehouses along the shore.

The boards gave way to sand, and he scrambled up the worn slope to the compacted gravel road that ran parallel to the shore.

On the other side of the crowded street was a neat line of faded shops, their awnings up to protect their wares from the noonday sun. The skies were clear, norrgel-free, but Fisher still felt antsy out in the open. He slipped between two shops, the narrow alley providing both shade and comfort.

Sweat dribbled down his back and he clenched his hands against the desire to hide in one of the garbage bins lining the narrow alley. It wasn't all about the norrgel. The last time he'd spent more than a few hours under the unending skies, he'd been ten. The catacombs in the desert, no matter how dangerous the people in them might be, never left him feeling as unprotected as an empty sky.

There were no catacombs in the Icy Wastes, where he'd lived as a child, just miles upon miles of undulating plains, green in the spring, brown in the short summer, and eye-blinding white throughout the long winter. His heart pounded as he stared at the strip of sky visible above him. He could live in the open again. It would be easy if there were no norrgel here.

Sweat slid down his neck and he wiped his damp hands on his thighs. He slipped his pack off and rested it atop his feet as he leaned against the rough brick wall.

Gradually, the lack of norrgel screeches became less scary and the sounds of sellers hawking their wares and buyers bargaining for the best price brought its own level of comfort. His breathing slowed and he began to separate the smells and noise around him into identifiable actions.

Time to go to work. He needed food he could carry easily and enough of it so he didn't have to stop and talk to people. The fewer people who noticed him, the better.

He watched and listened, practicing speech patterns and checking the application of the concealing paste was smooth on his cheeks. He adjusted his clothing so it looked enough like the locals' loosely-draped coverings that he'd blend in. There was nothing he could do about his height.

He left his position, slouched as much as he could, and matched the pace of the crowds of people wandering through the marketplace. He made one pass between the stalls, then doubled back, using the busy groups to camouflage his movements.

The shadows had lengthened by the time he had acquired all he needed. He stopped briefly at a gem merchant but quickly moved on, several small but perfect gems surreptitiously slipped into his hand. He stepped in front of a large and noisy group of men when a cry went up behind him. "Wait! Stop!"

Shit. Five years ago no one would have noticed. Five years ago, he had a home. The Exiles weren't everyone's idea of family but he had lived with them a long time. That was gone. After what he'd done to them, they'd kill him on sight.

"The tall one! Stop him!"

They were on his tail. Fisher darted between shoppers, shoving people aside when there wasn't enough room for him to move swiftly. Their cries and the clatter of wares falling echoed behind him.

The sounds of pursuit kept his feet swift, just as they had when he ran from the Imperials in the Analee Valley. In his mind, he heard again the call 'traitor' from the Yeudan prisoners, the call repeated by the Imperials, as he escaped back into the mountains. Any idea he'd had of allying himself to the Mafdeti had shattered when the dragons had flown overhead, searching for him.

There was nowhere he could go. No peoples in the north would take him in. Every one of them thought him a traitor. Foolishly, he'd thought it might be different here, that he could make a clean start, build a new life.

Perhaps he could, but it wouldn't happen if he was caught.

He ducked into a nearby alley, swiftly moved to the other end and wound a cream scarf around his head in the local style. A few more seconds saw the food, water bladder and gems moved into a hidden compartment in the bottom of his pack.

By the time he left the protection of the buildings, the area was quiet again, the people going about their business.

He joined the edges of a rag-tag group of youths.

"Oh ai," he said. "Where'n ya temple be?"

"Yon off t'boat from Grewin, he?" the tallest boy asked.

"Who t'know?" responded Fisher.

"Ah can always tell you Grewins," the boy said proudly. "Ya'n always talk odd, he."

Fisher drew out the syllables in his words, taking on the stretched tones of the uneducated fisherman he'd known in the Exile camps. "Oh ai. I's told ya temple'd have work for me."

"Ya. There's always hiring for t'farms near the demon now's they've stopped so many sacrifices." The boy pointed up the hill.

Fisher could see a castle at the top, the dark granite looming over the town. "Temple's utter side of the castle, he," said the boy.

If the priests granted him sanctuary, he could find work on the farms or even within the temple. Within a couple of months, no one would remember he was a stranger.

He turned toward the castle, ignoring the distance he was putting between himself and the coming battle on the mainland. He'd grown up in the Icy Wastes, born in the Yeudan capital, but that didn't make it his battle.

Checa, Heath, Rim and Ardelle had their armies and their dragons. They'd chased him away with the threat of death to traitors. They didn't need or want him, no matter how much information he could share with them about the people who'd banished his mother.

Outside the marketplace, the crowds thinned. The buildings were more widely spaced and the traffic was horse-drawn more than on foot. Fisher's coin purse swung heavily from the chain attached to the inside of his trousers, no lighter than it had been before he landed in Linspar.

He walked purposefully, nodding at anyone who focused on him, but not engaging them. One wide street curved into another, turning and twisting its way up the hill. At each juncture, he took the road that climbed toward the castle. After twenty minutes walking, he turned a corner around a tall building and came to an abrupt halt.

Less than a hundred feet away was a black gate. It was made of thin metal pipes intricately woven together to form a stylized crown. On either side of the gate was a thick hedge that hid everything except the pathway to a large black granite building. It had dragon gargoyles perched atop the corners of the symmetrically-designed portico.

In the shadows under the dragons was a large door inlaid with clear crystals that glowed in the same crown design as the gate. Guards wearing a white and blue-violet uniform flanked the door and several more patrolled between the gate and the building.

The castle.

Fisher stepped onto the road, intending to follow the fence around to the temple. As he stepped forward, a heavy hand landed on his shoulder.

"Got you," said a dark voice.

Even as he flinched away, another hand grabbed his arm. "Don't bother."

Two soldiers flanked him, and two more joined them, breathing hard from their pursuit. "Thought you'd got away, did you? You'll have plenty of time to think while you wait for the Viscount to hand down sentence." They tugged him toward the castle.

Fisher used the hold on his arms for leverage, lifted his legs and kicked. The soldier to his right when down with a scream, his knee bent sideways. Fisher wrenched free of the other soldier's hold and stumbled, his fingers scraping the uneven cobblestones, then ran again. Four steps, five. A dozen. He'd make it. He'd be free.

A weight barreled into his hips, crumpling his legs. His knees scraped along the road, and he landed, skidding, face down, with the weight still on top of him. He couldn't breathe. His knees and palms and face stung.

The weight lifted. Rough hands hauled him upright and he was finally able to draw a ragged breath. He cried out as his arms were wrenched behind him, his elbows held high enough to make his shoulders burn.

"Ain't it funny how they all think they can get away?" one of the soldiers said.

Fisher flexed his arms enough that his shoulders screamed and sweat broke out on his forehead. He wouldn't escape a second time. "You have the wrong man," he said in a futile attempt to deflect attention. He was taller than most here in Linspar, something he hadn't factored into his hasty plans for a new life.

"A'course we do." The first soldier chuckled. "Like we haven't heard that one before."

The heavy castle gates clanged shut behind them and the soldiers dragged him around the side and through a narrow door in the thick black stone. He blinked in the dim light of the corridor. Their steps echoed on the hard, smooth floors. Torches flared every twenty paces but made little impact.

Fisher slipped at the first step down, not expecting it in the darkness. The soldiers held him steady as they continued downward. The torches became smaller and more widely spaced.

"Why are we going downward? I thought the Viscount was going to interview me."

"You can take some time to cool your heels after fuckin' up Drannin's knee."

The deeper they went, the more Fisher was sure he'd never meet the Viscount, or see sunlight again. This seemed like the perfect way for the universe to show him how fucked his life was. Everyone he'd ever known had betrayed him. He'd lost every home he'd ever had. Now, when there was a glimmer of hope for something new, he was going to be thrown into a dungeon and forgotten.

Finally, they stopped and one of the soldiers thumped on a door to their right. A peephole was opened and low light glinted on the eye that peered out.

"Thief from the markets," said the soldier to his right.

The door swung open and they marched through. The corridor was a twin of the previous one. Smooth floor, black stone, sparsely placed torches heading downward. Always downward.

Fisher had lost track of time and built up a sheen of exertion by the time they stopped again. No one knocked on the door beside them this time. A soldier stepped forward and unlocked it with a large brass key then lifted the metal bar that secured the door.

The other soldier roughly dragged his backpack off his shoulders. As soon as the door was open wide enough, the soldiers holding his arms lifted him off his feet and tossed him into the room. He landed heavily on his hands and knees, agony wrenching an involuntary cry from him.

The door clanged shut.

Darkness descended before the sound of the door closing had fully registered. Fisher blinked and froze, instinct crying to him not to move. He could see nothing. If he didn't know his eyes were open and fully functioning, he'd think he was blind. For all he knew, he could be inches from a pit in the floor and certain death.

Somewhere nearby was constantly running water. There was no other sound; only his heartbeat pounding in his ears, loud in the complete darkness. He forced himself to breathe evenly even though his heart rate refused to obey.

The water was somewhere behind him and to the side but it wasn't close so the cell they'd thrown him in was large. He carefully stretched his hands out, feeling the floor in front of him. I was not as smooth as the floors in the corridors. Rough-hewn rock provided enough unevenness to have him tripping in the dark if he tried to walk.

He turned in a tight circle, feeling as he went. If he could get back to the door, he could find a way to break out.

"There's a gap between you and the door. I don't know how wide, but too wide for me to reach across. That's why they throw you in."

Fisher squeaked, wobbled and put his hand down. It landed on a sharp edge and he crumpled to the side. Another sharp point dug into his hip and he groaned. "Fuck. Who the hell are you?"

"I didn't mean to startle you."

"How did you know I was heading to the door?" He continued to move toward it. The man might have lied.

"It's the first thing I did and I could hear you shuffling around."

"How long have you been in here?" On his hands and knees again, Fisher moved gingerly away from the man, assuming the door would be that direction. He felt his way forward with his fingers.

"I don't know. A day. Maybe two. Not long."

"What did you do?" He kept moving away from the voice, his confidence growing that there were no obstacles between him and the door.

The man chuckled, deep and wry. "I said something the Viscount took offense to."

"What was that?"

"I told him he was a spoiled brat and I was going to put a stop to whatever he had planned then bring his father home. What's your name?"

Fisher continued his slow and steady crawl away from the voice. The rush of running water continued in front of him so he thought he was traveling in the right direction. Or at least, in a direction, and not wandering around in circles. "He doesn't want his father to come home?"

"I think he's very pleased his father isn't here. In fact, I think he's made arrangements with the Yeudan to ensure his father never returns home."

Fisher stumbled and landed painfully on his elbow. "The Yeudan?" He righted himself and reached his hand forward again, only to come down on air. He fumbled and fell forward, his right arm dropping onto nothing. His chest landed on the floor, his face over an emptiness he couldn't see.

The cry he released as he landed flew away and disappeared into nothingness. Cold damp air washed over him, rippling in time with the sound of rushing water. "It's a creek."

"An oubliette, I think. The guards who threw me in said they rarely have to get anyone out. Most of them end up down there and get washed away when they flush the system. I'm Gaelan."

Fisher felt his way to the right. As he crawled, he checked the area in front. Then, with his left hand, traced the edge of the rock that dropped to the water. He wasn't surprised to hear the guards wouldn't be coming to get them any time soon. "They flush the system? Just the oubliette or the whole cell?" He kept moving, systematically mapping the area.

"They didn't say." Gaelan's voice now came from his right and behind him. He was moving closer. "If they don't retrieve bodies, it's probably the whole cell. The walls were wet when they threw me in."

"How often do they do it? You've been here a few days? Daily? Weekly?"

"I don't know. Either way, if we don't find a way out, we'll either drown and be washed away or starve to death."

"Hmmm," said Fisher absent-mindedly. The burble of the water was louder now, rushing faster below them. "The water is moving. That means it's coming from somewhere..."

"And going somewhere else." Gaelan's voice was close. His warm breath washed over Fisher's ankles. He must have crawled closer as they'd been speaking.

"That's our way out," Fisher replied as his head bumped against a wall. He still couldn't see anything, but the blackness wasn't as empty as he'd first thought, not with the water rushing below him and Gaelan's warm body behind him.

"We don't know how far down it is, or if the exit for the water is the size of a horse or a tin can."

"There's only one way to find out." He ran his fingers along the waistband of his pants, feeling for the edge of the braiding that ran down the outside seam. When he'd picked it loose, he pulled, the ripping of stitching muted under the sound of the water.

"Can you use this to brace me?" He handed one end of the unraveling rope to Gaelan and quickly fed the rope out and looped it around his hand. "I'll go over the side and see if I can reach bottom." With the water roaring its way through, it couldn't be that far down, surely.

"What if I drop you?"

"Then we'll know for sure how far down it is."

Gaelan's cheek jumped under his clenched jaw. "What the hell. I certainly haven't found a way out in the time I've been here. Granite isn't my rock. What do we have to lose, right?"

"Is there anything you can anchor yourself against to help hold me?"

"Do you have any metal?"

"What?"

"Metal. Coins will do. Do you have any?"

"You want me to pay you to help me drop into the water?"

"No. The coins will help anchor the rope. What's this made of?"

Fisher scowled but fumbled inside his trousers for his coin pouch. He'd probably die anyway. Why would he need money? "It's norrgel thread encased in silk. Don't touch it if the silk tears; I don't want to get this far just to die of norrgel poisoning."

There was a soft sizzle and a flare of light that was gone too soon for Fisher to see anything other than the flickering afterimage of a broad-shouldered man. Then metal scraped on stone. "How did you do that? Do you have something to make fire?"

"Something like that. I made an anchor. Do you have another of these ropes?"

"How could you do that? I only gave you a few coins. And why do you need more rope?"

"I'm coming with you."

"But the anchor?"

"I told you. Taken care of. Come on. I think they're going to flush us out soon and I want to get out of here before then if I can."

A metallic clank echoed in the chamber. "That's gears or something." Shit. "You were right."

He ripped the braid from the other leg of his pants and groped for Gaelan's hand to give it to him, along with a few more coins. Another soft sizzle and brief flash of light silhouetting Gaelan's large body preceded the sound of metal scraping on stone.

"Okay." Gaelan's deep voice spoke close beside his face. "Let's do this. When we reach the end of the rope, take my hand. We'll drop together. It'll give us a better chance of survival."

He swallowed, uncertain whether he wanted to do this. But another clank of gears sounded, closer now. If he didn't take his chances in the oubliette, he'd be drowned before he reached whatever exit there was. "I'm going over now." He wriggled his legs over the edge of rock and began lowering himself down the rope. Beside him, arms brushing, Gaelan mirrored his moves.

The edge of the rock sloped back under the floor of the cell, making it impossible for them to gain purchase with their feet. Fisher slithered down the rope, his palms burning. "My hands better not be so calloused they tear this silk."

Gaelan chuckled then hissed.

"What?"

"End of the rope. Where are you?"

He slithered down a few more inches. "I've reached the end too." His feet met only air. "How tall are you?"

"Not tall enough to feel water under my feet. It can't be that much farther down. I can hear it closer and I'm sure that's spray on my ankles."

Gaelan's hand slapped Fisher's shoulder, then returned and tugged at his shirt so he swung toward him. Gaelan drew him into a hug that would have been awkward in any situation.

A loud clang above them heralded a noisy splash of water in the cell. "Let go! I've got you."

"Shit," whispered Fisher as he grasped Gaelan's arm with one hand. He let go of his rope and swung his arm around him. Their legs grappled together.

"Here we go," said Gaelan.

They dropped. Fisher counted to three in his head before they hit the water—hard. The cold stole his breath as it washed over him, drenching his clothes.

His hold on Gaelan was lost in that first tumble into the turbulent water and he'd have been washed away if Gaelan's grip hadn't remained firm.

Fisher wrapped his arms around Gaelan's neck and kicked, hoping he was kicking somewhere that would lead to air. Gaelan's arms around him were like steel, resisting all the water's efforts to tear them apart.

His lungs burned and he fought the instinct to inhale. The pounding of his heart was loud in his head, thumping against his eyes and closing his throat in growing panic.

They tumbled over again, helpless in the whirlpool. He slammed against the rock wall. Gaelan slammed with him, squashing him between the rock and his body. All the air rushed from his lungs; huge bubbles lost in the flow of water around them.

Fisher thumped Gaelan's shoulders, untangled his legs, fought against the iron-strong hold around him.

Air.

Fuck. He wasn't going to make it. His lungs burned, his eyes watered. He had to breathe. Inhale.

One of Gaelan's arms lost its hold and Fisher lunged, but was still caught by the other man. Gaelan's hand gripped Fisher's jaw, trying to pry his mouth open. He fought. He pushed at Gaelan's shoulders, his head, tore at his hair, every movement sluggish and uncontrolled against the pounding of the water against them, pushing them down and tumbling them over.

His lips pursed. His eyes opened wider, to find a way out. To breathe. He opened his mouth and...

Gaelan clamped his mouth over his. He sucked the air from him, but it wasn't enough. He fought against his hold, exhaling bubbles through his nose, breathing in again—through his nose. Choking.

He coughed but Gaelan pressed tighter against him, held him still with legs entwined and fingers digging into his jaw, holding him still. Gaelan's other hand skittered across Fisher's face until two fingers pinched his nostrils closed. He couldn't fight any longer. He sagged against Gaelan and inhaled.

And breathed in warm air.

He coughed again and gasped. He gripped Gaelan's shoulders and pushed away.

They tumbled again and slammed into the rock wall, smashing his breath from him again. Gaelan was wrenched away, leaving him with a forced exhale as he tumbled again. He was going to die.

Then Gaelan's face was back, his hands strong against his head and waist. His mouth landed on his again and, this time, Fisher held on. He took the air greedily, breathing out through his nose. Took another gasp of air from Gaelan and kept going until his lungs no longer ached.

The water pounded them. His legs flailed, his knees scraped against rock, and his grip tore free but he fought the current and gripped Gaelan's shirt. They slammed against the rock again, his hands squashed between the wall and Gaelan's back.

In the seconds before they tumbled again, he curled his fingers, one into Gaelan's hair, the other into his shirt, and gripped as tightly as he could. They tumbled again, over and over, until he thought they must soon be torn apart.

He slammed against rocks again. Sharp edges dug into his back and knocked his breath from him. His lungs squashed and spots danced across his vision, white against the constant blackness.

He pushed at Gaelan, instinct telling him to lift his head and take a deep breath. Gaelan pushed back, as buffeted by the swirling, angry water as he was.

The second time Gaelan's leg slammed against his, he realized they were still in the same position and it wasn't rock against his back but metal. Gaelan kept shifting, bumping against him, then a soft, cold hand brushed against his forehead. Another person. A dead person.

He fumbled behind himself with one hand, keeping a hard hold on Gaelan, even as the hand he'd released was caught by the water and slammed against the rock at his side. Only, that wasn't rock either. He fumbled and scrunched his eyes closed tighter in concentration. Finally, he could read the messages his sore, half-frozen fingers were giving him.

There was a grille through which the water flowed. He jerked his head, to lift it and tell Gaelan, but Gaelan's hold at his nape was solid. How were they not drowned by now? How could Gaelan still have breath left to give?

Even as he wondered, Gaelan breathed out again and Fisher sucked in another greedy lungful of air. How was he doing it?

Gaelan's legs shifted against him, a reminder that, while he was relatively secure in his position squashed up against the grille, the water still roared and pummeled them. He dug his fingers against the side of the metal and pulled. To his surprise, the grille groaned, low and agonized against the constant roar of the water, then began to move, opening slowly.

As it moved, so did they. Their bodies, again at odds with the water, were buffeted against the metal, sliding along it as it opened.

Before the grille opened completely, Fisher lost his hold on it and they slid through and were swept away with the water. Even as he clutched Gaelan, breathing from him more comfortably now, he wondered where they were heading. This was how they cleaned the black cells but who was going to be at the other end?

They'd be expecting dead bodies, not live ones.

CHAPTER THREE

FISHER BOBBED TO THE surface like a dead fish. He tilted his head back, his mouth separating from Gaelan's with a pop.

They were still locked together by their arms and legs, and his mouth tingled after the constant pressure of Gaelan against him, feeling naked in the cold air. He gasped in deep breaths of fresh air, shocked at the contrast from Gaelan's warm breath.

He opened his eyes and saw sky, gray and fading. The sun hadn't completely set, so it had only been an hour or so since the soldiers had taken him.

"Can you swim at all?" Gaelan's voice sounded richer now they were out of the cell. Thick and dark; like melted rock.

Fisher turned to look at Gaelan and gasped. Gaelan's black hair was plastered to his head. Beads of water dripped from black eyelashes that shaded brilliant blue-violet eyes. "Blue Goddess eyes."

Gaelan's eyebrows shot up. "You're Yuedan."

"No," Fisher lied. He pushed away and sank beneath the water. He kicked and flailed but he'd grown up in icelands and deserts. Swimming wasn't part of either lifestyle.

Gaelan grabbed him under his arms and pulled him back to the surface. "Idiot," he mumbled. His legs kicked next to Fisher's and they moved toward the edge of...

Fisher looked around. It was a pond, no larger than the small cave he'd used as his sleeping space in the desert. On its surface bobbed a half dozen bodies—prisoners like him flushed from the cells, dead before they could escape the water. They floated along with the current toward an outlet where the pond turned into a creek.

Fisher looked away. He didn't need the reminder that he would be one of them if it hadn't been for Gaelan. Guilt twisted in his stomach because he owed Gaelan his life but was going to run as soon as he worked out where he was.

Tall, slim gravestones surrounded the pool.

"If you can't swim, why were you so keen to jump into the oubliette?" Gaelan asked as they scrambled up the muddy bank onto dry grass.

They'd only been in the water a short time but fighting against it had made Fisher's legs and arms feel as limp as a dead snake.

Gaelan kept talking. "It's a good thing you're Yeudan. I need you to come there with me so you can—"

Fisher wasn't going to be taken back to the wastelands. It was just another place people wanted to kill him. He lunged at Gaelan and shoved against his shoulders. It was enough to unbalance him and send him back into the pond.

Fisher pushed himself to his feet and stumbled along the grass between the stones toward the cobblestone path that led to a building surrounded by wide cloisters. The temple. He ducked his head and ran, dodging around the gravestones and tearing down the path toward it.

"Come back!" Gaelan called.

Fisher didn't look back. He rounded a curve in the path, Gaelan's footsteps pounding on the cobblestones behind him. A break between two tall columns revealed a narrow iron gate with the sign of the Blue Goddess on it. He grabbed at the iron and fumbled at the catch to open the gate.

Gaelan's large hand grabbed at his shoulder. He shrugged it off and spun around, glaring at Gaelan. Behind his back, his fingers finally found the catch to the gate and flicked it up. As it swung open, he stumbled backward onto the paving stones of the temple grounds.

"Wait," said Gaelan.

Fisher took several more steps backward, moving farther into the grounds. He looked around, sighing when he saw two monks walking swiftly toward him. "I claim sanctuary," he called, still moving away from Gaelan, who had followed him through the gate. "I claim sanctuary from the Temple of Linspar, in the name of the Blue Goddess."

He wasn't fast enough. Before he could turn and run to the monks, Gaelan's large hand gripped his bicep.

"I knew you were Yuedan!" Blue-violet eyes blazed with excitement.

Fisher scowled and wrenched his arm, but couldn't free it. "Let me go." Close up, it was obvious Gaelan was older than he'd first appeared; probably a few years older than he. His skin was a warm caramel, almost the same color as the rocks that covered the mountain on the next island. One of the ferry passengers had pointed it out and claimed it was God's Island.

Gaelan looked at where he gripped Fisher's arm, his fingers digging deep into the muscle. He slowly pried them loose. He didn't step back, so Fisher did.

"I'm sorry," Gaelan said in a voice as rough as new cobblestones.

He rubbed his arm and scowled at Gaelan, then spun on his heel and ran—right into a monk. He flinched at the smack of their bodies hitting and the monk's nose slamming into his chest. He fell, tumbling over the monk and landing heavily on his elbow. "Fuck." Another pain to go with his grazed cheek.

A second monk reached them and helped the other to his feet. Fisher cradled his elbow and sat, contemplating never getting up. He was inside the temple grounds now. They'd have to throw him out if they wanted him to leave.

Gaelan crouched and held a hand out to help Fisher up. Now he'd reached the temple, he accepted the help.

"Are you alright?" Gaelan curled one hand around Fisher's shoulder while he gripped his head with the other. "Did you hit your head?

Fisher looked pointedly at his shoulder and stepped back. "What do you want? I've claimed sanctuary."

"If I was going to hurt you, I wouldn't have nearly drowned trying to save you. And you still haven't told me your name."

Guilt twisted in his stomach. Gaelan had saved him in the water; he'd shared his breath. Underwater. Long after he should have run out of air.

Was he a magician? Or a sea serpent from the legends? Exactly how dangerous was Gaelan?

He stepped closer to the temple buildings.

The second monk spoke. "Sir, may we know the name of the man we'll be harboring?"

Relief flooded through him, making him sway as he turned toward the monk. They would let him stay, and keep him safe from the soldiers and whatever Gaelan was. At least for a while.

He resisted the childish impulse to poke his tongue out at the blue-eyed man. "My name is Fisher. Can you offer me sanctuary?"

Gaelan stepped in close behind him. His warm breath on the back of Fisher's neck sent a shiver down his spine. He knew if he leaned back and tilted his head, Gaelan would easily be able to kiss the sensitive spot behind his ear. He kept his back ramrod straight and stepped closer to the monk.

"Why do you need sanctuary?" Gaelan asked.

Fisher whipped around at the rough anger in the man's voice and stumbled back when his hand bumped against his thigh. "Seriously, what is wrong with you?" He continued to step back until he was slightly behind the monks.

"You're Yeudan."

Panic nipped at his fingertips. Why was being Yeudan so important?

The first monk was still holding his nose. There was no blood so it probably wasn't broken. "Perhaps we could adjourn inside and discuss this. We'll be pleased to offer you both refreshments."

Gaelan nodded. "Thank you." He gestured to Fisher to precede him.

Fisher side-stepped first, keeping as much distance—and a couple of monks—between them as he could.

"Could you also let Brother Sand know I'm here?" said Gaelan.

The second monk bowed slightly. "Of course, Minstrel. Brother Sand will be pleased you're visiting again." He turned to Fisher and offered the same bow. "Brother Sand will also be pleased to meet you, Master Fisher, and discuss how we may help you."

As long as they didn't hand him over to this minstrel, he'd be fine. The promise of a new life, perhaps even a peaceful life, where he always had enough to eat, teased him. His stomach cramped with the yearning for it.

They walked through the cloisters, the shadows deepening the farther they went from the gates. Across the enclosed courtyard, the temple loomed—black granite shot through with gleaming crystal veins, like falling stars. Above, the sky gradually lost its color and the first stars of the evening echoed the temple walls.

The familiar feelings of comfort and claustrophobia washed through Fisher. He sighed, grateful for the respite from the open sky.

A rotund Brother Sand greeted them at the dining hall. "Welcome, welcome. You've arrived just in time to share our evening meal." He stepped forward and grasped the minstrel's hand, eyeing his wet clothing. "Gaelan. Always a pleasure to see you."

He waved his hands toward the door. "Unfortunately, if I give you both time to change into dry clothing, you'll miss the evening meal. The fires will soon dry your clothes and warm you up."

The large room was cold, the flames in the fire small and new, struggling to bite into the large log. As they walked between two long tables, two novices stood and carried their plates to the top table across the end of the room, under a large stained glass window. They placed their plates in front of empty seats then returned to their table, sitting quietly and staring at it.

"Brother Sand," said Gaelan, his voice forbidding.

"It's not what you think, Minstrel. They volunteered their meals for our guests. The kitchen will ensure they have food. It's the sacrifice that's important, not the starvation," said Brother Sand. "They'll eat a little later than the others, but they'll still eat."

Even as he spoke, Fisher noted a kitchenhand bring two more plates from the kitchen.

"My apologies, Brother Sand," Gaelan said.

Brother Sand smiled. Once they were all seated, he patted Gaelan's forearm. "You question every perceived injustice, Minstrel. It's one of the things that has made us friends." He took a bite of his food. "Now, let's dispense with the formalities and discuss why you're both here and how we can help.

"I'll admit," he continued as he ate, "I'm hoping it has something to do with bringing the duke home from Barthes and curtailing the Viscount's plans."

Fisher's mind spun. He looked around, almost frantic. He couldn't stay here, in another damned place full of political intrigue and danger—and connected to the Yeudan. Perhaps he could hire a boat, or steal one and sail over to God's Island. He could live alone and in peace.

Gaelan's arm brushed against his shoulder, bringing him back to the present. The two of them were squeezed between Brother Sand

and another monk. If they sat any closer, he would be in Gaelan's lap. He shuffled as far from him as he could and turned his attention to the conversation.

Gaelan was saying, "The situation with the ruling family will be a lengthy discussion. I need to meet with Aunty Cray before we can decide what's to be done there. Perhaps we should hear Fisher's tale first."

Fisher froze. Even though he'd been traveling for weeks, his only thought had been to get away, to stay alive, to find somewhere safe. He thought he'd ask for sanctuary and be granted it and that would be the end of the whole messy situation.

Of course they'd want to know what they were getting themselves into. What could he tell them?

He couldn't admit the truth—that he'd been instrumental in the murder of countless Imperials and Mafdeti, had orchestrated the kidnap and abuse of the Princess Royal, then led a force against his own people, seeing them defeated and incarcerated. He was a traitor to every people he'd lived with. What part of that would gain him sanctuary here?

He remembered his mother's most frequent advice—whenever possible, stick close to the truth. The whole truth would get him killed or banished again, so he chose the parts he could say.

"The Yeudan sent an invading force into the Analee Valley. The Imperials and Mafdeti joined forces and repelled them, then declared war on the Yeudan. I was recognized as Yuedan, so I'm no longer safe there.

'I also can't go back to Barthes." He couldn't suppress the shiver the thought of returning to the Icy Wastes brought. "My mother and I were banished from there when I was young and, now my home in the Stony Desert is gone, so there's nowhere else for me to go."

He sounded like a pathetic, whining child, but if it got him sanctuary, he'd do it. Anything if he didn't have to go back to the Imperial Counties or Barthes. That way led to certain death.

"Why were you banished?" asked Brother Sand.

That was his most pressing concern? Not war breaking out? His banishment was ancient history and had no relevance to why he had run from the desert.

Still, it was the easiest of the potential questions he could have been asked. "My mother became pregnant without sanction and refused to abort the child. That resulted in shunning. When the child came of age, she refused to give him to the military. For that she was banished."

They would have taken him as she left but she'd planned for that and, while she was stripped and beaten on her way through the city gates, he'd been safely hidden in an ice cave a mile to the south, as she'd instructed.

She'd been nearly frozen when she finally reached him. He'd had to remove two of her toes but that had been much easier than the prospect of being alone in the Icy Wastes in the middle of winter at ten years old.

"She was banished because she wanted to keep her child?" Gaelan exclaimed, horror dripping from every syllable.

Fisher shrugged. "The pregnancy wasn't sanctioned. No one knew who the father was." He tried to sound nonchalant but his lungs were so tight he couldn't draw breath. He felt again the tearing terror of hiding from the militia, not daring to move in case they found him and took him away. He'd seen what happened to illegals like him—the bruised and torn bodies, the tears. Once they were no more use, or stopped resisting, they were sent outside the walls. No food, no shoes.

His mother had taught him how to survive as well as anyone could in a land of ice so, when he was targeted, he'd escaped.

"You were the child," stated Gaelan. "When she was banished, you went with her."

Fisher couldn't look at them. He still felt the shame. The shame others had of his mother, shame for the way she was treated, shame for his cowardice. He should have been able to save her from all of that. It was like a dark fog that filled his nostrils and his eyes and ears, and pressed against his lungs so he couldn't breathe.

A large, warm hand slid up the back of his neck under the fall of his hair. Fingers squeezed gently, massaging the tight muscles. After a few minutes of the quiet pressure he opened his eyes.

Beside him, on his knees, one hand on Fisher's neck, the other on one of his knees, was Gaelan. His vibrant blue eyes were soft with compassion. Fisher fought against leaning into him and allowing that gentle strength to carry his load for a while. Instead, he pulled away, straightened his spine and looked out into the hall.

Nearby, monks ate and conversed, a stark contrast to the silent lives lived by the priests in Fisher's childhood home. Their worship of the Blue Goddess had been all-consuming—until they had decided she was never returning. Then their hatred took over.

Fisher remembered the shift in teachings when he was a child. Literally overnight, the Blue Goddess went from being treated with awe and reverence as they awaited her return, to disdain and anger.

The priests gained even more power from their campaign of hate. It had scared him when he was ten and it terrified him now.

"Why are they so happy?" he asked, indicating with a nod the monks before them.

Brother Sand regarded him with serenity. "What is there to be unhappy about?"

"There's war coming. Don't think it won't impact here because there's an ocean between you and them. Trade will fall off, borders will be closed. Your people will be weakened.

"If the Yeudan win, they'll keep moving south. Their numbers have been growing and they're looking to expand into the south where food is more plentiful."

"You say you left when you were ten," said Gaelan, "but your knowledge of the Yeudan is that of an adult."

Fisher glared at him. "I grew up. I didn't lose my hearing or my sight, or my mind." He'd done too many things as an adult that required him to be well informed of every potential danger to close his ears to the Yeudan just because they'd closed their minds to him.

"It seems we have been presented with exactly the resources we require in these trying times," said Brother Sand. He lifted a hand, summoning a young monk. "We'll all have a good night's sleep, then meet with Mistress Cray in the morning and decided what's to be done."

The young monk nodded and gestured to Gaelan and Fisher to follow her.

Fisher rose automatically but couldn't leave without making sure he'd receive sanctuary. "Brother Sand—"

"We'll discuss the conditions of sanctuary in the morning, Master Fisher. Prater Connie will show you to your quarters. Sleep well. Minstrel, if you and I might have a word in my study?"

Gaelan bowed his head. "Of course, Brother Sand."

As Brother Sand left the dining hall, Fisher harrumphed. "Since when does sanctuary have conditions?"

Beside him, Gaelan chuckled and stretched, raising his hands high above his head. His shirt was dry, not even damp patches at the thickest stitching.

Fisher glanced down; Gaelan's pants were the same. How did he get dry when Fisher's clothes were still damp and clammy, and chafed with every movement?

"You'll find Brother Sand will put conditions on anything if he thinks it will lead to improving the lives of his charges. He's probably the least priest-like brother you'll ever meet." Gaelan grinned at him.

"If you'll accompany me, Master Fisher," said Prater Connie. "I'll give you a quick tour as we go. If you're to be living here, you'll need to find your way around."

Fisher glared at Gaelan's retreating form, then nodded to Prater Connie and followed her out of the dining hall, even as he wondered if he'd ever see Gaelan again.

Just to thank him for saving his life, of course. Fisher didn't actually like the odd man, no matter how gorgeous his eyes were. Especially when he still couldn't understand how Gaelan had kept him alive.

CHAPTER FOUR

FISHER FOLLOWED PRATER Connie down the narrow corridor and up a tightly-winding staircase. His footsteps slapped the smooth stone floor rhythmically a few steps behind the monk.

Only the acute sense of direction he'd learned in the underground caverns of the desert allowed Fisher to maintain any idea of where they were. Connie's tour had been convoluted and random, lasting the better part of an hour.

Connie hadn't mentioned where Gaelan would be staying. Fisher winced at the twinge of guilt he felt of the way he'd treated Gaelan after he'd kept Fisher alive during their escape from the cells.

"I think you'll be pleased with your quarters, Fisher," said Connie, her narrow face breaking into a happy smile. They'd long since agreed to dispense with titles. "There've been quite a few changes to the guest quarters in recent months."

Fisher remembered stories of the monks' quarters in Barthes. "Have you put curtains on the windows so I can sleep past sunrise?"

Connie laughed as if that was the most ridiculous thing she'd ever heard. "No. Something useful. Brother Sanjay joined us eight months ago."

They'd reached a halfway point in the long hallway between two staircases to different levels. Prater Connie opened a door and Fisher went inside. The room was small, as all the rooms in the temple were. It contained a solid-framed bed with a white comforter, a narrow bedside table, a wooden chest at the end of the bed, and smelled faintly of damp.

"Brother Sanjay was a plumber's mate, so we now have running water in all the guest rooms."

"So I can take a bath without calling down to the kitchens?"

Prater Connie laughed again. "It's certainly a possibility now." She winked. "Between you and me, Brother Sanjay's decision to become a monk rather than remain in his previous employ was a good choice."

She leaned close to Fisher. "I've taken the liberty of leaving printed instructions in your night table for how to deal with unexpected leaks. There are spare towels in the chest at the foot of the bed. May your night be restful and may the dragon keep you dry."

Prater Connie bowed slightly, then was gone, the door closing softly behind her and her chuckles echoing in the corridor.

Fisher turned to inspect the room more closely, but before he could take in more than the narrow bed and a closed door, the door opened and Gaelan emerged from the bathroom. He still wore his pants, but that was all. His golden chest was front and center, the smooth satin of his pecs and dusky nipples drawing Fisher's gaze like iron filings to a magnet.

Fisher spun around and charged out into the corridor.

Gaelan followed and grasped his arm. "Where are you going?"

"Where'd that damned monk go? Why'd she show me to your room? Where's mine?"

"This is *our* room." Gaelan gestured to the room they'd just left.

"I've claimed sanctuary. You're a guest. We're not together. Why would they put us in the same room?"

"I've long since ceased to question all of Brother Sand's decisions. You can be sure, though, that we're both exactly where he wanted us to be tonight. Tomorrow, that might change, but for now, we're here. Sharing won't be too bad."

Sharing space wasn't what Fisher objected to. Privacy was a luxury he wasn't familiar with. Sharing with Gaelan was the problem.

Gaelan knew entirely too much of him, yet nothing at all, and everything Fisher knew of Gaelan only raised more questions. He didn't want his head to be riddled with them like an intestinal parasite. He wanted his only and last hope of a peaceful life to be here and now.

"I'm tired," said Gaelan. "I imagine you are as well, so why don't you come inside so we can get some rest?"

"I'm not sleeping here with you." Fisher stood in the doorway, arms crossed.

"The bath works—sort of. You could be clean and in dry clothes."

When Fisher didn't move, Gaelan sighed. "If it makes you feel better, I'll sleep on top of the covers, but I'm not giving up the first comfortable bed I've seen in weeks because you... whatever reason you have."

Gaelan ran his fingers through his hair and scratched at his scalp. "I'm going to finish washing, then I'm going to sleep. Whatever you decide to do, stay in this room. It would be the height of rudeness to wander the halls in the night, disturbing their rituals, when the brothers have shown you nothing but kindness.

"Rituals?" Fisher darted an alarmed look at the door. "What the hell kind of place is this where there are *rituals* during the night?"

"It's nothing bad. Just a lot of wandering the halls waving smoking lanterns and chanting. The halls become quite crowded at various times."

"I won't get any sleep." *What if they come in here? What sort of rituals are they?*

"I know. I'll wash up." Gaelan walked into the surprisingly spacious bathing room. He emerged a scant five minutes later, long black hair damp and curling around his face. He wore a long robe the color his eyes might have been behind a heavy mist. "Bathroom's yours. Don't use both faucets at the same time."

Fisher edged around the room and slipped into the bathroom. There was a large white tub in the middle with three pipes hanging from the ceiling, two faucets and a narrow nozzle that could be used to fill the bath or to shower. Along the wall, under a narrow window, was a toilet and beside that, a hand basin. A short open-faced cabinet contained a couple of towels and a jar of oiled cleaning salt.

There was a door on the opposite wall. Fisher darted across the room and tried it, but it was locked.

He raced back into the bedroom, ignoring Gaelan's startled gaze. "There's a door in here locked from the other side. There's no lock on the outer door." He checked the bathroom door. It didn't have a lock either.

The windows were his next port of call. Fisher opened the bathroom window and stuck his head out. "There are enough footholds in the brickwork that a toddler could climb up here."

Gaelan joined him in the bathroom. Fisher stood beside the toilet, hands on his hips, and scowled.

Gaelan shrugged. "Forgot to pee," he said as he nudged Fisher to the side, lifted his gown and began.

Fisher jumped and shot Gaelan a startled look. "Right." He retreated to the bedroom.

By the time Gaelan had washed, and brushed his clothes, Fisher had dragged the bed across to the door to the corridor. "It won't stop anyone coming in, but it will slow them down and give us some warning." He bent to the chest at the foot of the bed. "I'll put this in the bathroom."

"Do you expect to be attacked during the night?" Gaelan asked.

Fisher didn't pause in his efforts to drag the chest across the floor. "I like to be prepared."

After regarding him silently for several seconds, Gaelan shrugged and bent to help. Within minutes the chest was positioned against the locked door in the bathroom and Fisher had checked that both windows were locked.

He grabbed some towels and a blanket from the chest. "I'll sleep in the bath. You take the bed. That way, whatever happens, one of us will be able to clear an exit while the other holds them off. I'd suggest the windows."

He pushed the door between the bedroom and bathroom as open as it would go with the bed in the way. "Leave this open so I can hear if they come in through your door."

Fisher retreated to the bathroom and inspected the clothing left there. Thankfully, there were pants and a shirt similar to the ones he wore. He washed quickly, lamenting the loss of his concealing Cream, and put on the new clothes, then draped his clothes over the edge of the bath to dry overnight.

He used one towel to dry the bath thoroughly, then the rest to create a cushioned pad to sleep on. He was just settling after struggling to find a comfortable spot when Gaelan came through the doorway holding a blanket.

"If you put this down first, it'll keep the cold from the metal bath at bay. The towels will be better over you to keep warm." He waited while Fisher stood and rearranged everything. "I'll snuff the candles," said Gaelan. "Goodnight."

Fisher lay in the dark for a long time, staring at the locked bathroom window. It would be easy to slip over the sill and climb down the chunky walls but where could he go? This was the last bastion of civilization.

His heart thumped heavily as he thought through all his options—none—and formulated a second plan—there wasn't one.

The wee hours had arrived before Fisher realized it wasn't only his lack of options that was making his heart pound.

Within the darkness, water ran. He was back in the cell, with the oubliette a long narrow channel between the wall and the floor.

The creek ran, tumbling its way through the cell. Light glinted on the waves and Fisher knew the water was rising. The cold of it licked at his feet and ankles but he couldn't move. Frozen in fear, Fisher waited and watched the black water rise.

Fisher gasped and opened his eyes. Once they adjusted to the light, he could make out the shapes of the window and doorway. He was in the bathtub in the dark cell-like bathroom. It was almost as dark as the cell where he was supposed to die.

He kicked his legs, finally able to move. Water sloshed over his feet and crept up his back. The bath was flooding. He had to get out.

He slipped a couple of times, but eventually managed to roll himself out of the deep tub. Sweat beaded his face, not from the exertion but from the residual fear.

He stood and almost immediately dropped to his hands and knees again, then crawled to where he'd left his clothing drying. He hurriedly changed into them and crawled to the open door to the bedroom.

As he reached the threshold, he heard breathing. He swallowed the frightened whimper that swelled in his throat. Gaelan. Gaelan who saved him.

Fisher crawled to the bed where the sound of Gaelan's breathing was a comforting promise of life in the dark. He curled into a ball on the floor next to the bed and closed his eyes against the unrelenting blackness that threatened to swallow him whole.

"You'd be more comfortable if you slept up here." The warm molasses of Gaelan's sleepy voice made him shiver. "Come on, Fisher. I'm not going to be able to sleep if you insist on staying on the floor."

Fisher stayed silent, eyes staring into a darkness so thick it could smother him. Then he realized he was being ridiculous. He wasn't going to sleep here any more than he would have in the flooded bath. It was all he could do to hold the panic at bay.

He crawled onto the mattress beside Gaelan and lay stiffly. "I'm not going anywhere with you. I'm claiming sanctuary and staying here." He had to make that clear so Gaelan knew this didn't mean anything.

Fisher had finished with his previous life. He wasn't an Exile anymore and hadn't been Yeudan since he was ten. There was nothing left for him in the north and going back would mean his death.

"Roll over." Gaelan's hands pushed and tugged until Fisher was lying with his back to Gaelan. "This way, you'll be warmer and you'll still be able to move quickly." Gaelan snugged an arm around Fisher's waist and pulled him back into an embrace that was different but reminiscent of the way they'd held each other in the water.

Gaelan's warm breath on the back of Fisher's neck had irritated him in the cloisters but now it reassured him. If anything happened, he would still be able to breathe. He'd be able to escape.

And Gaelan now knew he was staying here.

Outside the soft chanting of the monks began, balancing the quiet shuffling of the others in the halls as they sang everyone to peaceful sleep. Thankful he wasn't one of the pond-dead being farewelled and buried, or whatever they did with their dead, Fisher allowed his muscles to relax and slept.

GAELAN CURLED MORE securely around Fisher, listening as his breathing slowed and he slipped into sleep. His heart ached for him, even as he wondered what Fisher hadn't told him.

It was obvious that only part of Fisher's story had been revealed at dinner, and Gaelan didn't think he'd learn anything more until Fisher learned he could trust him. He would make sure there was time to do that, provided he could convince Fisher to travel north with him.

He ran through different scenarios as he savored Fisher's warm body against his. He hadn't been sure what it was about Fisher until he'd seen the patchy skin under the half washed-away paste, but he vowed to keep him safe.

He'd listened as Fisher settled into the bath and wriggled to get comfortable, his breathing steady but watchful. Only after Fisher had fallen asleep in his arms did Gaelan close his eyes and begin to plan his campaign.

The first step would be to make sure Fisher stayed with him.

He was woken in the morning when the door bumped into the bed, unable to open more than a few inches. "Minstrel?" whispered Prater Connie.

Gaelan checked that Fisher was still sleeping then crawled to the end of the bed and peered through the gap in the doorway.

"Mistress Cray has arrived."

He ran a hand down his face. Wonderful. That meant he'd run out of time to try to convince Fisher to go with him to Barthes.

The mattress moved under him and he turned to find Fisher sitting up, his eyes dark with sleep. "We'll be there in twenty minutes."

"Is that Connie?" asked Fisher.

"Good morning, Fisher," called Prater Connie through the gap. "I sang a special ballad for your rest. I trust the dragon provided you a restful night."

Gaelan choked on air, coughing so much he fell out of bed.

Fisher looked at him oddly as he rose from the bed and tugged it out of the way, leaving room for Prater Connie to enter. Fisher grinned at her as she edged around the bed into the room.

Gaelan rose, his eyebrows drawing down. "You call her Connie?"

Fisher ignored him. "I did sleep well, thank you. I thought the chanting would keep me awake all night but it was nice."

Prater Connie grinned and moved closer to Fisher. Gaelan stepped between them, the air in the small room thick and dark, like the cell had been the day before. "Will Brother Sand be with Aunty Cray?"

"Gaelan?"

Fisher scowled at him but Gaelan couldn't stop. Fisher was his. The knowledge sank deep inside him and rested comfortably in the spot that he had always thought housed his sense of self. Fisher now resided there as well, and Prater Connie was going to end up flying out the window if she didn't get away from him within the next three seconds.

Two.

One.

"Brother Sand said breakfast would be ready by the time you join us," said Prater Connie as she edged her way out the door, eyeing Gaelan warily.

"Will you be at breakfast too, Connie?" asked Fisher. When Gaelan scowled at him, he grinned.

Prater Connie eeped and disappeared, the sound of her footsteps fading.

"Why do you call her Connie?" Gaelan blocked the exit, hands on his hips, determined to get an answer.

"What's your problem?" Fisher strode forward, the offensive taking Gaelan by surprise and making him step back. "We don't know each other." He waved his hand as if pushing aside anything

Gaelan might have said. "We met in a dark cell and escaped together. That doesn't mean we have to be joined at the hip."

"You're the one who wanted to sleep with me." Gaelan bit the inside of his cheek to hide his satisfaction that Fisher had sought him out during the night.

"The bathtub flooded!" Fisher's cheeks flushed a delicate pink between the uneven patches of brown. He pushed past Gaelan and strode into the hall. "We're going to be late for breakfast."

Gaelan allowed his grin to escape, quickly changed into his clothes and followed.

CHAPTER FIVE

"ACH, THERE YOU ARE, my boy," said the woman Fisher assumed was Aunty Cray as Gaelan and he entered the dining hall.

She grabbed Gaelan by the elbow, her wild gray hair bobbed as she moved, and the wrinkles cascading down her throat rippled like waves in the ocean. "There are things we need to discuss. Come and sit with me. I'm famished."

Gaelan glanced at Fisher but allowed himself to be dragged toward the head table.

Fisher hung back and looked around as Gaelan walked away. The only time he'd been away from Gaelan since he'd been thrown into the cell with him was when Gaelan met with Brother Sand.

He hadn't registered it at the time, but in hindsight, he had felt the release of tension rush through him when he'd seen Gaelan emerge from the bathroom. Then again, last night, the panic that took over him abated as soon as Gaelan touched him.

This morning, as he'd walked down the hallway away from Gaelan, his chest had felt tight, as if he couldn't breathe quite deeply enough, and had only settled once Gaelan caught up to him.

That proximal reaction had happened before when he first came of age, and Fisher refused to let it happen again. He wasn't going to be responsible for one more person's death.

He looked around the dining hall, catching sight of Connie, and made his way over to her table. "Good morning again," he said as he sat opposite her.

She darted a look at the table where Gaelan sat with Brother Sand and Mistress Cray. "Would you prefer I didn't sit here?" he asked, disappointed that their friendship had been so fragile it couldn't withstand a few scowls from Gaelan.

"The minstrel wields power here in Linspar," said Connie.

"He did with the duke," corrected the monk with her. "But the Viscount is a different person. I heard the minstrel was tossed out."

Connie looked back at Fisher. "Were you with him then?"

"No I wasn't." Fisher wasn't sure how they'd respond if they knew he'd been arrested and escaped so he didn't say anything more.

After a short, awkward silence, Connie spoke. "Fisher, this is Hagan. He's a diplomat posted here from the Imperial Colonies." Connie gestured to the slim young man who sat beside her. He had neatly trimmed hazelnut hair, green-gray eyes, a dimple in his square chin and a wide, angular jaw.

Hagan regarded Fisher with narrowed eyes. "They were missing two when they loaded the barge."

"Barge?" asked Fisher.

"The Death Barge. All Linspar's dead are loaded on the burial ships. They are taken out to sea for burial, the proper sacrifice to the sea serpent. There were two missing."

"You count the dead?"

"Of course. We can't leave them to rot here."

"There's a cemetery."

"That's for the ruling families, not commoners or criminals."

"They take *all* the dead out and dump them at sea?"

"It's a sacrifice to the sea serpent," reiterated Hagan. "And it's not a wasted trip. Before they return, they run the barge along the coast and trade with the Grewin, and return with shipments of the Elixir from the Icy Wastes." Hagan frowned as he said the word "elixir", emphasizing the contrast between his almost delicate brows and his solid jawline.

"What elixir?" *They're trading with the Yeudan? Nothing good will come from that.*

Connie gushed. "Oh, it's the newest thing for the healers. They swear by it. The way they talk about it, it's a magical cure for all ills. It removes pain and speeds knitting of wounds, reduces fevers and aids sleep. Brother Sand swears by it."

Beside her, Hagan was frowning again.

"You don't agree with Connie?" asked Fisher. He pressed his hand against the tightness in his chest.

"I don't trust miracle cures. There's always a catch." Hagan glanced at the top table where Gaelan still sat with Mistress Cray and Brother Sand, then leaned forward and lowered his voice. "I think it's highly addictive, although no one who has used it agrees with me."

"You haven't used it yourself?"

"No, nor do I want to. Not until I know for sure there are no ill side-effects."

"You sound like a physician, not a diplomat."

Hagan waved a dismissive hand. "My father is a physician. I learned to question from him, but don't have the stomach for illnesses."

"Have Linspar's dead always been taken to sea on barges?"

"Oh no," said Connie. "We used to take them to God's Island and offer them to the Dragon God but that practice stopped ten years ago. Two years ago, when the duke began to train the viscount to take over on his retirement, the practice was streamlined further."

She frowned. "I can't say I agree with the new harsher penalties given to the serious offenders but everyone gets a fair trial and the streets have never been safer, so I guess it's working."

"What happens to convicted felons?"

Even as Fisher asked the question, his mind screamed at him to step away from the table, to not get involved, but he couldn't. Alarm bells jittered across his skin.

"Minor felonies are punished by fine or a short prison stay. Only the major crimes are punishable by death. The murderers and rapists are euthanized then floated down the creek to the pond where we collect them and put them on the barge."

"The pond in the cemetery?"

"Yes, that's the one. Have you been there? I thought you were new in town."

Major felons? Euthanized? Fair trial? He wasn't a major felon. He didn't get any trial at all, let alone a fair one. And being drowned wasn't any kind of euthanasia he'd ever heard of.

Did Gaelan know about this? Did he have a fair trial, or was he thrown into the cell the same way Fisher had been? Did the dead people really get a burial? What else would happen to them? Why would anyone want dead bodies?

It seemed odd that this elixir everyone except Hagan thought was wonderful was only delivered after the dead left on the barges. A shiver ran through Fisher as he remembered the sacrifices that had begun while he was with the Exiles. That had been about two years ago too.

Damn it. There was a link. There had to be. He'd have to do something about it.

No. He could tell Gaelan. He was planning to go north anyway. "I just want a quiet life," he muttered, then stood. "Excuse me. I need to see Gaelan." He grabbed his plate of still untouched food—he wasn't idiot enough to starve himself—then wove his way between the tables.

Gaelan looked up as Fisher moved closer and watched his progress. Fisher ignored the intensity in those tanzanite eyes and the way his own breathing eased as he moved closer, and focused instead on the questions swirling around in his mind. And why he would care about strangers and their politics.

"Can I speak to you for a few minutes?" he asked as soon as he reached Gaelan. He placed his plate down above Gaelan's as he spoke so no one would hear. "There's something—"

Gaelan turned his head, his lips brushed Fisher's hair near his ear. "I know." He shuffled to the side of his seat, inviting Fisher to sit on the seat with him. "Eat first. Listen to Aunty Cray."

Fisher scowled at the half-seat he was being offered but squeezed in beside Gaelan anyway. As the warmth between them seeped through his clothing, the ache in his chest eased. *That is* not *happening.*

He turned to listen to Aunty Cray.

"Stop making 'scuses for that upstart, Sand. You know as well ah do that my position is bestowed by t'dragon. It don't matter how much t'Viscount dislikes what ah say, he can't do nothin' 'bout it, though he tried. His guards were all set t'drag me to t'dungeons when my pendant laid 'em all flat." She grinned proudly.

"You invoked your pendant?" Brother Sands eyes were wide and horrified.

Fisher sought the necklace in question, only to find a small, delicately set blue-purple stone nestled at the base of Aunty Cray's throat, almost concealed by the drooping folds of skin.

Aunty Cray smirked at Gaelan as she answered Brother Sand. "I did nothin'. The dragon invoked the pendant." She scowled. "Now that idiot is 'fraid o'me."

"You didn't want that?" asked Fisher.

"A little healthy fear with someone like that c'n be useful," she replied. "But not the sort 'at brings anger with it. He'll want me dead now." She returned her gaze to Gaelan. "He don't want you involved neither. That's why you were taken away. Did he throw you out?"

"Not exactly," said Gaelan. "He was going to arrest me, but I got away."

Fisher regarded him curiously. He didn't seem to want people to know they'd escaped from the cells. He was glad he'd kept quiet about it earlier.

Fisher was squashed so hard against Gaelan he had to eat his meal with one hand. The few times he struggled with a particularly large piece of meat in the stew, Gaelan had silently used his knife to cut it while Fisher held it still, all the while continuing his conversation with Aunty Cray and Brother Sand.

Fisher did the same for Gaelan when he needed it. They weren't doing anything but eating, but the cooperative mealtime felt more intimate than anything Fisher had done before. His face was hot with embarrassment long before they finished eating.

"If the Viscount is watching for you, Minstrel, it might be better if you weren't involved in any action that would bring you to his attention." Brother Sand shifted uncomfortably on his seat, tiny frown lines appeared between his brows. "We can find another way to bring the Duke home."

"Are you all right, Brother Sand?" asked Fisher.

"I had a fall a few months ago and hurt my back. I still suffer from the pain." He nodded at a young monk who was standing nearby.

As the monk disappeared through the doorway, Brother Sand said, "The healers gave me some of the Elixir the Viscount trades for. It's been a dragon-blessed thing, I'll tell you. Without it I'd probably still be bedridden."

The monk returned with a small glass filled with a viscous black liquid. "It doesn't look much, smells and tastes even worse, but it works." He tossed the liquid back with a grimace.

Gaelan snatched the glass up as soon as Brother Sand placed it on the table and sniffed the remnants of the Elixir, the displeased furrows on his forehead deepened. Fisher watched Brother Sand carefully.

Within seconds, Brother Sand's face had cleared and a small smile appeared. When he turned to them, Fisher saw his pupils were dilated.

"If you'll excuse me, the Elixir always makes me sleepy. I need to retire," he said. "And dance." He pushed his chair into place. "Dancing is always good."

The young monk came forward and linked his arm with Brother Sand. "Will you dance with me this evening, Pink? No? You never dance with me." Brother Sand tripped and would have fallen if Pink hadn't been holding him. They meandered their way out of the dining hall.

"Right," said Aunty Cray as soon as Brother Sand had gone. "The Receiving Parlor is empty at this time. Ah'll meet you both there in ten minutes." She swiped the last of her bread around her plate, leaving it almost as clean as it was before she put the food on it. She burped loudly, then scraped her chair back and waddled out of the dining hall.

"I know," said Gaelan when he turned to Fisher, "but that woman is the best warrior on God's Island, the fiercest protector and the funniest comic you'll ever see. She's also the mayor."

They quickly finished their meal then followed Aunty Cray to the parlor.

"You weren't travelin' through that 'orror, were you?" asked Aunty Cray as they entered.

Fisher looked at Gaelan because he didn't know what she was talking about.

She strode to a sideboard filled with bottles and glasses and splashed clear liquid into three squat glasses. Her hands were broad and brown, as time-worn as her face and neck.

"I was in the forest the night of the eclipse," said Gaelan.

Fisher jumped at the mention of the eclipse and his heart pounded. His mind replayed the night in a series of flashing images and sounds—the bloodshed, the clash of steel in battle, the red light, the four becoming one then separating again only to find themselves Bonded, the howl of Jun when he went feral.

He opened his mouth and tried to slow his breathing. Gingerly, he sat on a sofa and sipped at his drink to wash away the lingering blood-metal he thought he'd breathe and taste forever.

When he felt he was again completely present in the parlor, he looked up, straight into Gaelan's eyes.

"The light went a bit odd." Gaelan smiled as if he was part of an in-joke neither he nor Aunty Cray were aware of. He looked sharply at Fisher. "What about you? Did you see the eclipse from where you were?"

"See?" His voice sounded a little hysterical. Not surprising, considering his stomach tumbled at his memories and he struggled to take a deep breath. "I was underground at the time. I didn't see the eclipse." *I saw a person change from female to male in front of me. I saw four people move water in a huge funnel around them without touching it. And I saw the birth of dragons, but I didn't see the eclipse.*

"Tha's too bad. T'were a sight for sure, with the air all red and sparkly. Like some portent, it was." She sighed heavily, her significant bosom lifting and falling ponderously. "'Cause that were also the night all our men were taken."

"Taken? By whom?"

"Och, listen to you, talkin' all Imperial and everything. You'd never know you were really Yeudan, what with the fancy speech and them odd patches on your skin."

Fisher pressed his hand to his face where he knew the largest of the brown patches could be seen. He'd lost his concealing cream, as it had been in his backpack when the soldiers had tossed him into the cell. Until he got some more, there was no way he could cover them.

At least she'd stopped asking about the eclipse. He took a few careful, counted breaths and relaxed.

Aunty Cray waved her hand dismissively. "Don't you worry none. It's nice to see sompin' different, like our Gaelan here. No one round here has eyes like his. Same color as them God-stones, the tanzanite. Odd, that."

"Aunty." Gaelan frowned at her.

She grinned. "Orright, youngun." She turned back to Fisher. "Our men were taken during the eclipse by the Hoons. Tha's why Gaelan and I came here. Thought the Duke'd know sompin." She leaned forward conspiratorially. "Tha Viscount managed to get the Duke outta town. Sent him all the way to the Icy Wastes to deal with the Yeudan mebbe breaking the contract.

"Ya know who I saw in the hall with the Viscount? The captain of the Hoons! Tha were real friendly-like too." She glared at Gaelan. "Ya know what that means?"

"You think the Viscount ordered the raid?"

"I know it. They'd thrown you out by then, but that captain said the barge was loaded full, just needed a few more dead to make the trip."

"That doesn't mean they put our men on the barges with the dead." Gaelan stood and paced. "Why would they need the funeral barge fully loaded? There can't be that many people who die here."

"There's the cells, or dungeons, or whatever you call them," said Fisher quietly. "I'll bet a lot of people are thrown in there under false charges and don't get a trial." He looked pointedly at Gaelan.

Gaelan hmphed then paced some more. "They've been taking the dead. Now they also want the living. What does that have to do with the Yeudan supplying the Elixir? They trade for it so they don't come back empty, that's all."

Fisher didn't like the direct this discussion was heading. Every time either of them said something, it seemed to implicate the Yeudan.

Both Gaelan and Aunty Cray knew he was Yeudan, and both kept reminding him. As if he could forget. There was no reason for him to be included in this discussion unless they expected him to be involved.

Unless they wanted him to go to Barthes.

He jumped to his feet. "No way. Not a chance. Don't even think of it."

He strode to the door, but Gaelan got there first. How did he move so fast? "No. I've claimed sanctuary. I'm staying here and living in peaceful obscurity the rest my life." *No matter how bored I get.*

"You know the land."

"No."

"You know the customs," said Aunty Cray, as she sidled up to him.

"No."

"You know the people." Gaelan stepped forward, crowding him.

He stepped back and bumped into Aunty Cray. "No."

"Without your help, I'll be floundering around insulting everyone," said Gaelan. "I won't know how to get into the right places or talk to the right people. You can tell me what to do."

"I was a child when I left. I don't know anyone, let alone anyone influential." He stepped sideways, out of the Fisher sandwich they'd created. "This isn't my fight." He winced at the memory of fleeing from a fight that *was* his. *But that was to stay alive. Traitor.* The word haunted him.

"You'd walk away? Knowing people are being torn from their families? What if it's you? What will you do then? Your life won't be so peaceful or obscure then, will it?" Aunty Cray advanced on him, her hand held at shoulder height, her finger pointing and jabbing at him with each step.

He backed up. "Will you make that happen if I don't agree? Is that the deal? I go with you or you'll kill me and put me on the death barge?" He stood as tall as he could, towering over her. "Well, go ahead. The result would be the same."

"Aunty, stop it. You can't bully Fisher into helping if he doesn't want to." Gaelan held his position in front of the door as Aunty Cray deflated and stepped back.

She might have given ground, but Fisher could tell by her scowl she wasn't giving up.

"What about the dragons?"

Fisher gasped. She knew about the dragons? He didn't think the news would have traveled that far yet.

She had Gaelan's attention too, but he didn't look like he knew what she was talking about.

"Not the dragon god here," continued Aunty Cray. "Ah've heard rumors that dragons have hatched in the Aylmer Mountains. The first in a thousand years. You could enlist their help."

"What makes you think they'd be willing to help *me*?" Gaelan asked in a dark voice.

"Because you're—"

"No!" Fisher shouted. "No dragons. No, no, no." He put his hands on his face to hide his skin. The mottled brown and cream had been the bane of his life when he was young.

When he was a kid, they'd taunted him, singing that damned song over and over again until he screamed at them and threw rocks at them, and got beaten up for it.

He used to run then, whenever he could. He ran now, pushing Gaelan out of the way and fleeing back to their room.

He ran down one corridor after another. They all looked the same. One flight of stairs up, the wrong door opened, run again, another corridor. His breath rasped in his dry throat. He struggled to breathe. Down some stairs, turn a corner another corridor, another door, the familiar sound of water dripping in the bath.

He slammed the door closed and leaned against it, shaking, panting. It wasn't the fear making him gasp, just the running. He wasn't afraid of dragons he'd never meet. None of them were going to claim him as their concubine.

He slid down the closed door to crouch on the floor. He wasn't going to Barthes, he wasn't going to help Gaelan find out why their men were taken or where they were.

Fuck. What had he done? Fisher stood and ran his hands through his hair. He'd screamed at them and run away like a frightened child. He wasn't that child anymore. He didn't behave like that. He'd been the effective leader of the Exiles for years, covering the fact the old king was senile. He was calm and decisive, not hysterical.

There hadn't been dragons before.

He pressed his hands against his ribs and forced himself to breath slowly and evenly. That song from his childhood was simply a song. His mottled skin *didn't* make him part of any legend, just like Checa's silver eyes hadn't made him ... damn it. Checa's eyes *had* made him the Silver Shining from Rock.

That still didn't make Fisher anybody's bloody concubine. It didn't mean he had to go on some suicide mission to trace a whole heap of dead people. Gaelan could do it himself. It wasn't Fisher's fight.

He nodded to himself, relieved to have made the right decision. But the words spun in his head, as clear and taunting as they'd been when he was ten.

Concubine Mine
When the dragons return,
So will the concubine.

Indigo will tumble down mountains
And burn in ice that releases
Sapphire wonder.
Past and future collide.
Dragon king claims kin while
Air is washed away and shared.
The brown and cream comes home to
Silence loud and darkness lightened.
Heart-soul recognized, the Concubine
Wanders into dragon land,
Claimed.

CHAPTER SIX

FISHER LAY CLINGING to the edge of the bed as he had most of the night, but it was a wasted effort. He was alone, as he'd been most of the day before.

He dragged himself out of bed and washed his face. Each splash of water made him think he was drowning, so his wash was sketchy at best.

As ready as he could be, he made his way to the dining hall.

Hagan waved at him as he entered and indicated a seat at the top table near Brother Sand, Gaelan and Aunty Cray. Gaelan watched him, his bright eyes determined.

Fisher tried to breathe evenly through the fear and anger as he remembered the conversation from the day before. *It's not my fight. I'm not going near any dragons.*

He looked for Connie, but she was deep in discussion with another monk and there were no empty seats near her. Fisher sighed and walked the length of the room. *Eating with them doesn't mean I'm agreeing to go.*

"Master Fisher," called Brother Sand as he approached. "Sit with me. We have much to discuss."

His feet moved reluctantly but they didn't stop when that was what he wanted most. His manners must be better than he'd thought they were if he was so reluctant to disappoint the monk. But then, Brother Sand was the man who would determine whether or not

Fisher was to be granted sanctuary. That's all it was. It wasn't as if he knew the man well enough to like his ruddy face and full-bodied chuckles.

He sat in the seat indicated, between Brother Sand and Gaelan. As with the evening meal, he edged as far from Gaelan as he could.

That's when he smelled it—sweet and dark. Instantly alert, he looked around. The table was clear except for the bowls of vegetable stew for their breakfast. There were no suspicious-looking patches of oily sludge anywhere.

He looked up. The ceiling was sealed. Nothing would come in that way.

Yet he could still smell it. Norrgel.

"I trust you slept well," said Brother Sand. His esses slurred slightly and Fisher looked sharply at his face. Sweat dribbled down the monk's temples and he panted softly.

"You're not well," said Fisher.

Brother Sand gestured at the young monk who'd attended him last night—Pink. "It's nothing. The pain is becoming more difficult to manage. I've had to increase my dosage of the Elixir."

"I don't think that's a good idea," Fisher said slowly. He peered into Brother Sand's red-rimmed eyes and noted his shaking hands.

Brother Sand gasped and Fisher looked back to his face in time to see a ripple under his cheek fade away. "You sound just like my physician," he rasped as he reached out for the small glass Pink handed him.

The dark, loamy smell of norrgel grew stronger. Fisher's heart pounded. "Don't drink that."

He reached out to knock the elixir from Brother Sand's hand but Gaelan grabbed his arm.

"What are you doing?" Gaelan hissed against his ear.

"It's poison." He wrenched his arm clear.

It was too late. Brother Sand had already tipped the black liquid into his mouth.

Fisher stood, his chair clattering to the floor behind him. "Get water and bicarbonate," he yelled at Pink, who was waiting for the glass.

The only person that moved was Gaelan. "Fisher, sit down. Brother Sand simply needed his tonic."

"It's not tonic. It's poison. Norrgel excrement." He wrenched himself away from Gaelan again and turned to Brother Sand.

He was too late.

The ripple in the monk's cheek hadn't been his imagination. His whole face was moving now, as if there were rats running around beneath the skin.

Brother Sand groaned and pushed himself ponderously to his feet. Then his back arched, the tendons on his neck taut. He screamed.

Fisher backed away, bumping into Gaelan, who was reaching to help.

"No! Don't touch him. Get back! It's poison."

Brother Sand screamed again and collapsed to the floor at his feet, his body convulsing, jerking backward and forward sharply. Cracking bones splintered the shocked silence of the rest of the room, as loud as the monk's now constant screams.

Pink rushed forward. Fisher ran and pushed him back. "Don't touch him. You'll be infected." He dragged a shocked Aunty Cray several steps away. "Everyone get back."

"We have to help him," said Aunty Cray.

"There's nothing you can do. It's norrgel poisoning."

And it was his fault.

Fisher jumped away as Brother Sand fell to the floor. He crashed against Gaelan, pushing him back as well. They stumbled together, tangling limbs. Gaelan grasped Fisher's arms and held them both upright as the distance between them and Brother Sand increased. Aunty Cray, her elbow still held in Fisher's grip, came with them.

No longer tethered to them, Pink rushed toward the now writhing man.

"No!" yelled Fisher, but his voice was barely heard over the screams. He lurched forward a step, but the crunch of bone, accompanied by a hoarser scream stopped him. He couldn't get close, not if he wanted to live. "Don't touch him."

It was too late. Pink pressed his hand to Brother Sand's chest, perhaps to hold him still, perhaps to feel his heartbeat. The skin around his hand, unable to take the strain, burst. Blood and partially dissolved muscle, bone and organs sprayed out, drenching Pink. He jerked backward in shock.

The silence, stark and sudden, lasted several seconds. Brother Sand's body still writhed and bulged. Gashes appeared on his face and neck, his forearms and hands, muscle and sinew melted through and oozed onto the floor.

Pink whimpered as he watched his leader and mentor dissolve before his eyes. His whimpers gained in volume as Brother Sand's clothes began to disintegrate under the mess that had once been his body.

Then the whimpers became louder. The monk clutched his own clothes, the weakened threads tearing under his clenching fingers. He swiped at his face and neck where spots of blood and gore had spattered on him. Underneath, the skin was already gone, the muscle beneath exposed. Near his mouth, the damage was worse. His teeth gleamed in the torchlight.

The monk lifted his hands away and the whimpers returned as he looked at the clump of flesh in his palm. He panted, his eyes going wide with shock and fear and pain. Then he screamed.

By now, many in the main part of the dining hall had gathered around the table, horror the common mark on their features. Several of the monks pushed others out of the way and made their way through the crowd, fleeing from the room. Others maneuvered their way around the table, gazes intent through the horror.

"Stay away," yelled Fisher.

Aunty Cray pulled her arm from his grip and rushed to intercept those wanting to help. Gaelan released Fisher and went in the other direction. Both gave what was left of Brother Sand and the young monk, still screaming, a wide berth.

Fisher backed away, his heart pounding, throat thick with fear and guilt, tears burning his eyes.

Between them, Gaelan and Aunty Cray managed to clear the room. After seeing what happened to Pink when he touched Brother Sand, no one tried to get close to the screaming man, but many wanted to watch the gruesome sight, comparing the growing pool of liquid flesh that had once been Brother Sand with the slowly dissolving screaming, writhing mass that was the young monk.

The scream became a burbling cry, drawing Fisher's stunned gaze to Pink. His eyelids were gone, the eyeballs leaned drunkenly on the exposed cheekbones. Fisher gasped as one of the eyeballs wriggled in amongst the blood pooling in the eye socket and overflow over the ruined cheek and jaw.

Before he could fully comprehend that the wriggle came from the inside, a hole formed in the eyeball and the aqueous oozed out, threading its way through the blood and flesh as it all dribbled down his face and neck onto the robes that still covered him.

The noise cut off abruptly, as it had with Brother Sand. One minute the young monk was sitting there, falling apart, and the next his body quietly folded on top of itself, the outside lava-like ooze joining the lumpy excrement seeping through and beneath his clothes, and the whole lot gradually melting into a squirming mound of melting flesh and bone and cloth.

In the sudden quiet, Fisher's breathing was loud. Gasping. Wet. Panicked. Shudders wracked his body and he stumbled and fell to the floor.

He'd seen this before. Exactly this. Over and over. He'd fought against it, but it had happened anyway. He'd thought it was ended when the Exiles were taken by the Imperials and the Mafdeti. When the dragons came.

The hope that it was over and he could build a better life had swelled inside him, a fragile bubble that had burst when everyone had cried "traitor." Even then, when he'd escaped, he'd thought it was over.

But it wasn't over. Not by a long shot. This was worse. This wasn't sacrifices to a false god. It wasn't a power play. This was profiting from other people's deaths. This was murder.

And it was all his fault.

He rose from his inelegant sprawl, chest heaving as if he'd run all day, joints creaking like an old man's. He looked around the almost-empty dining hall. Cries echoed from outside, horror and grief mixing with the odor of violent death and the vomit of those who couldn't get out fast enough.

On the table, steam rose gently from bowls, the food still warm. Only one bowl was disturbed, knocked to the floor when Brother Sand began screaming.

At the other side of the table stood Gaelan, his somber eyes regarding Fisher.

"I'm sorry," whispered Fisher. "I thought..." He ran. The barge. He'd take it back to the mainland and fix this, even if he died doing it.

He stumbled to a stop in the entrance hall. If they saw him, they'd kill him. How was he going to get back to Barthes without being detected, without being caught and killed as a traitor?

He spun around, to go back... somewhere, and came face to face with Gaelan. "I have to stop this." He hoped Gaelan would know what he was talking about. "But I can't. They'll kill me before I get there."

"Where do you need to go?"

How could Gaelan be so calm about this? "Did you see what happened?" He pointed a shaky finger toward the dining hall.

Gaelan looked toward the dining hall, his expression gaining gravitas with each breath. When he turned back to Fisher, his vibrant eyes were dark with grief. "You seem to think you can stop it happening again." He waited, patient and silent, until Fisher nodded.

"The Exiles have been sacrificing people to the norrgel as part of their religious practices. The residue is collected and sent to Barthes." He stared down the long hallway toward the front door, unable to even glance in Gaelan's direction. "I don't know what they do with it, but I know the Yeudan will do whatever it takes to make this venture profitable. That's where the Elixir is coming from."

Aunty Cray walked to a tapestry and grabbed a rope hanging beside it. The mellow sounds of a dozen bells rang through the temple. "We need to farewell the dead." She nodded at Gaelan. "Minstrel, will you lead the chorus?"

Gaelan was silent for a long time, then strode to the center of the entrance. He stood in the middle of the ornate star etched into the tiles, lifted his arms wide and began to sing. His voice was deep and resonant. It wasn't loud, but it carried up the central staircase and reverberated through the temple.

As he sang, the monks returned and lined the stairs, their voices adding depth and tone until it seemed like the entire island sang the lament for the dead.

Fisher had only met Brother Sand and the other monk a couple of times, but by the time Gaelan had finished singing, tears rolled down his cheeks.

In the silence that followed, Aunty Cray stepped up beside Gaelan. "After the lament, comes the promise."

Gaelan lowered his arms and began another song, the monks again joining in.

When the dragons return,
So will the concubine.

A cry escaped Fisher as he recognized the words.

Indigo will tumble down mountains
And burn in ice that releases
Sapphire wonder.

His tears dried in the horror that swept through him.

Past and future collide.
Dragon king claims kin while
Air is washed away and shared.

His feet were welded to the floor as the words washed over him.

The brown and cream comes home to
Silence loud and darkness lightened.

He couldn't stay here.

Heart-soul recognized, the concubine
Wanders into dragon land,

There was nowhere else for him to go. The words chased him as he pried his feet loose and ran for the door.

He thumped into a broad chest. Hands were firm and steady landed on his arms. He looked up into tanzanite eyes, steady and serious. Gaelan's voice lifted, soared through the temple and landed with a thud in his chest.

Claimed.

IN THE AFTERMATH, WITH the echo of the music dying around them, three monks dressed in sombre black entered the dining room.

Aunty Cray clapped her hands. "We don't need to be here when they come aht. Come into the library and we'll work aht what will happen next."

Fisher walked along with them. The urge to run had died with the music. He wasn't going to be able to avoid going back to the mainland to fix this. Yes, he wanted to live, and he craved a life that had some measure of peace, but he knew he couldn't leave these people to fight the evil they were facing. Especially when they didn't even know what the Elixir really was.

The door was barely closed behind him when Aunty Cray asked, "Will you help us?" She closed the small distance between them. She was shorter than he, but he was intimidated by her gimlet gaze. He sidled around her and went to stare out the large window.

The sun was high in the sky now, even though they'd barely finished breakfast. The reminder of what had happened weakened his knees and he leaned against the window sill.

Below, in the garden beyond the cloisters, more monks dressed in black strode to and fro on errands he couldn't contemplate. Surely a sturdy bucket and a scrubbing brush would be the most useful thing in clearing up what was left of Brother Sand and Pink.

Beyond the garden with its neatly trimmed shrubbery and well-worn paths, was the wall separating the temple from the cemetery. Behind loomed the castle, dark and forbidding in its granite beauty. Beneath that were the dungeons he had Gaelan had escaped from.

Heart beating fast at the memory, he turned back to Aunty Cray and Gaelan.

He focused on Gaelan. "I'll go with you to sort out what's happening with this elixir of yours and help you find your duke, but there are conditions."

"I don't think you're in a position to demand—" began Gaelan.

Aunty Cray laid a hand on his arm. "Hear him out, Minstrel." She nodded for Fisher to continue.

He glared at Gaelan. "I want to know how we got out of the dungeons. I would have drowned if you hadn't..." He trailed off, unsure how to say it. *Kissed me? Breathed for me?* "How did you do it?"

Gaelan looked away but didn't respond. Fisher didn't know him well yet, but he knew guilt when he saw it.

"I want an answer to that, and I want you to promise we won't be going anywhere near the dragons."

"What?" Gaelan strode forward until there was barely a foot between them. He loomed over Fisher, but Fisher refused to back down. He'd faced off against fury like that before.

And there was guilt in Gaelan's eyes. Because of the water or the dragons? Fisher wished he could read the other man better.

Aunty Cray stepped forward again, wobbling herself between them. "Why don't we all sit down," she said to Gaelan. "Then you can give Fisher the assurances he needs, and we can get this job done before any more people die the way poor Brother Sand and Pink did."

Fisher flopping into the nearest seat.

Once they were settled, Aunty Cray smoothed her hands over her wide knees. "Gaelan?"

Fisher jumped. She knew his name? She'd only called him Minstrel before. Fisher regarded her closely and caught a calculated smirk aimed at Gaelan, who sighed and ran his hands through his hair. He stilled and focused his bright gaze on Fisher's face as if he'd come to a decision.

"The water first," Fisher said. He needed to know how they'd survived and he wasn't going to agree to anything more until he found out.

Gaelan stood and paced between him and Aunty Cray. "Okay."

"Might as well, just get it out, boy," said Aunty Cray. "Caint be more odd than some things I've seen."

"Why no dragons?"

"You don't get to avoid this, but I'll let you delay for now," said Fisher. Gaelan had looked so uncomfortable and worried, he had wanted to tell him it didn't matter. Except it did matter. If he couldn't trust Gaelan to tell him the difficult things, he couldn't trust him to keep him alive.

And it would fall on Gaelan to do that. Once it was discovered Fisher was back on the mainland, there'd be any number of people hunting for him. So. Dragons.

"I won't have anything to do with dragons. If you take me into their territory at all, even inadvertently, I'll leave. You won't know I'm gone until it's far too late to find me and bring me back. I'll refuse to help any further. You'll be on your own. I don't need to explain more than that." He held himself rigid as he glared, willing Gaelan not to challenge the issue.

Gaelan frowned and paced some more, then seemed to come to a decision. His face cleared and he sat next to Aunty Cray. "I'll make sure we know exactly where the dragon territory is on the mainland before we leave here. I'll do everything I can to make sure you stay out of their territory while we're there."

"But—" Aunty Cray said.

Gaelan held up his hand. "I'm not going to lead Fisher into dragon territory, Aunty Cray."

She narrowed her eyes at him but subsided.

"Good," he said, relief coursing through him. Then he sat straighter. "The water?"

Gaelan slumped. "The water," he intoned. He tilted his head. "You know of the sea serpent?"

"You're not trying to tell me you're the sea serpent?" Honestly, after watching the Mafdeti change into cats in front of him and dragons hatch and fly in the sky, Fisher would believe almost anything. But Gaelan didn't strike him as a sea serpent type, whatever that type was.

"No, of course not," Gaelan blustered before he slid further down in his seat. "But we're sort of... related."

"What does that mean? You can turn into a serpent and slither all over the place?"

"No, but I can breathe in places most people can't. Like underwater."

"How?"

"I grow gills." Gaelan still seemed reluctant to talk about it but he wasn't prevaricating.

"Show me," demanded Fisher as he stood. "Do you need to be in water to do it? Will the bath do?" He glanced out the window. "Or a pond?"

Gaelan stood as well. "You don't believe me? How else would you have survived? You know it's true."

Fisher was nothing if not stubborn. "I want to see." He jumped back as Gaelan whipped his shirt off.

"Watch," Gaelan demanded as he lifted his arms high.

Fisher studied Gaelan's neck for a few seconds, then realized he could have seen that without the shirt coming off so he lowered his gaze to Gaelan's broad brown chest. His gaze faltered and got caught on Gaelan's rounded pecs and dusky nipples, then movement caught his attention.

What had seemed like pale scars or white tattoos that followed the line of his ribs, rippled and separated until the skin gaped like fish gills. He stepped forward, reaching automatically to touch the flapping skin, but before he could, the gills closed and sealed, looking once again like thin scars.

Gaelan gasped, sucking in great breaths. He staggered and Fisher caught him and lowered him to a seat.

"You can't breathe out of water when you do the gill thing, can you? You could have died doing that stunt, you idiot." He pushed Gaelan down roughly and stepped back. "It would have been just as easy to jump in the damned pond. Don't do that again."

Gaelan shrugged.

"Don't you dismiss me, you oaf." Fisher was furious that Gaelan would have risked his life like that when there was a much easier solution. "You ever pull a stupid stunt like that again, you can go on this idiotic quest on your own."

Gaelan huffed a laugh. "Is that another condition?" He raised calm blue eyes to Fisher. "Are you going to add a condition every time I do something you don't like?"

"If it risks your fool life, I just might." He strode to the door.

"Where are you going?" asked Aunty Cray.

"I'm going to organize supplies for us. Work out who we have to talk to once we're on the mainland." He glared at Gaelan. "You work out how you're going to keep me concealed while we're there. I don't want to be killed on the first day. I'm sure you don't want that either, especially after you've gone to so much trouble to get me to agree to go with you."

Fisher closed the door when he left, refusing to feel guilty for piling all that guilt onto Gaelan. It wasn't as if Gaelan had arranged for Brother Sand to take the norrgel poison so Fisher would feel obligated to help.

And he didn't really need Gaelan to keep him safe. He had been doing that for himself for a long time.

He headed for the kitchens to talk to the cooks.

CHAPTER SEVEN

"ARE YOU SURE THIS IS a good idea?" Fisher asked as he boarded the death barge.

Gaelan glanced at the neatly stacked white-shrouded shapes as they walked up the gangplank. He'd hovered uncertainly on the dock as Fisher had tried to engage one of the crew in conversation while Aunty Cray negotiated their passage with the captain.

The man had given both of them such a practiced stink-eye that Gaelan was sure he had fleas crawling all over him. He scratched at the back of his neck reflexively as he watched the shoreline of the Lonely Isles recede, then moved to the side of the boat that was upwind of all the corpses. They'd been on board fewer than ten minutes and he was sure this wasn't a good idea at all.

"We'll have a small detour out to the open ocean, then they'll drop us at Grewin when they stop to trade," he said quietly, avoiding the question completely.

"Are they trading for more Elixir? Shouldn't we stop them?"

He looked around again but there were no crew close enough to hear them. "The only thing that will stop them trading is for us to stop it at the source. The Elixir makes too much money for anyone to consider stopping the trade."

"We're going through the swamps, right? Not to Hawkesby or the desert."

Gaelan didn't understand Fisher's reluctance to go to the seat of Imperial power. Hawkesby was a marvel in ancient technology, the workings of which had long been forgotten by most inhabitants on Thalazar. They could fly over the desert.

"Stopping at Hawkesby would give us more information on other things but we can bypass it for now. We'll go to Grewin to gather information so we know the best way to approach Barthes." Being Yeudan, Fisher probably knew the best way to get into Barthes undetected, but Gaelan didn't want to put more pressure on him than he already had to get him to agree to this quest.

"The military will see us coming miles away," Fisher murmured.

"Is there a way around?"

Fisher shook his head. "Barthes is in the middle of a vast plain. They can see for miles in every direction. The only way we'll get into the city undetected is if we approach under the ice. We don't have time to dig that sort of tunnel network. Not unless we can melt our way through." Fisher smiled as he gazed out across the sea.

Gaelan wondered what sort of memories Fisher had that melting ice could bring a smile to his face. His firm lips looked soft and vulnerable from whatever he was remembering.

"They aren't happy about us being on board." He wrenched his mind away from Fisher's lips. He moved closer so their shoulders brushed.

"It's only for a couple of days, right? They sail out to sea, dump the bodies, then follow the coastline back to Grewin."

"I think us being here has made them change their plans a bit." Gaelan wasn't sure what made him certain of that, but the sly glances he kept getting from a number of the crew made him suspicious.

He wanted to pretend he didn't need to be here, to get off the boat and disappear with Fisher until Fisher realized they were meant to be together, but he kept hearing Brother Sand's screams and knew fixing this was the only way to make the echoes of pain and terror stop.

The silence thickened and lengthened as the crew cast off and the barge floated into the Great Southern Ocean. Twenty minutes later, as they changed course from north to east, Gaelan spoke again. "The sea serpent is to the west of the Lonely Isles."

Fisher stared at the darkening water. "What's to the east?"

"Nothing. They must go north soon. I'd have seen from my home if they continued directly east or to the south." Even as he spoke the ship subtly changed direction, heading more northerly.

"What are they avoiding to the east and south?".

"God's Island. This way, no one will notice they don't go west."

"If there's nothing to the east, there must be something north."

"Only the mainland. Directly north of the isles are swamps. There are people who live there. To my knowledge, they don't interact with others."

Gaelan continued to stare northward.

Hours later, as the water turned indigo and the sky mirrored it, they came in sight of the coast, thick and black in the gloom, and turned east again.

Two crew members came and escorted them to a small interior cabin. "The burial ceremony is sacred and takes most of the night, so please remain here until morning."

The whole thing felt wrong. They were watched too closely, even as they were ignored. "I think we should find a way off—"

There was a knock at the door. Gaelan opened it to reveal a youth with a covered tray. He stepped back to allow the steward to enter. On his first forward step, the boy up-ended the tray and threw it toward him. He was too slow to defend himself and the edge of the tray slammed into his cheek.

On the heels of the steward, several sailors stormed into the room. Gaelan turned and struck the boy, knocking him to the floor, his head smacking loudly against the wooden surround of the bed.

A grunt from Fisher sent Gaelan across the room to grab the sailor strangling him. He lifted him by the back of his neck and flung him across the room and was about to turn and deal with the rest when pain exploded in his head. The floor smashed into his cheek.

Gaelan's head pounded in time with the slap of the boat on the waves. He clenched his eyes closed tight, convinced opening them would be a bad thing.

His stomach roiled and he tried to roll to his side in case he vomited. He tried again and rolled a bit but then slipped back. His arms locked when he tugged. Pain shot through his fingers and he pried his swollen eyes open.

"Damn." His voice was as thick as his head felt. Inside his head was as pudgy as his swollen fingers. He kicked his legs, but they were bound too. Sweat bathed him, pooling uncomfortably at the base of his throat and running from his navel and under his body. The air was warm and close.

"You're awake?" asked Fisher close by.

He turned his head. Fisher lay beside him, almost under the bed. His eyes were dull and sported dark shadows beneath them. His hands were bound behind his back. His legs were tied too.

Gaelan's head spun and his cheek throbbed. "I'm guessing they didn't stop overnight to perform any kind of ceremony to give the dead to the sea serpent."

"Not that I noticed."

"What are they doing with the dead then?"

The engines slowed, then idled throatily. Forward movement stopped and the boat bobbed gently. Outside, there was a grating slide then the splash of the anchor dropping into the water.

Orders were called although Gaelen couldn't make out what they were. Something thudded against the side of the boat, slipped away, then thudded again before dragging overhead and stopping.

"Have we reached land? Returned to the Isles?" asked Fisher.

"Not with the way we're tied up. I think we've pulled up beside another ship." He tugged at his hands again. "We need to get loose. We have to find out what they're doing and get ourselves out of this."

"Won't they come for us soon anyway?" Fisher began struggling against his restraints.

"By the time they come for us, it'll be too late." Gaelan closed his eyes and tried to concentrate. Most of his stones were in his backpack, but there was a small focus stone in his pocket. He just needed to channel enough heat to his wrists and he'd be free.

"If they're passing the bodies to someone else, rather than burying them, there's a reason for it. We're still alive. I think the only reason for that is because they need live sacrifices for the norrgel and we're it."

He kept talking to distract Fisher, hoping he didn't notice the smell of burning rope. "There's no way I'm sitting here meekly waiting for some bastard I don't even know to decide when I'm going to die. I'm not going to die by norrgel either."

He wove his body and kicked his legs until he'd spun around enough that his ankles were nearer to Fisher. "Can you get the knots undone on my feet?"

Fisher looked startled but then rolled so his hands closed around Gaelan's ankles and he began worrying the knots.

"We won't have much time," said Gaelan. "Once they transfer the bodies they'll come for us."

The knots at his ankles unraveled and Gaelan spun around again, ignoring his pounding head and clammy skin, and pushed himself into a sitting position. He grunted as he strained his shoulders and the weakened rope around his wrists snapped. Then he stood, sweating and swaying.

"There's a knife in my boot," said Fisher as he turned his back. "Under the cuff."

Gaelan squatted and lifted the cuff of Fisher's boot to reveal a small but sharp knife. Carefully, he maneuvered it out of its sheath with his thick, unwieldy fingers, and leaned over Fisher's awkwardly raised hands. He double-checked his hold on the knife, not trusting his aching hands to hold it steady, then sliced through the rope holding Fisher immobile.

Fisher chafed his hands as he looked around the room. "They took my new backpack. Bastards." He patted his clothing. "We've got a couple of knives and enough jerky to last four days between us. No water though."

Gaelan's throat dried when he thought about water and breathing for Fisher. He bent to listen at the door while Fisher rose unsteadily to his feet.

He reached to open the door, surprised when the handle turned. He looked back at Fisher, eyebrows raised. "That was careless. If we're close enough to land, I can get us both there alive."

Gaelan gently opened the door and poked his head outside. A sigh of relief escaped when he saw the short corridor was empty. He gestured to Fisher to follow then slipped out of the room.

A few steps brought him to steep stairs leading up onto the deck. He strained to listen but heard only a few softly spoken words far enough away he didn't think they'd be noticed as they left. He placed his feet on each wooden step carefully to mute any sound he made.

As his head cleared the top of the staircase, he gagged and dropped back a step, wrapping his arm over his face to cover the sound of his retching coughs.

He fumbled for his belt and unwove the narrow scarf Aunty Cray had given him. Fisher eyed him speculatively then retrieved a cloth of his own and wrapped it around the lower part of his face. Gaelan's eyes would still water, but he'd be able to move without coughing.

He tugged the scarf down a bit and whispered to Fisher. "It's ripe up there so be prepared." At Fisher's nod, Gaelan cleared the stairs and stepped to the side so Fisher could join him.

The sight that greeted them brought his nausea back full-force. The light was very low, only patchy moonlight through the clouds overhead and the occasional flash of lamplight to guide the men working.

He was glad he couldn't see more than he did. The deck was layered three and four deep in poorly wrapped corpses. There was order to the piles, with narrow paths between each row where sailors threw ropes around bundles of bodies and tied them off to a hand-operated lever that hung overhead.

As soon as the bundles were secure, the rope was tugged and lamplight flashed for a second, then soft grunts could be heard from the ship anchored alongside them. The arm of the lever lifted and the bodies swung across the gap between the boats and lowered.

They disappeared at the point Gaelan thought must be the deck of the other ship so he assumed they were being put into the hold. They worked in near silence.

Gaelan turned to Fisher and risked a whisper. "They're too quiet. We must be near land." He gripped Fisher's arm and tugged him to the left side of the boat as he brought his lips close to his ear. "I can see the shadow of land over here when the moonlight cuts through the clouds. It's not far."

"So we swim?"

Gaelan's heart pounded at the thought of taking Fisher into deep water. He'd sink like a stone but his chances in the ocean with him were much better than they would be if he stayed on the boat with the body smugglers.

He breathed slowly and deeply. Fisher already knew he could breathe underwater. It didn't mean he'd find out about the other. He nodded at Fisher, gesturing for him to move. "Now, while they're busy. Hopefully no one will see us go over the side."

They made their way across the deck, hugging any shadow they could find, stepping carefully to stay quiet and undetected. There was an open space between the wall they'd been following and the railing over the edge, so Gaelan crouched. He peered around as best he could in the low light. Above him, Fisher did the same.

When Gaelan rose, Fisher asked, "Don't you want to stay and find out where they take the bodies?"

He shook his head. "I don't like our chances of staying alive past dawn if we stay here. This coastline is filled with norrgel nests."

"What?" Fisher whisper-shrieked. "If we swim to the land, we'll end up right in the middle of the norrgel. How's that any safer?"

"I can get us past the norrgel if we're on land."

"So we'll either be norrgel sacrifices at dawn, or we'll wander into a norrgel nest and be killed there." Fisher looked around, his gaze once again falling on the rows upon rows of dead bodies.

"If we stay here, we'll *definitely* die at dawn. If we leave, we *might* die at dawn. At least we'll have a chance."

Fisher stared at the bodies. "Okay. Let's go."

Gaelan lifted his shirt over his head. Salt water was harder to breathe in than fresh, so he needed the clothing out of the way so he would suck water, not cloth, and be able to breathe. He checked the position of the sailors and froze when he met the startled gaze of a sailor.

"Stop!" the man yelled, and ran toward them. The cry grabbed the attention of other sailors who turned and joined their compatriot.

The sailors' footsteps pounded along the deck, getting closer, louder.

Gaelan bent and thumped his shoulder into Fisher's stomach, lifted him, and carried him away from the shadows toward the low railing surrounding the deck.

One of the sailors lunged, flying in a low tackle. Gaelan was sure he would fall and they'd be caught again, but he held his feet and jumped. The sailor slid harmlessly beneath them. The deck vanished from below, replaced by the dark, breathing water.

For the second time in three days, Gaelan plunged into cold water and sank. At least this time Fisher would know to hold his breath and not panic... he hoped.

He turned to Fisher and slid his arms more firmly around his stomach. Fisher leaned back, resting his head on his shoulder.

Gaelan's hand gripped Fisher's jaw and turned him. Fisher's mouth was open and waiting when he pressed their lips together. Their legs tangled comfortably together.

The naturalness and the rightness of Fisher's mouth against his seeped through him more slowly than the cold from the water, but just as inevitable. Air flowed between them; they breathed together.

Relief flooded Gaelan as he realized that it would be so easy this time. He almost laughed. It didn't matter how natural it felt to have his arms around Fisher; knowing he was breathing was better.

He shifted his grip and the water flowed around them as they moved. Any sounds from above were silenced in the deep water. For long moments they floated, entwined, through the ocean.

Overhead, a deep splash reverberated. Fisher groaned and almost tore his mouth from Gaelan's but he held him still. He undulated his body against Fisher, their torsos and legs rubbing against each other, working their way away from the ship and toward the shore.

Fisher wrapped his arms securely around Gaelan's neck and his legs around his hips, making it easier for Gaelan to kick. Gaelan took them down deeper than they'd been in the oubliette and pond, away from the surface turbulence and into the landward current. His ears popped. Water flowed more swiftly around as he increased their speed.

After ten minutes or so, he headed for the surface. His ears popped again and a short time later, cold air flowed over his forehead as they surfaced.

The odor from the ship had abated. He took his first deep breath since boarding. Nearby, waves crashed rhythmically.

"Why didn't they knock us out until morning? Just tying us up like that was almost an invitation for us to escape." Fisher panted slightly as he spoke. He'd been kicking his feet in time with Gaelan's but hadn't been a lot of help with the swim.

"Ssh," he whispered. "Noise carries over water. They're still looking for us."

Fisher clamped his mouth closed and allowed him to swim. After a while, the regular rhythm of their feet kicking together and their breathing synced, lulling Gaelan into an almost daze.

He looked up at the sky: clouds, dark and shiny-bright, covered most of it. Here and there, a star twinkled, but mostly there was only the gloom of an oncoming storm.

As they swam, the wind kicked up, blowing spray and tiny wavelets into their faces. "Keep your mouth closed if you can so you don't swallow too much water," Gaelan said. The turbulent ocean surface felt like needles piercing his forehead and cheeks.

Soon after, the waves became larger and bumped into them at increasing intervals. Fisher whimpered. Gaelan imagined that after the dungeons and the oubliette, drowning was running one of the top items in a list entitled "Ways He'd Rather Not Die."

"We're getting close to the shore now." Gaelan's voice betrayed his fatigue. "That's why the waves are getting rough. We just need to get over the reef and it'll get much calmer. Going underwater again for a while will make it easier even though the current has changed."

He was glad they were nearly to shore. It felt like they'd been in the water for hours and he was exhausted. He imagined Fisher was feeling much the same even though he hadn't been swimming. He lowered his face to Fisher's again, sharing breath as they sank below the waves.

Several minutes later they again rose to the surface. "Going over the reef," Gaelan rasped, then he grunted as coral scraped across the tops of his feet in a stinging strike. "Nicked me. Watch for sharks."

Just as he finished speaking, the water calmed. The wind still whipped across them, alternately stinging and freezing, but the waves were smaller, the crashing of them now behind them as they kicked their way toward the shore.

Much sooner than he expected, his feet touched sand. He lurched forward at the unexpected resistance and they flopped into the shallow water, going under. Gaelan pushed them up with his feet and Fisher coughed and gasped.

"Turn," he grunted. He flipped them over so Fisher's face went under. Before Fisher had a chance to panic, Gaelan clasped him around his chest and lifted him onto his feet. Fisher struggled to get his footing but with Gaelan's arm around his waist they stumbled their way onto the sand and collapsed, breathing heavily.

Gaelan rolled onto his back, then lifted himself up onto his elbows. Beside him, Fisher stared at the dark sky and dug his fingers into the soft sand. Water lapped at their feet, warmer in the shallows than it had been on the other side of the reef, and much warmer than the wind. Gaelan shivered and watched Fisher do the same.

Gaelan looked around. The sand was dark in the scattered moonlight and covered in short dark spikes like skin blemishes. He rolled over on the packed sand that was a little grayer than it had been a few minutes before. To the east, a thin strip of light limned the horizon.

A cry echoed across the water.

"They've seen us. We need to get off the beach." He stood on wobbly legs and hauled Fisher to his feet.

"Can they follow us? Will they be able to get over the reef?" Fisher stumbled. "How do you have so much energy? I wasn't even swimming and my legs are barely holding me upright." He stumbled again and kicked one of the dark spikes, sending his body heavily into Gaelan. "Ow!"

Gaelan sidestepped the mangrove roots Fisher had pushed him toward, but the side of his foot scraped painfully against one of the rough spikes. "Mangroves. Don't stand on them."

"We're still south of the Aylmer Mountains then."

Gaelan walked quickly, his feet sinking into the sand as they moved out of the high tide area and the mangrove jungle met them. Another cry echoed across the water.

"Why are they yelling now?" asked Fisher.

"I don't know. It didn't sound like a pursuit call. Probably no more bodies on board." He tugged Fisher's elbow. "This way. We need to be somewhere they can't see."

They wove their way through the close-set mangrove trees and onto more solid ground. Colors bled into the plants and the ground as the sun rose, the gray deepening until he could discern the difference between different shades of green and brown. "I don't think we'll have time to go to Grewin or Hawkesby," he added as if they were having an afternoon stroll.

He pursed his lips to control the smile that fought for freedom when Fisher predictably glared at him. "We weren't going to Hawkesby at all." He stumbled again, and Gaelan slowed his pace. "How are you moving so fast?"

It was darker amongst the mangroves and the short roots rising from the sand became painful obstacles. Going slower wouldn't make it any better so he didn't answer.

"We can go directly north from here," said Fisher. Did the man not appreciate the quiet? "We could avoid the Imperials and Mafdeti completely."

They walked a few more steps. "Dragons too," added Fisher quietly, as if he didn't want anyone to hear him speak of them.

Gaelan's amusement fled. Fisher's insistence on staying away from dragons was beginning to grate. Did he have no idea at all what they were to each other? His chest tightened at the prospect that Fisher might never recognize Gaelan, might never bond with him. That Gaelan would never be able to touch him, kiss him... fly with him.

"Don't you think we should visit Hawkesby and find out what's happening?" he asked purely to see how strong Fisher's objections were.

"If you want to go through that territory, you go ahead. I told you I'm not going there. I'll be recognized."

"That's a lot of territory."

"Yes. And the Imperials and Mafdeti have dragons now. That's a deal breaker. Definitely no dragons."

Cold, hopeless dread slid glacier-like through him, forming solid around his heart.

"You can go on your own if that's what you'd like," Fisher continued, oblivious.

As Fisher peered through the mangroves, Gaelan could almost see his plan to return to Linspar and disappear, never to see Gaelan again, form in his mind.

Gaelan held his hands up in surrender. "Okay. We'll have to be more vigilant and do our own reconnaissance, but we'll get there faster if we go directly north from here."

They left the mangroves and entered the forest, walking west until the trees had swallowed them and they could no longer see the sea. The air was briny and the ground still sandy between the close-growing shrubs and trees but there was enough ground cover to walk on greenery and hide their footprints.

Gaelan slowed his pace and loosened his hold on Fisher's arm. Every twenty minutes or so he veered toward the sunrise to peer through the undergrowth and out to sea. The first few times he spoke in a whisper, knowing how sound carried across the water, even during the day when the gulls were active. "They've come in closer to the reef, but I don't think they can get through."

The next time: "They're using their spy glasses to look this direction."

Finally, he could report: "They're pulling up anchor. I think they've given up." He sank behind the trees until there was no sign of the ocean and the susurration of the waves had faded into white noise.

"I haven't seen any norrgel," said Fisher.

That explained his preoccupation with looking into the canopy. In the few days he'd been in Linspar he'd been inside buildings most of the time, with no chance of attack from the skies. Now, out in the open, he looked twitchy and vulnerable.

Gaelan resisted putting a comforting arm around him. "They're around but their nests are to the west. They generally hunt in that direction too, usually avoiding the swamplands and ocean. The populations of the few fishing villages along the coast make pickings for the norrgel slim. The first well-populated seaport we'll come to is just north of the Seven Mountain Ranges. Yeudan. The norrgel don't go that far north.

"We'll be able to hunt for food along the way, even during the day, as long as we stay away from the norrgel nests."

"You must have traveled a lot to know so much."

Gaelan regarded him silently as they walked along, wondering what he was thinking about, if he had noticed the discrepancies in what Gaelan had told him before. Finally, he shook his head. "I'm a minstrel. I travel and sing. Traveling gives me material for my songs."

"Is that where you heard that song about the dragons returning?" Sweat dribbled down the back of Fisher's neck but Gaelan didn't think it was because they'd been walking for several hours. The concubine song terrified him and Gaelan couldn't work out why. It was *their* song, the one that predicted the majesty of their joining and magnificence of their life together.

"There better not be any dragons where we're heading," Fisher muttered, shattering Gaelan's warm and fuzzy imaginings.

CHAPTER EIGHT

FISHER TRUDGED ON ACROSS the now soft grass. Patches of sandy soil glowed bright between the verdant tussocks.

To their right, high dunes, grown over with grasses and shrubs, with the occasional stubby tree, blocked their sight of the ocean. The sea murmured softly beneath the screeching birds defending their homes.

The air closed in as the sun rose but Gaelan kept a punishing pace. Fisher's head throbbed with every step. His throat burned with thirst and swallowing did nothing more than block his breathing.

When the sun was directly above, cutting through the canopy and burning his nose, Fisher croaked out, "Gaelan."

Gaelan turned, his look of surprised query quickly turning to one of concern. "What's wrong? You're unwell?"

Fisher scowled. "We were poisoned and nearly drowned—again—and we've been charging through the wilderness without break for hours. Of course I'm not well. We need to find water at least, and have something to eat."

They'd neither seen nor heard anything that could be considered a threat the whole morning. He glared. "Then I'm going to nap for a while before we continue. You might be able to walk all day with no food or water and continue into the night, but I can't."

Gaelan immediately looked contrite. "I'm sorry. I forgot."

How could anyone forget they needed to drink and eat?

Gaelan took his elbow solicitously. "You sit here for a few minutes. I'll get something for you to drink."

Fisher shook free of the hold. "I don't need you babying me. We just need to stop for a few minutes so I can find some water and eat some jerky."

He turned studied the slope of the land and the density of the trees around them as he rummaged in his pocket for a piece of jerky. There'd surely be a stream not too far away that flowed into the ocean.

Gaelan patted his shoulder, raising Fisher's ire further. "Don't patronize me." He spun back to confront him but found he was talking to air.

His first thought was that Gaelan had simply disappeared but then he walked a few steps and peered into the undergrowth. There were newly broken stems and trampled mulch, indicating someone had recently passed that way, but Gaelan was nowhere to be seen.

"Gaelan," he called into the sudden silence, then clamped his mouth closed in case he'd attracted attention they didn't want. There was no response.

Fisher flapped his hands once, slapping them on the sides his thighs. "Idiot," he whispered, but he wasn't sure if he was referring to himself for believing Gaelan could just disappear, or to Gaelan for abandoning him without a word.

His throat itched with a need to swallow but was too dry to do anything. His stomach cramped around its emptiness. He pressed his fingers against his aching eyes, the momentary darkness providing minimal relief from the constant ache behind them.

Should he wait, hoping that Gaelan would return? Fisher huffed angrily at himself. He'd had enough lessons throughout his life to know he couldn't rely on anyone to come back; couldn't rely on anyone else at all.

To his left, a branch cracked. He spun toward the noise, heart pounding, as he stared with fixed concentration at the undergrowth. Nothing moved. What sort of animal could cause that noise? Was it dangerous? Could it be a person? He had no idea how close the nearest village was.

There was no point retracing his steps of the morning. He already knew there was nothing there. Imperial lands lay to the west, so he turned north again. After what he'd done as an Exile, he'd have a better chance of survival with the Mafdeti.

He thought of the ambush he'd organized and the number of Mafdeti killed. Or perhaps not.

Fisher picked up a small pebble and popped it into his mouth. The resulting saliva eased the ache in his throat but if he didn't find water soon, it wouldn't matter whom he ran into.

He walked purposefully, at least as purposefully as he could now that Gaelan wasn't clearing a path through the forest for him. He pushed aside low branches, stepped over and around fallen trunks and bushes. Within minutes he was panting, sweating and thirstier than ever.

Giving up wasn't an option though, so he pushed on, keeping the sun to his left as it slowly slid across the sky. His arms tore on thorns, his shirt stuck to his sweat-drenched skin and his toes and shins ached from the constant bumps of rocks and wood. He pushed the discomfort aside and kept walking.

A couple of hours later he stopped, chest heaving, sweat running off him in waves. He shivered and goosebumps sprouted across his skin. Every muscle in his body trembled, and his breath rasped painfully in his dry throat. His stomach clenched and his head spun. He swayed where he stood, and knew if he sat, he wouldn't be able to get up again.

Water. Rest. Fuzzily, he tried to calculate the time of day but couldn't gauge the angle of the sun through the trees. It was over his left shoulder, that was all he knew. At least he was still heading north, although his reasons for doing so were as fuzzy as his thoughts.

He blinked. And opened his eyes when he landed on a rock with his hip. His cheek bounced into a mulch-covered root. He blinked again only to wake when a hand gripped his shoulder and rolled him over.

He lurched away and brought his hands up in defense. "No."

"Easy." Gaelan's voice flooded his mind with relief. "You should have waited until I came back. I've had to track you." He pushed his arm under Fisher's shoulders and lifted him to half-sit, half-lean against his chest.

Fisher could sit on his own. It was hot. He was thirsty. He probably had heat exhaustion.

"Here." Gaelan held a leather bottle to Fisher's lips. Fisher gulped at the water, but Gaelan took it away. "Slowly. Sip it."

Fisher forced himself to take smaller mouthfuls and held himself still so he didn't grab the bottle and gulp it all down, no matter how much he wanted to.

Gaelan took the water away after a few minutes, then brought it back just as Fisher slipped into a doze. "Drink a bit more, then you can sleep." He wiped a damp cloth over Fisher's face and neck, reviving him.

"Where did you get the bottle?" See? Not confused at all, even though he was glad Gaelan took the bottle away again.

"There's a small village not far from here," said Gaelan in a non-answer Fisher recognized even in his weakened condition. "It's only a couple of hours away. We'll make it well before sunset. They'll let us stay the night."

More than anything, Fisher wanted food and sleep. A bath would be good too. He'd gone without all those things at various times in his life but knew he functioned better with regular meals and sleep.

THEY RESTED UNTIL THE sun had disappeared behind the trees and the heat began to dissipate. Fisher roused himself when Gaelan stood and they walked through the cool breeze.

The closer they came to the village, the more signs of life could be seen. Mounds of mushrooms grew under carefully placed logs. Where the trees grew wider apart, different foods made themselves known. Sorrel and spinach grew in clumps in small clearings. Later there were potatoes, carrots and herbs.

By the time the village came into view through the now sparse trees, pumpkin and zucchini vines had taken over most of the ground, their tentacles reaching away from the half-dozen thatched cottages nestled in a circle in the middle of the large, grassy clearing.

A short way westward, Fisher could see an orchard of evenly-spaced trees. It was too early in the season and the trees were too far away for him to tell what they were. On their right, the sound of the sea was louder, but he couldn't see it, even though only a few trees grew to the east.

Dogs bayed at their approach, but they were contained in cages attached to the cottages. He saw no people. Another twenty paces and a man stepped out of a building, a dog on a lead beside him. Fisher paused when the man glared at him. When Gaelan stepped around Fisher to speak to the man, his dog lowered his head and growled. The man yelled. At the same time, a bell clanged deep in the village and the man released his dog.

"Run," yelled Gaelan.

Fisher ran.

Behind him, iron clanked and squealed as cages and doors were opened and more dogs were released. The baying took on a new, frenzied note and Fisher lifted his feet and pounded along the narrow path, sure he was going to die. Crossing the creek was his only real option but he'd never make it before the dogs caught him. He ran under the trees and into the forest and up the slope.

Just as he was sure he'd fall and be mauled by the dogs, Gaelan's face swung down in front of him, upside down. Gaelan hooked his arms under Fisher's armpits and lifted him into the tree.

Fisher struggled to be freed and perched precariously on a swaying limb. "They'll find us easily here. The dogs track by scent. They'll notice my scent stops abruptly and will look up."

"Don't worry," said Gaelan as he dragged Fisher along the branch toward the trunk. "I've got it worked out." Gaelan climbed higher. "Follow me."

With no other options, Fisher followed. The barking grew louder and more frenzied. They climbed until they could see the white-tipped waves. Then they climbed some more.

The dogs still barked, the sound now directly below them. Fisher stopped when the branch he stood on swayed beneath him. "We can't go any higher. The branches will break."

Gaelan looked out over the treetops. He reached an arm out and casually pressed down until the branch broke and dropped away. They now had a clear view of the dark ocean and the multi-hued sky above it. The dogs still barked.

"It's a really nice view," said Fisher. "But it's not going to help us escape."

Gaelan turned to him, looking as solemn as Fisher had ever seen him. In his hand, he held a small brown stone. "I want you to promise me something."

"Promise? Now?" He glanced down. It was a long, long way down, but the dogs and now their owners were at the bottom of the tree.

"I want you to promise you won't judge me."

"Judge you? For what?" He shuffled his feet then froze as a crack sounded in response to his movements. "Gaelan, you've saved my life several times in the last few days. Anyone else would have let me die and saved themselves. You didn't. Why would I judge you?"

"Do you promise?"

He huffed impatiently. If they didn't so something soon, the branch he was standing on was going to break and promises would mean nothing. "Yes, of course. I promise."

The tension in Gaelan's face disappeared and he smiled a smile so sweet and happy, Fisher returned it even though he had a feeling he'd just agreed to something more than not judging Gaelan.

"Come up here." Gaelan gestured. "Wrap your arms around my neck and hold on."

"Gaelan?" Fisher gingerly raised himself up to the narrow branch Gaelan balanced on. It bent alarmingly under their combined weight but didn't break. Yet.

Gaelan reached out and pulled him closer. "Hold on."

He did as he was told. "Now what? This is a bit extreme just to get a hug. After what happened in the ocean you must realize I'd hug you anyway."

"Don't judge me. And don't let go. No matter what."

Gaelan jumped out of the tree.

Fisher yelled. He clamped his eyes shut. Perhaps he screamed. They were in freefall and would land, smash, on the ground any sec—

They lurched. Fisher screamed. He bounced in the air and gasped. His arms strained against the change in direction. Heart racing. His legs dangled and bounced along with them. *Can't breathe properly.*

Gaelan's neck felt different. Thicker. Rougher. Whomp. Whoosh. Whomp. Whoosh. The sounds punctuated their bouncing.

They stopped falling but kept bouncing. Then even that smoothed out. They hadn't hit the ground. *Open your eyes.*

The baying of dogs faded away.

Open your eyes.

Do I really want to see? Fisher locked his arms around Gaelan's neck, dug his fingers into his own flesh.

Don't let go. No matter what.

He opened his eyes a slit. New-day sunlight. Sky. Purple.

Purple?

His eyes snapped open. Empty sky. High. High. Very high. He scrunched his eyes closed again. Afterimages flashed in his mind. Blue sky, white clouds, growing sunlight. And purple. Or blue. Or a purple-blue. A huge block of purple-blue. Very close to him. What was it?

Fisher opened his eyes again in time to see—whomp—a wing. Whoosh. The sky. Whomp. A wing? A wing to what? He tilted his head back and looked up.

Scales. Skin. All different shades of blue and purple until they merged together so all his eyes saw was a vibrant tanzanite blue. Higher up, the line of a jaw tilted down. A bright purple-blue eye regarded him.

Gaelan's eye.

A dragon's eye.

Dragon!

Gaelan!

Fisher jerked backward, his hold snapping free. More of the jaw and head came into view. Air whistled past.

He was falling.

Fuck.

He screamed and flailed his arms then reached for the dragon. For Gaelan. His fingers closed on air. He'd missed. Air rushed past as he fell faster. *Don't want to die. Don't want to die.*

Claws grabbed. Tore clothing. Fisher fell.

The jaw opened, exposing huge teeth, sharp teeth that bit him around his stomach. Fisher's body snapped and flopped with the sudden change in direction. There were teeth around him, but he didn't feel any pain. Gaelan wasn't biting him. He was holding him.

Fisher stopped falling. Then he stopped screaming. He breathed. And screamed. Then stopped.

He wasn't falling.

A dragon.

"You're a dragon!"

The dragon head dipped down then up again. He'd fall! Fisher grasped upward, found an indentation, dug his fingers in. Held on. "Fuck, you're a dragon." He tightened his hold. "Don't drop me." Gasping breaths. "Don't eat me."

The dragon snorted, and warm, moist air washed over Fisher's hands. His fingers were holding onto, were dug into, Gaelan's nostrils. Ick. He twitched, then firmed his hold. "Not letting go."

They flew on. After a time, he noticed the air was cooler, cold around his middle where the dragon held him in his jaws. "I'm wet! You're drooling on me."

Gaelan snorted again.

Oh. "You can't close your mouth, can you?" Of course he's drooling. Fisher sighed. At least Gaelan hadn't dropped him. A bit of drool never hurt anyone.

That thought was so blase, Fisher was forced to realize he'd relaxed. At least, he was as relaxed as he could be hundreds of feet in the air, dangling from the mouth of a dragon. A dragon that had been a man half an hour ago.

Fisher's breathing jumped and jerked and he clamped his eyes closed again and counted every breath in and out until he breathed evenly again. "It's too late to panic, you idiot," he mumbled to himself.

The sun was high in the sky—late morning—when Fisher noticed he could see more detail of things on the ground. The trees had become more than connected green blobs, the valley more than a blurry patchwork of brown and green.

Gusts of wind swirled around them, forcing Gaelan to tilt his wings to hold steady. Fisher watched the action, fascinated by the precision and how quickly he could respond to every shift in the air.

He tipped his head back and to the side but couldn't see if Gaelan had a tail or how he was using it. He couldn't hold the position for long because it strained his already sore neck. He groaned.

He was going to be in a world of pain by evening after holding his head up in this position for so long, and keeping his arms locked tight in one position and fingers clawed in Gaelan's nostrils.

"Sorry," he said. "I hope it doesn't hurt too badly, but I don't think I can let go at all now."

They tilted. Gaelan banked, spiraling slowly downward. Fisher squashed an absurd impulse to yell "wheeee." He couldn't restrain his laughter. The sounds tore from him, floated away on the wind and echoed back from the mountains to the north, where they were heading.

Within minutes, they were skimming over treetops, then climbed halfway up the mountain until a large clearing came into view. Fisher bounced in Gaelan's hold as the dragon lifted his head and lowered his legs to come in for a landing.

Fisher tightened his grip, not wanting to be tossed away at the last minute. He closed his eyes and tucked his chin down. "Don't drop me," he whispered, knowing Gaelan wouldn't hear.

The cadence of their movement changed from gliding to a twisting sway. That slowed and stopped then Fisher felt earth beneath his back. The wind was gone. In the silence, the teeth withdrew, taking with them a tearing of Fisher's shirt. His arms dropped from the dragon's head.

He lay panting, his head spinning at the sudden cessation of all movement and sound. Pain spiked through his fingers and wrists and shoulders and he groaned.

Warm hands pressed against his shoulders and kneaded gently. Fisher opened his eyes to see Gaelan kneeling over him, a concerned frown between his brows, his bright eyes shaded.

"What are you doing?" Fisher asked.

"I bet your shoulders are sore. Are your ribs okay? Can you breathe deeply? I can't see any broken skin. There's no blood anywhere. How do you feel?"

"I'm fine," he replied, then he twisted away, rolled onto his stomach and vomited.

CHAPTER NINE

GAELAN FLUTTERED AROUND Fisher, wiping his face with a cool, damp cloth, offering him food and water, asking again if his ribs were sore and if he could breathe properly.

Fisher accepted the water, rinsed his mouth, washed his hands, and pushed the rest away, including Gaelan himself. "Leave me alone."

He curled into a ball and hugged his knees tightly to stop the trembling rolling through him. It didn't work. The shaking increased until he was shuddering, shifting along the hard ground in little bounces and bumps. He whimpered. Tears leaked from his eyes. His breath left him in gasps that punctuated the bumping of his body across the clearing.

Gaelan scooped him up into his lap, restrained his flailing arms, tucked Fisher's head under his chin and held on tight. "It's okay. You'll be okay. You've had a shock, that's all. A number of shocks. You'll be okay."

Eventually, the reassurances devolved into nonsense sounds. Then they evolved into humming and crooning, then words. After a while a song wafted through the air, the soft vibrations of sound humming under Fisher's cheek.

At first, he couldn't listen, couldn't make out the words, but the tune was soothing. Eventually, he relaxed, his tight muscles softening, and he rested comfortably against Gaelan, as the song washed over him and through him and drew him into sleep.

This song is for you
You know who you are
You are everything to me
Everything I was
Everything I am
Everything I will be
Is for you
Because of you
We'll meet in the water
And breathe each other in
We'll fly in the air
And float in the same breath
Your blood
Will be my blood
Your victories
My surrender
Our lives entwined
Together we'll
Merge and grow
Blue and gray
Under one sun
Two moons
Forever lovers

The song of the two moons followed Fisher into sleep. He hadn't seen the two moons on the night of the eclipse, but he could imagine how beautiful and horrifying their battle was. His mind flowed with red light bouncing around in the cavern under the Aylmer Mountains, the headwaters of the Crystal River.

He stood again amongst the rubble of the ruined cavern, a wall of ice at his back, an earthquake and flood still in his future, and watched as four people screamed in the light of the one moon. Their bodies merged and flowed—Mafdeti to Imperial and back again, male to female to somewhere terrifyingly in between, and Fisher screamed with them.

Strong arms held him and he flailed at them.

"Sh, it's alright. You're safe now."

Gaelan's voice. Even half asleep, Fisher knew he was safe. "Don't leave me." A single tear pushed its way between his lashes and rested, soft and lonely against the bridge of his nose.

Gaelan's lips pressed gently against Fisher's eyebrow. "I'll stay with you." He kissed Fisher's eyelid, his nose, then halfway between, scooping the tear up with the tip of his tongue.

Fisher slept again.

CHAPTER TEN

FISHER SLEPT THE REST of the day away and awoke to evening birds calling their warnings. *Stay awaaaay, stay awaaaay.* Whip fast and high-pitched. "Are there really so many threats around that those birds have to screech like that all night?"

"Perhaps they can't see in the dark."

"Then why let everyone know exactly where they are?" Fisher looked around. "It's not that dark." He stared at Gaelan and watched the same realization wash over his features.

They were not alone.

As one, they rose and moved to opposite sides of the clearing, seeking the shadows, stepping carefully to minimize the noise they made. Instinctively, he kept Gaelan in his line of sight. When a twig snapped to his right, too loud to be one of the small mountain creatures, he was able to signal Gaelan with a flick of his fingers.

A shadow loomed in front of Fisher, a large, broad man he recognized instinctively as Yeudan. A war cry echoed across the clearing, one he knew from his childhood spying on the militia. Clashing metal rang out: they'd engaged Gaelan. Fisher spared him a glance to see a man down, maybe more, then returned his attention to the man in front of him.

Fisher ducked under the raised sword and dove for the man's knees, knowing that was the weakest area. His shoulder connected with a knee-cap, drawing an agonized yell from the man.

Fisher landed and rolled back to his feet, in a crouch, hands out, everything balanced, ready for attack or defense. A branch connected with his shoulder. Hard. Pain bloomed as splinters flew from the branch. He lurched forward, off balance, and landed face-first on the ground. His mouth snapped closed, teeth over tongue. More pain and blood.

Rough hands grabbed him. He kicked. An arm pressed against his face so he opened his mouth and bit down. He kicked again, connected with something. *Crunch.*

He rolled free, then up onto his feet only to be thumped between shoulder blades so hard he landed on the ground again, a rock digging into his knee. He gasped as the spike of pain ricocheted up his leg, then he rolled away.

A body landed on his arm, tearing at his shoulder. He kicked out again, connecting with something that brought another scream to the clearing. He pushed at the man on top of him and rolled again.

Where's the other one? he thought. *The one with the branch.* He rolled onto feet and saw them both. One had a bleeding nose, the other a bleeding arm. He smiled in satisfaction as he rushed the one with the bloody nose, lowering his head and raising his arm at the last minute.

The heel of Fisher's hand slammed into the man's chin. The impact jarred and shook up his arm right to his already strained shoulder. Pain grayed his vision, but he shook it away. He brought his other hand up in the same motion and the man's head snapped back. A crack of bone preceded the man falling lifelessly to the ground.

Fisher turned to the other man, but he hadn't dealt with the first one fast enough. As he turned, he saw a branch. Then pain flooded his face. The world went white and he landed on the ground.

CHAPTER ELEVEN

WHEN FISHER WOKE, THE sun was rising. Or was it setting? No. The air had that expectant feel to it that always came with the dawn.

He opened his eyes, gritty with dust and tears. There were rocks and stubby bushes and sky and dirt. They were still on the mountain. He tried to move his arms, but pain shot through his shoulders and wrists. He groaned, inadvertently moving his head. Bright lights of agony spun through his head and tore another groan from him. What had they hit him with?

"He's awake." The voice was nearby and not one he recognized.

"The other one?"

"Nothing."

They had Gaelan too? Why hadn't he turned into a dragon and flown away? Fisher was sure he could have done that.

His head spun and threatened to turn his stomach inside out, so he stopped thinking and slipped back into whatever had been passing for sleep.

The next time Fisher woke it was afternoon and the air was filled with the scents of cooked meat and burned potatoes. It was enough to make him ill. So he was.

"He's awake again."

"He's chucked again. Probably got a concussion. I told you not to hit his head, you idiot. What good is he going to be to us if he dies from a fucking concussion."

"We're not going to keep him alive anyway."

"That doesn't matter. We need to find out why they're here."

"There are only two of them. They can't be an advance scouting party."

"How do you know? Just because we wouldn't be fool enough to send two men into enemy territory doesn't mean those southerners have as much sense. The heat has probably cooked their brains."

"I'll wake him up. He's so out of it he'll answer whatever questions we have."

"Fucking idiot. Don't you know concussion makes you really confused?"

"I had a concussion last month."

"Yeah. I know. You're still not over it."

There followed a grunt, a thump, swearing and punches. A foot connected with Fisher's hip and rolled him farther away from the fighting men and the fire.

Once he began rolling, he pushed himself over again and continued, over and over, with his head pounding and his stomach churning and a pain in his cheek that burned and throbbed with each twist and turn.

His cheek connected with a rock. Red hot spikes of pain shot through him and it sounded like a scream inside his head, but he knew it wasn't. A whimper. A groan. And blessed darkness took him again.

He was in a cage. They were underground, with water dripping nearby and the smell of lime strong in the air. There were metal bars, solid and immovable, a few inches from his face.

He'd kicked the bars for a long time but only succeeded in jarring his back and knees. His hands were still tied but he thought they'd changed the ropes. These ones didn't feel like they were cutting through to the bone.

There was a noise outside his cage, beyond where the light hid things. The noise continued and resolved into voices. People talking. Coming this way. "Grieving is fine, but his family seems to make saying goodbye difficult."

Fisher froze. A few minutes later, he noticed two men, one much older and shorter than the other, come into the light.

They were dressed in long robes that opened from the waist and flowed gentle as water around their ankles. Barthes Elders. The younger man's robe was plain black, making him look like an exclamation point; the older man's had heavy embroidery around the hem but little embellishment across his shoulders. Beneath, they wore light linen trousers tucked into suede ankle boots. The thick, squat heels clacked against the stone floor with each step, like a panicked death knell.

"He's an odd one," said the old man.

Before Fisher could begin to think why he would say that, the young one responded. "It's the life he's led."

His head throbbed and his eyes ached, but he knew the pain was better than the last time. At least they hadn't drugged him. He wasn't going to wish for a hit to the head next time. He shuffled a little, pressing closer to the cool, dark rock at his back. The pain eased further.

"Did he say why this one is so important?" The younger man dug into a cavernous pocket and extracted a let of large keys. "Do you think he's the one?"

The older man had a set of keys of his own. "There is that song."

"Are there other prophecies?" The younger man sorted through his keys and separated one.

"Not about the Concubine specifically, although some of the dragon ones could be interpreted to include the Concubine."

"There's only the one Concubine."

"And we have him." The two men approached the last small distance and inserted their keys into the slots at either side of the cage. Together they turned the keys clockwise and Fisher's door popped open.

He lurched to his feet. A vague notion of pushing between the men and escaping carried him forward a few steps. The pain came crashing down again.

His eyes blurred, his stomach heaved and he landed painfully on his knees, swallowing convulsively to prevent his stomach turning itself inside out again. The rock beneath his hands was cool so he lowered his head to the dark stone and felt immediate relief. Message received. Keep his forehead pressed to the cool granite and the pain was bearable. Move, and he probably wouldn't survive the night.

He rolled onto his side and peered up at the two men. "Is it night time?"

"Oh, he's not going to be happy about this," said the younger man.

"Play the love factor up big and he'll be fine. What's the worst he can do here, under the mountains?" The older man said.

"He could roast us!"

"That's nonsense, Tarron. The stuff of legends."

"So's he!" Tarron became more agitated with each sentence the older man spoke.

"What time is it?" Fisher tried again, even though he didn't know why he thought it was so important to know what time of day it was. It was easier than trying to make sense of what they were saying.

The men still ignored him as they helped him to stand and walked out of the cage with him sandwiched between them.

"What's going on?" He resisted their tugs on his arms. "I'm not going to do anything until you tell me."

Tarron turned to him with a scowl. "You don't have to be conscious for this, Concubine. He wrenched Fisher forward, the sudden movement throbbing through Fisher's head, making him dizzy. He allowed the two men to escort him into the corridors.

"What happened to my friend?"

"He wasn't necessary."

"You what? Killed him?" Fisher's stomach flipped at the thought of Gaelan being dead, but the tightness in his chest told him the dragon was still alive. The link wasn't anything he wanted; he didn't want to burn another man to death. But it was useful in letting him know Gaelan was at least alive.

"We're here." Tarron gestured to another doorway, indicating that Fisher should go in.

Fisher's heart jumped at the sight that greeted him. Eerily reminiscent of the Exile compound, the cavernous area was heavily draped in dusty tapestries depicting famous—and successful—Yeudan battles.

The large square table and chairs occupying the middle of the room were much better quality than those the Exiles had had but he assumed it would be used for the same purpose—for the Elders to meet and decide who would live and who would die.

Finally, he allowed himself to focus on the seven men seated around the table. Their white hair and rheumy eyes marked them clearly as Elders. Their embroidered robes told Fisher how much power each held in the Barthes Temple. He could ignore most of them, but one with a combination of thick gold and red leaves and branches sitting heavily on his shoulders like an ancient willow tree, scared him.

He recognized that design. When he'd last seen it, it had adorned only the hem of the man's robes. Fisher had thought he'd been powerful then, able to order the banishment of a woman and the enslavement of a boy. He wondered if the man would recognize him too.

As the thought crossed Fisher's mind, the old man looked up and grinned. His stomach dropped so far he expected it to seep out from under his toenails.

"Ah," Elder Evanson said. "I'd wondered if you'd survived." He gestured to an empty seat at the table. "Join us, young Gerard, join us."

Fisher narrowed his eyes at the use of his old name. It had been nearly twenty years since he'd heard it spoken, yet Evanson not only remembered it but used it as if they were close friends.

What the hell had happened after he and his mother left? He unrolled his still damp coat and tugged it on as he sat on the edge of the indicated seat, making sure he stayed far enough from the table to be able to run if he needed to, even if he had no idea where to go.

"You know, we searched for you after you disappeared. I thought your cousin—Kaod, isn't it?—knew something, but even after he lost a couple of fingers, he maintained you'd been taken by the militia."

A cold chill washed over Fisher. He'd wanted to say goodbye to Kaod but his mother hadn't let him. He'd even snuck out on their last night in town, intending to tell Kaod what he and his mother were going to do but she'd caught him less than a block away and sent him on ahead.

He'd hated her that day, but he'd done as she'd asked. He'd slipped under the barriers and trudged through the snow, trusting the overnight falls to cover his progress. It had taken him most of the night to reach their meeting place and another day to dig the snow cave so he wouldn't freeze to death.

Three days later, his mother had joined him, broken, bloody and half-frozen. He'd cut her toes off the next day. She'd bitten into a piece of wood so she wouldn't scream and bring the militia to them.

He had sobbed so hard he kept dropping the knife. It was only his mother telling him if he didn't do it she'd die that allowed him to go ahead with it.

Fisher wondered if Kaod had screamed or cried when his fingers were cut off.

Because of him.

"I wonder what your cousin will say when I tell him you've returned to the fold to follow your destiny." Evanson smirked as Fisher jumped to his feet.

"The only destiny I have is the one I choose for myself." He maneuvered his way behind his chair.

Evanson laughed. "There's no way out of here, at least none you're going to find. Did you enjoy your bath? Your clothes are the best we could provide here in the mountains." He scowled. "Lose that raggedy coat before we present you. You must look your absolute best for the dragons."

"Dragons?" Was Gaelan the dragon they were referring to? He breathed deeply and slowly, in and out. His chest wasn't tight at all, so Gaelan was close, but he could feel nothing that suggested Gaelan was in trouble. The Elders didn't have him.

And Evanson had said dragons. Plural. He looked around frantically as if the huge creatures would pop out from behind the tapestries. "Where are the dragons?"

Evanson laughed and clapped his hands, like Fisher used to do as a child. "Wonderful. You're as excited about the prospect of bringing the dragons under our control as I am. You'll make a wonderful Concubine." The smirk returned. "If you survive."

Fisher stumbled backward. He should have paid better attention when Tarron called him Concubine. He should have realized the Yeudan elders had some dreadful plan to gain power at the expense of others. It was what they did.

He kept taking small steps backward, putting as much distance as he could between him and the madmen sitting around the table.

Evanson laughed again. "You can run, if you like, but there's no escaping here unless you know how." He rose to his feet and grabbed a walking stick Fisher hadn't noticed before. It was carved from glossy black wood, the rare ebony that grew north of Barthes and east of the glacier. Only the favored of the Goddess were permitted to carry items made of the wood.

Bile rose in Fisher's throat. If Evanson was the Goddess's favored one, there was no hope for any of them. He took another small step back and tripped over something warm and furry. He landed painfully on his bottom, drawing laughs from most of those at the table. Only Evanson scowled.

"Where did that come from?" he demanded.

"That" was a cougar with dark markings. It was large for a cougar—a big, broad tom. The cat turned its back to the table, lifted its tail and shook it delicately. The thick odor of urine permeated the air. Fisher gaped at the cat. Surely it didn't do that on purpose.

The cat turned its face to him and it blinked one of its bright blue-purple eyes.

"Gaelan?" No, it wasn't possible. Gaelan was a dragon, not a cougar. The cougar sauntered over and rubbed his head against Fisher's calf, his intense blue eyes regarding him solemnly.

Fisher fought to get his breathing under control and rose to his feet. As soon as he was up, the cougar darted out the doorway. It might not really be a request for him to follow, but he took it that way anyway.

He ran, his boots alternatively sticking to the floor on uneven stones and slipping on shiny patches. He lurched his way down the corridor after the dark tail that disappeared around the first corner. Behind him, yelling erupted, followed by the patter of feet—two sets of feet from what he could tell without looking behind him.

Only Tarron and his companion would have the mobility to chase after him and he was betting he'd soon only have Tarron. He ran faster, not sure how fit the young monk was.

The cougar disappeared around another corner and Fisher careened after him only to have Gaelan reach out and drag him into a narrow alcove carved from the rock. It was wedge-shaped, narrower at the back, wider at the corridor where Tarron would soon find them. Gaelan pushed Fisher behind him and Fisher pressed his shoulders into the tight corner between the two walls of rock.

Tarron's footsteps grew louder and Fisher pressed back farther.

Behind him, the rock moved. In shock, he reached out and grabbed Gaelan's arm and pulled him with him as he fell through.

CHAPTER TWELVE

AIR RUSHED FROM FISHER'S mouth. His chest ached. Darkness swallowed him. Around him, unyielding rock crushed his ribs toward his spine and his nose flat. Granite sliced past his arm, his fist clamped tightly around Gaelan's bicep. Spots swam in front of him; ghostly lights in the darkness. Fisher chased them, thinking they were light, but soon realized it was because he wasn't breathing.

He couldn't breathe. Just like he was underwater.

Fisher opened his mouth, panic tossing a scream around inside his head, bouncing around like his fractured thoughts. Cool, metallic air rushed down his throat. In his head, he screamed. In his ears, it was a whimper. And still he fell backward, as if through molasses, suspended in time.

His heartbeat pounded in his ears, his head and his throat, like it didn't come from his chest but through every spurt of blood pumping in his veins. Thump, thump. Thump, thump. He screamed again.

Then he landed on his back on rough gravel, his breath knocked from him in a painful whoosh and Gaelan's arm wrenched from his hold. Gaelan landed beside him with a thump and a sharp elbow in Fisher's stomach.

"Oof." Fisher slowly opened his eyes, half afraid all he'd see above him would be granite. Stars blinked overhead, flickering in time with his out-of-control heartbeat. Stars. They were outside.

He lifted his head. They were on a mountain path that skirted the rocky wall of the mountain. As Fisher stared at the it, a gash in the rock rumbled closed. He wrenched his feet away from the narrowing gap, kicking Gaelan onto the path.

"What the fuck?" Fisher scrambled backward, pushing his heels against the gravel until he was far, far away from the granite wall, his shoulders hanging over the downward slope.

The air was cool and fresh on his face and around his neck. His chest heaved and his head spun like he was still short of air, even though he was in the open now. "No way," he panted. "No way." That couldn't have happened. There was no way he could move through rock. He couldn't have.

It must have been Gaelan. Fisher rose to his knees and crawled shakily to where he lay, unmoving, and shoved against Gaelan's shoulder.

"What did you do?" He pushed against him again. "What the fuck did you do?" His voice rose, hysteria edging his continued prodding at Gaelan, who still didn't respond.

Fisher knelt over him, put both hands on Gaelan's shoulder and shoved. Gaelan rolled, then coughed. He scrambled to his feet and stumbled away from the rock outcrop before looking wildly at Fisher. "What?" Even in the faint starlight, Fisher could see the whites of Gaelan's eyes. "What the fuck did you do?"

"Me? I didn't do anything. What sort of fucked-up trick was that, pulling me through rock?" Fisher shoved himself to his feet, knees wobbly and upper body trembling and swaying. "I couldn't breathe!" But then he could breathe—while he was still inside the rock. "How did you do that?"

Gaelan, bastard that he was, glared at him, immediately calm when Fisher's heart was still pounding in his throat and his gaze refused to settle on anything, flitting from the sky to the mountain to the path to the steep slope directly behind him.

Fisher stepped forward then back again, more afraid of getting closer to the rock that had just spewed them onto the path. Mercy of the Goddess, he'd moved through rock. That wasn't possible.

"I didn't do it," insisted Gaelan. "It's granite. I told you granite isn't my rock."

"What does that mean—granite isn't your rock? No one can push through rock. You're the dragon here. It must have been you." Fisher shuffled his feet but froze when pebbles tumbled down behind him.

Push one droplet at a time. Heath's voice washed through Fisher, more like a revelation than a memory. "Is that what happened?" he whispered. "Only not droplets. Bits of rock?" He turned to Gaelan who had at least stopped swaying like he'd fall over at any minute. "What are rocks made of?"

"What do you mean? They're rocks." Gaelan tottered down the path and looked out over the valley below.

"They must be made of something. Like water is made of droplets." Fisher followed Gaelan, gravel crunching as he walked. He stopped and looked down. He couldn't see anything with only starlight to see by, but his mind spun with possibilities. Could Gaelan do what Heath did with the water, only with rock? Did he not know he could do it?

"It wasn't me," said Gaelan. "I can't do anything with granite, or any rock other than tanzanite. It must have been you."

"I'm not the dragon here. I've lived under the desert most of my life and never been able to do anything like that. It can't be me." Fisher paced along the narrow path. They needed to get moving but if Gaelan was going to start lying to him—more than he already had—he needed to know about it. It would change everything about the way they worked together. Their whole relationship.

A squidgy feeling twirled in his stomach as he thought the word *relationship*. It was almost as if he was creating a self-fulfilling prophecy just by conjuring the word.

"The desert is sand, with sandstone and limestone underneath. There's no granite." Gaelan took Fisher's elbow and steered him to the cliff-face beside the path. "Touch the rock. Tell me what you see."

"It's nighttime. I'm not going to see anything." He resisted Gaelan's pull on his arm, reluctant to touch the rock again. "I don't need to touch the damned granite. I know it wasn't me."

"Prove it." The challenge in Gaelan's voice raised Fisher's hackles just as every dare he'd received in his life. He couldn't back down now. He stalked across the path and touched his fingertip to the granite. "Nothing," he said in relief.

"You're not trying." Gaelan crossed his arms and leaned his shoulder against the wall of rock.

Fisher scowled at Gaelan's comfortable stance. His heart beat faster, but Gaelan didn't sink into the rock. He took a deep breath and pressed his palm against the granite, then let it out in a sigh when the bumpy surface remained solid under his palm. He grinned at Gaelan. "I told you it wasn't—"

The rock warmed and became spongy. Fisher's hand sank into the wall as if pressing into custard. "Argh!" He jumped back and rubbed his hand against his thigh over and over as if the friction would remove the memory of it. "No!" His chest heaved and sweat popped out all over his body. "It's not possible."

He sidled up to the rock wall and gingerly placed his palm on the rock again. At first it felt solid, as it should, but as soon as he imagined his hand sinking into the rock, it softened and his hand disappeared. "It's not possible," he whispered. "It should be hard."

No sooner than the words had left his mouth than the rock solidified—with his hand still inside it. "Ahh! Out! Get it out!" He pulled his arm back, gripped his forearm with his other hand, but his hand was stuck. The rock cooled around his hand until he couldn't even wriggle his fingers. "It's stuck!"

Gaelan came up behind Fisher and leaned against his back. "Fisher, calm down."

"Don't tell me to calm down. What do you know? It isn't your hand stuck in a fucking mountain." He continued to pull and twist, wrenching his shoulder and back but not caring because his hand was still. Stuck. Inside. The. Mountain!

Gaelan pressed closer and rubbed his cheek against Fisher's.

Back off or I'll bite your nose off, Fisher thought as he continued to tug on his arm.

"I'll help you, but you must calm down. Stop trying to wrench your arm out and slow your breathing."

He wanted to yell at Gaelan, tell him to stop being condescending, that he was calm and his breathing was—bellowing in an out like a buffalo in rut.

He stopped struggling against the hold on his hand and began counting his breaths in and out. A whimper escaped as his panic subsided because he could now feel exactly how cold the rock was around his hand and how hard it was pressing against him.

"That's good," whispered Gaelan. "Remember what you were thinking when your hand sank into the rock."

A soft squelch punctuated Gaelan's voice and Fisher's hand slipped from the wall in front of him. Blood rushed into his fingers, bringing spiking hot pain. He stumbled back a step but stopped when Gaelan's arms came around him. He cradled his hand to his chest and began to chafe it, hoping to mitigate the pain more quickly.

"Oh fuck," he whispered as his knees gave way under him. "It really was me." His gaze skittered around them, settling briefly on the path, the shadowy valley, Gaelan. Everywhere except the rock wall beside him. *I moved through rock. I pushed my hand into a granite wall. I got stuck. Fuck, what if I get inside a rock and can't get out?*

"You know how to get out now," said Gaelan from above him. "It'll just take practice."

"You don't seriously think I'm going to stick any part of my body into a rockface again, do you?"

"This whole mountain range and most of the Icy Wastes are granite deposits," said Gaelan, irritatingly reasonable. "You're not going to be able to avoid touching it, so you have to make sure you can control it."

Fuck. He strode down the narrow path until he tripped over a large stone. "That's granite there." Even though he couldn't see the stone, he knew it was granite, almost as if the rock sang to him. "I didn't go through it."

He automatically imagined the way the rock softened under his hand. The next footfall sank, like it was on sponge. His heart jumped as he did. He hopped from foot to foot in large over-exaggerated steps. "Arghh, it's done it again. It was solid."

Again, when the image of the solid stone came to mind, his feet landed on hard ground. "It's all in my mind," he exclaimed, relief flooding him. If he didn't think about it, it wouldn't happen.

"We've come out on the northern side," said Gaelan as he picked his way downhill.

"Is that all you've got to say? I just pulled us through rock, and I can do it any time I think about it." The ground became spongy again, and Fisher quickly marshalled his thoughts. *Think hard, think hard.* His heart rate settled as the ground solidified again, but his body still thrummed with the sensation of being on the edge of... something. Something momentous, as long as he could make his mind think about it.

Gaelan's gaze was steady. "Beings doing unusual things isn't new for me."

Understanding flooded him. "You're dragon and a cougar."

Gaelan nodded regally. "That too."

Was there more that Gaelan could turn into? Wasn't a dragon and cougar enough? He turned to ask, but Gaelan had strode ahead and Fisher, still reeling from sinking into solid rock, decided he didn't really need to know right then.

The farther they walked, the more Fisher became aware of his surroundings. The air wasn't just cool as he had thought when he'd first burst from the rock. It was cold. His breath puffed in warm, moist spheres that washed over his cheeks and chin then cooled rapidly.

It was early in the season, but soon the air would freeze his breath to his chin and he'd grow little icicles. His jacket was still damp at the seams and he shivered against the clamminess. At least the rock beneath his feet still held some of the warmth of the day. That might help to keep him warm.

As with traveling through the rock, as soon as Fisher thought of it being warm, it was. By the time he'd pulled his panicked breathing back under control his feet were almost too hot and his jacket was dry and warm.

Okay. Okay, I can do this. Just don't panic.

He breathed deeply. There was the smell of snow in the air, a burning coldness that brought with it a clarity Fisher had never known anywhere else, but it wasn't nearby. He looked to the north, where the snow would be, then studied the stars that would tell him how heavy and far-reaching the snowfalls would be. The brightness and configurations in the sky were as familiar to him as his own hand.

Fisher stopped and stared into the darkness to the north. "We're on the border of the Icy Wastes." He crouched and rested his hands on the rocky path, trying to decide if the Yeudan would have forces between there and Barthes, or if they were concentrating most of their attention on the passes through the mountains.

"What are you doing?" asked Gaelan as he crouched beside him.

"I think if we go east a little we'll miss most of the Yeudan militia. They seem to be more numerous to the west, where the passes are." There was a dreamy quality to Fisher's voice that he never noticed before. Probably because he didn't usually talk to himself when he examined his surroundings and tried to work out where the enemy was.

"How do you know that?" Suspicion laced Gaelan's voice.

Fisher rose and brushed the dust from his hands. "How do I know what?" He continued walking. He recognized an easement off the path and down the mountain that would lead them east then north again.

"How do you know we have to go east first? How do you know the Yeudan are amassed to the west?"

Fisher glared at Gaelan. "I don't know what you're talking about." He wasn't doing anything he hadn't done thousands of times before. Anyone could read the landscape. He pointed down the slope. "This is a goat path that will bring us out down the bottom there." He pointed to the north-east. "We should be far enough to the east to give us a direct route north to Barthes without being accosted again." And perhaps he could make it more than one day without some bastard drugging him or knocking him out and kidnapping him.

Once they got off this mountain, Fisher was going to go through everything and work out why they kept targeting him. Was he just in the wrong place at the wrong time, or were they really after Gaelan? No, the Yeudan definitely wanted him. The Concubine. Bastards.

"We could fly," suggested Gaelan.

Fisher glared at him. "Don't push it, *dragon*." The word wasn't a compliment. "I've told you before and I'll tell you again—I don't want anything to do with dragons. The only reason we're traveling together right now is because you helped me escape from the Yeudan back there."

Fisher slipped a few feet on loose gravel before regaining his feet and continuing. "I'm still going to do what I can to stop the production of the Elixir. It's my fault they have so much of it and I don't want anyone else to die, but that doesn't mean you and I are bosom buddies, partners in crime, or whatever other cliche you can think of. I'm only working with you because I have to." He turned and jabbed a finger into Gaelan's chest. "And that means I don't have to fly."

He continued walking. "You could have dropped me, you bastard."

He was a dozen steps ahead before Gaelan replied. "I would never drop you."

"Drop, dig claws in. Bite me. Same difference." He slid another few steps down the shale.

They continued in silence.

The rock gradually changed to scrubby shrubs, then tall trees—conifers that survived the cold. It would be pleasant walking amongst the trees and on the soft pine-needle carpet between them. When the sun rose, Fisher stopped and sank to the ground to catch his breath.

"There'll be a stream not too far away," he said. "There are lots of them running down the mountains. Although most of them run to the south, there are about half a dozen that come down this northern section. The western ranges are drier." Fisher shut his mouth with a snap. He'd managed the whole morning not talking to Gaelan—the dragon—and now he was babbling about inconsequential things. "Why didn't you tell me you were a dragon when I said I wouldn't have anything to do with dragons?" That seemed to be the most important thing to know.

"We needed your help." Gaelan shrugged.

"So you decided to lie to me, when you knew it was a deal-breaker."

"I thought you were talking about the dragons cooperating with the Mafdeti. I'm not an ordinary dragon."

"An ordinary dragon? There's more than one kind? What exactly are you saying? Is it only the other dragons, the ones the Mafdeti and Imperials have, that will want me to be their concubine? Or is the concubine thing someone's idea of a bad joke?"

Gaelan shifted so he was facing Fisher. His face had fallen into serious lines, his brilliant eyes piercing. "It's no joke."

Fisher jumped to his feet, his heart taking wing. "No! I'm not going to be the dragons' Concubine."

"What is it that bothers you about it?"

"Wouldn't you be 'bothered' if everyone was trying to force you into something like that? I'm supposed to... what? Just accept that I'm going to be a sexual plaything for the dragons?" He stormed toward Gaelan and leaned over him in his most intimidating manner. "Fuck. You."

"What if you're loved?" Gaelan didn't cower from him but his voice was small and tentative, filled with something that could almost be called longing.

"Purely, deeply? Forever? Never." By all those dragons? It wasn't possible.

Gaelan ducked his head, but not before Fisher caught the devastation on his face. "Gaelan?"

If it was just Gaelan... but Gaelan would never be able to accept all Fisher had done before. No one could.

Gaelan stood, forcing Fisher to back up or be pushed over. "Let's find this stream you say is nearby, then continue." He took a few steps back. "How long do you think it'll take to walk to Barthes?"

He'd disappeared into the trees before Fisher roused himself to follow. "There's water farther to your right." He jogged until he caught sight of Gaelan's back disappearing around a tree trunk, the lines of his shoulders and spine stiff and unforgiving. "We're about five days from Barthes."

What he really wanted to say was something that would make Gaelan smile at him again. Fisher had never meant to bring such deep sadness to him but Gaelan didn't know Fisher at all. He was basing his desires on a myth, not a real person.

He jogged after Gaelan, determined to get them back to the friendly banter they'd just begun to settle into, but the longer he watched Gaelan's back, the less sure he was that it was possible. His stomach ached with the idea he'd hurt Gaelan, but there was nothing he could do or say to change it. Gaelan couldn't really want a murderer to be his Concubine?

They followed the sound of burbling water to the narrow stream flowing between the rocks, cascading over and around them in clear joy of being. Gaelan was already crouched, scooping handfuls of water up to drink while he held his waterskin under the water with his other hand.

Once the skin was full and fastened again across his chest, he stood and faced Fisher. Almost faced him. His gaze rested somewhere over Fisher's left shoulder. He picked up a fist-sized black rock and tossed it to Fisher who fumbled it before cradling it in his palm.

"Do you think there'll be any trouble between here and Barthes?" Gaelan asked.

"How would I know?" asked Fisher before he... knew. The granite was quiet and still. "No. There's no one between here and there. There are no norrgel this far north at this time of year. The first snows will come before we get there but won't hinder us."

The rock was warm in his hand. Very warm. He tossed the rock aside and stumbled back, his heart pounding in time with the knowledge of what he'd just done. "How...?" His fingers tingled from the remembered contact with the stone, the remembered knowledge.

"What did you do?" It must be something the dragon had done. Nothing like this had happened to him before. His mind wanted to remember all the times he'd been playing in the graveled streets and had hidden before the militia came around the corner because he'd known something dangerous was coming. He'd heard them marching, that was all.

Gaelan stepped close. His hand, trembling as much as Fisher was, cupped Fisher's cheek and tilted his face up. "It's you. It's always been you, only now you're ready for it, and it's ready for you."

"I don't know what you're talking about." Fisher moved his face so his cheek rubbed against Gaelan's hand. He clung to the contact as if it was the only thing helping him regain his balance since the rock. Without Gaelan's hands on him, he would sink into the rock and never be able to find his way out again.

"You might not know the rock, but you know this." Gaelan's face filled his vision as he came closer, closer. Their lips touched. Gaelan's were soft and dry, clinging, comfortable, like they belonged against his.

Fisher leaned into the kiss, opening for a deeper taste. Heat, comforting and searing at once, flooded through him, swelling his chest, fluttering through his belly, and landing firmly in his groin.

He groaned and shuffled forward, pressing every part of his body against every part of Gaelan's. Solid muscle, encased in smooth skin and soft clothes, pressed back, drawing an agonized groan from him. He jumped when Gaelan's hands cupped his buttocks. Drawing back from the kiss, Fisher gasped. Gaelan dug his fingers into the crease under Fisher's buttocks and lifted him inches off the ground until their groins were aligned.

Fisher groaned at the exquisite pressure against his cock. He hooked his foot around Gaelan's knee to get closer, to find more pressure. Heat rushed through him, tingling in his balls and pushing a blissful sigh from his lips.

A low rumble rose through Gaelan's chest and reverberated through his body, exciting and alien. It called to something in him; tugged at the base of his brain as if Gaelan was knocking on a door he didn't know he had.

He froze. He pushed at Gaelan's shoulders and dropped his feet to the ground. As he stepped back, Gaelan's hand fell away.

"What is it?" asked Gaelan.

"I told you I'm not going to be any dragon's concubine. Don't try to force me into it." He knew it was an unfair accusation, but he couldn't stop the words pouring from his mouth. He had to protect himself, so he went on the attack. He turned back to the path. "Let's go."

After half a dozen steps, he turned to find Gaelan still where he'd left him, as if frozen to the ground. "What?" he demanded, the swirl of guilt and painful denial cramping his stomach.

Gaelan regarded him silently for so long Fisher began shifting on his feet. "I think you'll find out more in Barthes on your own," Gaelan eventually said. His voice was flat, without any inflection at all, and Fisher wondered what he was hiding. "My presence will garner too much attention."

Gaelan straightened as he spoke, as if he was gathering invisible armor around himself, covering himself with impervious strength. "Gather as much information as you can without alerting anyone to your presence and then meet me near the glacier to the north. We can tackle the production of the Elixir together once we know what's happening and work out how to stop it."

Fisher stared at him, his mind refusing to understand what Gaelan meant. Then heat washed through him with the realization. "You're leaving?" It shouldn't make any difference. He should have expected that Gaelan would leave once Fisher rejected him. Fisher had been on his own for a long time, even when his mother was still alive. No one stayed.

Why then, did he feel bereft?

"I think it'll be better for both of us if I fly from here," said Gaelan. "Five days, then a couple more for you to find out what we need to know, and a couple more to reach the glacier. Will that work?" He handed Fisher another rock. "Keep that. Use it."

Cradling the rock as if it was the only thing holding him to the ground, Fisher nodded. Gaelan might say they'd meet again in nine days but he knew that wouldn't happen. What would happen was he would go to Barthes, destroy the ring creating the Elixir, and probably die while doing it. Or, he'd fail and die trying. Meanwhile, Gaelan would be off being a dragon, doing whatever dragons do—probably finding someone else he can pass around as a concubine.

Jealous heat tumbled through him, but he pushed it aside. He didn't have the right to be jealous; he'd rejected Gaelan, made it very clear he didn't want to be part of any dragon's weird sexual practices.

Grief ached in his chest and burned his eyes as he watched Gaelan change forms, knowing he couldn't ever expect that Gaelan would be his. The flash of blue light grew above the treetops then finally settled into the shape of the dragon that was the same color as Gaelan's gorgeous eyes.

"Call if you need me," Gaelan said as he lowered his head in a sonorous nod. Then he leaped off the mountain and flew directly north.

When he was no more than a sparkling speck in the sky, Fisher could admit that if Gaelan had offered himself, only himself, as single Consort to Fisher's Concubine, he would have accepted.

And been happy.

It was long after the glowing blue-purple of Gaelan's dragon had disappeared beyond the horizon when Fisher continued his trek down the mountain. The spongy needles underfoot became a means for the enemy to hide their approach. The trees, branches creaking in the subtly moving air, became careless footfalls of men surrounding him for an attack.

He found his footsteps increasing until he was running flat-out down the last slopes of the mountain, tripping, tumbling, coming to rest in a sweaty, panting heap at the base of a tree, with tears burning his eyes and violent sobs wracking his body.

He refused to be the Concubine of hundreds of dragons. He was worth more than that.

In the wee hours, Fisher dug into the deep mulch at the base of the tree and slept, warm and hidden, until the sun rose. He scrutinized his surroundings but could see no sign of the Yeudan who'd captured them, no sign he was being followed.

He remained vigilant, fully aware of his vulnerability now he was alone. There'd be no Gaelan swooping in to save him. If he was captured again, he'd be on his own.

Just like he'd always been.

He fell into a routine of half jogging, half walking throughout the early hours of the day, until the sun was high. Then he'd rest for a couple of hours, then walk again until the stars burned cold and high. Then he'd dig in somewhere protected and sleep until the sun woke him.

On the morning of the fourth day he rose to find Barthes on the horizon. He quickly ate and set himself to closing the distance. At midday he stopped, dug in between two scraggly bushes and watched the city gates. After a couple of hours, he carefully made his way around the city, keeping his distance, checking for any possible entrance points.

On the fifth day, the wind changed, coming from the north. Fisher stepped out from the shelter of the last of the forest trees and paused on the path to breathe the smells of late summer outside Barthes—yellowing grasses, sweet beehives and warm animal dung, overlaid by the lingering scent of maggots feeding off discarded food and feces. He adjusted the scarf covering the lower half of his face so that his nose was also covered, but his eyes watered with the acrid odor.

The scarf helped a little, but Fisher knew by the time he entered the city, the smell would have permeated his clothing, stronger and more noisome than three weeks without washing. The northern access, near the upper-class neighborhoods, would be cleaner but it was late in the day and the gates would be closed by the time he made the trek around the city.

Rising above the walls was the dome of the Temple of the Blue Goddess. Unless things had changed since he lived there, the brilliant sapphire blue was the only color in the entire city. During the spring when his mother had managed work on the farms, she'd brought wildflowers home. The sunny yellows, whites and oranges had brightened their room for a short time.

Outside the city stood a raised dais, similar to the one in the catacombs under the Great Rocky Desert. The gray rock had been used to worship the Goddess during the winter festival. Now it was stained with runnels of rusty brown. Fisher wondered when they began making sacrifices to the norrgel and making the Elixir. He continued walking around the city, keeping his distance and cover so he wasn't noticed.

At dusk, he found the stream flowing under the wall and into the city. He scrambled into the gully and waded through freezing water to the base of the wall.

A thick metal grille met his questing fingers. He tested the strength of it but it was solid and immovable. There was some rust forming where the grille was bolted into the rock but it hadn't cut all the way through the metal yet.

Instinctively, he pressed his palm to the dark rock wall. It warmed under his touch, like the rock Gaelan had given him. Granite. Would it work? Was it really him and not Gaelan? His mind shied away from the thought that he was like Heath, who could move water, but what if he was.

He pressed his hand to the rock around the metal pole dug into it. "Let it go," he whispered.

Nothing happened. He slumped, then sat up and tried it again. "Let it go."

Nothing. If he didn't find a way in before the sun rose, he'd be found out and captured, and that had happened often enough, thank you very much.

He tried pressing the rock again and again, but it kept its grip on the metal. Sweat trickled down his spine, the effort, even though he was just pressing and whispering, draining his strength.

He wriggled his toes in his shoes, cold and wet; a sharp contrast to the heat emanating from his torso. The sun had swung to the west, leaving him in freezing dimness. Temporary retreat was the only option. He'd dry his boots and find another way in come dawn.

In frustration, Fisher thumped the rock. "Let it go, you bastard."

Under his palm the rock slipped away from him with a deafening screech and rumble. His support no longer there, he lurched forward, tumbling off his perch, and slapped his forehead into the smooth granite surface. He scrambled back to see the grille still in place, with chunks of rock surrounding the ends of the metal that had once been solid stone. Now the rock was more than a foot away, giving him plenty of room to sidle around and under the wall.

"Okay," he whispered shakily as he stood just inside the grille, gravel beneath his feet and the water lapping at his heels. "You can move rock. Granite."

He looked outside, past where the rock and metal had plainly parted company. "That's going to be obvious." There'd been the noise too. Someone would have heard it and would come to investigate. Could he close the gap? Would he be able to open it again if he needed to?

He looked into the tunnel; at least he assumed it was a tunnel. The water had to go somewhere. "As long as it's all made of granite, you'll be able to move it," he reassured himself. "Right?"

There was no affirmation from the rock, or from himself. There were no guarantees. He could get the rock back in place around the metal, hide his entrance site, then get stuck somewhere downstream where the water met the ceiling and he had no way of getting through or back. He could die down here and no one would know until his fetid rotting body tainted the water.

"What choice do I have?" he asked, still whispering in case his voice carried to someone downstream. "I could leave now, return... return where, exactly?" There was nowhere for him. If he fixed this thing with the Elixir, there might be a place for him in The Lonely Isles. Where Gaelan lived.

No, there were other islands in the archipelago. He would go to God's Island and live there in splendid solitude. But he couldn't return to the Lonely Isles unless he fixed the Elixir.

He slumped against a jutting rock. He had to fix the Elixir whether he returned to the Isles or not. He couldn't pretend there wasn't a problem now he knew about it. He couldn't pretend it wasn't his problem either, because it was very much his problem. He'd been instrumental in providing the Yeudan with their raw materials for the last five years. It didn't matter that he'd thought he was doing the right thing at the time; all those deaths were on his head.

He returned to the grille and placed both hands on the separated rock. "Return," he said and leaned back. The rock, with a softer rumble this time, moved with him. At the last minute, he tore his hands away and watched as the rock slid into place around the torn-away sections still attached to the metal. The jagged lines were clearly visible to him but he thought no one else would notice unless they were looking for them. Either way, the rock and the grille were once again attached. No one else would get through.

Resolutely, Fisher put one hand on the rock wall and walked beside the stream. Within a dozen steps, the narrow bank disappeared and he stepped into the cold water again.

"I'll lose my damned toes in this if it goes on much longer." As he walked, his hand ran along the warm rock at his side.

When he put his hand on the rock it was cold. By the time he moved forward, the rock under his palm was warm. He stopped, let his hand rest on a small outcropping of rock and let the rock warm more while he held it. Then, with a grunt, he tore the small outcropping away and dropped it into the water. There was a hiss and a sizzle and steam rose around his knees.

Warm water seeped into his boots.

"Fuck." Fisher stumbled as his knees shook. He barely caught himself from tumbling headlong into the cold, but not-as-cold water, and leaned against the rock wall. "What the hell is happening to me?"

He scrubbed his trembling hands over his face. He didn't know who he was anymore, but he wasn't the man who could move rock, who could heat granite. How?

It had to be Gaelan. Fisher hadn't had any contact with anyone else unusual. Well, there were the four of the Warrior Pledge. Part of the Pledge ran through Fisher's mind—One Pure, prophecy revoked; One Great Heart Farseeing; One Changeling fooling wing; One Shining Silver from Rock. Ardelle, Heath, Rim and Checa.

They were all unusual but he hadn't been that close to them, hadn't touched them. Hadn't kissed them. Like he had Gaelan.

He'd kissed Gaelan. Taken his air. Breathed from him and with him.

That must be it. He'd caught something from Gaelan that allowed him to move and heat granite. But Gaelan said granite wasn't his rock.

So what? Gaelan said a lot of things. He wanted you to be the dragons' concubine. You can't trust what he said.

Fuck. He was talking to himself. What did it matter anyway? He was under the city, on his way to destroy any chance they could continue to make the Elixir, and it was day five.

He only had four days to accomplish his goal and get to the glacier.

If he survived.

And supposing Gaelan really was waiting for him. The tiny place in his chest that he'd begun to associate with Gaelan warmed pleasantly until he stopped doubting Gaelan would be there.

Fisher resolutely turned his mind away from what that feeling might mean and pulled another jutting chunk of rock from the wall, heated it and dropped it into the water. He continued, wading through warm water and misty air until the lowering ceiling made it impossible for him to keep walking.

Then he crawled. Then he slithered along the rocky stream-bed, barely managing to keep his head above the water so he could breathe. His palms and knees became inured to the dig of gravel but the scrape of rock across the back of his head echoed painfully with each contact.

Then it was gone, replaced by fresh air wafting over him. He put his hand down where he expected the bottom of the stream to be and met nothing.

He tumbled headfirst into cold, deep water.

CHAPTER THIRTEEN

FISHER AUTOMATICALLY arched his back, his knees digging painfully into the gravel. Finally, after what seemed an age, he lifted his head from the water.

He scrambled back, coughing and gasping. His concentration was shot, so the heat seeped out of the granite pebbles beneath him and the water grew icy. He shivered then waved his hands around to find where the rock wall had gone. Cool air continued to wash over him from above. He looked up.

To stars.

There was an opening above him. In the dimness he could just make out a thick bar across the opening at the top with a round thing perched on one end. A bucket? It was a well.

A way out of the water and into the city.

Fisher stood, found the wall and ran his fingers over the rock. It was too smooth to climb but surely it was granite, like much of the city. He found a rock with a flat top, pressed his fingertips into the edges and commanded it to slide out. It didn't, so he took a deep breath and imagined what the step would look like, then repeated his command.

The rock slid smoothly, with barely a sound, to exactly the right position. It was in the wrong place, though. Shoulder height was far too high for him to put his foot onto unless he built a number of stepping stones up the wall.

He looked up again but was unable to gauge the height of the wall. Hoping the whole thing was granite, he began making an uneven stepping ladder.

By the time he reached the top, he barely had enough energy to roll over the lip of the well and onto the dusty street, shivering in his wet clothes in the freezing night air.

He reached into his pocket for the rock Gaelan had given him. "Warm." He had say the word several times, partly because he stuttered so much in the cold and partly because as his clothes dried, the warmth leached from the rock.

Finally, only his boots were damp, but they were warm and his muscles had recovered enough from their long vertical climb that he could stand and take in his surroundings.

He recognized this place—the communal well in the middle of the western quarter.

There were lanterns strung along the street, the light directly beneath them bright yellow, then fading farther away. Just as the shadows consumed the road, the light of the next street lamp took over, the whole thing wavering like bric-a-brac around a woman's skirts.

Flanking the street were a hodge-podge mixture of shopfronts and houses. The shopfronts sported awnings and signs that advertised their wares. The houses had a single window above a dark narrow door. Fisher knew that behind all the doors were even narrower staircases leading up above the shops, most of them three levels, and down one level to a basement apartment.

The well, in the middle of a wide intersection, was flanked on four corners by two churches and two taverns. The sidewalk on the church side was dark and glossy, smooth from thousands of worshiping feet and regular cleaning. Opposite, outside the pubs, the path was just as smooth from just as many worshiping feet, but the glossy finish was marred by the refuse so common outside pubs—spilled ale and sawdust-covered vomit, left to dry and washed away only when it rained.

As he took in his surroundings, two men on horseback galloped out. He'd been there too long.

"What's your business here this late at night, stranger?"

Neither horseman dismounted. Both wore half chainmail under a leather jerkin and a battle helm that hid most of their faces, but Fisher remembered the short, broad scar under the jaw of the man sitting on the gray horse. He kept his gaze away from the rider's right hand.

"Can a man not return to his home, Kaod?" The lilting tones of his childhood returned to him without effort.

Kaod drew his sword and Fisher raised his hands to show he was unarmed. "Before my mother took me away, you weren't so quick to sword, although after I broke your finger, you treated me with respect at least."

The tip of the sword dropped. "Turn to the light."

Fisher obediently turned so his face would be visible in the light of the nearest lamp.

"It's the Concubine! The priests were right," exclaimed the second man.

"Shut it, you fool," said Kaod. "What's your business here, Fisher?"

Something settled inside him at Kaod's use of a name chosen only days before he had left Barthes. Someone had loved him well enough when he was a child to remember what he'd always said he'd wanted to be.

Thanks to Kaod's companion, Fisher had a starting point. "I've come from the Lonely Isles to see the priests. I know where the Blue Goddess is." According to the scriptures, the Goddess had once lived among the Yeudan but had disappeared and not returned.

The two men looked to the south. "She'd never go down there. Her home is here."

"I can only speak of this to the priests." He'd decided as a child that the Blue Goddess was a myth created to ensure children did as they were told. Believing in her hadn't made his life any easier. Not believing in her hadn't made it less difficult. There was no Blue Goddess, but saying so would get his guts run through by Kaod's sword.

The sun took that moment to bathe the skies in the eerie blue light of pre-dawn, seeming to punctuate his claims.

"We'll escort you." Kaod kept his sword unsheathed and at the ready. "You go ahead."

Kaod hadn't said the words, but Fisher knew he'd just been arrested. The chances of him being delivered to the temple were even with his chances of being delivered to the militia. Either way, he'd just been "recruited," and the chances of him completing his mission were almost nil.

He should have remembered what happened to strangers. He had remembered. What made him think he'd be exempt? The fact he'd lived here before? Anyone of age caught on the streets at night or without purpose during the day, was taken. He should have remembered that.

"Who's the Captain of the Guard?" he asked. He had to bargain for his freedom with the information he had about the alliance formed between the Imperials and the Mafdeti.

"I am," Kaod responded gruffly, as though it should be obvious.

Fisher looked more closely at Kaod's clothing. The chain mail was better quality than the other horseman's, and there was an insignia on his helmet.

Fisher was losing his edge. "My apologies, Kaod. Congratulations. My only defense is that I was but a child when I left."

"You were ten summers, same as me. I've been fighting since my training finished at fourteen." Kaod looked Fisher down, then up again. "Although you always were a scrawny one."

Fisher forced a chuckle through the memories that term brought back. Being scrawny wasn't an advantage in Barthes.

He trudged through the summer dawn, the only sound the jingle of horse's harness following too close behind him.

When they reached the wall surrounding the center of the city, where the government, the temple and the militia were housed, the gates swung open silently. Several newly-risen civilians lined the road. They all watched Fisher but none spoke.

The silence is new. Fisher kept his head pointed firmly ahead but darted his gaze around as much as he could without making it obvious. Dirty clothing, sunken cheeks, hopeless eyes. Either his memory was defective, or things were much worse than they'd been when he and his mother had been run out of town.

Fisher veered to the right when they entered the Wheel—the network of roads and buildings that radiated from the temple—expecting to continue through the gates. Kaod's horse nudged his shoulder and pushed him back onto the main thoroughfare that circumnavigated the wall.

"I need to see the priests," said Fisher. He had a chance of surviving if Kaod let him go to the temple. His life expectancy would be significantly shorter if he was pressed into the military. It wasn't that he couldn't fight—he probably had skills Kaod only dreamed of, after his years under the desert with the Exiles—but conscripts were always put on the front line, in the most danger.

Kaod's horse nudged Fisher in the back, making him stumble the few steps that took him past the gates. The temple gardens behind the iron gates beckoned him. There lay relative safety.

His heart rate increased with every step they took beyond the gates. With every step the uncertainty increased. Would Kaod take him to the barracks or the dungeons? Would he die there, in the place of his birth, with less fanfare than he came into it?

"What are you doing back here at this time of day, Kaod?" The strident voice preceded the opening of the door to a small cottage across the laneway from the temple walls.

A short, angular, middle-aged woman stepped out, a scowl deepening the frown between her heavy brows. The horses behind Fisher stopped at the same time the woman did. In between them, he froze.

It couldn't be. She'd been arrested the day he fled. He'd believed her long dead, executed or sacrificed to the Goddess for her sins.

Before he could say anything, Ma Jeffries strode up to him, swung back her arm and slapped him hard across the face. He stumbled sideways and would have fallen if Kaod, down from his horse, hadn't grabbed his arm and righted him.

"That's for the stupid racket you made that nearly got you and your mother killed. I told you to be quiet, you idiot, and what did you do? Scream the place down because the priest and constable wanted to talk to me."

"They arrested you for blasphemy!" Two decades had passed but fearful sweat still broke out on his forehead whenever he thought of what happened to blasphemers in Barthes.

"They wanted to know if I knew where you and your mother were." She crossed her arms over her flat chest. "By the time they asked the question I didn't have a clue where you were, so they couldn't detect the lie on me. Why do you think I refused to let your mother tell me where she was headed?" Ma Jeffries humphed. "I suppose you were only a child, but my Kaod knew enough to stay quiet long before *he* was ten summers old."

Fisher felt he should shuffle his feet or drop his chin in shame but those would have been the actions of the boy he'd been the last time he saw his mother's sister.

He reached under his tunic to the small pouch he kept at his waist and pulled out the last item his mother had been given by the Exile King. With his other hand, he took Ma's hand and placed the sapphire and diamond brooch in it. "She wanted you to have this and to tell you she loved you... and that you saved her life." His mother hadn't really said that, but he was sure she'd meant to.

Ma didn't look at what Fisher placed in her hand. She stared at him, her eyes filling with heavy tears that ran down her cheeks and dripped off her chin. "How?" Her voice as broken as her expression.

"She saved some people. They're good people but they're bringing war to us, and we can't win."

"No one can beat us!" Kaod stepped forward indignantly. "The Imperials are too focused on their hierarchy to know how to fight properly and the Mafdeti have been beaten since the first invasion a millennium ago.

"Our organization and training is far superior. We're a much stronger people, used to fighting and thriving through all hardships. We've had spies in place for the last decade. There's nothing we don't know about their military or training procedures."

That was all true. He could refute none of it. The fact that he thought the Mafdeti, as the original inhabitants of the country, should be the ruling power, wouldn't hold any sway here. The Yeudan had long believed they were the chosen people, beloved of the Blue Goddess, and therefore deserving of supreme power. Nothing would sway them.

There was one thing Kaod didn't know. For a second, Fisher wondered if he shouldn't tell him, but the telling might get him what he wanted. It would at least keep him alive a little longer.

Decision made, he smiled at Kaod, enjoying the suspicious narrowing of his cousin's eyes. "They have dragons."

Shocked silence greeted him. Then Ma Jeffries moved swiftly, gripping his bicep with hard fingers digging in. "Have they taken you yet?"

"What? No! I'm not the Concubine." He tugged his arm but she didn't release him.

Ma peered at his face in the growing light, then relaxed her hold. "No, they haven't. There's still time to make things right before it happens." She turned to Kaod. "He needs to see the priests; the Abbott if you can get an audience. If we leave it any longer, the dragons will have him and there'll be no chance for us to win."

Fisher stumbled backward. "What are you talking about? You can't win. The dragons can breathe fire." He was sure they could by now. Heath had begun teaching them before he had escaped. "They'll incinerate us all."

Us. It had been twenty years since he had been Yeudan, yet as soon as he set foot in his birth town, he once again identified with them.

"They won't attack us if we have the Concubine." Ma gestured to Kaod, who stepped forward.

Fisher stepped back. "I'm not the Concubine. There is no Concubine. There's no way I'm going to let you... what? Bargain with them for peace if you hand me over? I'm not going to be the dragons' Concubine."

He turned and ran, ignoring Kaod's roar of "Fisher!" behind him.

"Kaod! Get him. It has to be us to hand him to the priests or we'll all be dead."

Fisher darted down the road, then turned sharply off the wheel, weaving his way through progressively narrower lanes as he left the ordered center of the city and entered the slums. The horses, hurriedly mounted by Kaod and his companion, had fallen behind at the first narrow alley he ran into, but pounding footsteps, even now recognizable as Kaod's, still followed him.

Fisher slowed. Kaod was no taller than he was but he was more heavily built, more muscled. Why hadn't he overtaken him yet?

At the next corner, he risked looking behind, only to see Kaod pause as he did, maintaining his distance. What was his game? He shrugged. It didn't matter. What did matter was that he had to gain access to the temple and find out how to stop the production of the Elixir. He rounded another corner, smiling as he saw where he was—exactly where he expected to be—at the wall of the temple again.

"Fisher, don't," called Kaod. "They'll kill you."

Fisher turned and backed against the wall, resting his palms against it. The granite hummed, welcoming him home. "I have to stop them making the Elixir, Kaod. I can't let them keep killing people with it."

"You want to stop the Goddess potion?" Kaod came to a stop several feet in front of him.

"Is that what you call it? It's nothing to do with the Goddess. It's norrgel poison, treated so it isn't immediately deadly. They use it to kill people, wealthy and influential people who can afford their prices. They're murdering people and making money from it."

"I know." Kaod's shoulders slumped. "The Abbott is the only person who has the complete recipe but many have the parts. You would have to destroy them all—all the recipes, all the people involved—if you expect the Elixir to be destroyed."

"That's what I'm here for."

"I can't let you do that." Kaod stepped forward, his face a study in desperate choices.

"Why?"

"Things are different from when you were here. A lot of people died after you left and those of us left had to do whatever we could to stay alive."

Fisher waited, but Kaod said no more. "What aren't you telling me?"

"Ma is one of the mixers. If you want to destroy all chance of the potion being made, you'll have to kill her too."

"Won't she just stop making it?"

Kaod shook his head. "She can't. She needs it to survive."

"I'll find another way for her to make a living."

"You don't understand. It isn't a choice for her. I know she said the priests only talked to her when they took her, but they tortured her. Badly. The potion is the only thing keeping her alive and she receives a dosage only if she continues to make it. If she stops, so does the potion, and she'll die."

Fisher's breath left him in a rush and he stumbled backward until he leaned awkwardly against the temple wall. Guilt gouged a hole in his chest and grief filled it. It was his fault she'd been taken. His fault she'd been tortured. His fault she was going to die.

Fisher couldn't allow the Elixir to be made. He couldn't be responsible for one more death. Except he would be.

He always was. The Exiles. The Mafdeti. His mother.

Now her sister.

"She's never been much of a mother, Fisher, but she's all I've got."

"I'm sorry." One tiny spark told him it was a good thing Gaelan was gone. He would probably get him killed too. If he didn't, the Elixir would.

He pressed back against the wall, the rock humming gently in his mind. "I have to, Kaod. I'm sorry."

As Kaod raised his sword. Fisher closed his eyes and allowed the granite to take him.

CHAPTER FOURTEEN

THE FALL THROUGH THE rock was easier this time. Dust and metal filled his nostrils, but he could still breathe.

He kicked his feet languidly, like he had when he and Gaelan had been swimming, but this time he didn't need Gaelan to breathe for him.

He kicked again. The pressure of the rock around him increased, thick and tense, and something inside his mind twigged that time was passing—more time than he'd spent inside the rock last time.

What if he got stuck? What would happen if he never fell through the other side. Would he die there? Or would he float, sustained inside each particle of the wall, moaning every time someone passed in an effort to attract their attention, to get out. Would he become the "ghost of the temple," with this section of the wall to be avoided for the next hundred years?

Fisher kicked out and twisted, trying to move through the molasses. His head bumped against something and he twisted and kicked again, his breath thick and labored. Each kick with his foot jarred, each push with his hand strained his shoulders.

Around him, the rock cooled and thickened. What was wrong? Why couldn't he get through? The other times had been swift and easy. Almost comfortable, if at first terrifying.

He kicked again. Something cracked and warmth jumped through the rock again. He kicked again and again, each time causing a crack that brought with it warmer rock and cooler air rushing through his lungs.

He kept kicking, even though he was tiring. The cracks sounding only every second or third kick. His lungs were tight, more so than they'd been since Gaelan had left. This time, it was like someone was sitting on his chest. He couldn't get a deep breath. He really was going to die here, inside a wall.

No, he wasn't.

He rested a moment then gathered as much energy and momentum as he could and kicked out with both feet.

The crack burst through his head, then crashed beneath him and he shot from the wall and landed with a thump on the floor and skidded several feet. Skin tore from his elbows and his back shredded on the sharp points of whatever had fallen onto the floor with him, then he stopped, gasping in fresh air and coughing up dust and phlegm.

He opened his eyes in the ensuing silence to be greeted by four militia men holding their spears at the ready, pointed at him. Beyond them were three pale, wide-eyed priests, each of them gripping their prayer beads as if they'd save them from anything that happened.

Still gasping for air, Fisher looked at the wall he'd burst from. The granite was solid, intact. The sandstone veneer, however, had a great gaping hole in it, the shattered pieces of which lay uncomfortably under him. He rolled to his side, groaning at the sharp pain in his back, but froze when the guardsmen surged forward with their spears.

"Stop!" called one of the priests. "Take him to the Abbott." He stepped back as one of the guardsmen hauled Fisher to his feet. Shards of sandstone dropped from his skin, the staccato shattering of them making the priest jump. He looked so like a marionette bouncing at the end of strings that Fisher laughed, then coughed up a couple of small pebbles of sandstone.

"I've always hated sandstone," he said as he spat the pebbles out.

Another guardsman grabbed his other arm and, together, they marched him out.

Warm liquid slithered down Fisher's back and he realized he was bleeding. The blood was a trickle and the wound more of a sting than anything else, so he wasn't too worried. It would be another small injury to join those he'd gained on this journey.

Of greater concern was that he'd been captured immediately and was being taken to the Abbot. His feverish mind ran through all the possibilities.

The Abbott could welcome him with open arms and say he'd been waiting for him to arrive and show him how to defeat the insidious evil of the Elixir.

He could rush the Abbott with one of the knives still secure in his boot and kill him, destroying a key part of the Elixir recipe in the process. Some people would die from the withdrawals, but the world would be saved.

The Abbott could order him summarily executed and production and sale of the Elixir would continue unabated.

He didn't anticipate what did greet him.

The Abbott sat in a large, heavily upholstered throne-like chair. His robes, rich, heavily embroidered purple trimmed with gold braid, flowed over the floor surrounding the chair and cascaded down the stairs from the dais.

The over-abundance of purple velvet wasn't what caught his attention, though. What drew his attention were the gilded cages sitting on either side of the throne.

In the left one crouched Checa, his tawny hair matted and dull. He'd lost weight since Fisher had seen him last and looked tired and worn.

The cage to the right held Checa's mate, Heath. Heath's hair was glossy and smooth but the dark circles under his eyes belied his attempts to appear well.

"What's going on here?" he demanded as he tried to tear himself from the guardsmen's grips. "Why are they confined? Why are they separated?"

He almost asked, "Where are their dragons?" but stopped himself in time. It was possible that the Abbott didn't know that Heath flew the golden dragon, Kimi, and Checa's was the dragon king.

The Abbott looked up and smiled. Even from this distance, Fisher could smell the norrgel on him and see his glassy eyes. "Oh good, you're here. Now we can begin negotiations for peace."

Peace? Negotiations? "Is this about that stupid Concubine song again? You know it's not real, don't you?" If he could convince them it was all a joke, perhaps they'd drop the subject once and for all and let him live his own life. Going by the look of rage on the Abbott's face, though, he didn't like his chances.

As he spoke, another cage was wheeled up beside Heath's and the door opened. His guards dragged him over to it. He dug his heels in. He hated being confined and knew he'd never be able to escape.

"I'll admit, I never expected to see you here," said Heath, his usually cheerful voice flat and low.

"You know me," said Fisher. "Always where the highest paying job is."

Heath chuffed, for a second sounding as disenchanted as Checa usually did. "Some job you've landed inside a bloody cage no one can break out of. You know the bars are set into granite, don't you?"

Fisher jerked then tried to hide his response by slamming his palms against the bars. He dropped to sit cross-legged on the floor of the cage and reached his hands out to feel the stone. For the first time, it struck him how comfortable this pose was and he realized he'd been doing it instinctively for most of his life.

Fuck. That meant it wasn't some magical voodoo that Gaelan had done to make him weird. He'd always been weird. He'd just never known exactly how weird before now; never noticed how often he read the stone to find things out.

Under the granite was more gilded metal. After his experience with the sandstone, he wasn't going to push himself through anything other than granite.

I have to stop the production of the Elixir. He looked around the large room, remembering the Elixir wasn't the only reason he'd come north. Gaelan was also on a quest to rescue his duke. "I don't suppose you've seen a duke around here at all?" he asked.

Heath did nothing more than glare at him.

"Where's your... young lady friend?"

The Abbott guffawed. "He won't have a lady friend."

"Kimi says you'll help us," said Heath. To Fisher, it sounded like an accusation but he ignored the tone. "She and Staton are coming but are too far west."

The Abbott gestured to Checa, ignoring Heath. "He's Bonded to this one. Can't you see the deliciousness of their suffering because they're separated?"

"Delicious?" asked Fisher. "Why is separating them such a good thing?"

"I've read the scriptures. I know it means their strength is halved." He reached into his voluminous sleeve and pulled out a small glass vial. He unstoppered it and took a small sip. A violent shiver shook his frame then he settled languidly against the back of his chair.

"Without the freedom to touch, they're useless. They can't control their strength and they can't summon their dragons." The

Abbott laughed. "They're totally under my control." He peered myopically at Fisher. "And now so are you—Concubine."

Fisher clenched his fists. Why was everyone so focused on the bloody concubine thing? He didn't care what his skin looked like. He wasn't going to be the dragons' bloody concubine. He'd seen the results of multiple partners for one person during his time with the Exiles and he knew he didn't want any of that for himself. He wanted the fairy tale that his mother used to tell him as a child. He wanted a relationship based on trust and respect, and he wanted it to be exclusive. And safe. But all anyone wanted was for him to be the dragons' whore.

As he sat in his cage, idly feeling the extent of the granite surrounding him, he wondered if anyone even knew what the Concubine did. If he, an ordinary man, could have such an affinity with granite, what might a legend such as the Concubine be able to do? For the first time since falling through the wall, he smiled.

"I wonder why you're so desperate for the Concubine. What could he or she possibly have that you want? Isn't he just a sex toy for all the dragons?"

Beside him, Heath coughed. Checa covered his face with his hands. Were they laughing? Bastards.

The Abbott wasn't laughing, so Fisher focused on his red face. "What could you possibly hope to achieve with a whore?" He inwardly cringed at the word. Even if someone did find pleasure in multiple partners, it didn't make them a whore, but he knew it was a term the Abbott would understand.

"You know nothing!" Spittle flew from the man's lips. The skin on his hands stretched taut over his knuckles as he gripped the arms of his chair.

"If I'm supposed to be the Concubine, I should know something about it. So tell me." Some of his anger seeped out but he relaxed when he realized he'd dug his fingertips into the floor of the cage.

The Abbott smiled beatifically. "The Goddess Potion is for the Blue Goddess."

"She instructed you to make it?" Apart from the fact the Blue Goddess didn't exist, and they believed she'd been missing for hundreds of years, encouraging a deadly addiction didn't seem like something the Goddess he'd learned about as a child would encourage.

He shifted until he sat with his back against the bars and his arms curled comfortably behind him, hands resting on the stone where the metal was embedded.

"The potion will bring her home." The Abbott shifted in his seat so he could recline farther. He tipped his head back and closed his eyes. "She'll see her people in trouble and she'll return to save us all."

"It's a poison. It kills. How many have already died from it?" The bars behind him wobbled so he moved to the next ones, his back now fully to Heath.

The Abbott's smile returned. "She'll come soon. She'll see how dire the situation is and she'll come to us."

Are you mad? The question was on the tip of Fisher's tongue, but he suppressed it. "That explains why you have the potion here. Why have you been selling it to others?" The next two bars wobbled. Another two would give him enough room to get through.

Heath's movements behind him had stopped. On the other side of the Abbott, Checa was crouched, his head still down but his muscles tense.

The Abbott waved a languid hand. "We'll need those lands once the Goddess comes." He sat forward, making Fisher jump. His gaze was sharp, all evidence of the potion, except the odor of imminent death, was gone.

"The potion will take care of the rich and powerful. You'll bring the dragons under control." His grin had a manic quality. "We'll have it all, just as the Goddess promised." The Abbott leaned back again and began to hum distractedly.

"What about these two? Why do you have them in cages?"

The man flipped his hand then turned sideways in his seat, drew his legs up and settled his head upon the arm, apparently preparing for a nap. "They're insurance. No one will attack us while I have them. Their dragons are subdued with them here, and the Imperials are too busy strutting around claiming superiority to be able to work together effectively. By the time they finally get themselves organized, the Goddess will be here, and she'll kill them all."

"If I'm to bring the dragons under control, why do you need them? What sort of insurance can they offer if I'm all you need?"

A squeak from Heath startled Fisher. "What?" he asked. "You like being in there?"

"You think he's just going to release us?" Heath responded with a sneer.

Fisher laughed as Heath's defeated posture changed. He and Checa were ready to fight, no longer hiding their alertness. "I always knew your resilience was what would save you." He winked then turned to the Abbott. "Are you going to release them, or shall I?"

The Abbott gaped, then threw his head back and laughed. "The only way those two are leaving their cages alive is if everyone in this room is dead first."

"Okay." The next two bars wobbled free of the granite and he lunged back.

He tumbled in a backward somersault, reaching for the knives hidden in his boots as he flew through the air. He landed lightly in a deep crouch, flinging one knife at the Abbott, even as he raised his head and checked his surroundings.

The guard closest to Heath's cage caught his second knife in the neck a split second after the Abbott screamed and collapsed, his hands tugging at the blade sunk deep between his ribs.

Blood gushed as the Abbott pulled the knife free, and the guard stopped screaming as his legs folded under him. He landed face-first on the floor, the knife skittering toward Heath's cage, blood flowing swiftly underneath him.

Fisher raced to Heath's cage. He jumped and raised his hands. When he landed, he brought his fists down between the bars and smashed the granite base. Heath slid out and immediately went to release Checa.

Fisher slid toward the guard, retrieved his knife and threw it underhand into the stomach of the second guard, who was almost upon him. The guard fell, but not before he swung his sword, taking a slice off Fisher's jacket at the shoulder and drawing blood.

Fisher's gaze darted around the room, noting the converging soldiers, too numerous for him to fight on his own. There was no time to retrieve his knives. He pulled the last two from the slim holsters in his boots and backed up against the Abbott's chair.

"What's the plan?" asked Checa as he stepped beside him, the snick of his claws releasing in the sudden silence of soldiers pausing to consider a changed landscape.

On the other side of Checa, Heath crouched next to the cage, the door hanging open. His claws were extended and his dropped canines dripped saliva down his chin.

The first wave of soldiers, those who'd been standing guard outside, rushed them, swords drawn. Fisher crouched, conscious the only way to counter the longer reach of the man's sword was to attack.

He jumped in a long tackle, using the hasp of one knife to redirect the sword above his head rather than through it, then punched his other knife deep into the soldier's stomach. Keeping hold of his knife, he pulled back, not caring if he enlarged the puncture wound or not.

A second soldier was behind the first, another next to him. They weren't going to wait patiently and attack one at a time. He was going to go under. He dodged another sword strike, but knew it was only a matter of seconds before he became a human pin-cushion.

As he fought, his mind raced with possible scenarios, but none of them left the three of them alive. Not unless the dragons were close enough to get them out of here. "Where are your dragons?" he asked, panting as he slashed and danced away. Not quickly enough to avoid another glancing blow on his left arm.

His fingers tingled and his knife slipped in his hold. He slammed his hand against his thigh to close his barely-responsive fingers harder around the hasp so as not to lose the knife.

Checa blinked, his gaze distant for a second. "On their way." He snarled and sliced his claws across the stomach of a soldier who dared to lunge toward Heath. He ignored Heath's scowl and engaged another soldier in combat. "They were destroying a potion factory but now they seem to be making friends with another dragon. Is he yours?"

"No," responded Fisher automatically, ignoring the sweep of pleasure the thought of Gaelan brought. "Blue-purple? Huge wingspan? Black claws?" He slashed at another guard as he ducked under a sword coming at him from the side.

"Um."

"I know him. He can be trusted."

"Uh-huh," said Checa as he slashed the throat of the guard Fisher had ducked. "He's on his way. Staton says he seems a bit angry. Move away from the windows."

The soldiers near them paused as Checa's resonant voice reached them. As one they looked up to the long row of stained-glass windows along the southern wall. Outside, three shadows were visible, growing with each second, heading straight for them.

"Oh, fuck," said Fisher as he dodged another sword thrust and ducked around the other side of the Abbott's chair.

The air tinkled and sparkled with shards of blue, red, yellow and green exploding from the windows above a split-second before the roar of three dragons reached them. A second roar, piercing enough to make Fisher's ears hurt, followed and the glass shattered again until sparkling dust fluttered down around him, covering the floor and everything else in the room in rainbow glitter. He expected the dragons to follow but when nothing but silence ensued, he looked up.

Three dragons, black and gold close together, blue slightly apart, perched on the window sills.

Gaelan. He was there, not in the Icy Wastes. He'd come when Fisher needed him. Fisher's chest tightened and he had to suck in a hard breath to stop the burning in his eyes. He looked away to see smoke waft from the gold's nostrils. Scarlet fire burned deep within the black's red eyes. The two dragons looked at each other then turned to the center of the room and roared fire.

Soldiers screamed and ran, some of the them with flames licking at their clothing and sizzling in their hair. Some fell, eventually silent, but most escaped.

When the searing heat abated, Fisher emerged from the protection of the Abbott's chair and looked at the dragons. The black and gold grinned; Fisher wasn't sure how he knew they were grinning because their fangs looked anything but happy, but he was sure that's what they were doing.

His supposition was confirmed when Checa walked forward. "Stop looking so pleased with yourself. You two are late." He stood below them with his hands on his hips. The gold looked contrite, but the black lifted his chin and glared back at him.

"You forget yourself, Rider." The deep voice rumbled through the now-empty room.

Fisher would have cowered if a dragon spoke to him thus, but Checa merely raised his eyebrows.

"'Twas but a few days, Rider, and we brought a friend." The black, which had been superior seconds before, was now as excited as a puppy. "He's the son of—"

"My name is Gaelan." Until then, Gaelan had been watching the spectacle with bored amusement, but his attitude became sharp and secretive, his wary gaze on Fisher.

Fisher glared at him. *What are you hiding? The son of whom?*

He jumped as the main doors exploded inward, small and large splinters arcing into the room. Almost faster than he could track, a black ball flew toward him. With no time to react, he stood frozen, fulling expecting to die.

Blue light filled the room as a thin narrow stream of blue fire flew through the space and stopped the ball, like it had hit a rock face. It crashed to the floor and flowed, molten, leaving a small mound of metal surrounded by a flat spill.

Fisher's gaze darted back to Gaelan in time to see the blue glow in his eyes fade and his irises return to their usual vibrant blue-purple. Gaelan blinked at him then turned to the broken door and let loose another narrow blue flame that melted the rock surrounding the destroyed doors until no gap remained. Only once the rock solidified, sealing the room, did Fisher realize the noise of charging soldiers was abruptly cut off.

"We need to leave here now if you intend to finish what you've begun," said Gaelan. "They're surrounding the castle and will attack from different aspects within minutes."

Fisher kicked over a soldier and retrieved one of his knives, wiping it clean on the soldier's trousers. As he walked to the next one, he glared at Gaelan. "How do you propose we get out now that you've melted the only exit?" He should be more shocked that Gaelan could melt rock, and he probably would be once the danger was completely passed, but he had seen Gaelan turn from a man into a dragon and back again. He could grow gills and breathe under water. He could be a cougar. It wasn't that unbelievable that he had other skills Fisher would have naturally attributed to a dragon.

He retrieved his last two knives and checked his holsters sat correctly inside his boots.

"Are you ready to leave now?" the annoying blue dragon asked.

Fisher ignored him and all the aches the fight had reawakened and walked to stand directly below him. He lifted his arms, raised his eyebrows and waited, refusing to allow anyone to see how his hands trembled in the aftermath of the fight, or how his heart pounded with residual fear. Or how his heart soared because Gaelan came back for him.

Gaelan chuckled then shifted slightly and lowered his tail through the opening.

Fisher scowled at the tail hanging before him, then mounted it like a broomstick, leaned over and held on tightly. "Don't bang me against anything, dragon," he grumped, then closed his eyes, not wanting to see the building fall away below him or how close he came to having his head smashed against the roof overhang.

As he lifted off the ground, he heard Checa ask, "Is your tail long enough to do that, Staton?" There was a low growl, a slap, a call of "Hey," and laughter from Heath, but Fisher didn't look back.

The air cooled as they rose into the sky and soon he was shivering so hard he thought he'd fall off. Immediately he had the thought, his trajectory changed and his eyes flew open to find himself swinging through the air under Gaelan's belly. Then he was grasped in black claws, the sensation at once familiar and alarming. At least he wouldn't fall unless Gaelan dropped him. He flung his arms around one of Gaelan's claws anyway, holding as tightly as his trembling body allowed.

They landed in the commons a few minutes later, Gaelan hovering to gently lower him before landing softly beside him. The sun was high in the sky and the air filled with the screams of market owners abandoning their stalls and fleeing.

He stepped forward and slapped Gaelan's chest. "Why did you land here? You've terrified everyone." He cast a glance around, expecting to see the square empty, only to find most of the people creeping back onto the edges of the common and dropping to their knees.

"What the—?" Then the murmurings began, prayers Fisher hadn't heard since his childhood.

"Oh, for the Goddess's sake," he muttered before turning to the largest group of people. "He's not the Blue Goddess, you idiots. He's male." Fisher pointed to Gaelan's hips but stopped short at the idea of trying to lift the dragon's leg so everyone could see exactly what he meant. "And he's not blue."

He walked back to Gaelan and slapped his foreleg. "Let me up."

Gaelan obediently crooked his leg, forming a convenient step for him to climb. The crowd gasped, and he heard cries of 'Concubine' amongst them. "Idiots," he grumbled as he settled himself on Gaelan's back at the base of his neck.

"Where did the other two go?" He surveyed the sky but couldn't see the black or the gold of Checa and Heath's dragons. "We need to go see Ma Jeffries and make her tell us how we can find the master recipe for the potion now the Abbott's dead."

I can take you there but there's something else I must do.

Fisher jerked at the sound of Gaelan's voice in his head. He'd been surprised that Gaelan spoke out loud to him before, but now the quiet words in his mind shocked him. "How do you do that?"

The crowd around him had moved closer and Fisher noted a few priests amongst them, chanting that stupid song from his childhood.

Never mind how, he thought with a frown, trying to push his thoughts out. *Can you hear me too?*

I could hear you even if you didn't yell. For now, we can speak like this if we're touching.

What do you mean for now?

Where is this Ma Jeffries?

You'd better tell me everything once we're finished this. He tried to make his mind-voice as threatening as he could his real voice, but he wasn't sure he succeeded. He gave up and focused on the more urgent problem. *In the slums on the other side of the castle, near the barracks.*

I can take you there but then I have to leave.

"You're leaving me? Again?" It was ridiculous to feel abandoned. Fisher didn't like the stupid dragon anyway. "Where are you going?" *Why do you keep saving me if you don't want to be with me?*

Gaelan snorted a laugh as he jumped into the air, drawing gasps and more screams from the crowds below. Musical instruments had joined the priests and that stupid song echoed on the air. "Will you join me on my Adventure, Concubine?" Gaelan asked.

"Don't call me Concubine." It was probably a futile request. Then his curiosity pinched at him. "What sort of adventure?"

"Once you stop the production of the potion, join me at the glacier."

That was the original plan. "What are you doing there?"

"I'm going to rescue the Blue Goddess."

"What?" He slipped sideways, only a quick tilt from Gaelan buying him enough time to grasp one of the spines on Gaelan's neck and right himself. "The Blue Goddess doesn't exist."

"You won't help me?"

It was ridiculous for Fisher to imagine disappointment in Gaelan's voice.

Gaelan's wings lifted and they slowed and dropped. Fisher looked down, recognizing the lane behind Ma Jeffries' house.

Gaelan dropped. Just as Fisher was convinced they'd get stuck in the narrow opening between the rows of houses, blue light shimmered over everything, then Gaelan dropped to the ground on two human feet, Fisher held awkwardly on his back.

Fisher dropped his legs from around Gaelan's waist and stepped away, stumbling a couple of steps as he found his feet. Gaelan turned, his hands cupping Fisher's elbows until he was sure he was steady, then he stepped back.

"Would you like to help me?" Gaelan asked again.

The Blue Goddess didn't exist, did she? Fisher wasn't so sure. Even if it wasn't the Goddess, Gaelan clearly intended to rescue someone. "Where?"

"She's trapped in the glacier."

In the glacier? He shook his head. Gaelan must mean *at* the glacier. "That's a damned cold place."

"It is."

"How will you free her?"

"I don't know yet, but I have to try."

"What can *I* do?" He wasn't really going to help. He just wanted to know what he would do if he decided to.

"Be with me of your own free will." Gaelan stepped forward and cupped his hand around Fisher's cheek. He bent closer, his lips pressing against Fisher's mouth.

Warmth flooded him, jumping under his skin, scalding him, lighting a fire deep within. Fisher clasped Gaelan's wrist and leaned into the kiss.

This was vastly different from the water when Gaelan shared his breath. It was different again from the kisses they'd shared on the mountain. This was past and future colliding and bringing heat and want. This was what truly living meant.

He stepped closer, his free arm wrapping around Gaelan and drawing him as close as he could get without their bodies merging into each other. Becoming one. He gasped as Gaelan groaned. *One with you*, Gaelan growled in Fisher's mind. *I would be part of you, and you part of me. Forever.*

Fisher pulled away, shocked that a large part of him found what Gaelan suggested appealing. More than appealing—everything he wanted. But Gaelan didn't really know him. he didn't know how many deaths stained he soul. "I have to stop the Elixir."

Gaelan stepped back, his fingers sliding away slowly. He stared at Fisher for a long time and Fisher saw the hurt and longing in his look. No one had ever longed for Fisher in any way except to have him gone. Could Gaelan want Fisher for himself if he knew what he'd done?

Once the contact between them was gone, Gaelan was all business. "Ma Jeffries is the key. She knows more than she's told you."

Fisher gasped, his mind rejecting the idea that his aunt would advocate the addiction and death of so many people. To what end?

Gaelan leaned forward again. "It wasn't you who brought the militia after your mother, Fisher. If it was, you'd have been taken too." Then he crouched and jumped, shifting mid-jump, blue wings scraping the ground and the buildings as they pushed air downward. Then he was gone, and Fisher stood in the dusty lane alone.

He turned and ran to the gate at the back of Ma Jeffries' house, his mind churning with long-suppressed memories. Yes, he'd screamed for his mother, but she'd been there. She'd pushed him down the laundry chute and told him to run to their meeting place.

Then she'd gone, him still screaming after her. She'd been long gone before he stopped screaming, but no one ever came to find out why he was making such noise. Not even the militia.

His mother had been somewhere else when she'd been caught. It couldn't have been him.

Tears streamed down his face. Relief. Grief. Betrayal. He gripped the rough wood of the gate as he caught his breath.

When he looked up, Ma Jeffries stood in the doorway, her hands, encased in long, thick gloves, streaked with black and red, a scowl on her face.

"It was you all along. You reported her to the militia. You lied so that she would be blamed and you could continue to produce that poison."

"You know nothing. You were a child and you're still thinking like a child. I've secured our future in the only way open to me and I won't allow you to destroy it any more than I allowed your mother to."

She took a threatening step forward, but he wasn't going to stand there and wait for her to come and kill him.

He jumped the fence and rushed her. He dodged, stepping sideways, avoiding her blackened hands. He twisted and kicked out, tripping her. She screamed as she went down, anger and frustration swiftly turning to searing pain when her arms collapsed under her and she fell, chest and face, onto her gloves.

Fisher paused only long enough to see the blackness, probably almost pure norgell excretions, burning her, eating into her flesh. He turned away, his stomach churning, his heart aching.

Inside the kitchen, cast iron cauldrons bubbled on the aga. Shelves were filled with glass vials, some empty but most filled with black liquid and stoppered. On the table was a thick book, opened about a third in.

Fisher studied the stained and spattered page until he was sure it was the complete recipe for the Elixir. He flipped a few pages over, reading other spells that were heavily notated. His aunt's heavy hand was clear on several of them.

He paused at one that held more of his aunt's notes than others. Amongst other hands, he recognized his mother's as well. On the left leaf was a heading, "Banishment of gods" with a notation in his mother's hand "Was this the one used against the Blue Goddess?".

On the right, "Entrapment and Release," and his mother's note—"Nadya could help me free her."

Nadya now lay dead and dissolving outside the back door. He tore the two pages out, roughly folded them and shoved them inside his shirt.

The door of the aga opened easily beneath his fingers. He grabbed a taper from the shelf above, lit it, then turned and set it to the book.

As the crisp pages caught alight, he looked around. What he needed was the dragons' ability to spew fire to totally destroy this place. He noticed a pile of papers and kindling beside the stove. So it was to be the old-fashioned way.

By then, the taper had burned down low, scorching his fingers. He flicked it away, into one of the cauldrons.

A whooshing gaseous explosion engulfed the room and knocked him to the floor, singeing his eyebrows. He gasped, hot air filling his mouth and lungs like liquid. Golden red flames shot above the cauldron at the same time his heartbeat slammed. Within seconds, the wall above the aga was aflame. One of the liquid flames slid down the wall above the next cauldron.

His legs, frozen with the first shock of heat, finally responded to his progressively more panicked commands. He scrambled to his feet and ran.

The resulting explosion lifted him from his feet and threw him into the backyard. He tucked and rolled, bumped against the back fence, stumbled to his feet and fled.

Behind him flames crackled and roared, the heat at his back growing as the fire jumped from house to house, hungrily devouring them all. Screams began. Feet pounded. Fisher exited the lane and joined the fleeing crowd.

CHAPTER FIFTEEN

SEVERAL BLOCKS DOWN, an arm reached from an alley and dragged him into it. Kaod's dirty face scowled at him. "What did you do?"

Fisher panted, hands resting on his knees as he caught his breath. "You told me your mother wasn't willing. She was the fucking mastermind!"

Kaod roared and threw him against the building. "What did you do to her?" He looked at the crowd, his eyes wild, then he shook Fisher again. "What did you do?"

"Nothing! She was making the Elixir."

"Liar! She never makes it at home. They make her go to the university to mix her sections. She doesn't have the whole recipe."

"She does. She did. She had a whole book of potions and spells designed to harm people. I burned it."

"Burned what?" Kaod looked around wildly again. "'The whole bloody city? And where's mother now?"

"She tried to kill me!" Fisher yelled. "She said I should have died when she set the militia onto my mother. She had norrgel poison and she tried to kill me."

The first waves of shock rippled through Fisher. Up to then, he'd been too focused on staying alive and saving others, but now... his aunt had tried to kill him.

His eyes burned, and he grasped Kaod's biceps. "She tried to kill me," he whispered, willing his cousin to understand.

Kaod stared at him too, his expression a mix of horror, grief and distrust. "I have to find her." He released his hold on Fisher.

Fisher tightened his grip. "You can't. There's nothing left. I told you—she had norrgel poison and tried to kill me with it. When I dodged, she fell and landed on the poison. She's dead." He sucked in a breath that had a thread of panic to it now he'd stopped reacting and begun to think. He trembled with cold, even though the city burned. "I set the book alight, to destroy it, then the taper burned down and..."

He closed his eyes as the images flared again in front of him. He swallowed, his throat parched. "Apparently, norrgel poison is extremely flammable. It exploded, and then spread."

Another sound was growing louder than the screams of the crowds still running past the alley. He looked to the street and saw the crowd had thinned to a definite ebb and flow, and most of those limped and clutched at others, skin red and black. An eerie orange-red light filled the air around them. He looked up to see flames jumping across the alley.

Kaod looked up too and swore.

"Run!" yelled Fisher as he pushed his cousin out of the alley and into the street. Almost immediately they were separated by the crowd. After a few minutes futilely trying to spot Kaod, Fisher focused on outrunning the flames.

A block later he ran into an intersection and looked right and left. Flames leaped over the rooftops and exploded from windows. Thick, oily smoke filled the air and burned his eyes and his throat.

He tugged up the thick scarf he'd been wearing since Linspar. It helped but wouldn't help for long. Even as he stood there, jostled by the reducing number of people, flames burst from a building halfway down the block. The two side streets were now engulfed to street level but he might still make it.

He turned to chase after the straggling crowd only to stumble to a stop when screams erupted amongst them. People turned and raced back toward him, pushing aside those that hadn't noticed the fire's direction or the changing path of the crowd.

Too late.

With the fire closing in from four directions, the smoke increased until he could barely see a hand's-breadth in front of him. Terrified faces materialized out of the smoke, pushing and shoving him out of the way.

There were fewer screams now; people needed their breath simply to breathe in the thick, rancid air. Any screams he heard were high-pitched, filled with pain and terror.

The roar of the flames grew louder, the air more impossible to breathe. He was bumped and fell to the ground. The air was clearer there so he stayed down.

Someone trod on his fingers, grinding them painfully into the cobbled road. He dropped lower, onto his elbows, curling his hands close to his body but still pulling himself along.

He lowered his head so his hunched shoulders would take the brunt of all the thumps and bumps of people tripping over him. His hips and ribs were kicked painfully; several bodies landed heavily on his back before he could wriggle out from under them and keep moving.

The air was hot now, waves of heat washing over him. His eyes burned and ran. He breathed in shallow, quick breaths through his scarf but they burned his throat and set him coughing.

He stumbled as the road dipped, only to rise again a few feet later. His muzzy head recognized a cover for the city's storm drains. Had the fire reached there yet?

The metal beneath his fingers felt marginally cooler than the scream-filled air above him so he curved his fingers around the edge and pulled. The metal lifted then snapped shut again.

The second time, the same thing happened, then Fisher realized it was because he was kneeling on the cover. He shuffled to the side, shoving a body away. Hazily, he noted the screaming had reduced but the crackle of the flames was closer and clearer.

Sweat poured down his face and slicked his hands as he struggled to lift the manhole cover and slide it aside. Cool air washed over him and he gasped in a deep breath that turned into a painful coughing fit. As soon as there was enough room between cover and cobblestones, he lowered his upper body over the edge of the hole. There was a metal ladder, warm to the touch, so he grasped it and pulled himself down.

His hands slipped and he fell.

His shoulder landed with a crunching wrench and a searing pain he knew meant dislocation. He opened his eyes and saw liquid flames dancing across the hole above him, the metal cover glowing red in the heat.

Coughing, and gasping with the pain, he rolled to his feet, clasped his useless arm across his body and stumbled his way down the sewer, splashing through foul ankle-deep water. After what felt like an hour, he paused to try to catch his breath. Every second breath resulted in coughing but there was little he could do about that. At least he was out of the smoke for now.

He felt around his shoulder, identified where the joint was protruding, then positioned himself against one of the regular upright pilings in the tunnel. He took a few breaths, then shoved his shoulder against the piling. Bone scraped against bone, clicking into place.

He screamed with pain and dropped to his knees, his stomach emptying itself of whatever food he'd managed to eat that day. He stayed there, the murky water rushing past him until the nausea passed, his head stopped spinning and the pain was down to a bearable level.

The air wasn't as clear as it had been when he'd first opened the manhole cover. Smoke. The flames wouldn't be far behind, and he wasn't so far gone that he'd think the stones would stop the fire. Most of the uprights were wooden and the waste he was wading through would surely burn as well, once the water boiled away.

The thought of the water heating and boiling while he was still standing in it was enough to get him moving again. He used the pylon to steady himself as he pushed to his feet then walk-jogged as quickly as he could with the current. His fuzzy head told him the water must be running to somewhere, so he followed it.

The light quickly faded, leaving him stumbling in the dark, one hand tucked into the waistband of his pants to hold his shoulder still, the other trailing along the damp rock on his left, the only thing that told him he was upright and moving, rather than simply imagining it.

It was probably a good thing there was no light because his eyes still stung, tears streaming down his cheeks. He closed them, hoping whatever made them sting so badly was soot and smoke that would wash out eventually, not burns that would make him blind. Either way, there was nothing he could do about it, just as there was nothing he could do about the pain in his chest with every breath, his swollen throat, and his shoulder, which throbbed with sickening pain every time he stumbled over something in the water.

Eventually, the water cooled again. Shortly afterward, he noticed the air washing over his forehead was also cooler. He lowered his scarf and opened his eyes briefly but they burned and he couldn't see anything, so he closed them again and continued on.

He stopped when the burning in his cheeks wasn't from heat but cold. Again, he opened his eyes, surprised there was enough light to see the shape of the tunnel and the glint of water at his feet. His eyes watered and stung but not as much as they had before.

His vision was blurry from the tears still filling his eyes and streaming down his cheeks, but he was so relieved to be able to see anything, he didn't care. He increased his pace to a limping jog as the light grew, pale and clear, into the shape of a flat-bottomed circle.

With thick metal bars running across it from top to bottom.

He stumbled to a stop, resting his forehead on a bar, jerking his head back as soon as he registered how cold it was. A small part of skin from his forehead stuck to the bar and warm blood ran down his forehead and trailed down his cheek. As he stepped back, he noticed also that his feet were numb and probably had been for a while.

He stepped out of the rank water and onto the wide stone floor beside it. He frowned at it, his sluggish mind wondering why he hadn't walked on that the whole way instead of in the water, but a glance behind revealed that the stone floor narrowed and disappeared less than twenty feet into the tunnel. Outside, it followed the same pattern, its widest point where the bars prevented anyone entering the city.

As he stood, he shivered and his teeth chattered. The pain in his jaw told him he'd been shivering for some time but hadn't noticed. At least he was coughing less now.

He needed to get warm but his sluggish mind couldn't work out how. He sank to the floor and pulled his knees tightly against his chest. He tilted, nearly toppling to the side but automatically put his hand out to hold himself upright.

Pain shot through him as his weight pushed at his shoulder. His arm collapsed under him and he screamed as he landed on his shoulder once again. He flopped onto his back, panting through the pain, as he reached across his body and pulled his useless arm back into position so the pressure on it was relieved.

As the pain receded, he noticed a hum emanating from the rock beneath his head. He grinned, tears welling in his eyes, this time from relief. Granite. He could get warm at least. He dropped his good hand to the floor beside him, palm flat on the stone beneath him.

For a while, he thought nothing happened but eventually his back began to warm. After a while he stopped trembling. He knew he should take his boots off to dry them faster but was too exhausted. Keeping his hand on the granite, he closed his eyes and drifted.

WHEN HE WOKE, HIS EYES were crusty. His lips were dry and cracked and stung with every movement, like a bad sunburn. Any part of him that was exposed was the same. The fire had been both hotter and closer than he'd realized.

He moved gingerly, hissing at the pain in his shoulder. His boots and socks were dry but his toes hurt. He sat up and clumsily untied his boots, removing them and his socks to check his feet. Relief washed over him when he saw them pink and moving freely, albeit with blisters rubbed raw on toes and heels. He wished for his backpack and his spare set of clothing. An extra pair of socks would be welcome right then.

He emptied his pockets and took inventory. He had one small water bladder, enough trail food to last five days if he was careful, a slim coil of rope, his scarf, the two pages from the spell and potion book, and four knives.

He measured the scarf then cut it into three pieces. One piece, he tied around his head. The other two, he wrapped under and around his feet to provide more insulation against the ice. His coat was sufficient for short trips around the city but was inadequate for a trek across the ice.

He dug his fingers into the granite and pried loose enough small stones to fill his pockets. He rested while he ate and drank, touching each of the rocks until they were warm, staring out at the landscape beyond the bars. Eyeball-searing white greeted him. On the horizon, the ice rose in a blue-white wall.

The glacier.

He stood and slipped a few warmed stones into the folds of the scarf around his head as well. It wasn't perfect, but it was the best he could do.

Pressing his hands against the rock at the top of one of the bars, he crumbled it, like he'd done in the temple where the Abbott had caged him. Crouching, he did the same at the base, then pushed the bar out. The resulting gap was just wide enough for him to sidle through.

A few hundred yards away from the wall, ash wafted over him. He turned back to the city that had once been his home. A dark, smoky haze hung over it, poised like chocolate ice-cream above a square cone. Red-orange flames lazily licked the haze on one side, but they shrank and disappeared as he watched.

"May the Goddess save you." He hoped there were survivors and that Kaod was one of them. The Yeudan wouldn't survive if the only ones still living were those in the south waging war on the Mafdeti and the Imperials. "I pray you survive, cousin."

He turned his back to the city of his birth and began the long trek to the deceptively close glacier.

ON THE THIRD DAY, FISHER ran out of food. He'd underestimated how much fuel his body needed in the desperate cold when the only way he had to stay warm was pushing his own energy into rocks.

He scooped more ice into his water bladder and hung it inside his coat, against his side, to thaw. He shoved his hands into his coat pockets and curled his fingers around the stones in there. The burned skin on the backs of his hands caught in the fabric and crackled and tore as it caught in the fibers. At this point, he was no longer sure if the dried, blackened skin was from the fire or the ice.

He raised his head and stared blearily through the single layer of the scarf he'd raised over his eyes to reduce the glare from the ice. The glacier seemed closer. The first two days, he wondered if he was moving at all as the ice wall remained steady. Now, it loomed over him but still too far for him to estimate how close he was. Another day? Two?

The sun dipped low on the horizon when he first stumbled. He righted himself and walked more carefully, slowing his steps, picking his feet up over the uneven ground. He didn't know if he'd have the energy to rise again if he fell. He had to keep moving or die.

His mind wandered after that. The only thing that kept him moving was his steady gaze on the face of the glacier. He had to get there, although the reason escaped him. Something was waiting there for him. Warmth and comfort. Arms around him, holding him close, a deep voice murmuring soothingly in his ear.

He tripped and landed face-first on the icy ground. Stinging prickles burst across his cheeks. He groaned and untangled himself from the tendrils of ice holding him flat. It took more effort than it should.

Eventually, he was upright again and peered around to get his bearings. Where was the glacier now? It had moved, no longer directly in front of him. He must be imagining it. His head was woozy enough to be playing tricks on him.

He continued walking straight, the blue-white haze from the ice shining on him from the left in a dappled array.

The fourth time he fell, he laughed. He was tired, hungry and thirsty and all he wanted to do was sleep. His feet agreed with him, refusing to lift high enough over the mounds of ice. His arms agreed with him too, preferring to remain warm and snug beneath him. His hands, still in his pockets, curled around the cooling stones.

He put his head down, snuggled into his scarf and closed his eyes. He'd rest a while before continuing.

Blue flame flared briefly behind his lids, then was gone.

CHAPTER SIXTEEN

"THE FOOL," GAELAN MUMBLED. "What's he doing here in such a state?"

"What state did you think he'd arrive in?" asked his mother. The ice wall of the glacier shimmered as she moved, one piercing cool blue eye becoming visible before retreating again.

Gaelan bent and scooped Fisher up in his arms. "He said he wouldn't come. He had to destroy the Elixir."

"Would that have taken the rest of his life?"

"He doesn't want me, Mother. There's nothing either of us can do to change that." He walked to the edge of the glacier, where it met the mountain and where the movement of the ice was most visible. As he surveyed the area, small shards of rock and ice fell, spearing into the ground. He retreated. "Move back into the ice, Mother. I'm going to build a cave."

"You'd better replace it all once you're finished. If you melt this glacier, I'll be dead."

He scowled. "I know. I'm doing my best to work out how to free you."

The Blue Goddess sighed. "I know you are, my son, but without the original curse, your chances are slim." The blue faded from the ice as she moved farther away.

Gaelan focused on a small section of the glacier wall, then blew a thin stream of blue flame to melt it and form a narrow tunnel. Droplets pattered down as he walked through a freezing waterfall.

About ten feet into the glacier, he stopped and redirected his flame to create a circular cave. Once it was ready, he placed Fisher carefully on the smooth ice floor.

"He's alive then?" his mother asked, the blue eye once again pressed against the ice and shining blue light into the igloo.

"Barely. I need to get him warmed up. See if I can save his toes and nose. He needs to eat a hell of a lot more than he has been if he's going to survive in this cold."

"You should take him somewhere warmer." The blue glacier lost its color as his mother's presence faded from it.

"I can't leave yet. You're still trapped. The longer you're in there, the more difficult it will be for you to separate."

"None of your other attempts have been successful. It's not such a bad life."

"That doesn't mean I shouldn't keep trying. And it's a terrible life to be trapped like that. If you had chosen to stay here, that would be different, but you didn't."

She chuckled. "You and your choices. Most people don't get a choice in how they live. They're trapped in the life they're born into."

He didn't bother responding. It was an old argument and one they'd long since agreed to disagree on.

The whole time he was speaking with his mother, he watched Fisher. Too still. Too pale. "I'll be back in an hour or two with some furs. If you can, please keep him warm."

"I'll try, my son, although my powers weaken every day."

That was exactly why he needed to free her from her prison.

He strode outside, swiftly changed to his dragon form, and flew south. Two hours later, he returned, changed to his human form and dragged the cumbersome bundle into his ice cave.

Swiftly, he unraveled the furs and spread them out, wrapping Fisher securely once he'd removed Fisher's outer clothes and boots. He pulled out several raw tanzanites from a bag and breathed blue fire onto them. Once they were brilliant blue-purple and warm, he tucked them into the furs.

He set a container of snow on a triangle of tanzanites to melt. Once the water was warm enough, he dipped a cloth and began to gently clean Fisher's face. He used small, sharp scissors to cut away some of the flaking, dead skin then put a healing salve on him. He did the same to his ears and any other skin he found burned either by fire or ice.

Fisher groaned when Gaelan touched his shoulder. Gently, he removed Fisher's coat and shirts to find his shoulder black and blue with bruises. He used the stretched and ruined scarf to secure his arm across his chest so the shoulder couldn't be moved. Then he reheated the tanzanites, rewrapped Fisher, curled up around him, and waited.

A short time later, Fisher began shivering. Gaelan held him tightly, careful of his shoulder, so he wouldn't injure himself further.

He'd begun to doze when Fisher shifted restlessly. He opened his eyes to find Fisher's black gaze on him.

"How—" Fisher's voice strained and pushed and cut off in a cough that had him curling in on himself. He twisted away and spat out black sludge.

"Don't try to talk. You've obviously been through some things." He ran his fingers through Fisher's black hair, clean and silky after he'd washed out whatever had made it so crusty and matted. "I'm sorry. You said you wouldn't come to the glacier, so I wasn't expecting you. If I'd known, I would have met you and saved you—" he swept his hand down the length of Fisher's body "—all this."

He ducked his head at the guilt flooding him. If he hadn't been sulking over Fisher's rejection he'd have felt that he was so close. He reached over and lifted a cup of soothing tea kept warm over the stones. "Try to drink something, then sleep some more. There's time to find out what's happened to you."

He gently lifted Fisher's head and held the cup for him to drink from until he shook his head. He put the cup down and drew Fisher more securely to him. "Rest now, my love," he whispered as Fisher slipped into sleep.

Gaelan cradled his mate gently, conscious that if he let the anger and worry he felt take over, he'd hurt the only man that who could make his life whole.

IT WAS ANOTHER TWO days before Fisher was up and about again. He was still weak from his ordeal but recovering quickly. He'd refused food from Gaelan that morning, insisting he was strong enough to feed himself. Gaelan scowled at him but gave in eventually. He sat close by, ready to help if he was needed.

"I'm fine," said Fisher. "You don't have to sit gleefully waiting for me to drop something. I'm not helpless."

No, you're mine. He didn't say it out loud but Fisher jumped and stared at him wide-eyed.

"I thought you said that only worked if we were touching and you were in dragon form." Fisher edged away from him until he sat close enough to the ice wall that the ice glistened as it melted.

"It's probably just because we've spent so much time together?" He didn't mean for it to sound like a question, but he was sure Fisher didn't want to know the real reason they could now speak to each other mentally.

He certainly wouldn't want to know the ability would grow stronger the more time they spent together, until finally coalescing into a permanent bond when they mated. When they became Dragon God and Concubine.

Silence fell between them. It was as uncomfortable as sitting on the tip of a poisoned spear.

Eventually Fisher cleared his throat. "Where did the Goddess go once you released her?"

Gaelan glared at him. "Nowhere. I haven't been able to break the curse and free her. Everything I've tried has driven her farther into the ice and weakened her powers. If I keep trying things that fail, she'll die, and the northern lands will be left with no one watching over them."

He slumped, his anger leaving him as quickly as it flared. "There's one more thing I can try," he said quietly, "but if it fails, she won't have the strength to withstand another." He looked beseechingly at Fisher. "I don't want her to die."

The cave filled with blue light, making Fisher jump and dart over beside Gaelan. He automatically put his arm around Fisher and pulled him close.

Any time Fisher was near him, Gaelan wanted to pull him closer, to keep him warm and protected. The first few days, when Fisher was weak, he'd accepted it. Then he had pulled away and sat upright, several inches of lonely air between them. This time he snuggled closer. Gaelan hoped it wasn't only because of fear.

"Gaelan, I've told you before—stop worrying about me. What will happen will happen. You have your own life to live with your mate."

"Mate?" squeaked Fisher.

Gaelan pressed a kiss to Fisher's forehead. "Don't worry about it. Build your strength first, then we can argue." At least he hoped they would. He'd shown a worrying pattern of leaving or pushing Gaelan away when he didn't want to do something.

"Do your final chant this evening. I've held on for three hundred years, hoping someone would recognize the curse, but even I know how difficult that would be when the only thing I can remember is the screech of norrgel and black rain pouring from the sky."

Fisher sat up straight. "There were norrgel when you were cursed?"

"Of course," said the Blue Goddess. "All the blackest curses involve norrgel."

Fisher scrambled over to the furs he'd been sleeping on and pulled his ragged coat from the pile.

"What's wrong?" Had the mention of norrgel terrified him so much he was going to leave? "You're not leaving without me." He rose and began to gather his own belongings, then dropped them all in a pile when Fisher grabbed his arm and wrenched him around.

"Look at this." He shoved a folded paper at Gaelan who gripped it reflexively. "I found this when I..." he cleared his throat, "when I killed Ma Jeffries."

Gaelan looked down at the papers he held, then gingerly unfolded them. "Banishment of gods?" He looked at the other page. "Entrapment and Release." He looked at Fisher.

"They were in a book she had." Fisher shuffled his feet.

Gaelan read the pages, excitement bubbling up inside with every word he read. "Mother, look at this!" He strode to the ice wall where his mother's eye could still be seen.

"She's your mother?"

Gaelan ignored him. "Does that sound like what was done to you?" Once his mother was free, he'd have all the time in the world to explain to Fisher what his mother meant to the way they were going to live their lives.

She laughed, the clear bell tones fresh from his childhood memories when the world was calm and his family was whole. "That's exactly what happened. Does it say how to reverse it?"

Gaelan flipped to the other page. "The first one is the chant that goes with the actions described on the first page. The second one must be it. It must be." He grinned at his mother, then turned and grabbed Fisher by the shoulders, releasing him almost immediately at his pained grunt. "Sorry."

He threaded his hands under Fisher's arms and lifted him in a high swinging hug. He was sure he sported a stupid grin on his face as well but couldn't bring himself to care. "I'll be able to free her at last."

He dropped a fast, hard kiss on Fisher's stunned lips, then grinned some more. "I'll have my mother back."

He dropped Fisher back on his feet then strode to the exit.

CHAPTER SEVENTEEN

ONCE GAELAN WAS GONE, Fisher turned to survey the small cave. He'd only been there a few days, but it had been more a home than he'd had since before he and his mother were banished. He could kick himself for letting his guard down, for believing in the impossible.

"It's called the impossible because it's actually impossible, you idiot."

Gaelan wanted to free his mother then return with her to his island home. Whatever he felt for Fisher must be an illusion because he didn't know Fisher at all, and was relying on the legends of his Concubine to guide him. Once Gaelan knew Fisher better, he'd realize it.

Better to leave now, rather than get in deeper and be cast aside when Gaelan finally realized the kind of man Fisher was.

Slowly, he picked up his clothes. His knife sheaths in place, he put on his boots and coat, then gathered all the small granite stones he'd brought with him. He was going to need them to get back to Barthes. Hopefully there was enough left of the city that he could find supplies and move on.

Where would he go? The Lonely Isles were supposedly the last place for him to be. His mind raced as he absently filled his pockets with food, then swung the water bladder over his shoulder and tucked it beneath his coat.

Perhaps he could go to the Mafdeti. He'd saved the Dragon Rider and his Bond Mate in Barthes. Surely that counted for something. At least they wouldn't kill him outright.

Probably.

Fisher wound his ragged scarf remnant around his head and face, tucking the ends into his coat. He took a last look around then snatched up one of the furs. Gaelan owed him for the means to save his mother.

He dropped to a crouch, his breath ragged and knees weak. He'd been avoiding thinking about it but Gaelan was the son of the Blue Goddess. A fucking goddess. What did that make *him*?

His mind spun with images of all the things they'd done together—the dungeons, the ship, the ocean, the village. At every turn, Gaelan—the son of a goddess—had saved him. It didn't make sense. He was nothing. He'd been abused throughout his childhood and used as an adult. He'd never been able to save his mother from the abuse she'd suffered and hadn't prevented her death. He'd done nothing worthwhile. Ever.

He'd begun to think things could be different with Gaelan, that someone, just one person, thought he was capable of being more, and sometimes he thought—with Gaelan—he could be. He was wrong. Gaelan wanted to free his mother from the glacier and Fisher had given him the means to do that. Even with Gaelan's promises, there was nothing left that Fisher could give him.

Fisher had achieved what he'd set out to do as well. He'd destroyed the recipe for the Elixir as well as all the stores Ma had had.

Pockets full, and with no reason to linger, he left the protection of the ice cave. He looked across the ice to the south, imagining walking all the way back to Barthes and feeling nothing more than... tired.

That's what he was. He was tired of walking the ice, tired of fighting every day to stay alive, to find a place where he could be safe.

Tired of looking for somewhere to belong, someone to belong with. It wasn't going to happen. He'd been a fool to think it might.

He stepped away from the glacier, his first step toward he didn't know what. There was no sign of Gaelan. Fisher told himself he didn't care, but the twist in his chest and tightness of his throat called him liar.

He sighed resignedly and kept walking. He'd either make it back to Barthes or he'd die along the way, not that Gaelan would care. Fisher didn't want to die but couldn't think of a reason to keep living. Perhaps one would come to him later. Until then, he'd put one foot in front of the other, his gaze resolutely on the southern horizon and the smoky haze that was Barthes.

Gaelan walked to the edge of the glacier, where it met the mountain and began to climb the rubble and shattered ice there. He needed to be on the glacier to bring his mother out. It was the only aspect that was large enough for her dragon form to fit through.

He could change to his dragon and fly to the top, but he was afraid he'd drop the papers Fisher had given him. The pages that would free his mother were too precious to risk, so he stayed human and climbed.

It wasn't long before he'd lost sight of the face of the glacier and the small hole leading to their ice cave. He smiled as he remembered waking with Fisher in his arms. He'd never felt that level of contentment before, but he knew what it was.

He'd sat alone in the dungeons, waiting, for what, he wasn't sure. Then Fisher had touched the granite, and the echo resonated through him, calling to the tanzanite in him. He was Gaelan's mate, the peasant who would be Concubine to his Consort, but he'd known if he had announced it then Fisher would have fled.

Tip-toeing through the minefield of his relationship with his mate had kept Gaelan busier than even the disappearance of the duke and the advent of the Elixir in the Lonely Isles combined.

Maneuvering around Fisher's disbelief, his insecurities, and his past, challenged Gaelan in a way nothing else ever had. He couldn't wait to learn more of his mate.

He walked to the middle of the glacier, read the instructions again and turned to face the north. He took a deep breath and centered himself.

"I hope this works, Mother."

"It will work, or it won't."

"Now isn't the best time for that philosophy. I'd really appreciate it if you wanted it a bit more."

"No one could want my release from this frozen wasteland more than I, but it won't be your fault if I perish here."

Gaelan didn't answer. His mother could no more command his lack of guilt than he could command Fisher to love him. The thought of Fisher brought an almost uncontrollable urge to find his mate and hold him close, sure if he didn't he'd never be able to hold him again.

But he could feel his mother's strength ebbing, so her needs were more urgent than his own.

"Okay. Are you ready?"

"Of course. Don't drain too much power into it. You'll need enough to pursue your mate."

"Thank you," Gaelan said dryly.

He read the paper one last time then folded it and pushed it deep into his pocket. "Let's do this." He shifted his feet so they were sturdily planted on the ice and focused his gaze along the frozen river. He took a deep breath and allowed the resonance of his voice carry the length and breadth of the ice.

Beloved locked in frozen world
Trapped by fear and hate
Rising new freedom
Back into being
Everyone that sees

Everything you need
Never could be
Swimming in the blue depths
Falling sparkling
Forever through the clouds
Of the ancient river.
The danger has passed
The black has risen
And so must you.

He roared the last word, throwing all his power into it. It surged and rippled across the ice and echoed back to him in waves that forced him to stagger backward. He barely held his feet, stumbling right to the edge of the ice, but held his ground there.

Absolute silence followed. Not even the wind stirred. Panting, he dropped to his knees, ignoring the way the sharp ice dug through his clothes. His head pounded, his stomach churned. He bent forward and watched saliva dripping from his open mouth to freeze in shiny puddles, his entire being too exhausted to do anything. He toppled to his side, unable to hold himself upright any longer.

Beneath him the ice shivered. A low rumble bounced through the glacier. The uneven ice, sharp and imperfect, shattered and toppled until the sunlight glinted painfully off each tiny shard. It shook until he was covered by powdered ice that melted on contact with him until his skin became too cold to heat it. He lay, too exhausted to shiver, as the melted ice refroze, trapping him in a clear, glistening layer.

He bounced as another shudder flowed through the glacier. The ice coating his cheeks cracked, pieces of it falling to join the rest of the bouncing particles.

Thunder rumbled and cracked, and the glacier heaved—a huge rippling wave that settled with a screeching crack. Just as he was convinced he'd fall over the edge, a shadow fell over him.

"You idiot," his mother said.

The last time he'd seen her in human form, a thousand years before, her eyes had been the clear blue of sapphires, her skin milky pale, her hair golden. Now her eyes were the crystalline white of the glacier, but her skin and hair were the pale, pale blue of an aquamarine.

"I told you not to use all your power to get me out." She brushed his hair back from his forehead, flicking the ice away as she moved. "It's going to take some time for you to recover, and even longer before you can reclaim your dragon. It'll sleep for a long time after this."

Gaelan opened his mouth to ask about Fisher, only to find he hadn't closed it yet. And still couldn't. He groaned, but all that came out was a pathetic whimper.

His mother scooped her arms under him and lifted him easily. "You're still a silly boy, aren't you? I could feel the power building with each word. You really shouldn't have pushed like that at the end. The words had all the power you needed."

She jumped over the leading edge of the glacier, landing easily in front of their ice cave. "Let's get you inside and bundled up so you can rest."

If Fisher had entertained the idea, even for a minute, that Gaelan would come after him, he'd have been bitterly disappointed. He'd managed to keep himself alive, thanks to his granite rocks and Gaelan's fur, but he didn't want to go beyond Barthes for a while. He needed time to recover.

The city gates were locked securely but there were no guards to call. The smoke haze was still thick, but it was less dense than it had been.

He leaned against the gates and breathed in the air. The smoke was a few days old and clung heavily. There wasn't enough breeze around to disperse it and probably wouldn't be until the autumn storms arrived.

As he rested, he wondered if he had enough energy left to push himself all the way through the thick outer walls, or if he'd get stuck in the rock like he almost did in the temple. Before he could decide whether or not to risk it, the small door in one of the gates swung open.

Kaod stepped out. "I've been searching for you for a week, you bastard. I thought you'd died in the fires like everyone else." He looked away, blinking rapidly, then heaved a sigh and turned back to the door. "Are you planning on standing there until you freeze to death?"

Fisher straightened. He wanted to grin at his cousin the way he'd always done when they were children, but he'd been away for nearly two decades and when he'd returned, he'd killed Kaod's mother, so he wasn't sure of his welcome. "Are you going to arrest me? Or execute me?" He cringed at the reminder that Ma Jeffries was already dead.

Kaod scowled at him. "For what? It's not as if you deliberately started the fire that killed more than three thousand people, is it?"

Fisher swayed, light-headed. "Three thousand? Fuck."

"You probably wouldn't stay arrested anyway." Kaod grasped Fisher above his elbow and dragged him into the city. Snow still fell inside the walls, but it was warmer inside than out. "Apparently Ma had quite a business going. The explosions rocked the city for three days before all the potion plants were destroyed. There's still some fire in the western quarter but it's contained. We've evacuated everyone we could."

He kept hold of Fisher's arm as they walked toward the temple. "The temple is the only building not destroyed, probably because it's made of stone, not wood, although some of the priests say there's goddess magic in the walls. We've taken over the largest prayer rooms for hospitals and most of the rest for accommodation for as many citizens as we can fit."

They continued in silence, wading through thick, soupy air. The sky was more charcoal than blue. Fisher's throat tickled with the residue he took in with every breath. He lifted his scarf up to cover his mouth and nose. It helped.

"Why didn't you tell me about that thing you can do with rock?" His cousin's voice was quiet and held a level of pain Fisher had never heard from him before, not even when Kaod's younger brother had died when they were children.

"I didn't know until recently. I'm still figuring it out."

"You're a wizard or something?"

"I don't think I'm a wizard. I don't know what I am."

Kaod's hand fell away.

"What are you doing for food?" asked Fisher, wanting the awkward silence to end.

"The food stores have been hit hard, I can't deny that." Kaod shrugged but a worried frown marred his forehead. "We've set up a rationing system and I have people in the Temple basements checking their stores. We might have to approach the Mafdeti for help."

"Not the Imperials?"

Kaod shook his head. "They've placed embargoes on us pending an investigation into the kidnapping of Princess Ardelle. They can't prove it wasn't an independent Exile undertaking, not unless they can identify the man who acted as liaison between the Exiles and our advance forces. They say he was tall and skinny and had funny—"

Kaod stopped walking, pulling Fisher to him. "Shit. It was you, wasn't it? No one else has skin like yours." He looked around the street they'd been walking down, then tugged Fisher to the side, under the burned remnants of a shop awning. "How many people know you're Yeudan?" he whispered. "And that you're here?"

"No one! Only Gaelan. And Aunty Cray in the Lonely Isles. I was there a few days, no more. They arrested me and then I was at the Temple." He hadn't spoken to many people at all.

"There was Connie, and Hagan," he said, guilt growing like sludge in his stomach. "And other brothers." He sighed. There really were a lot of people who knew about him. "Possibly the soldiers who arrested me, and all the sailors on the ship we left on, and probably whoever else they met while we were captive." His voice ran down to a whisper. "I don't think the villagers realized I'm Yeudan."

By now, Kaod was squeezing the bridge of his nose as if he had a headache. Then he chuckled. "You haven't changed a bit. What did they arrest you for?"

"They arrested anyone they thought wouldn't be missed. Then they drowned them and sold the bodies to the Yeudan for the Elixir."

"The Goddess Potion? It's a mix of norrgel poison and herbs to make it less toxic. I know it's addictive and they hooked Ma on it to make her help, but it's mostly sold as pain medication."

"That's why you're not more upset with me."

"What are you talking about?"

"It's not only norrgel poison. They make the Elixir from people killed by norrgel poison and people who died by other means. They distill the corpses down until there's only a black, oily sludge, then they mix them together with the residue of the norrgel deaths. The herbs are only to make it more palatable."

"You're wrong. Where would they get all the bodies from?"

"How long have you been worshiping norrgel? How many sacrifices are made each day? What happens to your criminals? How long are they held in the cells before being moved? Where do they go? You're Captain of the Guard. You must have seen what happens to them."

"Exile is the most common punishment. After the trial, they're escorted to the gates and locked out." He must have seen something in Fisher's face because he continued quickly. "They're given supplies to last a week and we don't expel them during winter anymore. They stay in the cells until spring." He frowned as if he just realized something. "A lot of people in the cells over winter die."

"What do you do with them?" Fisher didn't remind Kaod that he and his mother were expelled during winter.

"We deliver them to the Temple for disposal," he said grimly as he grabbed Fisher's arm again and continued walking.

Fisher assumed the conversation was over even though there were still a lot of things he needed to know. He should have spent more time talking to Kaod when he first arrived, before he went to the temple. He might have saved himself a lot of trouble.

"There haven't been as many arrests in the last couple of years. The streets are quiet most nights."

"Even on the Day of Thanks?"

"We didn't do that this year, or the last. There were wreaths left at the statue of the Goddess throughout the morning, but most people chose to stay at home in the evening. There were no other celebrations."

His grip on Fisher's arm tightened but he didn't think Kaod realized it. "The year before that, there were a lot of arrests, though. There'd been reports of violence in the square. When we got there, it was over. People were drinking and dancing, but everything was under control. They were just having fun. We were ordered to bring everyone in for questioning about the incident, so we did that.

"There were a number of reports of missing persons from that night. We searched but never found any of them. We all thought they were so drunk they'd wandered outside the city and dropped into a crevasse or something."

Kaod shook his head like a dog with fleas. "We're off track. We have to work out what to do with you now. You can't go back south if everyone will recognize you and assume you're the reason all their people died before the eclipse. You can't stay here, not since the fires."

"You said—"

"It doesn't matter what I said. You're a stranger here now. You came into town and within days most of the place has burned down, thousands are dead, and our main source of income for the last five years is gone with them. Whatever way you look at it, we're looking at a pretty bleak future and a lot of people are going to look for someone to blame."

"And they'll look for an outsider to blame."

"I know." Kaod's gaze was full of knowledge and sorrow. Fisher wasn't sure if the sorrow was because of Ma Jeffries and her actions or that he was going to be the target.

They stopped walking and Fisher looked up to see the Temple steps before them. At the base of the steps was the statue of the Blue Goddess.

It was made of granite with a veneer of pale blue sapphires so thin that the granite showed through and turned the pale blue into navy. The statue's eyes were made from brilliant sapphires so clear and blue they looked like a summer sky. When he'd been a child he'd been sure the eyes smiled at him. One day, he thought the Goddess had winked.

"I can't go in there." He dug his heels in. "They tried to kill me before."

"We're under martial rule. The priests have little power since the fire, although that will change quickly once we've worked out how to keep everyone fed through winter."

"Why are you taking me there?"

"Where else am I going to take you? Most of the housing is destroyed. The Temple itself is in an uproar after the death of the Abbott but there's nowhere else to stay."

Fisher quickly changed his plans. "I'm not staying. I came back here to get supplies and find out where Duke Zanderfeld of the Lonely Isles might be, that's all." Finding the duke wasn't his problem. Gaelan was the one who'd wanted to find him.

Fisher just wanted to destroy the Elixir and any possibility of it being made again. He'd done that and could leave, so he didn't know why he was risking his life to find a man he'd never met and meant nothing to him. All because Gaelan wanted to find him and he wasn't there to do it himself.

Fisher wondered if he was a fool to believe in the future Gaelan offered him but he was beginning to trust that he could have the future Gaelan promised him. Until he doubted it again. He rubbed the warm, comforting ache in his chest that made him feel like Gaelan was thinking about him.

"Who would know where the duke is?" Kaod hadn't argued with him about leaving so he assumed he wanted Fisher gone as much as Fisher wanted to leave Barthes behind.

There was a long pause as they made their way to the kitchens. Kaod began stuffing a bag full of food for him. "Lord Zanderfeld left here three weeks ago. He and the Abbott had a disagreement and the duke left shortly after. I personally escorted him to the gates." He frowned. "He left in the dead of night. I stayed at the gates long enough to ensure he wasn't pursued so he probably reached his destination."

Fisher's heart ached that a good man like his cousin lived in such times. "I'm sorry you constantly have to do that."

"Do what?"

Now he was on the spot, he was hard-pressed to explain it. "Protect people."

Kaod laughed. "It's what I do." He held his hand out in a "wait" motion. "I'm not so simple I can't see what's been happening in my own town, but my purpose is the same—keep the citizens of

Barthes safe from threat. I'll admit the people I'm protecting others from have changed drastically in the last few years." For a second, he looked lost. "This is what I do, and I'll do it to the best of my ability for as long as I can."

He nudged Fisher's shoulder. "Perhaps if things get so bad that I can no longer do my job, I might find a safer place for them to be. Then we'll move from here." He handed Fisher the oilskin bag full of food and a flask of water. "I'll show you where you can wait until dark and how to get out undetected."

At Fisher's querying look, he chuckled. "This isn't my first time around the circle. I'm Captain of the Guard and proud of it, but that doesn't mean I blindly follow orders and allow innocent people to die. Not if I can do something about it."

"Is that why you're not more upset your mother is dead?"

Kaod closed his eyes in a long blink, despair washing over his features. "The things I've discovered since the fire have convinced me my mother left a long time ago. The woman who died was nothing like the one who raised me. I'll always miss my mother, but I'm glad Ma Jeffries is dead."

They left the Temple. "Why's the duke so special? The Mafdeti were also looking for him."

"His son is ruling in his place. It's not a good choice." It sounded simplistic put like that, but he thought Kaod would understand the implications.

"I was going to take you to the gate closest to the path you need, but I don't think I need to, do I?"

"What do you mean?"

"You can walk through rock. Why do you need a gate?"

"I can move through granite. Nothing else."

Kaod's head tilted to the side as he regarded him. "They've been putting veneers over much of the walls lately, but there's still one section that's the original granite. Did you ever learn to swim?"

Fisher groaned. "Tell me there's air and I won't be stuck underwater for hours."

"You can breathe underwater too?"

"No. Gaelan can, but he's not here." His chest tightened at the reminder, but he pushed the loneliness away. He and Gaelan couldn't be soul mates or anything else, regardless of what had happened at the beach. And in the mountains. And at the glacier. He didn't need Gaelan with him all the time. "Where was the duke headed?"

"The Pass of Nines."

Of course he was. Where else would he go from here except directly to the Mafdeti, who wanted Fisher dead? The old man was probably in talks with the Matriarch. It was probably unnecessary to take him back to the Lonely Isles, but Gaelan couldn't.

While most of him dreaded going into Mafdeti territory, part of him wanted to see how being Bonded Mates and dragon riders had changed Checa and Heath. Their short meeting in the cages didn't give him an opportunity to do more than watch them escape.

"Where is your man, then?"

"He's not my man." His face heated at Kaod's smirk.

"Yet you immediately knew who I was talking about."

He decided to ignore the comment. "His mother is at the glacier. He needed to stay and help her."

"The glacier? That place is a death trap. Why would his mother be there?"

"She was trapped there. He's releasing her." It sounded silly in his own ears, but he kept going. "It's the Blue Goddess."

They rounded a corner and were faced with the wall. Kaod didn't stop, though, and led him along the wall until they stepped on a large metal plate in the middle of the road.

"I don't know what you've got yourself into, or why you think bringing the Blue Goddess into it will help, but..." He sighed. "I wish you well, wherever the Goddess guides you."

Tears sprung in his eyes at the formal farewell. He hadn't considered it as a child when he left, but as an adult, he was aware that this was probably the last time he'd ever see Kaod. He flung himself against his cousin's broad chest and clung to him.

"Thank you. You're the reason I survived as a child, and you're the reason I'll survive now." He stepped back and regarded Kaod solemnly. "You're good at your job, Kaod. You're a good man."

Kaod nodded then bent to slide the metal panel aside. Under it was a black hole. "That's the Life River down there. There's enough depth to the water that you won't break every bone in your body once you land. It flows from the city, under the Seven Mountains and comes back to the surface at the river outside Amadon in the Analee Valley.

"Go through Amadon and head south-west to get to the Pass of Nines. Your duke was heading there. If you miss the exit and continue to follow the river, you'll reach the Lake of the Dead and Fyoder in the Aylmer Mountains. From there, go west, through Mafdeti territory to the Pass of Nines."

Fisher nodded as he stared down into the hole. More water, probably freezing. He still couldn't swim properly, even though he knew enough now to kick his feet and keep his head up. He couldn't breathe underwater and there was no chance of Gaelan conveniently coming across him down there. Gaelan was at the glacier trying to release the Blue Goddess. Fisher wouldn't even warrant a stray thought. He rubbed his chest absently as he wished that Gaelan would come and find him soon.

"Goddess keep you safe, cousin," said Kaod.

"And you, Kaod, brother of my heart." He tucked his waterproof bags close to his body, took a deep breath and jumped into black.

CHAPTER EIGHTEEN

GAELAN WOKE AND LURCHED upright, furs and tanzanites dropping randomly around him. He spun in an excited circle. "It worked, Fisher! It worked! She's safe."

He looked for Fisher then slid to a halt. Except for a few furs with his tanzanites scattered on top, the cave was empty. "Fisher?" He was sure his heart was breaking.

"Go after him."

He turned to face his mother. She stood inside the cave entrance, roughly dressed in furs, swaying with fatigue. He rushed to steady her and led her to the pile of furs. "What are you doing walking around like that? You need to rest."

"Go after your soul, Gaelan. Don't deny him."

"I'm not denying him. *He* left." He helped his mother to settle comfortably.

"So he's taking a long time to accept you belong together. You need to go after him, and keep going after him until he understands you won't let him down like everyone else has."

"You need me here with you."

She waved a negligent hand. "Nonsense. Take me to Barthes. I can recover quietly there."

"Mother, you're blue. You won't go unnoticed."

The hand waved again and Gaelan was reminded why he and his mother chose to live thousands of miles apart. They loved each other but he became annoyed at the way she dismissed everything he said.

"I'm sure they won't worry about that," she said.

He opened his mouth to argue. There was no way the people of Barthes wouldn't notice that her skin and hair were blue, and her eyes were white, but if she wanted to go to Barthes, he'd take her there. Then he'd find Fisher and make sure the man knew running away wasn't the answer to his problems. Whatever those problems were, he intended to be there and help Fisher through them.

His mother began shivering. Gaelan rushed over to her.

"What is it?" She was the Blue Goddess, the Goddess of the north where there was nothing but ice and snow for most of the year. The cold didn't affect her.

"I-I-I don't think the curse is completely broken," she stuttered.

"Fuck." He never swore, but this situation surely warranted it. Frantically, he pulled out the pages Fisher had given him and checked the chant. He'd done it all exactly as it was written. He flipped the page over to see what was on the other side. A few sentences in a spidery hand.

"Only the Descendant can break the link once the curse is vanquished."

"The Descendant?"

His mother shrugged. "I don't know who it will be, but there'll be someone of that family in Barthes. The link would have broken with the curse if the family was gone." She struggled to her feet. "Take me there, then find your soul."

They flew at night, reaching Barthes before dawn, not wanting to draw any more attention to themselves than was unavoidable.

The odor reached them before they were halfway there. They'd been burning norrgel. And people. Lots of them. Soon after, they flew through the first noxious clouds. Gaelan lifted over them until they were near Barthes. He tucked his feet close to his body. His mother, comfortably resting in the bed formed by his claws, drew closer and shielded her face against his chest. He circled down through the oily fumes.

He did three circuits of the city before she pointed to a place near the southern wall. He drifted down and landed in a nearby common.

He'd barely changed to human form again before there was a harsh cry of "Halt!" He stepped in front of his mother, who'd curled into a fetal position as soon as he'd laid her on the ground.

"Why are you out during curfew?" the soldier asked. His sword glistened as he moved it to point directly at Gaelan.

Normally Gaelan would deal with the soldier and go on his way, but his mother was on the ground behind him and, while she was a goddess, her strength was seriously depleted. She couldn't defend herself.

"I need to find someone to help my mother." Worry was clear in the tone of his voice.

The soldier looked around. He eyes widened comically and he stumbled back several steps. "What the fuck is wrong with her?" His gaze darted frantically over Gaelan as he stepped back again. "What's she got? You'd better get her back home or something. Get her out of here and don't let her near anyone else."

Gaelan stepped forward but stopped when the sword waved wildly in front of him.

"You stay away too. You've probably got what she's got."

Gaelan almost chuckled at that. She was his mother. Of course he had what she had—godliness.

The soldier pulled a short wooden pipe from his vest, put it to his lips and blew. The shrill whistle made Gaelan cringe. "Stay right there. I've called for backup."

For someone who wanted him to keep his mother away from everyone, he thought it was strange the soldier was calling others close to them. Pounding footsteps echoed in the empty streets.

Gaelan turned toward the sound to see a dark-haired man running toward them. He wasn't as tall or thin, and his eyes were gray rather than black, but there was something about him that reminded him of Fisher.

"What is it, Corporal?"

"Don't go near them, Captain. The woman has something and it's probably contagious."

The captain eyed the corporal for a second. "How did you plan to help her without going near them?" he asked, his voice deathly soft.

Even in the darkness, Gaelan saw the corporal's face drain of color. He stuttered but didn't reply, nor did he move any closer.

The captain nodded. "You're dismissed."

The corporal sagged with relief then jerked to attention when the captain continued to speak. "Report to the armory in the morning for your new uniform."

"New uniform, sir?" He looked down at his clothes. "I've only had this one a couple of months."

"And you're clearly not ready for it, *Private*. Have it changed to one more suited to your attitude and station in the morning."

The newly-made private squeaked, sketched a shaky salute, then fled.

The captain was crouched beside Gaelan's mother before the footsteps had faded. "Can you tell me what's wrong, miss?" he asked in a soft voice.

Gaelan shifted, allowing what light there was to illuminate his mother.

The captain gasped but didn't draw back. "How may I serve you, my lady?"

Gaelan relaxed. This man knew what he was about, even if his soldiers didn't. "She was trapped in the glacier. I've broken the curse, but she's still linked to the family that cast it. I need to find them to break the link."

The captain scooped his arms under his goddess and lifted her. Gaelan stepped forward to take over but stopped when he noticed his mother's relaxed posture. Something about the captain eased her pain.

Before he could ask if the captain was the Descendant, the man said, "You must be Gaelan."

"How do you know me?"

"I'm Kaod. Fisher is my cousin." He walked past Gaelan toward the center of town.

Gaelan stood frozen until the captain disappeared around a corner with his mother. He hoped the captain wasn't the Descendent. If he was, and Fisher was his cousin, then Gaelan had to rethink his plan to kill everyone in the family to break the link that tied his mother to them. The captain meant nothing to him, but there was no way he'd be able to kill Fisher.

The captain led them past the temple and toward the attached guardhouse. "These are my quarters." He opened the door and took Gaelan's mother into the small set of rooms. "There's not a lot of space but you won't be interrupted here."

He lay her gently on his bed then brushed her hair off her forehead. He frowned as his hand rested against her skin, then he opened a chest that doubled as a bedside table and drew out an embroidered quilt. "This might help warm you." He bent to tuck the quilt securely around her but before he could draw back, she reached up with both hands and cradled the captain's face.

Gaelan froze. What was his mother doing? They needed to test this man to make sure he was the Descendant so she could be cured. Instead, he was standing there watching as his mother kissed a man.

And not just kissed. It was like she was inviting him inside her, absorbing his strength.

When she finally released him, the captain staggered back and almost fell before he righted himself. He leaned against the wall as if his knees wouldn't hold him upright.

"Mother?" Gaelan asked.

She smiled at him, her white teeth brilliant against her dark lips. "I'm fine. This young man is all I need for now." She looked at the captain. "I'll need a blood oath to break the hold your family has over the curse placed on me, but the kiss was enough for now."

"What does a blood oath entail?" the captain asked.

Smart man, thought Gaelan. *It won't do him any good. He's going to end up mated to my mother before he's come to terms with the fact the Blue Goddess has returned.*

He regarded the two for a few seconds. They looked good together and Kaod already seemed besotted. His kindness to strangers said a lot about his character. Perhaps, in time, he'd be able to look past the Goddess and see the woman who was perfect for him.

Even from an acquaintance of only an hour, Gaelan was positive this man would be good for his mother. Already he had held her attention more than the last man she'd taken as mate. Perhaps this one would last longer than it took for her to conceive. "Will you be alright if I leave, Mother?"

"Of course, dear. Now I have the captain to look after me." Her attention was firmly on Kaod. "What's your name, dear?"

The captain pushed away from the wall and stood at attention. "I'm Captain Kaod Jeffries, my lady. I'm happy to serve you any way I can."

"Kaod," the Blue Goddess purred. "That's a strong name. If you don't mind, my dear Kaod"—she seemed to like the sound of the man's name on her tongue—"I'll need some food and rest. When you bring it back, stay with me and I'll tell you what needs to be done to break the final strands of this curse."

She turned abruptly to Gaelan. "Go and find Fisher. Try not to lose him again."

Gaelan looked around the small room then scoffed at himself. As if there'd be some indication where Fisher was. Then he remembered Kaod was his cousin. "Do you know where he went?"

Kaod's gaze remained glued to the goddess, but he responded readily enough. "He's in the underground stream that runs through the mountains. He's heading for the Pass of Nines to find Duke Zanderveld."

"He's what? He can't swim!"

That brought Kaod's head up. "He said he'd been in the stream under some dungeons and then in the ocean. Why did he jump in if he can't swim?"

Gaelan was already striding for the door. "The idiot thinks all he needs to do is kick his feet occasionally. Where do I get into this stream?"

Kaod opened a small cooling cupboard and drew out bread and cheese and a half bottle of white wine. He placed it all beside Gaelan's mother then cupped her cheek. "I'll return as quickly as I can, my lady." He bent and placed a gentle kiss on her lips then stepped back. He joined Gaelan at the door, all sign of gentleness gone. "I'll show you where he went in."

Once out on the street, Kaod broke into a run. He turned down an alley a couple of blocks from where Gaelan and his mother had been accosted by the corporal-who-was-now-a-private.

Kaod skidded to a halt near a metal plate in the middle of the street and slid it away. "It's deep enough here to jump in but is shallower for most of the way until it joins the river near Amadon. If he survived the first jump, there are a couple of places he can crawl out to catch his breath."

He grasped Gaelan's shoulder before he could jump into the hole. "May the Goddess guide you." He ducked his head in embarrassment. "Sorry. You probably don't need that blessing as the Goddess is your mother."

Gaelan clapped Kaod's back. "I'd never turn down my mother's support. Thank you." He stepped over the lip of the hole and fell.

CHAPTER NINETEEN

THE FALL WASN'T LONG, but the water was deep. And freezing cold. It sucked the air from him and his lungs ached for want of air for several seconds until his gills activated.

Had Fisher survived even that first drop? Gaelan took a few precious seconds to dive down deeper and search for him. He couldn't see even his own hands in the blackness and felt nothing but icy water.

One of the small tanzanites in his pocket came free when he shoved his hand into the wet cloth. It gave him enough light to see a few feet away. The water reflected the light back to him, making it impossible to see clearly. He abandoned the search, hoping that Fisher made it into the creek and had floated downstream.

He bobbed to the surface, identified which direction the current was flowing, then swam. It was slow going. Every bump he felt on the riverbed had to be investigated to make sure it wasn't Fisher. Every time the water slowed, he had to determine whether or not there was a bank wide enough for Fisher to have climbed onto.

There was no light, none at all, except for the small tanzanite. It was too difficult to keep hold of it, power it and continue swimming, so he shoved it back into his pocket and swam on in the darkness.

If it wasn't for the constantly flowing water, he would have long since lost any sense of direction he had. He could see how easy it would be for someone to go mad down there. The total blackness affected not just his sight, but his balance and his hearing.

Those few times the water was shallow and the ceiling high enough for him to kneel or stand, he kept falling over, the splash of the water echoing strangely around him. Without his eyesight to orient himself, he couldn't tell if he was leaning or not. He ran a hand along the rock above his head as he floated downstream, his eyes straining to see something... anything.

With each small section of the river traversed and still no Fisher dead in the water, he began to relax. He imagined getting to the end to find Fisher drowned and washed out into the open, but it made his chest ache and his eyes burn so he suppressed that thought.

He lost track of time—forgot what time of day it had been when he'd left Barthes, couldn't work out what time of day it should be. He didn't know how long it would take him to float down the river and come out on the surface but knew it must be days rather than hours.

The cold seeped through him until shudders wracked him. He rolled onto his back and floated as he pushed his hands into his pockets and curled his fingers around the tanzanites. Warmth radiated up his arms and through his torso. He breathed his first deep breath since dropping into the water. When he was warm enough he released the stones, he rolled over again and continued swimming.

The constant darkness pressed in close. In the Aylmer Mountains, the granite was shot through with silver threads that glowed in the dark. This place had nothing. The only color was black, the only sound the gentle tumble of water over its course.

He began counting, but he stopped after 10,000 when he realized he'd said the same number four times and could no longer remember what he was supposed to be doing. He dug his tanzanites out again to warm up.

Eventually, the current slowed until it was little more than a gentle wash as the water spread out into a wide pool. Gaelan felt his way across the current to a stony beach where he could warm up a little and rest before continuing. The act of resting would also allow him time to clear his thoughts and remove himself from the troubles plaguing him.

He dragged himself out of the water and fumbled in his pockets for his tanzanites. He blew a steady stream of blue fire onto one of them to give it a stronger light, then closed his eyes against the sudden flare.

Once his eyes had adapted he looked around. A barking laugh escaped him. Lying sprawled on the opposite bank was Fisher.

Gaelan surged to his feet and waded through the water. He reached out a hand to touch him. Before his hand made contact, Fisher jerked and sneezed. A violent shiver traced through his body, then he settled again.

Gaelan laughed, his joy at finding Fisher safe and alive overtaking everything else. He laid down behind Fisher and wriggled until his front was firmly pressed against his back. Then he reached an arm over and did his best to will warmth into him. They were both still damp when he fell asleep.

An hour later, Fisher's occasional shiver had developed into regular shudders, accompanied by pained groans. Gaelan roused to lean over him and gently shake his shoulder. "Fisher," he whispered.

His hand brushed Fisher's hair off his forehead, cool against Fisher's hot skin.

FISHER GROANED, PARTLY from pain and partly because he wasn't surprised that his body had recognized Gaelan immediately.

"Wake up, Fisher. You're ill." Gaelan moved away.

The loss of his touch brought the cramps back to Fisher's stomach and the shivering increased. "It's nothing you can help with." Fisher ground the words out around another full-body shudder. "It's happened before. I just have to let it run its course." He had no idea what would happen if he did that, but it was definitely better than Gaelan burning alive.

"Is it a cold? Or something worse?"

"Worse. But it'll pass." It had passed the first time. Fisher squeezed his eyes tightly closed, refusing to remember what made it pass last time. This time felt much, much worse than it had when he was young, but he wasn't going to kill Gaelan.

Gaelan hovered over him for a couple of minutes, his body warm and comforting. He tried to move away, but every wriggle brought him closer until he realized that Gaelan was following him and they were inching their way across the ground in a weird, slow-motion game of chase.

He froze, but Gaelan slithered close again as he brushed his hair back. The shuddering eased. He calmed more when Gaelan slid his palm across his forehead again and slid closer so that his front was plastered against his back.

Fisher sighed, going limp, reveling in the relief even as he knew he'd have to move away again soon. The sharp pain in his chest and stomach eased into a heavy ache in his groin.

"Is it over or just a reprieve?" asked Gaelan.

He sighed. "Touching you will ease it for a time but there's only one thing that'll make it go away completely." He rolled over and tucked his head beneath Gaelan's chin. "I'll rest a while, then we can continue our journey." He snuggled closer, his breathing calm and even, a sharp contrast to the pained gasps it had been a minute ago.

"Tell me what's wrong. Why does touching me help?"

He remained silent until Gaelan shifted against him. He wasn't going to let it go. "I don't know exactly what it is, but it's happened before. I didn't know what the consequences were the first time, so I didn't try to control it."

"Why do you need to control it?"

He pushed himself away so he could see Gaelan's face. "You'll die."

"Why?"

He jumped to his feet. "I don't know why. I just know it'll happen." He glared at Gaelan. "Didn't you hear me when I said it's happened before? I didn't control it, and someone died."

Gaelan stood as well. "Tell me what happened."

A shudder so strong that it made Fisher stumble swept through him. Gaelan took two steps forward and drew him into his arms. Small tremors continued to sweep through him, but the shudders abated.

"It's getting worse," said Gaelan. "Tell me."

"I was sixteen. There was a boy my age in the same group. We'd just been moved from the youth group to the soldiers' barracks and had to share a bunk. He had the softest, finest hair I've ever seen. Every time he moved, strands of it wafted across my face.

"One day I grabbed a handful and pulled it away. It put our faces very close; I could feel his breath panting across my chin. I pulled him closer... and he came." Fisher shuffled on his feet but didn't break Gaelan's hold on him.

"After that, every time we were alone, I grabbed his hair. I kissed him, I jerked him off. We... he liked it best when I was a bit rough, pulling his hair, holding his hands down so he couldn't move away.

The more we did, the more I craved it. I thought it was normal, the way I trembled and ached if we hadn't touched for a while." Fisher shifted in Gaelan's hold, not sure if he should like being there or not. He craved it, but it wasn't safe. He'd thought just kissing would be safe, but now he was like this again. He'd have to leave, to get far away so he didn't kill him.

"What happened?"

"The jerking off was good, the oral better, but I wanted more. So did he." His voice dropped to a whisper, all his strength consumed by the lingering grief and horror at what he'd done. "At first it was good, better than good. He was so hot and tight. I held his hands and hair the way he liked it and moved. I thought his groans and whimpers were ones of pleasure like they usually were when I hurt him a bit."

He pulled out of Gaelan's arms and stepped away. He wrapped his arms around his stomach, the tremors there more than pain, more than memory.

"Then he screamed. It was right when I was coming so my eyes were closed. I thought he was coming too." He tightened his grip on himself so he didn't double over in remembered pain and shock. "Then I smelled it—burning hair, burning meat. I opened my eyes and he was on fire. It wasn't just his hair, but all of him. Bright orange flames danced over his skin.

"I fell off the bed. He kept screaming. I tugged a blanket off the next bunk and beat the flames with it, but they wouldn't go out. The blanket caught fire as well. By the time he stopped screaming, that whole end of the bunkhouse was alight, and the fire was spreading."

He walked in a small circle, threading his hands through his hair and pulling, as if that would tug the memories from his head.

He flicked a look at Gaelan but kept walking around, now slightly hunched, protecting his stomach. "I thought it would be different with you. You were in charge, not me. You didn't want me to hold you down. I didn't touch you with my hands. It was only the one time." A sudden cramp caught him off guard and he gasped, bending at the waist to try to ease it. "But here I am."

Gaelan walked toward him.

Fisher put his hands out, warding him off. "You can't come near me. I know I let you before, but I barely controlled myself. If we do it again, you'll die."

"Fisher—"

"I'm not going to kill you too."

"You know what I am."

"I can't kill—"

"Fisher, pay attention. I'm a dragon."

"I know you're a dragon. That's another reason we can't."

"Specifically, I'm a dragon that lives in a volcano."

Fisher glared at him. Was he being obtuse or did the idiot dragon not get it? "If we have sex, you'll be consumed by fire."

"What is inside a volcano?"

"Why are you talking about volcanoes all the time? Don't you understand what I'm telling you? If we have sex, I'll burn you."

Gaelan laughed, the bastard. "Bring it on. Let me feel you inside me and see if you're hotter than lava."

Fisher opened his mouth to warn him again when what he'd been saying finally sank in. "Oh." Not the most intelligent thing for him to say but the best he could manage since Gaelan's comment about lava had washed over Fisher like... well, like lava. He was hard as rock. "You want me inside you?"

Gaelan laughed. "To start with. We can try it the other way later, after you try to burn me from the inside out. Perhaps when I'm in you, you can try to burn my dick off."

He jumped back, his hands automatically cupping his dick and balls.

Gaelan laughed again and began to unbutton his shirt. Fisher scowled at him. "Why are you taking your shirt off?"

"So I can get naked."

"I've seen you magick your clothes on and off. Why are you taking your shirt off like that?"

Gaelan blinked. By the time he opened his eyes again, his clothes were gone. "I thought you'd like the show, but I can do it either way." He stalked toward him.

Fisher backed up.

"You're right," he said as he came closer. "It's easier when I only have to concentrate on getting your clothes off."

"Gaelan." He had to try to save him. "We can't. I told you—" he let his jacket fall to the ground when Gaelan slid it off his shoulders.

"Yes, you did. I can't wait to feel your heat inside me." He cupped Fisher's face. "I promise I'll be careful. I don't want to burn you too badly."

"Burn me? But—" Fisher gasped. "You'll burn me?"

"I'm a dragon that lives in a volcano. What do you think? You felt it at the beach." He dropped a kiss on Fisher's lips. "Shall we try this?" He didn't wait for Fisher's response, just tugged Fisher's shirt up and over his head.

"I thought that was me." Fisher gasped then laughed even though his stomach still clenched with worry. "Don't blame me if you end up with scorch marks." Chances were, Gaelan was right and he wouldn't be affected by Fisher's fire, but there was still a chance he was wrong.

"Stop worrying," said Gaelan as he nibbled on Fisher's neck. His tongue flicked out, shooting warm tingles down his spine as he swiftly dispensed with his jeans.

Fisher stepped out of his jeans, then leaned down the scant inches needed to touch Gaelan's lips with his own. He anticipated an easy, gentle exploration to make sure they weren't going to kill each other with this, but he should have known better. Their last erotic interlude hadn't killed them, so they'd have to go a lot further than that to find out exactly how dangerous he would be to Gaelan. "Tell me the moment things get too hot for you. I won't hurt you."

Gaelan's response was to pick Fisher up and lower him to the sand. His eyes flared blue fire for a second then Fisher felt smooth fabric sliding beneath him. "We don't want the sand to get into awkward places." Gaelan grinned before he slipped away, his mouth trailing down his stomach until he took Fisher's cock deep.

Fisher jerked and cried out at the sudden sensation of being completely enveloped in wet heat. Gaelan's lips slid back toward the tip, until only the head was in his mouth. He teased Fisher with his teeth just under the helmet, but before Fisher could decide if it was uncomfortable, or the best thing he'd ever felt, Gaelan plunged down again.

Fisher screamed as the intense heat enveloped him, shooting sparks skittering across his skin. He pushed Gaelan away, onto his back and straddled him, plunging into a deep kiss. Gaelan groaned and gripped his hips. Fisher grabbed fists-full of Gaelan's hair and pulled, breaking the kiss.

"Are you sure?" he asked breathlessly.

"More than anything. I want you inside me." Gaelan wriggled, lifted Fisher at the waist then pushed his legs wide so Fisher could settle between them.

Fisher wanted to ask again, make sure Gaelan knew what he was risking, but decided Gaelan's legs wound around his hips and holding tight was answer enough. He spit on his fingers and pressed against Gaelan's opening.

"It's fine," he ground out through gritted teeth. "Get in me."

"I *won't* hurt you."

"Fuck's sake, Fisher. I'm a dragon. You're not going to hurt me." Gaelan pushed his hand between them, grabbed Fisher's cock and guided it to his hole. He grunted as he lifted his hips and the tip of his cock slipped inside.

"Gaelan," Fisher ground out as he pressed inside. He panted at the snug heat that engulfed him, searing his resistance. He pushed inside, his breaths faint gasps as Gaelan's heat engulfed him, almost too hot, but exactly what he needed. What he craved.

When he bottomed out, he lifted his hips again, the rhythm building automatically as he pushed Gaelan's legs wider and higher so he could lean down and taste the sweat beading on his forehead. Gaelan gripped his hips and lifted his face for a plunging kiss that was all tongues and teeth.

The heat built in tandem with the pressure at the base of his spine and in his balls. He drove into Gaelan over and over, harder and harder, needing more, needing everything from him.

His fingertips tingled. His eyes burned. Scalding heat danced up and down his back and legs.

His hips punched down once, twice, as he buried himself inside Gaelan as deeply as he could. On the third time, he screamed again, fire erupting through him with his climax. He opened his eyes to see red-orange flames flicker between him and Gaelan.

With the first pulse from Fisher's cock, Gaelan surged up, blue fire dancing in his eyes. Fisher tightened his hold on Gaelan's hair, watched it catch alight at the same time he felt thick liquid land on his stomach and chest.

"More," growled Gaelan.

Fisher punched his hips against Gaelan's buttocks, his thickness stretching Gaelan wide open. It burned, but with the flames arcing between them, from one to the other and back again, everything burned.

Fisher couldn't catch his breath. He'd just come, but hadn't come down from it. His cock was still hard, still pulsing with every movement Gaelan made. "Come with me inside you. Burn for me." He leaned down to take an awkward kiss, crunching Gaelan's body into a tight arc. "Let me burn with you."

Gaelan groaned. "Yes," he hissed.

Fisher's lungs were tight and aching from lack of air. His stomach clenched painfully from keeping the punishing rhythm. Gaelan's legs bounced against his back as if they were no longer part of his body. There was no control; they were consumed. Taken.

The heat built, drying his mouth and his eyes, shredding his throat. Gaelan kept shooting even as yellow-orange flames skittered across his skin. If he kept going, Fisher would explode, and they'd truly burn.

"G-G-G." His mouth wouldn't shape Gaelan's name, couldn't form even one word. Couldn't say *enough*.

"Give it all to me," said Gaelan, his voice as raw as Fisher felt all over. "Burn me." The tendons on Gaelan's neck stood out as he flung his head back and roared. Flame erupted from his mouth, yellow and white, and tanzanite blue right at the center.

Fisher screamed as he came again, Gaelan's body clenched tightly around his pulsating cock, Gaelan's blue flames blending with his own orange ones.

They collapsed together, the flames snuffed out, their sweaty skin slipping and sliding until Fisher lay half-on and half-off Gaelan. He panted, his throat raw, feeling like little spikes of glass pricked the surface. Or little flames. He tried to swallow but his mouth was too dry. Parched. Tasted like smoke.

Gaelan's arm, where it lay across his hip, flopped as if he tried to get up but didn't have the energy. Fisher knew how he felt. All his energy was going into trying to remember how to breathe.

A huffed laugh escaped. Cool air rushed in as he finally took an independent breath. He was still alive. Gaelan's arm flopped again, then his hand slid up Fisher's back and neck to cup his cheek.

"You're still alive," he said, his voice a husky rasp.

"Yeah," breathed Gaelan. "Fuck, that was good." He rolled them so they were on their sides and Fisher could see his face. "My whole body feels like mashed potatoes." He grinned at Fisher's horror. "I love mashed potatoes. We're definitely going to do that again."

Fisher returned the grin and continued breathing. Pretty soon, his body would remember how to do it automatically, and it wouldn't take so much energy. He closed his eyes and relaxed.

An hour later, they woke, washed, dressed, gathered their belongings and plunged back into the cold water. Fisher carefully kept his thoughts on the present. What they'd done, how they had both burned yet survived unscathed, was tucked tightly into a corner of his consciousness. Waiting. He would deal with that when he must. For now, he'd continue their search for the duke and the Elixir.

The chill water didn't seem to affect Fisher as much as it had before. It was almost as if Gaelan had transferred some of his body heat to him, no matter how unlikely that seemed. He put the oddity in with other things he'd decided he didn't need to question. He'd enjoy the warmth while he had it.

There was no talk of what they'd done or what it might mean, but he could feel Gaelan's intent. They'd be doing that again. And more. He floated along with the current, one thought in his mind. He wouldn't hurt Gaelan. He loved that Fisher burst into flames whenever he fucked him, because he did too. He shook the thoughts from his head before he began to panic, and focused on the water.

He hadn't been lying when he'd said he could swim now. It wasn't graceful or efficient, but he could keep his head above the water when he needed to breathe, and he could steer himself through the current. As much as he wanted to stay with Gaelan and find how far they could push their individual fires right now, he knew he had to keep moving.

He didn't know why but finding Gaelan's duke was something he had to do. Perhaps it was because he had landed on the Lonely Isles with the intention of making his home there.

Part of him thought it was because he didn't believe the Elixir was completely destroyed. Barthes was little more than rubble, and the book Ma Jeffries had was destroyed, but the duke hadn't been there. If the viscount had sent his father to the headquarters of the Elixir, then he should have been in Barthes.

Fisher was missing something and until he was completely sure the Elixir was gone and not coming back, he'd keep searching. Finding the duke was the next logical step.

"Why wasn't the duke in Barthes?" he asked, spluttering as he dipped too low in the water.

Gaelan frowned. "Focus on your swimming." Several feet farther along. "The viscount said he'd be there. I don't know why he wasn't, but I don't think it's anything good. We need to talk to the Mafdeti. If there's someone new wandering around the Aylmer Mountains or in the catacombs, they'll know about it."

"We should talk to Checa and Heath, not the Matriarch."

"We can't go into her territory and not let her know why we're there."

"She won't give us the information we need, whether she has it or not. We'll end up under arrest for something and imprisoned deep in the mountains."

"What type of rock are the mountains made of?"

Fisher glared at him. "You're not taking this seriously. What difference does it make what the mountains are made of? Checa and Heath are the Mafdeti we need to see, no one else."

"What rock are the mountains made of?"

"I don't know. The desert is sandstone. The only section of the mountains I've been inside of are to the west where the Lake of the Damned is. That's a combination of granite and other igneous rocks. There's lots of crystal. The granite is coarse."

"And where the Mafdeti live is the same mountain range, right?"

"Of course. It's the Aylmer Mountains. There are five of them in a row, running west to east. We're under the Seven Mountains now. They're the same, only there are seven of them and they reach farther west."

"The Matriarch might imprison us under mountains made primarily of granite." Gaelan's brows lifted as if he was missing something.

"What?"

"Did the sex fry your brain completely?" Gaelan swam across the stream they were desultorily floating down. "You can move through granite, Fisher."

He shoved him away, splashing water in Gaelan's face as he did so. "I know I can. Stop talking to me as if I'm a child."

He could move through granite. If the mountains were made of granite nothing could keep them there if he wanted out.

He splashed Gaelan again. Just because. Then he rejoined the current and kicked to widen the gap between them.

Gaelan's laughter followed him down the river.

CHAPTER TWENTY

IT WAS AFTERNOON WHEN the river spat them out of the mountain. For a moment, Fisher was airborne, flailing in the heavy spray, then he dropped with the water, thudding painfully on his back onto what felt like rock but was actually water. The air whooshed out of his lungs and he couldn't breathe in, which was actually a good thing as he was so far underwater he didn't know which way was up.

By the time he surfaced, his lungs were burning with the need to breathe and his eyes felt like they were going to pop out of his head from the pressure. As soon as his chin cleared the water, he gasped in great lungfuls of air. He sank again but kicked himself back to the surface so he could breathe.

The current carried him swiftly downstream as he struggled to keep his head above water amidst the spray and wavelets. Every now and then his knee or hip scraped against a rock beneath the water as he tumbled along.

Finally, just as he thought he had no more breaths to gasp and the water would take him, his knees scraped the riverbed. He grasped handfuls of gravel as he pulled himself out of the current and into calm shallow water at the bank, then collapsed, coughing, his cheek pressed against soft sand and grass, his legs still in the water.

Once he'd coughed up most of the water he'd swallowed, he dragged himself out and flopped onto his back. He tried to take in his surroundings through watery eyes and convulsive coughing.

The sky was brilliant blue with fluffy clouds lazily drifting by. A gentle breeze teased his hair and clothes, bringing with it the smells of eucalyptus and lemon. A few lazy birds twittered desultorily in the hazy afternoon.

When he could breathe without coughing he forced his rubbery limbs into motion. He sat, for the first time wondering where Gaelan could be. He wouldn't have drowned because he could breathe underwater, but he might have hit his head and be unconscious, or he could have been washed farther downstream, or—

He jerked upright at the sound of something crashing through the undergrowth. The sounds came closer. Whatever it was, it was large. He jumped to his feet and backed away. Where was the heart-pounding, sweat-inducing, screaming fear that should overtake him with an unknown threat like this?

He'd barely made the thought conscious when the beast crashing through the bush, burst free and stumbled the last few steps into soft sand.

Gaelan.

Fisher shook his head. "Do you think you could have made more noise? Perhaps you could have roared out a warning or something." He gestured to the south. "That might have let the Mafdeti know we were coming."

Blue-purple light shimmered as Gaelan changed to his human form. He watched with the same fascination as he had the first time but without the stomach-cramping fear. He didn't think he'd ever get tired of seeing Gaelan change.

"You couldn't... I was coming for you."

"I couldn't what?" Fisher narrowed his eyes.

"You." Gaelan pointed at the water. "In the water."

The irritation drained from him quicker than the water ran down his skin and his face warmed. "You're not making any sense." He turned away before Gaelan could say a word. "Let's get moving. We need to see the Mafdeti to make sure they have the duke, then go to the desert."

Gaelan joined him, walking quietly by his side. His fingers touched Fisher's head before gently threading through his hair and away. He automatically leaned into the touch but didn't return it.

"Why do we have to go to the desert?" asked Gaelan.

"The Exiles began sacrificing to the norrgel a couple of years ago. I'd bet my left nut we'll find an Elixir plant in the catacombs."

"Wouldn't you have seen it when you were there?"

"I was in charge of offense and defense against the Imperials and Mafdeti. There were significant areas I wasn't involved in at all." His mother might have known about it. Why wouldn't she have told him? He sighed. She was dead; there could be no answers from her.

"We should fly. It will be much faster and there'd be no time for messages to be relayed should we be spotted."

He glared at Gaelan, but the softly pleading expression in his brilliant blue eyes deflated him and he couldn't maintain the fiction that he still hated flying. If he was honest with himself, he'd never hated it. He'd just been afraid of falling. He knew now that Gaelan would never drop him.

He heaved a great, put-upon sigh. "Fine. You want to fly, we'll fly. But if you let me fall, I'll break your nose."

Gaelan grinned, rushed to him and planted a swift kiss on his lips. Then he was gone again, striding into the water, looking around at the trees. Fisher supposed he was gauging the space he had for his wings. "This time, mount me and sit between my shoulder blades. You'll find it more comfortable."

Most of the words following "mount me" came to Fisher as if through water, his mind filled with images of Gaelan kneeling in front of him, his round buttocks thrust toward him, his brown-pink pucker barely visible between them.

Between one breath and the next, Gaelan disappeared and, in a flash of blue light, stood before him in his dragon form. His breath caught at the beauty of the beast even as the sexual urgency faded.

He walked slowly into the shallow water and ran his hand over a glistening purple scale. "I've never had the opportunity to really look at you like this."

Gaelan's head swung around so he could see one brilliant blue eye regarding him. "You're beautiful." he said, maintaining focus on the eye. It blinked, but he didn't know if Gaelan was winking at him or blinking at the unexpectedness of his declaration. His face flushed hot and he looked away, searching for a way to climb up onto the dragon's back.

Gaelan bent his foreleg so his toes and knee formed a couple of steps—enough for him to climb up so he could grab hold of the thick edge of a scale and clamber along his neck and onto his back. He settled himself just in front of Gaelan's wings, in a natural divot.

As he wriggled to find the most comfortable place, his legs naturally fell beside a line of scales along the dragon's shoulder. The backward edge of the scales lifted slightly and he was able to slip his legs under, held firmly. Gaelan hunched his shoulders, raising his wings, and Fisher felt his seat shift under him as if it was molding itself to him, cradling him securely. Experimentally, he leaned forward, back and to each side, but he was held securely. Unless Gaelan turned upside-down and deliberately released him, he wouldn't fall. "You're right. This is much better. Let's go."

The jump into the air was still as terrifying and exhilarating as it had ever been. Gaelan's wings rose above him, pushing his body downward. His stomach lurched with the plummeting sensation before the wings swept down again and they lifted higher. The dragon rose in an ever-increasing spiral until they lazily circled the river where it burst from the foothills and tumbled toward Amadon.

Before they reached what he assumed was Gaelan's preferred cruising height, several norrgel screeched and raced toward them from the south-west. "We have company." Tension tightened his voice.

Gaelan circled lazily. *They're just worried about another "bird" in their territory.*

Gaelan's voice inside his head made him jump, and he knew he'd have fallen if he wasn't seated so securely. "I forgot you can do that."

We can do it.

The norrgel came so close, he could see the way the light glinting off their beady black eyes contrasted with the flat black of their feathers. They screeched again, the sound far too close, and he broke into a terrified sweat. His heart pounded and his grip on the smooth scales slipped. "Gaelan." His throat was so tight, the yell he'd intended emerged as a strangled whisper.

Gaelan huffed and a puff of smoke drifted over his head and washed over him, enough to make his eyes squint, but not thick enough to make him cough.

The norrgel came closer. "Gaelan!"

Beneath him, Gaelan's body expanded, a deep breath widening his chest. His long throat grumbled and groaned, and Fisher wondered if there was something wrong with him and they were going to crash.

Then the dragon blew out his breath, a great whoosh of sound and heat and flame shooting out in front of them, the acrid smoke washing backward, hot enough to singe Fisher's eyebrows. He ducked his head.

The norrgel screams cut out. The smell of freshly-cooked meat permeated the air around them.

Gaelan dove.

Fisher screamed.

Thunk, thunk, thunk. The motion of Gaelan's grabbing the norrgel, one in each claw and one in his mouth, made barely a blip in their mad fall. The sounds of flesh tearing, slurping and chewing followed, then Gaelan's neck moved in an obvious swallow.

He gasped. "Are you eating them? They're norrgel!"

Mmm. Roasted norrgel. Yum. I haven't had any in ages. Another swallow. *You want some?*

"No! It's poisonous." And... yuck.

You'd handle it. Their flight dipped and twisted as the dragon ate with relish. Fisher decided that each bird was about three mouthfuls for him.

Once the norrgel feast was over—no other norrgel had come near them after Gaelan started eating their buddies—he dove toward the river.

Fisher screamed. Then he stopped, ashamed of his reaction. The ground rushed toward them and sound bubbled up in his throat. He swallowed to control it.

Fuck it. It was a sudden drop, and a long way down and he felt like he was falling. He screamed again.

The river filled his view. They were going to dive straight into it. Then Gaelan leveled out, his claws washing through the water. He dipped his snout, and water splashed over his head, drenching Fisher. It was so cold it made him gasp then cough at the mouthful of water he'd inhaled. He leaned over the dragon's neck and held on tightly.

After a few seconds, they lifted again and flew steadily southward. Fisher shivered as the cold air hit his wet clothing.

Sorry. I needed to wash my face and hands. Gaelan belched, a bubble of stinking sooty smoke drifting from his mouth. Fisher coughed.

Excuse me. I forgot.

"Forgot what?"

Norrgel always give me indigestion. Unfortunately, there's worse to come.

"Worse?"

Gaelan's body responded for him. By the time they landed in the mountains an hour later, Fisher couldn't wait to get off the dragon and somewhere that wouldn't try to suffocate him with noxious belching and farting.

He took a few seconds to work out which direction the wind was blowing, then pointed downwind. "You go that way far enough that I can't hear you or smell you, and don't come back until that's over with."

Fisher...

"Forget it. It's disgusting. You stink and I need some fresh air or I'm going to be ill. Go."

Gaelan hung his head. *But they're so tasty, and I only had a few.*

"A few was more than enough. The next time you decide you simply must eat roasted norrgel, tell me first so I can get far, far away. I'm going to have some water to wash away the lingering taste of your burps, then I'm going to sleep." He turned away and deliberately ignored Gaelan's continued apologies. Finally, after another nauseating belch, the dragon slunk away.

Fisher settled under a rocky overhang and sipped water from his waterskin. With Gaelan downwind, his stomach settled and his head stopped spinning. After about ten minutes, he eyes stopped whirling and he could focus on things again. He no longer felt drunk.

He wondered if the gas from Gaelan's indigestion could be bottled. He'd bet it was similar to the Elixir in the effects it wrought, apart from the gut-clenching nausea. Perhaps that as well. Not ever having taken the Elixir, he didn't know.

He dozed for a little while, only rousing himself when Gaelan, again in human form, sidled up to him.

"I'm sorry. I truly forgot how ill they made me." He turned his head and burped softly.

"Gaelan."

"No, it's over. I promise. I'll eat something to settle my stomach a bit." He sighed. "They're such a delicacy and I so rarely have an opportunity to have any."

"That's probably a good thing." Silence filled the air between them and he almost dropped off to sleep again but he shook his head and blinked several times to make sure he stayed awake. "What's the plan now? Are we going to keep flying?"

"I had thought we'd fly directly to the Pass of Nines tonight and arrive there shortly after sunrise." He rubbed his stomach, which growled ominously. "But I think it might be better if I rest here tonight and we can continue tomorrow."

"Fine." He was reluctant to enter Mafdeti country. In spite of the more relaxed attitudes of Checa and Heath when they left him in Barthes, he was still branded a traitor. He'd lay even money on him being killed on sight, rather than them listening to him first.

He lay down, pushing back under the overhang until his back rubbed against rock. Still granite, although he knew the southern side, particularly closest to the desert, was all sandstone. He wouldn't be able to read that.

His eyes snapped open as soon as he realized what he'd thought.

He was reading the rock. Just like Heath had.

He threaded his arm behind him and pressed his palm against the ragged rock, closing his eyes to focus more fully on it. Sensations washed through him and a surprised laugh burst out.

"What is it?" asked Gaelan, sitting at his feet, immediately alert.

"I can tell how thick the rock is," he said in wonder. "I know what's on the other side of it."

Gaelan lay down again, shifting so he was lined up with him, his buttocks snuggled against Fisher's groin. "Of course you can." He yawned.

Fisher pushed him away and sat up. "What do you mean *of course I can?*"

"That's part of the skill-set."

"What *skill-set*? How do you know there's a skill-set? What the hell does skill-set even mean?" Until he'd gone to Linspar, he was just a normal person. No special skills or anything. Of course, he'd spent most of his life in the desert, surrounded by sandstone.

But Gaelan was talking like it was expected. Like Fisher being able to sink through granite, being able to move the rock out of the way and being able to read it were all perfectly normal things for him to do.

Gaelan sighed and sat up, the tilt of his head making it clear he was eyeing Fisher warily. "Umm."

Fisher twisted around so he could see Gaelan more clearly in the shadows. He couldn't see his features but, against the slightly lighter blue-black of the sky, his body language was easy to read. "Tell me."

Gaelan shrugged. "You're the Concubine."

Fisher pushed him away, scrambled out from under the rock and stood. "I am not the bloody Concubine. I'm never going to be the Concubine."

Gaelan slumped. And sighed. After a long silence, he nodded. "I'm sorry."

"What are you sorry about?"

"I... I can't take you any farther." He stood.

"What? Why?"

"You won't be the Concubine."

He was missing something. "Why can I only travel with you if I'm the Concubine?"

"No one else can ride me." The whisper barely floated on the breeze, but it was strong enough to freeze him in place.

Gaelan's head tipped up as if he watched Fisher through his lashes. "Or mount me," he said, his voice a little stronger. "No one else can sire my children."

He stumbled back, cracking his head against the rock. "Children? Who said anything about children?"

"You don't want children?"

His heart wept at the sadness in Gaelan's tone. "Why are we talking about children? I just said I'm not the Concubine. I refuse to be used by any bloody dragon that decides he needs a little relief."

Gaelan surged forward, grabbing his shoulders, almost lifting him off his feet. "Not *any* bloody dragon. Me! Only me. Do you understand?"

"That's not a concubine. A concubine is anybody's."

"A Concubine is one not eligible for Bonding because of status."

"Right. A whore anyone can have."

"Is that why you're resisting it? Because you think it would make you a whore and anyone could have you?"

"I'm not a whore. I know others can be and enjoy it. They don't want to be restricted to just one person, and some make a good living from it. But that's not for me. I'll never be anyone's whore."

"The Concubine isn't a whore, just lower status."

"If that's the case, Checa would be Heath's concubine. He's much lower status. But they're Bond Mates. Status has nothing to do with it."

"It does if you're a god."

Even the air paused at that pronouncement.

"You're not really a god, though, are you?" asked Fisher. "You're just a dragon."

"Not *just* a dragon."

"The Blue Goddess. She's not really a goddess. She's just a dragon too." One who'd been trapped in a glacier for hundreds of years. "How long do dragons live?"

"Normal dragons, five hundred years or so unless they manage to Bond to a wizard."

Fisher scoffed. "Wizards are a fairytale. So, five hundred years. Anybody would think someone that long-lived would be a god." He was avoiding the real question but couldn't allow the conversation to circle back around. Gaelan was suggesting that Fisher was his Concubine. His alone. He wouldn't be used by everyone. Only Gaelan. "How old are you?"

Gaelan stepped closer, until the distance between them was no wider than a breath. "I'm three thousand years old, and have been looking for my mate, my Concubine, for most of that time." He drew Fisher into an embrace. "Now I've found you, I'm not letting you go." As Fisher stiffened in denial, he continued. "I won't force you into anything you aren't ready for, but know that you're mine and you'll always be mine."

Fuck.

Just. Fuck.

His mind swirled like empty clouds. What was he supposed to think about that? It was a declaration of ownership. Of possession. He wasn't anyone's possession. He wouldn't be owned by anyone.

But why did Gaelan's hold on him feel more like comfort and belonging than it did capture and restriction? His heart sang a song of belonging so strong it almost shattered the memories that assaulted him, the visions spinning through his mind. Locked in a closet at three, seven and tied to a bedpost, in a cage underground as a young man.

He couldn't. He just couldn't.

He pulled away. "I'm going to sleep. If you still want to go to the Mafdeti, you do that. I think I'll go directly to the desert and see what the Exiles are up to."

"Fisher—"

Fisher didn't turn to look at him, didn't lean back into the heat he could feel at his back. "I'm not anyone's concubine, Gaelan." He couldn't lose himself like that. It had taken too many years to find himself in the first place.

"Not anyone's. Mine."

Placing his feet one in front of the other as he made his way back to the overhang, felt more like wading a mile through mud than walking the few feet it really was.

FISHER WOKE ALONE AT first light. He pushed himself to his feet with a sigh and gathered his meager belongings.

To the east, the first norrgel screeched and he scowled. The day before, after Gaelan's feast, they hadn't seen any norrgel in the vicinity. Without Gaelan to scare them off, this would be a different kind of day.

Fisher left the outcropping and scrambled down to a more easily traversable section of the foothills. He'd probably spend most of his morning running from tree to tree, trying to avoid the notice of the norrgel as they hunted.

He wondered when Gaelan had left, both accepting that he'd had no choice and disappointed that he hadn't argued against his insistence he wasn't the Concubine. There was just his strange and repeated pronouncement that Fisher was his.

Fisher didn't understand how that could be. Gaelan was a three-thousand-year-old dragon, for all intents, a dragon god. There was no chance that he could be the only person Gaelan could want as his... *not*-Concubine.

Fisher still couldn't and wouldn't agree to that. His companion, perhaps. And what was that about children? They were both male. Could male dragons bear children?

The sky darkened. Fisher looked up to find a blue belly above him, claws clamped around a derafawn, its spotted rump and fluffy white tail stained with blood.

Gaelan dropped the fawn in front of Fisher, then breathed fire on it. Fisher stepped back from the heat, his mouth watering at the smell of succulently cooked meat. Once the meat was done, Gaelan stopped hovering above and dropped to the ground, changing to his human form as he landed.

He regarded Fisher silently and seriously for a few seconds. "I brought breakfast. I think you'll like this a lot more than the norrgel." He gave a shy smile. "I know you'll like *me* eating it a lot more than me eating norrgel."

Fisher bit the inside of his cheek to stop the smile blooming. He looked again at the derafawn, then back to Gaelan. "I thought you'd gone."

"I should, but I can't leave you. We'll travel together." He stepped close to Fisher but didn't touch him. "Together we'll find the duke and ensure he goes back home. We'll go to the Exiles and destroy any Elixir they have then we'll go back to the Lonely Isles where we can live in peace."

He lifted his hand and stroked a few fingers lightly down Fisher's cheek. "Together." He lowered his mouth and pressed a barely-there kiss on his lips.

Fisher swayed when Gaelan stepped back and let his hand drop away. Then he scowled. "You did that on purpose."

Gaelan's gaze was serious. Piercing. "Know this, Fisher. Everything I do with you is on purpose. You aren't some random person I've decided to torment. Whether you acknowledge it or not, you are my Concubine. Everything with you is something I choose to do. One day, soon hopefully, perhaps you'll choose me too."

Fisher gaped. His thoughts swung between rejection of the ownership he heard in Gaelan's voice and craving the belonging he seemed to offer.

His indecision was interrupted by a low growl in his stomach. Gaelan laughed. "Eat something, then we'll fly the rest of the way to the Pass of Nines."

Fisher retrieved one of his knives from an ankle sheath, cut away a portion of skin and the layer of fat, and began slicing meat from the derafawn's haunch. He shoved a few small pieces into his mouth then passed some over to Gaelan. "Do we have to go right to the Pass of Nines? Isn't the Mafdeti community east of that? We could go directly there."

"We should go to the palace at some stage to let the Matriarch know we're in her territory, but the Dragon King lives in the Pass of Nines. He's our first stop."

"Why the dragon?" He slurped at some juice that dribbled down his chin as he spoke, then sliced some more meat and wrapped it tightly in supple sorrel leaves. He drew out a leather pouch and began filling it with the meat parcels. It would still be good for their midday meal. He frowned at the rest of the derafawn.

"There are animals here that will welcome the food we leave. There won't be any waste from this kill," said Gaelan.

After they ate their fill and Fisher was satisfied they had enough for another meal, they walked out of the foothills and into the valley where Gaelan had enough room to change forms. Fisher was more comfortable with the change and barely blinked when the man he was traveling with was consumed by blue flame and replaced by a massive blue-purple dragon.

Gaelan cocked his foreleg as he had the day before and Fisher climbed to his place between Gaelan's shoulder blades, locked his legs in place and gripped the rounded edge of the scales that appeared to be placed specifically for him to hold. Within seconds, they were in the air and flying west.

Twice, norrgel flew directly toward them, but Gaelan roared and belched flame each time. After the second time, Fisher only saw the carnivorous birds from a distance. "It would have been handy to have you in the sky when I was in the desert," he said after the third time a flock of norrgel came close only to veer away once they were close enough to recognize the dragon.

When the sun was high overhead, they flew over the Pass of Nines and continued west. "We should be landing."

It's rude to drop in unannounced. We'll land soon and walk in via the expected route.

Fisher was used to the protocols surrounding the Exiles. There were often criminal and political Imperials exiled from Hawkesby and other centers. None of them bothered to walk in by "the front door;" there was no real front door in the Exile compound. All entrances were guarded, and all intruders were arrested and brought before the king for sentencing. "Will we be incarcerated long?"

There was a long pause before Gaelan responded. *Unless these dragons are markedly different from all others before them, we won't be incarcerated at all. We'll either have an Adventure for them to be part of, or we'll be roasted for invading their territory.*

"Roasted!" His heart rate increased at the thought of dying in such a way, but then he relaxed. Gaelan wouldn't risk their lives like that. At least, he didn't think so. "What sort of an Adventure can we offer them? Aren't they already on an Adventure with the Mafdeti, fighting the Yeudan? Isn't what we're doing more of the same?"

It is, but it'll give the dragons more things to do. They like being useful, and they're serious adrenaline junkies. They love it when they have the most dangerous jobs.

"Why do you speak of them as separate from yourself? You're a dragon too."

I am separate from them. I was separate from them when they lived before, and I'm separate from them now. Fisher was jostled in a way that made him think Gaelan just shrugged. *They don't live as long as I will.*

"How long will you live?"

I don't know. I'm still young yet, according to my mother.

Three thousand years was young for Gaelan. Fisher couldn't even conceive of living for the five hundred years the other dragons would live. "How do you cope with everyone you know dying when you just keep going?"

The dragon tipped to the side, spiraling down to the mountains west of the Pass of Nines. He still hadn't responded by the time they landed.

CHAPTER TWENTY-ONE

THEY CLIMBED FOR A couple of hours, then stopped to eat and rest. Fisher leaned against the mountain and sidled along the ledge until he could see around the rock. The blockage in the Lake of the Damned was finally cleared and the Crystal River was flowing. In the valley below, the river ran bright and furious, still mottled with debris from the Lake of the Damned.

From this distance, he could only make out glistening blocks of ice in the torrent, melting rapidly after it emerged from the mountain and met the warmth of the sun. There were people, like ants, rushing up and down the riverbanks.

Scattered across the landscape on either side of the river were large lumps, all the colors of amber, from pale gold through all ranges of yellows, greens and browns. Every now and then one of the lumps moved, the sunlight glinting off scales. Golden wings unfurled and Fisher could no longer doubt what he was seeing.

Dragons.

He'd seen a dozen of them hatch and had thought that was all there was, but there were hundreds lazing around the valley. After a millennium, dragons truly had returned to Thalazar. They were the stuff of legends, warrior companions to the Mafdeti, the first bastion of defense and a truly terrifying offense. He squinted at the closest ones. "They seem smaller than you." The two at Barthes had been smaller too, but not as much as these.

"They are." Gaelan settled on the small ledge beside him. "I don't know how big I was when I was young. They might be the same size I was."

"Are there other stories about the dragons? Ones the Mafdeti don't know. Where do they fit with you and the Blue Goddess?"

"Legend says all dragons are descended from one family. There's a song about them. Shall I sing it for you?"

Fisher pulled out their lunch of cold meat wrapped in sorrel leaves. "After lunch." He handed several wraps to Gaelan, amused when he immediately unwrapped the meat. They settled against the warm rock to eat and watched the dragons as they sunned themselves and stretched their wings.

When Gaelan finished his last piece of meat he began to sing.

When the world was young
And people swam in the sea
The dragons ruled the land
Each one
Hard as the stone they bore.
The eldest, Diatera,
Carves a life for her people
Deep beneath the earth
And forgives not one transgression
Far in the north where ice flows
Sapphirus, beautiful and determined
Nurtures her wards
And becomes one of them
Rubéo, fierce and protective
Rides the plains
Reading the sky
Through tall grasses
Laperoni, warm and beloved
Guards the jungles

Walking amongst them
To protect the ones he loves
Opalesa, pale as the sands that give her life
Weeps for her people
Abandoned in the dust.
Each dragon will find
Of the people
Their one Concubine
Blessed to live and serve
A treasure above all.

As Gaelan's deep voice rang sonorously through the mountains, Fisher remembered Temple stories from his childhood, about how the world came to be, and that the Blue Goddess had come to the Icy Wastes to protect the Yeudan and show them how to thrive.

The ringing silence after Gaelan finished singing made Fisher gulp. He stared at Gaelan as his mind swirled and twirled. Was there truth in the words? "Is your mother descended from one of them?"

"No."

Fisher relaxed against the rock and lifted his face to the sun. It was just a legend, then. Not history. Gaelan wasn't really descended from the gods.

"My mother *is* Sapphirus, ageless and ever, one of the dragon gods."

Fisher narrowed his eyes. Gaelan seemed to believe what he was saying. Could the Blue Goddess just be a dragon like him? "I never really believed she existed. I thought it was all simply a way for the temple to control everyone."

"Some of them use her that way, but that doesn't mean she doesn't exist."

"Stop sounding so reasonable. You're talking about a whole heap of dragon gods ruling the world. Where does that leave us?" He waved in a wide arc to indicate the whole land and all its people.

"It leaves you exactly where you've always been. Whether or not you believe in us, we exist. Nothing has changed beyond your understanding of the world."

"Bullshit. Everything has changed. Three months ago, I was an Exile working my way through the ranks and protecting my mother the best I could. There were no dragon gods, except one legend of the Yeudan. There were no dragons at all. Now... He was unable to take a deep breath. Spots swam in front of his face. If he'd been standing, he'd have fallen over.

Gaelan shuffled closer and cupped his cheeks. "Breathe. Everything is going to be fine."

"Fine?" he squeaked. An honest-to-gods squeak. "There really are gods, aren't there? You're not just very old dragons."

"I'm not old at all!" Gaelan snapped, then he took a breath and smiled sheepishly at him. "Sorry. Yes, there really are gods, and we're dragons."

Fisher looked out into the valley where the dragons still sunned themselves. "Are they all gods?"

"No. I told you. Most dragons only live a few hundred years—normal lifespans. There's only my mother, and my aunts and uncles, and their progeny... and ours."

Fisher couldn't take a breath. "Yours? You have children?"

Gaelan chuckled and planted a quick kiss on his lips. Fisher recoiled and bumped his head against the rock. "This isn't funny."

"I know." Although he still grinned as if he thought Fisher was hilarious. He slid his arms around Fisher and drew him closer.

Fisher sighed and snuggled in. He knew he was avoiding what could possibly be one of the most important pieces of knowledge he'd ever have, but Gaelan's arms around him always seemed to make him think everything would work out in the end, no matter how bad it seemed at that moment.

"I don't have any children yet." He drew back enough to kiss Fisher's forehead. "I hope we have children at some time in the future."

"We can't have children. We're both men." Belatedly, Fisher realized he should have protested the having children at all and him being party to it, not the gender thing. Gaelan was a self-confessed god; an actual, real-life god. If he wanted to have children, he could probably make it happen.

Gaelan kissed his forehead again. "We'll work it out together." He glanced down into the valley. "Time to meet the king." He stood, holding a hand out to Fisher.

The words had barely left Gaelan's mouth than there was a crack of air and wings, and the first dragon lifted into the air. As if there'd been a call to action, one by one the dragons rose, and settled into a loose formation and flew toward them.

Fisher stood. "Did you do that?"

Gaelan grinned and shrugged, gesturing to the narrow pathway around the lip of the mountain. They climbed some more then stopped in a large, flat clearing before the mouth of a cave.

A large golden Mafdeti stepped from the gloom. The sun caught the red, orange and gold in his long, flowing hair. His eyes, at first green, flashed silver briefly as he scowled at them. "Fisher," Checa said. "You keep turning up." He turned his glare to Gaelan. Fisher shifted so he was between them.

Heath burst from the cave and jogged toward them, his tortoiseshell hair streaming behind him in a sensuous waterfall. "Fisher! You came back." He tugged Fisher into a rough hug. "We never thanked you for getting us out of those cages. Where did you disappear to?"

Fisher pushed him away and stepped back, more because he wasn't used to such casual intimacy than the scowl Checa had on his face. "You're the ones who disappeared. I stayed there to clean up the mess you left behind."

"We already got the information we needed and our dragons Kimi and Staton were getting worried. It was better to go with them before they destroyed the city." He walked over to Gaelan, his eyes narrowing and his smile hardening. "You've been here before."

"Not for a long time. I'm Gaelan."

Heath continued to stare at him, then jumped and looked at Checa, a guilty flush coloring his cheeks. "Staton says you're all right, so come on in. Kimi found some new fruit on one of her expeditions west. She's decided she's going to explore as much of the country as she can while she's waiting for our Adventure to begin. Bran and Dawn go with her as often as they can."

"Bran and Dawn?" Fisher shared a stunned look with Gaelan before he glanced at Checa, who was shaking his head but wore an amused smile.

"Rim and Ardelle's dragons. They don't get out as much as they'd like because Ardelle is a princess and there's a war coming and Rim has his own people to look after, but we still see them when the moons kiss."

Fisher instinctively looked at the sky but the moons weren't there. Since the eclipse, the moons' orbits had been diverging until they chased each other across the sky. Once a month their edges merged in a gentle kiss that lost depth each time. Soon, the moons would once again follow separate paths.

The breeze gusted strong enough to make Fisher stumble. He turned and was confronted by a large black dragon with red eyes who snuffled at Checa before landing and blocking the entrance to the cave. A gold dragon with swirling golden eyes landed beside him. The other dragons from the valley hovered around and above them until Checa spoke.

"Staton, could you ask Rock and Walrus to patrol this area? Jade can take a team and do a sweep of the Pass and the lower reaches. Make sure we're undisturbed." He turned to look at the black dragon. "I know." Checa ran his hands through his hair and sighed. "If you'll move your butt, we can get them inside and you can do your thing."

Fisher gripped Gaelan's arm as he went to walk past him. "Wait." He looked around, noting the strategic positions of the dragons flying around them and the two on the ground near them. "We came to tell you most of Barthes has been destroyed by fire, but the militia wasn't there. They're probably already in place. I hope you're ready for it." He looked around again. "You don't need to monitor us or anything; we aren't staying."

Heath slumped. "Oh, we thought..." He cut a glance at Checa and shrugged. "Company would be nice. You can stay for lunch, can't you?"

Fisher had orchestrated too many ambushes and kidnappings to accept that at face value. He held his ground. Gaelan stayed quiet, allowing him to retain his hold on his wrist. "What's really going on?"

Checa stepped forward. "I know why you don't want to stay." At Fisher's raised eyebrows, he amended his statement. "Why you can't stay. We won't hold you against your will, but Staton says there's something in the cave you must see."

"What is it?"

Checa's eyes briefly glowed silver again. "He won't tell me. Just keeps saying you must see it. You're the only one who can."

"Why me?"

"From one dragon to another." A grin spread across Heath's face.

"He must mean you," Fisher said to Gaelan. "Go and have a look at whatever this is, then we can go to the catacombs and find out what the Exiles have been up to."

Checa stepped in front of him. "Staton is the Dragon King. He means you." He turned to Gaelan. "I'm sure you understand that he can't have such a powerful dragon in his sanctuary until you're needed."

"How is Fisher permitted?"

Fisher scoffed. "Obviously because I'm not a dragon. Wait here and I'll go and have a look at whatever I'm supposed to." He looked into Gaelan's brilliant eyes. "If I don't come out in ten minutes, come find me."

"I'll come for you." Gaelan glared at Checa, then at Staton. "I'll destroy the mountain if I have to."

Fisher's lips twitched at the image that presented and he patted Gaelan's shoulder. "I'll be back soon."

"Be nice, Staton," called Checa as the black dragon ducked under the dark rock and disappeared into the gloom.

Fisher followed, holding onto the warm fuzzy flowing through him after Gaelan's declaration of rescue if he needed it, and refusing to allow the trepidatious butterflies following an unknown dragon into a pitch-black cave brought to his stomach.

After half a dozen steps, a red light flared, two pinpoints about fifty feet in front.

You aren't aware of your worth, are you, Concubine?

Fisher jerked. Until now, Gaelan was the only person—dragon—who had spoken in his mind.

Only kin and mates have that ability.

"I'm not a dragon. How could you and I be kin? We're certainly not mates." He took a few more tentative steps, not sure he wanted to be closer to a dragon that thought he was going to be his concubine. "And I'm not a concubine," he said, asserting his position.

A snort was followed by a spicy smoke wafting in the crimson light. *It's always hardest for those chosen.*

The light moved, panning across the cave floor, picking out all the dips and ridges Fisher had to avoid. "You're the light. It's your eyes glowing red." With the almost constant state of adrenaline-fueled excitement of the past couple of weeks, his heart felt like it would never beat at a normal rate again.

It must be some sort of change fatigue or something, for him to respond to seeing a huge dragon with glowing red eyes with little more than statement of fact. He was more exhausted and overwrought than he'd thought. It wasn't the sort of thing he would ever become used to. Until a few months ago, dragons hadn't existed.

Staton didn't respond other than to move his lumbering body out of the way and shine his red light into a shallow alcove.

Fisher stepped forward curiously, categorizing the shapes he saw. Judging by the drawings of the sun and moons at various stages of waxing and waning, the mural was designed to tell a story over a period of time. It took a few minutes for him to work out which direction the story was told.

He began at the top because of the sun and moons marking time. The drawing directly below was of two dragons, necks and legs entwined intimately, wings spread in flight. They were obviously lovers. Fluttering around them were several smaller dragons. There was nothing childlike about the images, but Fisher was certain the small dragons were children.

His gaze wandered down the wall, taking in the other sets of images, but kept returning to the lovers at the top. A need to find out what happened to the lovers had him skipping over the rest of the story and focusing on the image at the bottom.

Low on the wall, sections were missing, possibly because the paint could have easily been rubbed off. He could just make out the image of a man with a sword fending off a dragon. The picture reminded him so strongly of his first altercation with Gaelan in his dragon form that he laughed.

That's when he realized the top wasn't the beginning of the story. It was the end. In between the bottom and the top were various sets of drawings. The central one showed a direct progression from the initial conflict to the happy family above. Others showed divergences; what would happen if the man rejected the dragon.

Of the five stories, three showed the death of the dragon, one the death of the man. Only the central story led to the happy image above, but it too indicated the man would die. It wasn't difficult to put himself in the place of the man, and Gaelan as one of the dragons.

Choose the path you want to follow.

He jumped at Staton's voice in his head, so absorbed in the tales in front of him he'd forgotten the dragon was there.

Choose the path you want to follow, Staton repeated. *Touch it.*

Mesmerized, he reached out. And paused. He'd instinctively been going to touch the central path, the one leading to love and family—belonging—but was that what he should do? Shouldn't he want to destroy the dragons? They presented a threat to the status quo. With their strength and abilities, no mere human could ever hope to win a war against them. How many people would he condemn to death if he chose a path that left the dragons alive?

You must choose, Concubine. Your will determines the future.

"I'm not a concubine," refuted Fisher without heat. In his mind, he saw the way Gaelan rolled his eyes every time he said that. Even he was getting tired of hearing it.

He turned to look back at the entrance of the cave. A man stood there, silhouetted against the light. Fisher couldn't see any features, but he knew it was Gaelan waiting for him.

The way he always waited for him.

"Fuck it," he mumbled. He might be condemning his people to a lifetime of war, but they were heading to war anyway, even without the dragons. He couldn't bring himself to condemn Gaelan—for he was sure it was Gaelan in the paintings—to death. He didn't know who the other dragon was with Gaelan in the paintings, but it didn't matter. Gaelan deserved happiness, and choosing a future that would provide him with that was the best he could do, even if he died in the attempt.

He reached out and touched the center path.

His hand sank into the stone, a sensation at once familiar but also terrifyingly different. He stepped back and tugged his arm, but this rock wouldn't release him.

Blue-gray light sparked around his hand as if the rock itself was exploding and reforming around him. The rock sucked him in farther, his wrist disappearing into the cool black depths.

He slammed his other hand against the wall to push, but that hand sank too. He cried out, scrabbling his feet against the graveled floor, trying to pull out of the wall.

The sparks of light increased in frequency, becoming brighter and lighter until the blue was almost leached out of them. Fisher sank up to his elbows. He intensified his struggles but none of it helped.

Don't fight it. Gaelan's voice was in his head, dark and soothing.

"I can't get out!" he panted, unable to draw in a complete breath as the granite ate its way up his arms. Cold enveloped his hands, pricking at his fingertips like dressmakers' pins.

It is as it's meant to be, intoned Staton.

"Not helping! Get me out of here."

Gaelan's arms came around his chest as he rested against his back. Fisher wasn't sure when he'd begun associating Gaelan with warmth and security, but his immediate relaxation clearly indicated he did. *You know you can breathe through rock*, said Gaelan, his hot breath gusting over his ear.

"What if I can't get out? Ever?"

Gaelan's chest pressed against his back and his hold tightened, his arms crossing over Fisher's stomach and chest. *Whatever happens, I'll be with you.*

"By the Goddess, I hope you are. That way I can kill you as soon as I'm free of this." He tugged at his arms again but only managed to strain his shoulders.

Relax, Fisher. Let it happen.

"Why are you talking to me in my head? You're right here."

In the rock, that's all we'll have. He kissed Fisher's neck, causing an entirely different kind of shudder to overtake him.

"We can't go through this rock, Gaelan." He struggled again. "It's too thick. We'll get stuck there."

The rock will release us once it's over.

"When what's over? What the hell did I do? All I did was touch the picture."

Whichever path you chose will come to fruition. When we're released you'll understand.

"You keep saying that I'll understand, but you never bother to explain anything to me. Why won't you tell me anything?"

I can't explain what I don't yet know. My trust is in the Goddess, just as yours needs to be.

Fisher was just about to assert that the Blue Goddess didn't exist, but he'd seen her in the glacier. "She's a dragon, not a real goddess."

That doesn't change the fact that we must await her pleasure with this ritual.

"Ritual?" He sounded hysterical, which was understandable because he felt bloody hysterical. Every tiny nerve ending quivered and jumped in protest at the cold rock gradually oozing over his skin.

He squeaked as his boots tore from his feet. He'd never lost his clothes in the rock before. He was sure, regardless of every other time he'd entered rock, that he wouldn't be able to breathe in this one.

He was going to die, and he was going to take Gaelan with him. They'd both be dead, and there'd be no one left to remember them. Gaelan's mother would remember him and Checa and Heath would probably remember Fisher for a few weeks. He was nothing to them, so it wouldn't be any longer.

Gaelan released his hold on his chest. Fisher was just about to protest when Gaelan's hand cupped his jaw and turned his head. He lost all will to argue once Gaelan's lips covered his. He groaned and relaxed into the kiss, leaning back against Gaelan, trusting him to hold him up.

Cold rock crawled up his legs and around his groin. His pants melted away and the cool stone met Fisher's warm flesh. He jerked but Gaelan held him steady and deepened the kiss. He sighed, trying to get his heartbeat to slow. Gaelan was there, so Fisher would still be able to breathe.

Wait. Gaelan's gills only worked in water. *He* was the one who could breathe in rock. It was up to *him* to save Gaelan this time. *Don't let go*, he thought frantically. *Stay with me.*

Wherever you are, I will be. Wherever you go, I will follow, until the end of my days.

The words sounded like a promise, not just the reassurance he clearly intended. They sounded like a vow that would follow them much farther than the thickness of this rock.

It would follow them to the ends of time.

They were deep in the rock now, completely surrounded. The cool silence enveloped him and calmed much of his panic. He turned, swimming in the viscous rock, until he and Gaelan were pressed chest to chest, groin to groin, their kiss shifting and settling into a devotion he had once dreamed could be his... until others ripped his life from him and threw him away.

Gaelan pulled him closer, the brush of his hard cock against Fisher's, tossing all thoughts from his head.

They rutted against each other. Fisher grew harder and fuller until his skin stretched and itched. He felt as if his whole body had grown and would explode when he came.

He groaned into Gaelan's mouth and clutched at him, his fingers digging into his flesh, bruising in their need to be part of him. One with him. Gaelan's fingers dug into his as well, cupping his buttocks, grinding them together.

You complete me, whispered Gaelan as he pressed against him.

Stay with me. It was more than a plea for them to come together. It was his need to always have Gaelan by his side. A companion, a friend, a lover. Partners through life.

Always.

The vow whispered through his mind and settled deep into his body as it strained toward Gaelan. Fisher deepened the kiss, breathing with Gaelan and for him, but also memorizing his taste and the feel of his lips against him.

Around them, the rock pulsed and breathed with them, squeezing and scraping gently, heightening his pleasure until it had nowhere to go but out. His orgasm began with the usual tingly tightening behind his balls and rapidly spread through his body until every cell felt ready to disintegrate in a shower of multicolored sparks.

And then they did.

Tightness that edged toward pain dug into his skin and seized his muscles. Beneath his fingers, Gaelan also went rigid. Fire raced through Fisher from the base of his brain to his tailbone and fluttered throughout his body, searing nerves and muscles and mind before it settled, scalded in his balls and pulsed through his cock, shooting icy-cold semen to mix with Gaelan's as he came too.

After the first volley, Fisher slammed his mouth back on Gaelan, swallowed his struggling breaths and returned them.

The rock pelted them with stinging grains and sucked up their combined semen, then pushed them out to tumble down the side of the mountain.

Fisher landed in an untidy, painful heap on a narrow outcropping, his legs dangled over the edge and his shoulder wedged under a rock. As the sound of rocks and pebbles tumbling down the mountain faded, the sharp pains made themselves known and he groaned. He opened his eyes to find the sky above milky-white with a rapidly graying center. As he watched, the sky rolled over and darkened some more.

Clouds. A fat drop of rain landed on his cheek, almost warm against his chilled skin. A second later, another landed on his chest. *It's going to rain.* He tried to roll over, but his shoulder was still wedged under the edge of a rock and he couldn't get any traction with his legs dangling off the mountain.

On the third attempt, after the skies had opened up and heavy rain washed over his naked body, his battered brain finally kicked in and he remembered Gaelan had been with him. He wasn't on the outcropping with him.

He craned his head but could see nothing through the trees marching down the mountainside, green-gray sentinels in the downpour.

"Gaelan!" His voice was drowned in the roar of water crashing through the leaves of the trees and washing its way down the mountain. A high-pitched *ping-ping* heralded another rockslide, led by stones and pebbles bouncing down the slope.

The rock at his shoulder moved, rocking first toward him, making him cry out in pain as it rolled onto his shoulder, then away from him, releasing its hold on him.

He quickly rolled and scrambled more securely onto solid ground. He tucked his legs close to his torso and ducked his head, trembling as the earth shook and increasingly larger rocks pelted past him, some bouncing glancing blows on his back.

As quickly as it began, the rockslide finished. Fisher opened his eyes to see earth and rock inches from his face. Gingerly, he tested his range of motion and found he could roll over. He groaned as the movement put pressure on his shoulder but was soon able to sit upright, only to find the rock surrounded him. Where he sat was rock-free, but there was little room for movement. Between the rocks, he could see the sky—brilliant blue, sparkling through the clouds, chasing them eastward.

Fisher pushed his hand at the rocks, targeting the gaps but none were large enough for him to push through. The rocks remained solid.

He pushed harder, straining his muscles until his injured shoulder screamed with the pain. He pounded his fists against the spot that showed the most light. "Come on, you bastard," he ground out as a fist-sized rock. "You're barely even resting there. There's nothing holding you in. Why won't you move?"

His breath came faster, billowing out of him in time with his panicked pounding. Sharp edges cut into the meat of his hands until the rock face glowed red and blood ran down his forearms.

Finally, he stopped, sweat running over him, dripping from the ragged ends of his hair. His breathing was loud and hot in the small space.

He leaned back, his arms limp beside him. Every muscle ached from the exertion. He glared at his rocky prison. "Bloody granite. At least with sandstone, I could grind bits away." His breath caught in his throat.

The rocks were granite.

He'd be able to move through them.

He sidled forward to peer through a gap. To the front was a drop down the mountain. Behind him was the mountain itself. Beside him was the only viable option.

He reached out and pressed his hand against the rock, shocked when he met resistance. He mustn't be concentrating the way he should. He took several deep breaths, closed his eyes, imagined moving through the rock like he had before, and pushed again.

Nothing.

There must be another type of rock on the other side, like there had been sandstone at the temple. He leaned against the rock and focused his thoughts but couldn't read the rock the way he'd been able to since he arrived on Linspar.

He couldn't read the rock.

He couldn't pass through the rock.

His heart pounded, his eyes burned, and he felt stupid. Until a few weeks before, he hadn't been able to do any of it. Now he couldn't again and it felt like it was the end of the world. It wasn't just because he couldn't escape from his impromptu tomb. It was that it was the only thing he could do that no one else could. Not even Gaelan.

Gaelan! Was he trapped too? He had been with Fisher when the mountain spat them out.

"Gaelan!" He called again and again, but there was no answer. No rescue. He was alone again, as he'd always been. Maybe Gaelan was dead. He couldn't come.

His vision blurred as he imagined a similar tomb near the one that confined him. Only Gaelan was in there. And he was dead.

"Gaelan!" He screamed as he pounded on the rocks in front of him. He kept calling until his voice was little more than a ragged whisper and his breath came in hot, burning gasps and his tears mingled with the stinging sweat.

The sobs overtook him. He curled into himself, reaching one limp fist out to thump the rock. He froze when a low rumbling accompanied a grating screech of rock sliding against rock.

He looked up instinctively, his tears drying as his stomach rolled in fear. No light showed between the rocks above him. What light permeated his small cave came from in front of him—where there was nothing but air and a long fall to certain death.

His breathing fractured and his heart pounded, but the new rock slide had at least broken his mindless panic. He refused to give in. He'd keep fighting until he couldn't fight anymore.

He pushed his back firmly against the mountainside, braced himself and began pounding at the rocks in front of him with his feet. If he could knock a couple out, he'd have enough room to crawl through and make his way down the mountain—provided the rocks above weren't relying on them to hold them in place so they didn't crush him.

The first kick accomplished nothing. The second, the same. The third time, his heel caught a glancing blow on a different rock and it shifted with a rolling groan. It twisted, creating a small indentation in the nearly perfect wall of his enclosed cave and all the rocks above it moved with it. By the time the noise and dust settled, his ceiling was several inches lower.

"Gaelan!" He screamed again and again, knowing it was pointless. His voice was so ruined, the sound would barely travel further than the rock surrounding him, but he could no more give up on believing—hoping—Gaelan was alive, than he could give up on himself.

"Gaelan!" His eyes burned as he thought of ending his days alone as he'd lived his life.

The ground began to shudder, a deep rumbling encompassed him and the rocks above him groaned and shrieked. He looked up warily, raising his arms above his head in a futile attempt to ward off the inevitable crushing. A new wave of sweat beaded his forehead, his skin prickling with heat.

The rocks began to glow, growing hotter and hotter until the center of each one was a vibrant orange-red overlaid with black tracings.

One of the rocks wobbled, then the one beside it did too. They were melting. He curled his legs up, crying out as pain lanced through his injured shoulder, but he couldn't move out of the way. The area was too small. His skin burned and blistered in the scorching heat.

The rock elongated, a long blob sagging, reaching for him. Then it dropped and landed on his leg, right over one of the pale patches of his skin, now red in the heat. It seared right to the bone.

He screamed.

CHAPTER TWENTY-TWO

ONCE, WHEN FISHER WAS a youth, a fire had swept through the catacombs and killed more than twenty people. In the aftermath, many were left horribly burned. He had been tasked with administering potions to ease the lives of those worst afflicted.

One victim, a burly soldier, was reduced to a shivering blackened husk. He took the potion offered, but told him in a hoarse, pained whisper that he didn't need it. While the burning made him scream so much his voice was gone, and the heat and smoke made his throat bleed and his chest cramp, his burns didn't hurt him at all. He just felt cold.

Fisher hadn't believed him.

He scrambled back as much as he could, brushed the thick, orange blob away, only to have it stick to his hand. He watched in horror, hands still brushing and shaking, as the molten rock sank into the flesh of his thigh, so deep he no longer felt it.

Another rock dipped and oozed, a red-hot bole ready to follow the previous one. His heart beat a frantic tattoo, his fingers scrabbling at the rocks in front of him, his body still functioning even as his mind refused to deal with the horror of what he was seeing.

Blisters on his chest and arms burst, the liquid running hot and sizzling over his hotter-than-hot skin.

That he felt.

The air, steamy from his own body fluid, was thick in his throat, searing the membranes, breaking his screams into hoarse whimpers.

He fumbled around, finally got his feet under him and his hands against the lowest of the rocks in his fiery tomb. Steam billowed around his palms as he pressed into the scorching granite. The scent of burning flesh made him gag, but he had to get out.

His muscles strained with his effort. Even over his hoarse screams and frantic, uneven breaths he heard them pop under the pressure as his tendons strained and snapped. He pushed harder, a roar building in him, coming out as a pained whisper.

The rocks bulged and bent, no longer scraping against each other but stretching like taffy. He kept pushing until he slid through, the molten rock gliding across his body like a caress, taking what was left of his skin with it.

He fell.

There was no ground beneath him. Only sky all around. The wind seared his burned eyes, but he refused to shut them. He would not die baked and broiled; he would choose his destiny and die flying through the cloud-scudded sky.

He screamed again as he forced his crippled limbs away from his body, stretched out, the pain soul-deep. Below him, thick red liquid rained down and spattered over the land far below. He watched it for a few seconds until his fevered mind told him what it was. His blood.

Fisher! Fly!

The words filled his mind and he embraced them. Yes. He was flying. He would fly right into the earth and the searing pain that skittered over his back and other parts not too badly burned would explode into nothingness.

Fisher!

A dark cloud scudded close to him, deep blue-purple. His tortured mind reached for it, knowing he would find comfort in its arms.

Fly with me. Damn it, Fisher. Fly.

The voice in his head was filled with a pain that mirrored what he felt. The voice shouldn't feel pain too. He had chosen the path that would let Gaelan live. Gaelan had to live. The Dragon King said so.

Yes, Fisher. It's me. Come fly with me.

A forgotten tune floated through his mind; something his mother used to sing to him as a child. *Come fly with me, fly away. Into the blue. Into the blue. Into the blue.* The phrase ran around his fractured mind. He snapped his arms out, then up and down, and closed his eyes. *Come fly with me*, he crooned. *Fly away, into the blue, blue, blue.*

The wind whipped at him, flayed every part of him, as hard as the burning rock had been, but it was good too. It made him feel larger. Impervious. Inviolable.

Free.

His arms snapped again, but this time, a sharp pain exploded in his back and a crack accompanied it. The wind lessened. So did the pain. His throat still burned, full and raw. He opened his mouth wide in a scream and heard a crackle. He opened his eyes to see yellow-orange flames shooting through the air in front of him.

He screamed again. More flames erupted.

From his mouth.

The flames were coming from his mouth. He clapped his hands over it, but they didn't reach. He looked down to find short arms covered in gray scales and tipped with charcoal-colored claws.

He swung his head to the side. A large, translucent gray wing stroked downward. He twisted to see where it came from, but the wing twisted away from him. Then he was on his back. The wind returned, folding two wings around him. He kicked out to get away from them, but his feet weren't feet. They were claws.

Fisher!

He swallowed the scream that built inside and looked for Gaelan.

There, at his feet, blue-scaled Gaelan flew toward him. He slid between his wildly flapping wings, over his clawed feet, folding his own wings at the last minute. Gaelan opened his mouth wide and sank his teeth into Fisher's neck. Needle pinpricks accompanied the pressure and shot white-hot pleasure through him.

Gaelan. For the first time since Fisher had pressed his hand against the mural, he relaxed. Gaelan was with him.

Open your wings, Fisher. You must fly or we'll both die.

You can't die. The mural said you'd live. He closed his eyes, swallowing against the pain in his throat and in his heart. Gaelan would live and find that other dragon and have babies, and be happy.

We live and die together, so you need to decide now. Is this the day we die? Or is it the day we live?

Together? His mind was fuzzy, still singed from being melted by burning rock. *You want us to be together?*

I made the promise in the rock. Do you remember? A promise in rock is as permanent as the rock it was made in. Granite is hard, the kind of rock that will last forever. That's how long my promise to you will last.

You really want me? Fisher cringed at the neediness coursing through him. He thought they'd dealt with this already, that he'd accepted that Gaelan did want him. But no one, save for his mother, had ever wanted him. No one had ever sounded like they needed him. It was difficult to believe, completely, that someone—this one person—needed him like air. *You're not just saying that so you don't die?*

Gaelan gave another tiny shake of his head, his teeth slipping between the small scales and sinking deeper into his neck. He shivered as Gaelan's teeth entered him, became part of his body.

And he knew. Gaelan would die for him. More than that. He would die with him.

Together, said Gaelan.

He wanted to laugh, felt it bubble up into his ruined throat, but he didn't trust only a laugh to come out and more flames right now would terrify him all over again.

He lifted his legs and sank his claws into Gaelan's hips, bringing their groins together. Then he rolled, twisted until he was on top with Gaelan clasped securely under him.

His wings snapped out of their own accord and they slowed their maddening descent. He lifted his head, his body following, and their dive corrected. He was flying, not falling.

They flew in a wide arc. The tops of the trees bowed under the force of their passing when they bottomed out. Fisher's tail—he had a tail—skimmed the leaves as they began to rise again.

They were still sunk deep into each other, teeth and claws, and each strong downward stroke and graceful upstroke of his wings rocked his body against Gaelan's abdomen. Another sensation swept through him, almost too much after the pain and terror he'd just endured. He groaned.

Yes.

Fisher froze—as much as he could with his wings still rocking their bodies together. *You're a dragon.*

So are you.

But— He wasn't a dragon. He caught sight of his gray wings, knew they were part of him, and felt particularly foolish. *I'm a dragon.*

And so am I.

Then...

It's perfectly fine. Gaelan groaned deep in his chest. *It's perfect.*

And it was.

Fisher took them high enough they could see over the mountain peaks, across the valley straight to the distant peaks that formed the barrier to the Icy Wastes.

The tension between them built the higher they climbed. Gaelan's teeth were still sunk into his neck but there was no pain, only a warm sense of belonging that grew into a raging need the more they rutted against each other.

Be sure of this, said Gaelan. *There's no going back from this.*

He laughed aloud, clamping his mouth closed when flame erupted. He swallowed and snorted when some smoke escaped his nostrils as if he were smoking a pipe. *I'm a fucking dragon. Literally, a fucking dragon. I'm pretty sure I got the message there's no going back.*

Gaelan shifted his hold on his neck, biting closer to his shoulder. Raw sensation flooded straight to his groin. He dug his claws deeper into Gaelan's hips, twisted his head and bit Gaelan's neck, exactly where Gaelan was clamped onto him.

Heat built, radiating from his chest until they were enveloped in a brilliant red glow, as if they were rock heated to melting point. Beneath him, Gaelan groaned, the sound of his climax as recognizable in this form as his human form. His semen washed between them like ice on a burn and triggered his own orgasm.

He lifted his head and roared, flames erupting from his mouth and shooting high into the sky. Unable to keep them open while pleasure roared through him, his wings folded and they plummeted, but he only noticed because the wind flowing past them fanned the flames of his desire and lengthened his orgasm. He screamed again, rutting against Gaelan's soft underbelly until he was empty and limp.

He opened his eyes to see the desert rushing toward them, so close he could see the dark pockmarks of the openings to the underground caverns carved into the dunes.

They were about to die and he couldn't find any fear within him. In that moment, he had everything he'd ever dreamed of. Until now, he'd never been good enough. Never worthy.

At least he'd had this one perfect moment of belonging and acceptance. That one moment was worth every other hardship he'd ever faced.

Thank you, he whispered in his mind. He closed his eyes to savor the feel of Gaelan's body crushed against his.

They twisted and turned again until Gaelan was on top. Then there was the crack of Gaelan's wings extending, catching the air, slowing their descent. Not enough, though. The sand still raced toward them no matter how much Gaelan strained to lift them.

They smashed into the ground. Fisher's claws and teeth were ripped from Gaelan and he bounced like a stone skipped on a still lake. He tumbled, his head smashed against a rock, his leg caught and bent painfully backward before releasing on the next somersault.

Finally, he came to a rolling stop, his head tucked under one leg, the other stuck awkwardly into the air and his tail trailing over the lot like some drooping flower after heavy rain. He groaned as he straightened himself out.

"Well, that worked better than I thought it would," said Gaelan beside him, back in his human form.

Fisher looked over in time to see clothes grow from Gaelan's rich brown skin. Jeans, boots, shirt, backpack, exactly the same as he'd worn the whole time Fisher had known him.

How did you do that? Fisher had opened his mouth to speak in the same manner that Gaelan did, but all that came out was a bellicose grumbling and a puff of smoke.

"Change to human." Gaelan placed a small granite stone on the ground in front of him then stepped back, his hands on his hips.

Fisher leaned forward to touch him but Gaelan stepped away and he tumbled forward.

"Change," Gaelan insisted.

He picked up the stone and huffed at it, sending a thin stream of smoke over it. *I don't know how I changed to dragon. How am I supposed to know how to change back?*

The smoke slid over the rock and billowed around them. By the time it cleared, he stood in the sand on two feet. Naked, heart pounding. He slapped his hands over his body—shoulders, arms, chest, legs, butt, groin—reassuring himself all his bits were back where they should be. Then something odd caught his attention.

"Where are my patches?" His skin was a smooth even-toned caramel color. "There are no scars either." All the injuries he'd gained recently were healed. He ran his hands over himself, everywhere he could reach but his fingers met only smooth brown skin. "I was burned." He broke into a sweat, as if it was happening again.

Gaelan embraced him, ran his hands up and down his back. "Easy now. It's over. You're fine." He stepped back but kept his hands cupped around his shoulders. "That was the conversion. It blended both parts of you into one. That's why your skin is now a blend of the two original colors."

Fisher's mind spun with questions. His fractured breathing told him he was a couple of breaths from panic, but he found he could push it down with Gaelan close. If he started asking his questions, he'd revisit the molten rock sinking into his skin and nothing would bring him back from that.

He stared at Gaelan's clothing. "How do I get some clothes? Mine were destroyed when I went into the rock." He still held the granite stone and, as he spoke, the air swirled around him, twisting and turning in a mini whirlwind that eventually settled.

His clothing was the same style as it had been since he'd settled in the desert—thick-soled desert boots, wide-legged pants tucked into them, knee-length tunic, lightweight robe and a large cashmere scarf.

The difference was in the colors. What was once the sandy colors of the desert was now all gray like the smoky quartz embedded in granite.

Fisher exhaled. "I could get used to this." The self-reassurance was shaky, so he brushed his hands down his tunic, pretending there was sand there, but really needing time to steady his legs so he knew he'd be able to walk without stumbling.

"You're going to have to," said Gaelan. "This is your life now." He turned away, gazing southward. "Where do we go from here?"

Right. He had just been sucked into a mountain, spat out to fall down a cliff, trapped in an impervious rock cave which then melted all over him. He'd been burned alive, had fallen off a cliff, almost died, turned into a dragon and had the best sex of his life—twice—and all Gaelan had to say was "get used to it" and "where to now?"

He swallowed against the hysteria bubbling inside. Gaelan was right. He couldn't give into it now, not while they were standing in the middle of the desert with no shelter, water or food. The desert was the primary hunting grounds of the norrgel, and they were miles from anything that could protect them.

The mountains were at their back, several miles away, but looming over them like benevolent monks. Fisher stared at them for a long time before he realized what concerned him. When they had entered the mountain, they had been in the valley—on the northern side. Now they were on the southern side of the range. Their trip through the rock had taken them right through the mountain. "They're miles deep."

As far as he could see there was sand and dunes and, every now and then, a sandstone spire; a monument to the origins of the desert. "I lived here for twenty years and never noticed how big it is."

All of him was different, not just his skin. His essence, whatever it was that made him *him*, had changed.

He looked at the stone in his hand. He curled his fingers over it and the tips sank into the stone until they met his palm. The stone remained the same, solid for everyone but him. He could move through rock. He could breathe in rock. He could turn into a dragon. He'd even learned to swim when he couldn't before. Was there any part of him that was the same? Who was he now?

"Fisher." Gaelan stood in front of him, his hands rubbing up and down Fisher's arms, like sandpaper on his new, sensitive skin, even through the clothes. When had Gaelan moved? Why hadn't he noticed?

Fisher was trembling again, great wracking shudders that threatened to knock him off his feet. Only Gaelan held him steady. There was only Gaelan to pull him against his body and hold him close and warm against the sudden chill of fear. Only Gaelan who whispered, "You'll be all right," and other nonsense he couldn't promise. Only Gaelan who waited through the storm until he could breathe again and wipe his face dry and could stand on his own again.

"Better?" Gaelan asked.

Better than what? He wanted to ask but didn't. He was better than being drowned or trapped in rock or burned alive. He didn't know about anything else. He nodded, then walked into the desert.

After half an hour, Gaelan broke the silence. "We could fly, you know. It would be good for you to get some practice."

He looked at the sky, white-pocked blue with black spots of hunting norrgel. His body remembered the sensations of flying with Gaelan, in his claws, in his mouth, on his back. He remembered falling off the mountain and the ground racing toward him, the pain of rushing wind and raw flesh, and shuddered. "I'll walk." Walking was normal, and he desperately needed normal.

Gaelan nodded then continued in silence for a dozen paces. "What made you think the Exiles have the Elixir?"

"Something the Abbott said about sacrifice. It might be nothing, but we can't risk anyone continuing to make it."

"You know it doesn't matter how much we eradicate it. Someone will reconstruct the recipe and begin production again."

"Then we'll find them and shut them down as well. Enough people die from norrgel poisoning without someone turning it into a business. Not even the Goddess has power over who lives and who dies, or how or when that happens." It felt strange to be thinking "we", not "I" when he hadn't been sure if what they had would last past the desert, but Fisher was beginning to believe Gaelan meant what he said, and would continue to mean it. He and Gaelan were partners.

"So we go in, blow the place up, make sure there aren't any hidden stores, and go back home?"

"We're not blowing anything up." He glared at Gaelan.

"With them making the Elixir, most of them will be addicted anyway. If they stop taking it, they'll die."

"We don't know for sure they're making the Elixir or taking it, and I'm not storming in there blowing things up and taking over on the off chance they might have some of it there. We go in carefully and only destroy the Elixir. Nothing else."

Barthes going up in flames was enough to give him nightmares for years. "People live in the catacombs. It's the only home they have. I'm not going to destroy that, or them. We're only after the Elixir."

Gaelan sidestepped until he was right beside him and flung an arm around his shoulders. "You're a good man, Fisher. So we'll do it your way, then go home. Right?"

"Right."

It wasn't until Fisher saw Gaelan's grin that he realized what he'd said. He was going home with Gaelan.

Wherever that might be.

CHAPTER TWENTY-THREE

AT SUNSET, THE NORRGEL began flying east, toward the mountains where their nests were. Their flight path brought them directly over Fisher and Gaelan.

Fisher knew when they'd been spotted as an ear-splitting screech split the air. "You are *not* eating any norrgel. We do this my way." He looked for cover. There was nearly always a sandstone outcropping he could dig under enough to be out of range. Sometimes he'd laid down in the open with just his sand-colored clothes as camouflage. Those had been harrowing times and not always successful—he'd lost good people to the norrgel.

There were no outcroppings close enough this time, and his clothes were gray, not ochre. "This way," he called to Gaelan.

He began running to the closest lump of sandstone, knowing it wouldn't be enough cover for even one of them, but with no other options. He hated being caught in the open.

Behind him, there was a whoosh. A flurry of sand washed over him. He looked back to find Gaelan, his blue scales glinting, lift off and fly directly toward the norrgel.

The norrgel scattered, black dots exploding across the blue sky like a starburst. Flames erupted—brilliant orange-red with a tanzanite blue center. Norrgel dived and wheeled evasively.

Darker blue glinted against the pale blue sky as Gaelan turned. Fire shot across the sky again and one bird was caught in the flames.

Still burning, it plummeted with Gaelan in pursuit. The rest of the norrgel wheeled south before continuing their flight east, leaving Fisher unaccosted, and the desert air once again silent.

The dying light revealed a darker blue shape separating from the sky; Gaelan returning with roasted norrgel. The smell of burned feathers and entrails was enough to put Fisher off the birds as food, even without the fact they were highly poisonous.

"Why are you bringing that here? Why did you even cook it? Surely there was another way you could have scared the birds off?" He nearly echoed Gaelan's derisive snort. He'd spent his life in kill-or-be-killed societies. There was no reason for him to avoid killing anything that stood in the way of his continued survival, particularly something such as a norrgel that could kill him with one swipe of its feathers.

Gaelan used a claw to neatly slice into the bird, cutting off a chunk of succulent-looking breast meat. It didn't smell any better than the rest of it. Fisher stepped back.

Gaelan changed back to his human form and stood holding the meat out to him. "It's a ritual—me providing for you."

"I can provide for myself."

"I know you can but I'd still like you to try this."

"It's norrgel. Poisonous."

"You're a dragon now. You can eat it."

"It stinks."

"But it tastes wonderful." His smile took on a dreamy quality.

Fisher stepped forward and snatched the meat out of his hand. "There's no way *you're* going to eat any of this. Not after last time."

Gaelan gave him a sheepish look. "This can be all for you."

Fisher sniffed at the meat. Okay, it didn't smell as bad as he'd said it did. "You're sure this won't kill me?"

"As a dragon, you're immune."

He bit off a piece of meat and chewed. Strong. Gamey. He swallowed. Ugh. Bitter aftertaste. He tossed the meat on the remains of the bird. "No offense, but it's disgusting."

"You don't like it?" Gaelan sounded bewildered.

"No."

"Not at all?"

"If there was nothing else available and I was starving, I'd eat it, but it'll never be a food of choice."

Gaelan stared at the cooked bird as if it had personally insulted him. Then he grinned. "But you ate it. I provided for you."

He rolled his eyes. "Yes, you provided for me." Why did that seem so important to Gaelan?

He wiped his hands on his trousers and continued walking, only to collapse after half a dozen steps when his stomach cramped and his chest tightened. He couldn't breathe. He needed to vomit.

He dug his fingers into the sand, retching, spewing up bright blood. His insides were melting, the pain so fierce he couldn't make a sound, even though his mind was screaming.

Norrgel is poisonous. The threads dissolved you from the outside, the meat dissolved you from the inside. Either way you ended up as black sludge on the ground—norrgel food.

He retched again. This time the blood was aflame; a deep, rich red around the edges, brilliant blue in the center. He closed his eyes, dropped to his side and curled into a ball in the futile hope his arms around his stomach would hold him together.

Bright spots flickered and he squeezed his eyes closed tighter, tighter, burning liquid dribbling from his mouth and nose and leaking from his eyes.

"What's happening?" Gaelan's voice echoed as if he was in the catacombs.

Stupid dragon. Pain hit him again and he groaned. Couldn't Gaelan see what was happening?

He was dying.

Immune! Fucking dragon.

He rolled, cramped, and cried out with pain. He buried his face against his knees, wishing he'd lose consciousness. Wishing it was over already.

He got his wish.

HE OPENED HIS EYES to a sky full of stars and a silence that only ever happens in the desert. Not even a breeze stirred the air, except for the small puffs of warm air at his nape. Gaelan.

That meant the norrgel meat hadn't killed him. Fisher moved his leg but stopped on a groan as every muscle in his body protested.

Behind him, Gaelan stirred. "Don't move yet. It'll take some time for your muscles to repair."

"Fuck you," he rasped through his burning throat. *You poisoned me, you bastard.* He thought the words as loudly as he could but even then they echoed through his mind in a barely-there whisper.

He closed his eyes and concentrated on breathing evenly and slowly. Deep breaths hurt. Moving hurt. Squeezing his eyes closed hurt.

He groaned. That hurt too.

"It'll pass soon. You're going to be fine."

Why should I trust you? You fucking poisoned me. A careful breath. *I should be dead.* Another careful breath. *Why aren't I dead?* Fisher shouldn't still be talking to Gaelan. He should get as far from him as he could.

"I'm so sorry. I thought it would be all right. You're a dragon. Norrgel shouldn't affect you like that."

You thought. Fisher held himself very still as he panted through his anger. And everything hurt, even his eyelashes as they rested against his cheeks. That was the only thing that could explain the tears leaking from between his lids.

"Your dragon saved you. It took over, came out when you needed it." A tentative hand scraped down his arm but retreated when he groaned from the pain.

He couldn't have Gaelan touch him. As long as he kept perfectly still the pain was manageable. Finally, his breathing eased and he slept.

He woke with the first cries of norrgel returning to their hunting grounds—black dots against the streaked pink and blue sky. None of the flocks came near where he lay in the rapidly warming sand.

He lay still, unwilling to revisit the agony. His throat was thick and thirsty, his lips beginning to peel and crack. He needed to find water soon, and to do that he'd have to move.

Lethargy tangled with his fear of pain and he stayed where he was, nestled in the sand with the growing heat of the sun soaking through his clothing and burning his face and hands. He drifted in a powdery haze until his dry throat forced him to swallow, bringing a groan and a grimace.

He rolled onto his back. The sky was a faded cerulean blue streaked with golden light. The norrgel were gone, flown west in their never-ending search for food.

Beside him, Gaelan looked around the desert. "I don't know what is edible in the desert, except for norrgel."

Fisher shuddered. "Neither of us is ever eating norrgel again."

Gaelan grinned like he'd been given a prize. "Let's find these Exiles and any Elixir they might have. Then we can go home and you can berate me about the norrgel."

He held his hand out to Fisher, who eyed it suspiciously before giving in and grasping it. One short tug had him on his feet and stumbling into Gaelan's chest. Gaelan steadied him, keeping hold of his hand, and began walking to the south-west. "How far away is the first entrance to the catacombs?"

Fisher shrugged as he looked around. On the horizon, a red lump shimmered. That was probably the mesa under which the Exile headquarters was located.

Between it and them were several lumps of rock, like pimples on the corrugated surface of the desert. Any one of them could be entrances, but none looked familiar.

"My area was closer to Hawkesby. Before that, I was stationed in the west. I don't know the northern territories very well on the surface. I could have walked past a dozen entrances and not seen them."

He looked around, feeling more at home in the wide-open desert than he had in the crowded streets of Linspar or in Barthes. Here, he could see the norrgel in the distance, and had plenty of time to find shelter. In the city, they'd be on top of him before he knew what direction their cries were coming from.

"Would you recognize them from the air?" asked Gaelan.

"Some, probably. I've never been up high over the desert. Some of them are open to the air but surrounded by boulders so they'd be visible from the air but not at ground level."

He pointed to an outcropping of sandstone boulders worn into fantastical shapes by the blowing sand. "We should check those out. There's probably a section that would be easier to get through."

He pointed to a shallow indentation in the sand. "That dip there is probably nothing more than sand blown over to that dune but it seems a little too oddly shaped for just the wind." He changed direction to investigate.

"It's farther away than it seems," said Gaelan after a few minutes.

"Things in the desert always are. And you always need more food and water than you think you should." He frowned at the empty water skin.

"Is there water underground?"

"Of course. That's how the Exiles survive. They live near huge underground reservoirs and even grow vegetable plots in sections that are somewhat open to the surface."

"Why don't we fly?"

Fisher stopped. "You're bound and determined to fly everywhere, aren't you?"

Gaelan shrugged. "It's quick and it's easy, and we don't have to carry a lot of food and water with us all the time."

He sighed, loathe to admit it but knowing he had to. "I don't think I can change to a dragon right now. Between the norrgel poisoning and dehydration, I'm too tired to concentrate." Both times he'd changed to dragon had been out of his control and full of searing pain: not something he wanted to revisit.

Gaelan grasped his shoulder. "Because you weren't born dragon, it might never be an easy thing for you, but you don't have to change. You've flown with me before so we can do that again."

"You don't mind me sitting on you while you're flying? I thought that was just those few times because it was an emergency."

"You can fly with me even when it's not an emergency."

Fisher was more tired that he'd been willing to admit to Gaelan or himself. "Okay. Let's fly. We'll go to an entrance I know well. That will put us close to the Exile headquarters."

Gaelan grinned, leaned forward and planted a quick kiss on his lips, then stepped back. "You remember how to position your legs to be secure?"

At Fisher's nod, he took a small blue stone out of his pocket and breathed on it. There was a flash of blue light, then Gaelan the dragon stood before him, an excited gleam in his eyes. *Mount up, Fisher. Let's get this Adventure started.*

"Adventure? You sound just like those other dragons when they first hatched." He placed one foot on Gaelan's raised leg and climbed into place. "Are all dragons so fascinated by adventures?" he asked as he settled in the indentation between Gaelan's shoulder blades and pushed his legs into the grips along his neck.

We live for a long time, so we need to make sure we never become complacent about life. There's always something to enjoy if you look hard enough.

Sand swirled over them as Gaelan lifted into the air. He spiraled upward then evened out and flew to the south-west. *I've never enjoyed any Adventure as much as I'm enjoying this one with you.*

You have a strange idea of adventure. I've nearly died half a dozen times since I met you.

Nearly, but didn't. Gaelan's tone was smug.

CHAPTER TWENTY-FOUR

THE ENTRANCE TO THE catacombs was hidden at the base of a tumble of sandstone boulders that looked like they'd once been carved into the shape of a norrgel. Wing-like protuberances cast thick black shadows over golden-red sand.

Fisher stumbled a little as he climbed off Gaelan and landed in the shifting sand. He turned to survey the area.

A sand haze hovered over the land, stirred by the light breeze that punctuated the distant calls of norrgel returning to their nests. Rising to Fisher's calves, it obscured any traps that might have been laid, so he approached the outcropping cautiously.

Gaelan pointed past him to an obvious gap between the boulders. "That looks like a likely spot."

"It is." He went the other direction.

"Where are you going?"

"Checking for traps. Stay still before you trigger something."

Fisher went flying as an explosion slammed him into the ground and smashed his legs against the boulders. He landed face-down close to the outcropping under a rain of stinging sand.

Too late, said Gaelan from above as a blue shadow crept over him.

Fisher stared at the sand in front of him, judging whether or not it was safe to move, and if he could move his legs through the pain that pricked every hair on his body.

Sticking up from the sand, about a foot in front of his face, was the corner of a thin sheet of metal. The trigger mechanism was hand-made; crude, but effective. First contact would allow the flint detonator to spark against the saltpeter and the bomb would explode.

He had apprenticed briefly with the man who'd designed them. He knew how to construct one in the dark, the exact angle to place the flint to ensure immediate detonation, and knew the only way to disarm one was to let it explode. That usually meant someone died.

Exile lives were cheap; they'd never worried about triggered bombs before. But this was Gaelan...

Who was a dragon and hovering above him. "Exactly how quickly can you change and become airborne?"

Pretty fast.

"How badly hurt are you?"

Claws scraped rock as Gaelan settled more comfortably on top of the boulders. *I'm not hurt. Well, except for a sore toe. I changed and flew up at an angle as it exploded so I could avoid the worst of it. What about you?* Guilt tinged his voice.

Fisher moved his gaze away from the metal, only to find evidence of another device less than a foot away, neatly pinning him exactly where he was. He could probably stand if he ignored the pain that was beginning to swirl into identifiable throbbing at different places but wouldn't be able to move away from the boulders.

He pushed his hands underneath his chest and lifted himself, falling and crying out when his right wrist collapsed under him. He panted against a depth of pain he recognized as a broken bone. His shins reminded him, with stinging certainty, that they'd been flung against a boulder. At least he could still feel everything.

"A broken wrist. Bruises. I think everything else is fine. There are two more devices directly in front and to the side."

I'm going to clear those devices so I can get to you. Shield yourself from the explosions.

"Stop! The bombs are directly in front of me. There's nothing around here that can be put between me and them to shield me." He gingerly pushed himself to his shaky feet and wedged himself between the boulders as best he could.

You're a dragon. You're impervious to small pieces like that.

"Am I impervious to projectiles in the same way norrgel meat won't poison me?"

Oh. Stay there. I'll be back soon.

There was a flurry of wings and a swirling of sand and then silence, except for the soft ping-ping-ping of grains of sand landing on the rocks around him.

Up and behind him, one of the boulders in the grouping shuddered, rock grinding against rock. Fisher twisted and looked up to see Gaelan flying above, claws sunk deep into the boulder he was lifting. Behind him, another boulder rocked, then tilted sideways, exposing a hole in the ground—the entrance underground.

Can you reach it? Once you're safe, I'll join you.

Fisher squeezed between the two boulders and slipped into the hole, his injured arm protectively cradled against his chest. He landed about ten feet below and rolled, crying out in pain when his broken wrist became squashed between his body and the ground and all his other scrapes and bruises made themselves known.

Up above boomed and shuddered. He scrambled away from the opening as debris rained down around him.

"That idiot's going to get himself killed and I'll be trapped here under a rockfall," he muttered as he wriggled upright and stumbled in a crouch to the farthest corner of the cave.

The ground rumbled again, the aftershock of the explosion traveling underground, and he dropped to his knees. His eyes burned, partly from the dust swirling through the cave, but also partly from the thought he'd never see Gaelan again. No one could survive that blast.

He sank back onto his heels and pressed his face against his knees, his burning wrist pressed close.

More rocks slid down and rolled close to him. They crunched rhythmically and he clamped his eyes closed so he wouldn't begin searching for something that couldn't be. "Gaelan," he whispered.

Warmth slipped around his shoulders. "Let's take a look at that wrist."

He jerked his head up, his crown connecting painfully with Gaelan's chin. "Ow!" He sat upright. "I thought you were dead."

Gaelan chuckled. "Not from that little puff." He leaned closer, cradling Fisher's face in his hands. He pressed a kiss to Fisher's forehead. "You're my Concubine now. You'd know for sure if I died."

He gently lifted Fisher's arm and probed the break. Fisher hissed, but Gaelan continued until he rested his thumb against one spot. "There it is," he murmured as he leaned forward and breathed warm blue flame onto Fisher's arm.

Fisher jerked but settled when he realized the flame wasn't hurting. The burn he felt was inside his wrist as the bone and torn flesh mended under Gaelan's ministrations. "How are you doing that?"

Gaelan rubbed his thumb over Fisher's now blue-ish skin. "I can only do it for you." He looked up at Fisher. "Because you are mine."

Fisher frowned. Gaelan kept saying things like that as if they were significant and he should understand, but there was nothing in his history to prepare him for what this concubine thing was turning out to be.

It was clear all the stories and songs he'd grown up with, the threats of being nothing more than a dragon-whore were wrong. He didn't know what he should replace them with, no matter how much he yearned for what Gaelan seemed to be suggesting. It wasn't just permanence, but caring and protection, and so much more that his mind whirled with the possibilities.

Fisher was changed too. Could he commit to anything if he didn't who he was anymore? Or could he learn what he'd become at the same time he explored what he and Gaelan were building together? He wanted that. He wanted not to be rejected by everyone. He wanted to have a place he belonged, and a person he belonged with. He wanted what Gaelan was offering.

Gaelan pressed another kiss to his forehead then moved lower, trailing kisses down his cheek until Fisher lifted his head and Gaelan pressed against his lips. Another slow, deep kiss that sank into his mind and body as if it belonged. He'd crave kisses like this for the rest of his days.

He leaned forward, deepening the kiss, and fumbled for Gaelan's crotch. The movement jarred his wrist and he hissed. Grimacing, he sat back and surveyed his still-blue skin. "I thought you fixed it. Is that color permanent? Am I going to turn blue?"

"I did fix it, but it'll be a while before the swelling settles and you're pain-free. I don't think the color is permanent."

"You don't sound sure."

"I've never had a Concubine before and I never met my father, so I don't know how everything works."

"Great." It had been bad enough being mottled cream and brown. He wasn't like the Blue Goddess with a whole people worshiping her. At least Gaelan didn't seem to care if he turned blue.

He used the rock wall to steady himself as he rose, then looked for the exit. To his left was a dark shadow almost hidden by a fallen pile of rocks. He clambered over them and through the narrow opening.

Gaelan carried one of his blue rocks. It glowed faintly, but enough for them to see a couple of feet ahead. The tunnel was more of an obstacle course and they crawled over and around fallen boulders and sank elbow-deep into fine dust.

The exertion, and the way their movement stirred the dust, made easy breathing impossible. After the first coughing fit, Fisher wrapped his scarf around his head desert-style.

After a couple of hours, they stopped in a slightly larger dusty depression.

"It's late," said Gaelan. "We should rest here before continuing."

Fisher crawled around the low-ceilinged cave, carefully inspecting the walls for markings. "No one's been here for a while, so we should be safe for a few hours."

"I didn't think of that."

"It's not a problem. We never enter at the same place we exited from, but this one hasn't been used in months. That usually happens when resources in an area dry up. I doubt anyone will come through this way until the Imperials begin to trust this route again."

Gaelan looked startled but eventually began shifting sand around him. Fisher laughed when he saw what he was doing. "Are you making a nest?"

He glared at him. "If we're going to get any decent sleep here, we need somewhere large enough and smooth enough to be comfortable."

He stepped over the lip of sand and rocks into the nest. He ignored the electric shiver that washed over him as if he'd passed through some kind of barrier.

He also ignored the sense that he'd finally found home, and Gaelan's grin and air of satisfaction. "Lie down and go to sleep." Following his own advice, he settled on his side, facing away from Gaelan.

He closed his eyes and listened as Gaelan continued shuffling sand around. Finally, he lay down behind him.

"I've provided for you," Gaelan whispered, his warm breath washing across the back of Fisher's neck. "Gave you food and water." Gaelan shuffled closer, and sweat beaded and dribbled down Fisher's back. "Now I've given you a place to rest. Do you know what that means?"

"It means we can sleep." He deliberately blocked out what he wanted it to mean. It was natural that Gaelan would want to... no it was more than that. All those things Gaelan said to him when they were in the mountain... gods, Fisher wanted that. With everything Gaelan did, they moved inexorably closer to it.

His mother had nurtured him, fed him and clothed him and made sure he knew how to stay safe. She'd rescued him too, and she'd promised to always be there for him. But it was different from what Gaelan promised. A mother's love was sweet and gentle, fierce and protective. This thing with Gaelan wasn't. It was raw and powerful. It consumed Fisher, until he was a shadow of what he'd once been; and until he was more than he'd ever thought he could be.

With his mother, he could do anything.

With Gaelan, he could *be* anything. With Gaelan, he could be... fuck, he could even be a dragon.

His mind recoiled at the thought, increasing the tremors wracking his body. He'd always been himself, but nothing he'd been had ever been remotely dragon-like. It wasn't until he'd met Gaelan that strange things began happening to him. He'd never been able to sink into mountains before and had never noticed how comfortable he'd been with the rock. Now, he could slide through granite, he could burst into flames and survive.

He sniffled. He could change into a dragon and fly.

"Fisher," whispered Gaelan. His warm, thick arm slid around Fisher's ribs and pulled him back into the security of his body. He held tight until Fisher's trembling sobs eased. "It's all right. Everything will work out the way it's meant to."

Fisher rolled over and thumped Gaelan's chest. "Shut up. You don't know that. I was fine until I met you. I was making a life for myself, but now... now I've been drowned and drugged and burned. I turned into a dragon!"

His breath rushed through him faster and faster until he was dizzy. "I don't want to be a dragon! I want to be me." His eyes burned and tears pooled against his nose before slipping over the bridge and dropping onto Gaelan's bicep.

Gaelan drew him in close and kissed his eyes, drying the tears with his too-hot breath that felt perfect on his new skin. "I promise you, you'll be exactly who you're meant to be. The dragon didn't surface until you needed him. If you want it so, he'll stay deep inside you, where he's always been, until you need him again. Only you can call the dragon forth."

"Where he's always been?" He could feel the hysteria bubbling up, tearing away his ability to breathe evenly or speak calmly. His mind scattered, unable to settle on one thing. "Are you saying I've always had a dragon inside me? Waiting to burn me alive?"

"It's not a separate being living inside you. It's you. You've always been dragon, even if you were born a man. You've always had fire."

Once he'd grown past his teen years and begun moving up the ranks of Exiles, Fisher had believed he was as good as anyone else. He'd worked hard to achieve what he had, had suppressed the horror he'd felt at some of the things he'd had to do to not just survive, but thrive. His skin hadn't mattered as much. He'd been just like everyone else. Sometimes better.

Now, he had a dragon inside him and Gaelan said it had always been there. Visions of his first attempt at anal sex flashed through his mind. "I really *am* a freak." The broken whisper made his throat ache. Inside, he cringed at the childish weakness he was showing.

Gaelan pulled him closer, and Fisher let him when all he wanted to do was tear free and run. "Fisher, look at me."

Reluctantly, he looked into Gaelan's eyes, the rich blue almost glowing in the dim light of the stone. At first his breathing was as erratic as his thoughts, but as Gaelan continued to watch him, calm and accepting, the heavy rasp of it quietened, matching Gaelan's rhythm.

His heart stopped pounding its way through his chest and into his throat and his breathing slowed, slipping through his lips like an early-morning desert breeze.

Gaelan brushed the back of his fingers against Fisher's cheek. "Let me show you what I see."

He closed his eyes and Gaelan's fingers speared into his hair, pushing the strands away from his face. He leaned into the pressure against his scalp, his breath leaving on a contented sigh, but immediately straightened, and frowned at the attempt to distract him again.

"Your hair is gorgeous," said Gaelan as he sifted Fisher's hair through his fingers. "It's soft and silky, nothing like what you'd expect from a warrior such as yourself."

Fisher scoffed. He was no warrior. He was a misfit Exile who had risen through the ranks only because of his tenacity.

Gaelan's hand slipped down the back of his neck and kneaded the tension there. He leaned forward and pressed a chaste kiss to Fisher's forehead. "You're quick. There isn't a problem you couldn't find a solution for, even if it's a situation you've never been confronted with before. You don't panic."

Fisher huffed.

"Okay, you panic when you're on fire. But only a little bit, and only because you're in pain. Hopefully that'll be the last time that happens."

"Hopefully?" Fisher pulled away. "What do you mean 'hopefully?'" Sweat broke out on Fisher's upper lip and a full-body shudder ran through him. He wasn't going through that again. If that's what it took to bring the dragon out, the animal could stay where it was... wherever that was.

"Ssh," Gaelan soothed. When Fisher once again settled, he continued. "You're kind to others, even when they're not kind to you."

"Rubbish."

Gaelan shook his head as his finger continued wandering over Fisher's body. He unraveled the ties on his shirt. "Others have deliberately hurt you, but you've never retaliated, even when you had a perfect opportunity to do so.

"I burned Barthes to the ground." He lifted his arms as Gaelan pushed his shirt up. As the fabric covered his face, warmth surrounded one of his nipples. He jumped, but Gaelan lifted the shirt away and his hands returned to Fisher's back and held him still.

Gaelan groaned. "That was an accident."

Fisher, drowning in the heat of Gaelan's mouth, forgot what they were talking about.

Gaelan's lips moved against his nipple; a smile amidst the passion. "You didn't know the Elixir was that flammable."

Oh. Barthes.

Gaelan's hands wandered over his chest. He jumped when Gaelan tweaked his nipples then slid his hands down his ribs on their way to the fastenings on Fisher's trousers. "You're strong and decisive." He pushed Fisher's pants over the swell of his buttocks when Fisher lifted up, and down his legs.

Gaelan knelt at Fisher's feet and gently removed his boots before leaning forward to nuzzle at his groin. Gaelan groaned. "And you smell wonderful."

"I haven't bathed in days." He pushed ineffectually at Gaelan's head as he hummed against Fisher's balls.

"Rich and earthy."

He jerked when Gaelan's tongue darted out and painted a wet stripe from his balls to the tip of his cock. He tensed and waited for Gaelan's mouth to engulf him, but it didn't; his wandering tongue returned to Fisher's balls, laving them with saliva.

Fisher shifted restlessly, then froze as his buttocks sank more securely into the sand. He pushed more firmly at Gaelan's head. "Sand," he said breathlessly.

Gaelan paused then lifted his head. "Perhaps you're right. I want this to be perfect and it won't be if you're worried about getting sand stuck in places."

He breathed blue fire onto one of his stones and silky cloth flowed under him. He kissed Fisher's balls. "Remember where we are here so I can continue as soon as we return home."

Warmth washed through him as Gaelan talked about his home.

He wrapped his arms and legs around Gaelan as he slid up Fisher's body, pressing them together, soft skin, hard muscle and harder cocks digging at each other. "How are you still talking?"

"You inspire me," said Gaelan with a smile before he dipped his head and pressed his lips to his. He deepened the kiss as he wriggled on top of Fisher until their bodies were aligned.

Fisher slipped a hand between their hips and shifted his cock until it pressed perfectly against Gaelan's and rode in the sweat-slippery groove between it and Gaelan's hip bone. He left his hand there, squashed between Gaelan's cock and his stomach.

Gaelan tore his mouth from Fisher's and trailed sloppy biting kisses along his jaw and down his neck. "You taste like raspberries."

"What?" He pushed at Gaelan's shoulders but all Gaelan did was move his kisses to the other side of his neck.

"Like strawberries and mango, new lemons, and mint picked from the garden."

"I'm filthy. I don't taste like anything but sweat and desert."

Gaelan finally lifted his head high enough so Fisher could see his face. There was no teasing in his serious eyes. "You taste like home."

"You're mad." He threaded his fingers through Gaelan's hair and drew him back to him. He had the notion that their mouths and tongues melded, as if kissing each other was exactly what they were meant to do. Forever.

He drank in the dark wine taste of Gaelan. Lost himself in the heat and padded solidity of him. The air was cool and dry when he withdrew his hand from between their bodies, and he dug his fingers into the flesh of Gaelan's buttock to pull him closer.

He strained upward, grasping, gasping, pressing. Always needing more—more flesh, more movement, more kisses.

Instead of coming closer and harder, Gaelan lifted up.

"No."

Gaelan's hand slid between them, where his had been minutes before, and he gripped their cocks in his tight fist.

Fisher groaned and jerked, the sweat and pre-come providing slide; the lack of lube burning enough to be on the edge of pain, but still perfect. His hips jerked spasmodically, all control gone in the intense rise to orgasm. His skin tingled, from his toes to his scalp. Every hair on his body stood upright as searing heat flooded through him.

He froze, his hips punched forward, and the warmth flooded his body and shot out of his cock, dark flames licking over Gaelan's skin.

By the third pulse Fisher's muscles relaxed enough to allow a groan to escape.

"Home," whispered Gaelan as he tensed and his warm come joined Fisher's cooling between them.

The word floated between them and wafted in the air around them. He opened his mouth to ask what Gaelan meant, then closed it silently

He wanted to pretend that *they* were home, not a place, and this was the kind of life Fisher could have now that no one else would die from the Elixir and the Yeudan were no longer a threat to the Mafdeti or the Imperials.

He could be finally free to choose his own destiny. And that would be Gaelan.

Gaelan's hair slipped through his fingers so he threaded into it again, loving the softness against his skin. He lay awake a long time, secure in the familiar comfort of being surrounded by sand and wondering if he could make his destiny what he wanted it to be, now that he was free.

Whether or not he could achieve his dream depended on who he was now.

CHAPTER TWENTY-FIVE

TWO DAYS LATER, HIS fingers were raw from clawing his way past rocks, and his body covered in so much dust Fisher was sure it coated the inside of his nostrils and the roof of his mouth. They came to a tunnel he knew well. It was narrower and the rockslide made it almost impossible to move through.

He remembered exactly where he'd placed the small charges to bring those rocks down exactly where he'd wanted them and where each of his men had been positioned to inflict the most damage with the lowest losses, and also to hide their scent from the Mafdeti. It had worked perfectly, and they'd taken the two women the king had wanted.

The air was full of the smell of dust and the scent of his own sweat. The last time he had been there, there had been a thickness to the air—rancid and rotting. Most Exiles weren't too vigilant about their personal hygiene.

"Once we go through here," he said, "the tunnel will be clear for about fifty feet, then it curves. After that there's only another few junctures with clear, well-used tunnels and we'll be at the main cavern."

They clambered over rocks to the other side of the rockslide then, with a nod from Gaelan, broke into a jog. He was glad to finally stretch his legs in the larger tunnels after spending days crawling through narrow openings.

They paused at a wide intersection. Fisher took the lead at the last minute, signaling Gaelan to wait.

He shot a quick look around the corner. Only two guards were on duty and neither of them seemed alert; a far cry from the discipline Fisher had insisted on when he had been in charge.

"This is the Exile community," Fisher whispered. "Most of them are ordinary people but we have to stay hidden. It would be better if Maris is the only one who knows I'm here."

"Maris?"

"The women's deputy—" Fisher shuddered at his last memory of his mother. "She's the women's Elder."

After about ten minutes the guards nodded to each other and wandered off in different directions. Fisher assumed they were patrolling the tunnels but they could as easily have been taking a break. "Come on, this is our chance."

Silently, they ran down the tunnel and slipped into the cavern, moving sideways behind a dusty tapestry. Moving as little as possible, Fisher peered around the edge of the tapestry. As far as Fisher could see, nothing had changed since he'd last been there.

The large, almost-round table still dominated the cavern with the short stools surrounding it. Several Exiles sat around the table eating from a large platter piled high with roasted meats and root vegetables.

The floor was covered in threadbare rugs, none of them quite square, their garish colors patchy against the soft sandstone floor. Boxes were lined up around the edges of the cavern, their contents spilling over.

The king had forbidden anything to be moved or cleaned, declaring it was his treasure and no one was permitted to touch it. Silks and pearls competed for space with brass cups studded with glass or semi-precious beads. On top of one of the boxes balanced a child's wooden carriage, one of its wheels broken in half.

Fisher noted the position of all the people in the cavern. Gaelan pressed close behind him.

Together they made their way around the cavern to the opening that led to the sacrificial chamber and all the other tunnels and caves of the Exiles. Fisher measured the distance between the edge of the tapestry they were behind and the next one, then checked the people in the cavern.

Some distance behind the table, the king's huge throne-like chair leaned drunkenly to one side. There were more boxes behind the chair, but Fisher knew they'd been raided years before, with the king none the wiser.

He knew where some of the jewels had gone. Before he left, he would make sure Maris knew where the stash was. Perhaps she and some of the other women could get away and start a life of their own.

As they made their way around the cavern, trying to keep the tapestries as still as possible as they moved behind them, he vowed to get the rest. He didn't plan to return.

They paused before leaving the dubious protection of the tapestries near the entrance to the adjoining chamber. Fisher sidled forward to make sure they'd be able to cover the distance without being noticed.

"When's this shipment being collected?" It was Laec's gravelly voice. He'd once been Fisher's second. The other two with him glanced at each other before the blond, a man Fisher didn't know, answered.

"It was supposed to be this afternoon, but we haven't received the signal. It's still in the storeroom." He spoke through the food he was chewing and followed the sentence by shoving a whole potato into his mouth.

Laec backhanded the blond. Food sprayed across the floor as the man tumbled from his seat, coughing. "Find out what the problem is. Move that stuff now." He pointed to the other man, a brunet. "You go to the stores and start moving it out. I want it ready to be picked up as soon as they get here." He stormed from the cavern, into the tunnels they'd just come from.

Fisher grabbed Gaelan's hand and hauled him out of the cavern and into the sacrifice chamber. He spared a split-second for a glance around to make sure there was no one there, then ran to the entrance to the women's quarters.

"Is this where the brunet went?" asked Gaelan. "It's the stores we want, right?"

"Right, but I have to do something else first." He continued to run and skidded into the women's quarters without checking. The only people there would be the women too unwell to work, or new mothers. All the others would be in the kitchens or laundries.

The men weren't permitted access to the women until after the evening meal was served. Then they could do what they wanted with them as long as they didn't kill them or injure them so much they couldn't work.

He skidded to a halt when he entered the room as he realized it was almost full. Gaelan bumped into him from behind, the momentum pushing him forward a couple of steps.

"Fisher!" Maris's eyes carried more wrinkles underneath a new bruise that overlayed a series of aging ones.

"Maris." Fisher glanced at all the other women in the room. "What's going on? Why are you all here?" He reached toward her but pulled back when she shied away, revealing more bruises on her neck and arms. "This is worse than normal."

Maris shook her head at Fisher. "Not anymore." She pointed to each of the women in turn. "Pregnant, pregnant, injured, recovering from childbirth, in labor, pregnant, injured, miscarrying, injured, pregnant."

She pointed to the last woman, a young girl barely out of her teens. "Baby died, but don't tell anyone until I decide she's ready to go back out there. She thumped herself on her chest. "Overseer."

Fisher gaped. Most of the women sported visible bruises. Those who were injured were young, possibly still teens, and looked terrified.

"You were ten when you came here," Gaelan said quietly beside him. "I'm sure your mother shielded you from the worst of it."

"I'm not ten now. I've only been gone a few months." He spun around, only settling again when he saw the way most of the women cringed at his sudden movement.

He swung to her. "I should have—"

"You should have done your job, and that's what you did. You protected us when you could and trusted us to protect ourselves when you couldn't." She crossed her arms under her breasts and scowled at him. "Now tell me why you're here and how you're getting out without them killing you and *us* in retaliation."

Fisher recognized the determined glint in her eyes. "I'll show you where my mother kept some things. You might be able to use them to help some of the women get out of here and somewhere safer." He rubbed at the tension sitting over his eyebrows. "But first, I need you to tell me how to access the back door to the main storeroom."

A collective gasp filled the room. All the women stared at him, fear whitening their faces.

"I know there's another way in because Mother used to top up your rations from the stores and no one ever caught her."

"You knew she was doing that?"

"I knew that much, but I never asked her where it was in case someone questioned me."

"And now?"

"I've already been branded a traitor. I might as well know something that's considered treasonous." He tried to sound flippant but knew the pain he'd felt at being rejected by his adopted people still floated on the top of his heart. "My mother had a stash."

For the first time, Maris refused to meet his gaze. "Your mother didn't have a stash. You know we're not allowed to keep anything."

Calling Maris on her lie in front of all the others wouldn't achieve anything except to undermine her authority and put even more of them in jeopardy.

He mentally sifted through everything he knew his mother had. "There are only a couple of things I need. I think you and the other women here would be better able to use most of it than I would."

"How do I know I can trust you?"

"You trusted my mother. You helped raise me. You know you can trust me not to hurt you, or to steal from you. Whether or not you decide to trust me to keep my word is something only you know."

Maris scowled at him. "Jenny, watch the door." She motioned to Fisher to follow her. She stopped when Gaelan followed them.

"He's with me," said Fisher. He made sure he voice was flat and certain, brooking no argument. He was half convinced they'd turn Gaelan in as soon as he was out of sight.

Maris led them down progressively narrower corridors until they reached one that he couldn't stand upright in. He recognized the low opening they faced.

In the bottom left corner were the letters "M & F." He remembered carving those letters deep into the stone on his eleventh birthday, the day he decided on his new name. He'd moved out of these quarters when he was twelve, into the youths' cavern, and he had believed he'd never set foot inside the small cave again. It had been barely big enough for him and his mother to curl up together to sleep, although most nights she didn't join him until almost dawn, so it wasn't too bad until he'd grown to almost six foot.

"She showed me where she hid the box," said Maris defensively.

"Have you taken anything from it?"

"No." Maris's quick sideways glance showed that for the lie it was.

"There are only a few things I want from it. You can have the rest." He crawled into the alcove. He sat and twisted, grunting as he bumped both his head and his knee, then reached above the lip of the opening onto the shallow ledge he'd carved out as a child.

There lay a cigar box the king had tossed away and forgotten, which he had rescued. Inside was the sum total of his mother's life, less the brooch he had given to Ma Jeffries. There were two small figurines, both dragons, one made from quartz-grained granite and the other palest sandstone, worn smooth by hopeful fingers.

There was also a silver locket that his mother said his father had given her. The front was crudely carved with what he had always thought was a gnat, but now he thought could be a dragon. Inside the locket had been empty for as long as he'd known.

There was a small bag of silver coins and another of gold. Both had been nearly full the last time he had added a coin. Now there were only five gold coins and seven silver left.

He pocketed the granite figurine and the locket. He'd managed without money in his life and Maris would need it more than he did.

On impulse, he also grabbed the sandstone figurine. He didn't recognize it, but it might be worth something. He could sell it if he needed to.

He crawled back out. "What have you been using the money for?"

She ducked her head. "Mostly medicines for the girls. Two gold coins were used to get one of them out of here before Laec could kill her."

"Where did you send her?"

"Hawkesby. I have a cousin there." She hesitated, but eventually went on. "If you go to Hawkesby, call in to see Nadya in the laundry and check that Lowell is all right."

"I'll do that." But he wondered if he'd have time to stop at the city and if he'd get out alive if he did.

Gaelan fumbled with his backpack then held out a blue leather sack to Maris. It jingled as it dropped into her hands. "This will help you all go somewhere safe."

Maris gaped at the tumble of gold coins and tanzanites in her palm, then a lone tear slipped down her cheek. She nodded and turned away to stash the coins on the hidden ledge. "Come this way." Her voice was rough and harsh. "I'll show you how to get to the storeroom."

At the end of the tunnel was a narrow opening. It was barely wide enough for Fisher to fit his hand in. Maris slipped her hand in about a foot above the floor. A click preceded a soft groaning swish and the entire wall moved several inches toward them.

"Don't touch the sharp edge. If any shards break off, it'll be obvious this is used for something." She motioned for them to be quiet then slipped through the narrow opening.

Fisher slipped in after her then turned to help Gaelan. His extra bulk would make it almost impossible for him to move through.

Gaelan eyed the gap with a frown etched deep between his brows then he pulled out a small tanzanite from his pocket. "Step back." He raised the tanzanite above his head, stretching his arms high, then kept stretching until his body was as tall as the gap and could slide through without touching the rock.

Behind Fisher, Maris gasped. There was a soft thud and he turned to find her on her knees with her hands pressed firmly against her mouth.

Gaelan's body bounced back into its usual size and shape with a soft slurp and wavering of skin and muscle. Fisher pressed his hand against his mouth as Maris had, but wasn't sure if that was because he needed to prevent a noise, or something else, from escaping. He pressed his other hand against his churning stomach.

Gaelan brushed his fingers gently over his cheek and slid briefly into his hair, then he went to Maris.

"It will be alright, grandmother. If we had time, we could help you take the women to safety, but our mission is time sensitive. Remember if you can find no other safe place, come to the Lonely Isles. I'll make sure there's somewhere for you all to settle and live in peace."

He leaned forward and pressed a gentle kiss to Maris's forehead. She gasped then gazed at Gaelan reverently.

"Will you show us the way?" he asked.

Maris nodded dazedly then crouched to move a stone bucket aside. "Follow this tunnel, always taking the left fork. You'll think you're going in circles, but you'll eventually come to a dead end.

"Down low, there's a square red stone. Pull it out to check if the coast is clear. Once it's out, and you're sure it's safe, reach your hand through the opening and find the bracket for the shelf above. Twist it to your left. The door beside you will open and you'll be able to get through." She glanced at Gaelan. "He might need to…"

"Thank you, Maris," said Gaelan with a smile in his voice. Fisher, having been on the receiving end of her temper a few times, knew better than to laugh.

"Take the women somewhere safe, right now, far away from here," said Gaelan. "As far as you can go."

"When will it be safe to return?"

"You'll know once it's over, but there probably won't be anything left in the storeroom."

Maris frowned then looked back the way they'd come. "We should have enough supplies packed. I'll send out scouts to get everyone moving." She slipped away, quickly disappearing into the narrow tunnel.

"Let's check what's in there, and who, then we can decide the best way to deal with it," said Fisher as he reached for the red stone.

He glanced at Gaelan, who nodded, then he maneuvered the stone toward him.

He had to lay on the ground to see through the small opening and almost choked on the odor. He knew whatever he would see would be bad news. He lifted his scarf and peered through.

The storeroom was a large square divided into different sections, the perishable foods kept separate from the non-perishables, which were kept separate from household items such as bed linens and cleaning products. At the far end were the military supplies and medicinal stores.

Several years before, the stores had been his domain and he'd organized them so products were always rotated according to useful life. That system had been followed throughout his tenure as Head of the Militia.

The arrangement of the room now bore little resemblance to anything he was familiar with. The narrow rectangle he could see through revealed a tangled jumble of household stores, cleaning products and non-perishable foodstuffs pushed into a corner with a narrow path leading toward the door.

In front of the tumble of boxes and fabrics were haphazard piers of thick green glass jars sealed with circular sandstone stoppers. The liquid in the jars was black and viscous; the jars so poorly sealed the rank smell of norrgel residue made his eyes burn, even from this distance. He sat back.

"No wonder Laec wanted this stuff moved so quickly." He kept his voice low. "It stinks, and there's so much of it in there, one careless spark will set the whole place alight."

Gaelan laid down and looked through the opening. "We could set it alight."

Fisher pushed him back so he could have another look. "The liquid will explode. Everything will go up. There'll be glass shards everywhere and liquid shot out through the doors. If they have things stacked in the tunnels to make room for the jars, all that will go up as well." He sat up. "We could destroy everything down here. Everything will burn."

"They're Exiles, criminals who—"

Fisher didn't let him finish. "That might be how the Exiles began and where some of them still come from, but they aren't all criminals. Many were born here, many came here when there was nowhere else for them to go." He sucked in a deep breath, willing his pounding heart to calm down. "I won't risk killing all those people just because some of them were criminals. It's not up to us to decide who is worthy of life and who is not."

A small smile played around Gaelan's lips. "We'll evacuate everyone then, just as you told Maris. Or we wait until they take the jars to a place they can be destroyed without killing everyone."

Fisher thumped him on the shoulder. "Bastard. That's what you always intended. What was that supposed to be about? Was it a test? Did you think I'd find it funny?" He curled his fist tightly into his shirt and pulled him close when the distinctive sound of a trolley being wheeled into the storeroom distracted him.

He pecked a swift kiss to Gaelan's lips instead of the punishing one he'd planned, then peered through the hole. One of the towers of jars wobbled before a hand came into view and steadied it. There was a soft clink, then another and another.

Eventually, the tower wobbled again and the jar at the very top tipped over. He gasped, was about to cry out, when the jar steadied and lowered gently. The trolley rolled away, and another came close.

He turned to Gaelan. "They're moving it now," he whispered. "There are too many possibilities for a collection point. I wouldn't know which one to go to unless we knew exactly where it's being taken so we have to follow it to the collection area."

Gaelan nodded. "How easy will that be? If they see us..."

"Maris might know." He slid the red stone back into place. They turned around in the narrow, cramped space and began the laborious journey back to the women's section.

Screams and shouting echoed down their small tunnel well before they reached it. Fisher froze.

Gaelan kept crawling until he was half on top of him, his mouth next to his ear. "What do you think is happening?"

"It could be a routine inspection or someone might have noticed something odd. Or someone could be on a rampage." Shame and helplessness twisted in his chest. "If we go out there we'll only make it worse. If we're found there, all the women there will be killed as traitors, and so will we."

He lowered his head until his forehead rested on his hands. They waited. The yelling and screaming continued unabated for what felt like hours. Sweat dripped from Fisher's face, the only outward sign he allowed of how difficult he found it to remain still.

Finally, the noise died down. he wiped his face, sniffed and raised his head.

"Do you think it's safe?" whispered Gaelan. His voice was ragged.

Fisher leaned against him for a second, then shuffled forward and reached for the rock. Before he could grasp it, it slid away from him and dropped onto the ground outside. Maris's face appeared in the hole. She jumped when she saw them but calmed quickly.

"They know you're in the caverns and are heading to the storeroom." She darted a glance behind her. "You can't come through here again. They're guarding these rooms." She shot another glance behind. "None of us here can leave now."

"They'll be guarding the storeroom too." They should have gone through there while they had the opportunity, except there hadn't been an opportunity. "What do we do now?"

"Maris," said Gaelan. "Lock us in here again. If there's a way to make sure that entrance stays blocked, do it."

"They need access to the stores," protested Fisher.

"They need to stay alive more." He glared at Fisher then turned to Maris. "Are you ready to leave? Get as far away as you can. Don't let yourself get trapped anywhere without a way out. Don't go anywhere that the air in the storeroom will go."

Maris flicked a look behind her.

"What we're doing will give you the distraction you need. Get as many out as you can."

She nodded warily then backed out and replaced the stone.

"There's a slightly wider section back a bit." Gaelan tugged on Fisher. "Go back there and turn around. Once we're back at the storeroom, I'll create a diversion. When we're both outside the storeroom, you can set fire to the jars. The room should keep the fire contained."

They wriggled back along the tunnel. When the space widened, Gaelan performed a liquid somersault so he was facing the opposite direction. Fisher tried to turn but got stuck with his knees up against his ears and a jagged rock digging into his shoulder.

"Hold still. I'll get you free," said Gaelan. He removed the tanzanite from his pocket and held it against the rock at Fisher's shoulder. Heat radiated through the sandstone, growing in strength as Gaelan held the tanzanite. "Move now."

He rolled forward, diving along the tunnel until he rested on his stomach, facing the correct direction. Something plopped beside his knee and he twisted to find a glob of golden glass, grains of sand swirling inside it. Gaelan grinned at his surprise.

His shoulder was still hot, likely burned from the melted sandstone, but the pain was nothing like molten glass should cause. He ignored it and scowled at Gaelan before commando-crawling toward the storeroom again.

The red stone came away easily.

"Hurry up. Get moving. Those jars have to be moved now. Right now." Laec's gravelly voice reverberated around the room. "No, you stand guard. Keep that knife ready. He's coming here. Move. Move. Move."

"I'll draw them away," whispered Gaelan. He planted a kiss on Fisher's temple then turned into blue smoke and disappeared through the small hole into the storeroom.

First it was a cougar, then the wriggly, stretchy thing, and now it was smoke. Being able to slide through granite didn't seem at all remarkable.

Fisher peered through the hole but couldn't see anything beyond what he'd seen before. The tall piles of jars were shorter, but everything else remained the same. Behind the unchanging view, the trolley wheels rattled toward the door, replaced by others. Glass clinked against glass as more jars were loaded.

To his right a wisp of blue smoke wound its way around boxes, sliding toward the door. They'd see it soon, surely.

There was a startled cry then a thump. Glass clattered but didn't shatter. More cries. Yelling. Boxes tumbled. Running feet.

Fisher felt for the lever and pushed the stone out of the way. He crawled through the opening and sidled between the stacks of supplies, wary of any guards left in the storeroom.

The yelling and pounding of feet were receding, leaving him alone with a room full of green glass jars filled with black norrgel residue.

To his left was where the firelighting equipment should be kept but the labeled shelves were nearly empty. He searched nearby shelves with no luck. Still no tapers or matches or torch triggers.

He widened his search and eventually found an untidy pile of matches half-hidden behind a pile of dishes. He could see tapers and torch triggers in random piles between enamel mugs. He grabbed an iron fire poker, a couple of packets of matches and a few tapers then ran to the door.

Three trolleys, each half-loaded with jars blocked half the entrance. He lifted one of the jars, unstoppered it and began drizzling thick black liquid over a couple of the others, then continued in a thin line out of the room and down the tunnel. The residue sizzled as it touched the stone floor and began seeping into it. Some splashed up the walls and onto Fisher's boots.

He moved faster, less focused on maintaining an unbroken line—the flames would jump the small gaps—and more on getting as far from the storeroom as possible before the whole thing exploded.

He rounded the corner into the tunnel leading to the sacrifice chamber and found all the people who'd been missing from the tunnels as he ran.

A blue glow flared then settled and he looked up to see Gaelan standing on the altar, blue-purple smoke wafting from him and forming an image of his dragon form above. A wave of noise washed over him; the cries angry, fearful. Some of them held wonder in their tone.

Above it all, Gaelan's voice carried. "You will be judged on your actions today. Many of you will die. Some innocents will die this day because of the actions of others. Your souls will be revered and remembered as long as dragons live. These chambers will be destroyed now, all past evils washed from them."

Gaelan pointed to the main chamber and the tunnels beyond. "Go now. Run fast, before it's too late."

Panic ensued. Fisher was jostled, the jar in his hands went flying and smashed, black liquid spraying in a wide arc, drenching those nearest. Screams rose as the norrgel residue ate into flesh and bone. One woman, splashed on her back, turned to her companion, clutched at her, begged for help, only to be met with wide eyes rolling with terror and clawed hands prying her away and tossing her aside.

Fisher fought his way to the edge of the cavern so he wouldn't be swept along in the current of terrified people.

Above him, on the altar, the smoke dragon dissipated and Gaelan looked around anxiously. When he spotted Fisher pressed against the wall, he smiled. *You made it.*

You idiot. Why did you have to panic them like that? He was so angry he didn't moderate his tone. He grunted as a child was flung against the wall, his elbow slamming into his thigh. He tugged the child against his side, protecting him from the worst of it.

The child's cries were barely audible above the continued screaming of the crowd as it fought and tumbled its way out of the cavern and into the tunnels beyond. Some poured into the tunnel he had just come from and he yelled at them to come back. They didn't hear or ignored him, and he couldn't move enough in the crush to redirect them.

I had to get them out. I didn't think they'd act like this.

How did you think they'd act after you told them their home was going to be destroyed and they were going to die?

I didn't! Only some will die.

And they don't want to be part of the "some."

By then, the crowd had thinned. Only the injured, the elderly and a few children were left. The ground was littered with bloody bodies. Some moved and groaned, others lay ominously still.

The boy beside him squirmed then broke free and ran to one of the bodies. "Mama!"

Fisher rolled the woman over to find sightless eyes staring up at the ceiling.

"Mama!" the boy wailed. He looked around but everyone was gone, only the panicked cries of the fleeing crowd remaining. After a last anguished look at his mother, the boy fled after the fading noises.

Fisher waved Gaelan closer. "Come through this way." He pointed to the entrance to the women's quarters. "Take the left fork. It'll lead you to the edge of the mountain range. Once you're there, fly. The mesa we're under, and this whole section of desert is going to go once I light this." He gestured to the black liquid splashed around.

Gaelan glared at him then gasped as he saw the state of his boots. "Get those off now."

He shook his head. "Once I'm in a better position to outrun the flames. Now go."

"If you don't show at that exit soon, I'll come back for you." The words were heavy with promise.

"If you don't stay away and safe, I'll beat you until you're black and blue."

Gaelan grinned. "You'll want a hug then," he teased before treating Fisher to a serious gaze. "Stay safe."

He nodded and pulled out the fire starter and long taper from his pocket.

He stepped carefully between the splotches of black that was gradually eating into the sandstone until he was in the same tunnel he'd sent Gaelan through. After checking his hands and clothes for residue, he used part of someone's jacket to wipe his boots off.

Then he held the fire starter as far from his body as he could and ignited it to light the taper. He tossed the taper toward a large puddle of black, expecting a soft whoosh as the liquid caught fire. Instead, there was a roaring whomp with flames bursting large and loud, swamping the ceiling and exploding down the tunnel.

Toward him.

With his hastily-wiped norrgel-covered boots.

"Shit!" He fumbled with the ties around his ankles then grabbed each boot and flung it into the fire, even as he ran from it. He pelted down the tunnel, knowing he'd never outrun flames.

One turn, two. A small alcove, then a dog-leg that might slow the flames down a bit. He slipped around the protruding rocks, tearing his shirt, scraping his palms, feeling the heat searing the hairs on the back of his hand, then took off again.

The fire followed, feeding off rock so porous the residue from all those norrgel sacrifices had seeped into it, making it as flammable as a stick of dry wood. All around him, the rock heated and began to glow as the flames worked their way through it, eating at the air trapped between the grains.

In front of him a protruding rock exploded, showering the tunnel floor with stones and liquid flame. He leaped. Flame licked at his body and his clothes, but he didn't stop to check if anything had caught.

One more bend in the tunnel and the opening was in front of him, tall and narrow with glimpses of green leaves and blue sky.

The flames were behind him, roaring, consuming, licking at his back, singeing his hair. He tripped on a rock, stumbled, pushed his foot under him and dived through the opening.

He landed on gravel and grass and rolled. He slid right off the edge of the path and fell. A long, wide stream of flame burst from the rock and shot straight into air above him.

He bumped and bounced his way down the slope as short, stumpy trees—the only vegetation that grew in the hilly parts of the desert—were consumed by the insatiable flames. Beside him, sand and rock exploded in violent spits, followed immediately by hungry flames.

Fisher tumbled and grasped at anything he could find to try to control his descent. He had to get off this rocky hillock and, while tumbling down it would work, he'd rather be alive at the end.

A shadow consumed him a split second before black claws grabbed him around the waist and lifted him out of the dust and smoke, wheeling away as more flames exploded through the rock, scattering half the mesa into the flat desert beyond.

He coughed, only now realizing how tight his lungs were from smoke and dust, how hot and tight his skin was. How close he'd come to being burned alive. Again. "Better than dissolving in norrgel poison."

Above him, Gaelan laughed, a deep rumbling roll through his chest and belly that had the effect of simultaneously warming Fisher and cooling his burns. He chuckled weakly as he closed his eyes and let Gaelan take him wherever he wished.

CHAPTER TWENTY-SIX

THEY LANDED ON A GRASSY verge above a verdant field. Fisher scrambled out from Gaelan's protective hold then Gaelan shimmered and flashed blue, standing before him in his human form.

He rushed forward. "You're burned. Look at your clothes. Where are the worst ones?" His fingertips patted and hovered over him. "At least you got rid of your boots?" He tugged Fisher to turn around. "Your clothes are ruined. There's not enough here for me to repair. Oh, look at your poor skin. Those blisters must hurt."

He noticed the stinging burn, the puffy tightness that restricted movement and ached deep inside. "It was fine until you mentioned it. Stop fussing. I'll be fine."

As he spoke, the sting faded. He brushed a hand over his ruined tunic. It had been a good one, too; soft and comfortable.

The leading edge of his hand rubbed against crinkly, blackened fabric. As it passed over it, the fabric healed itself until all his clothes looked the way they had when he'd first imagined them into being. His boots reappeared, sturdy and comfortable. His hands were still blistered but already looked better.

He humphed and looked across the field. There had been too many amazing and startling things happen in too short a time for him to maintain any surprise or trepidation. He'd probably fall in a screaming heap when this was all over and he had time to think.

In front of them, the green land stretched calmly to the horizon. Spaced a man's height apart, silver-domed grilles shone like dusty crystals amidst the waving grasses as the midday sunlight beat down on them.

Thin streams of steam wafted through small vent holes in the closed grilles covering each vent and hung in the still air; the only outward sign a huge city lay belowground. Most of the coverings were for ventilation, but every fifteenth one opened to one of the many corridors running through the underground city. "Why are we here?"

"To warn the Imperials about the Elixir and take the duke back to the isles."

"Once we finish this, I'm going back."

"Why?" asked Gaelan. "We gave them as much notice as we could."

"I need to find Maris and the others. Take care of them."

"What if you can't find them?"

"I have to try."

Gaelan nodded. "Let's find Princess Ardelle." His expression turned serious. "They only know me as the minstrel here. They don't know who I really am."

They walked a dozen steps before Gaelan bumped his shoulder against him. "Give me some warning before you blow this place up. With all the levels underground, and its larger population, it'll take longer to evacuate."

"We won't be blowing anything up."

"That's what you said about the Exile caverns."

Fisher sighed to release the defensiveness he felt at the disaster they'd left behind. "I didn't realize they'd been so careless with the substance. It was soaked into the stone." He was surprised the fires in the fireplaces hadn't set the place afire ages ago, but the spillages seemed to have been confined to storage areas and might have been relatively recent.

Norrgel wheeled in the air in the distance. From their cries, Fisher knew they'd been spotted.

"They won't come near us," said Gaelan with a reassuring pat on his shoulder.

After a few seconds to prove he was right, Fisher started down the slope to the city.

As they walked between the rows of grilles, he wondered if this was what his life would be now—traveling from city to city, sneaking in and destroying everything before escaping and moving onto the next city. Would Hawkesby still be standing and functional after he left?

Was he now to be known as a destroyer? Not just an Exile and traitor, unfit for any other society?

He stopped at a row far enough into the city to be beyond the infrastructure and hydroponics, but not so far they'd be in the inner residential areas. He crouched and tested the grille. It was heavy and resisted but they should be able to pry it up far enough they could slip down.

"You go first. You'll fit better than I will," said Gaelan. He heaved the grille up, his shoulders straining. "Drop straight down. Watch your shoulders."

Fisher stepped off the lip of the grille. Air whistled past his ears and whipped his hair around as he fell, his shoulders and elbows bumping against the smooth wall of the shaft. The floor hit him hard, buckling his knees. He rolled. The breath rushed from him and his head thumped onto the ground.

He lay still in an effort to gain control of his winded body. He groaned and rolled to his side, just in time for Gaelan to land behind him and kick him in the kidney.

He gasped for breath while he waited for the pain to dissipate. Behind him, Gaelan scrambled to his feet.

As Fisher's breathing evened out, he became aware of voices around them. He opened his eyes to see they'd landed in a large laundry, right next to a long conveyor belt.

"Don't move." A voice hissed and cold metal pressed against his neck.

He stopped breathing and his heart thudded unevenly in his chest before he took another breath.

Slowly he moved his eyes and looked towards the voice. It was a boy, barely five feet tall, shrouded in a too big flak jacket and hard-cased face helmet. He looked to be in his teens, but there was nothing small or fragile about the knife he was holding. One slice and Fisher was dead.

The boy held it with confidence. It wasn't his only weapon, either. There were three in a band that ran diagonally across his chest, another in a holster at his hip and Fisher was sure there'd be others hidden at ankles and wrists, possible on the boy's back as well. His pale green eyes held the kind of knowledge only a seasoned fighter would have.

He glanced at the trio of soldiers behind the boy, noting their practiced attention. Gaelan was in front of them. Fisher raised his hands in surrender.

At least they were in the city, exactly where they'd intended to be. The rooms and corridors in this section of the city were painted a dull blue-gray. They were in the utilities and amenities quarter. Now all they had to do was find the princess and tell her how dangerous the Elixir was, although that might not be easy with the soldiers.

He slowly drew himself up to his full height even though he knew size wasn't always an indication of power.

The boy gestured with the knife. "Move." The knife gestured again, and they started moving through the laundry toward the exit.

He pushed it all aside to face the boy who was obviously in charge.

"I seek an audience with Princess Ardelle. Please tell her Fisher from the Lake of the Damned is here with intelligence."

The boy froze and narrowed his eyes. "Fisher!" he spat.

He gasped, recognition washing over him at that small show of temper. He grinned and bowed perfunctorily. "My apologies, Princess. I didn't recognize you with the helmet."

"What do you want, traitor? Tell me quickly before I kill you."

Ah. It was to be like that, then. He ignored the sense of betrayal and loss that rolled through him and lifted his chin to hide his shame. "I passed on information to Checa and Heath at the Pass of Nines and they suggested I should also share it with you as I was coming this way."

"Why do you have the Minstrel with you?" She turned to Gaelan. "Is he holding you by force?"

"Of course not."

She scowled at Fisher again. "I know about Barthes. It burned."

"You don't know about the Exiles."

Her scowl deepened. "Watch him," she said to the soldier beside her, then she sheathed her knife and looked into the middle distance. Her face went slack.

Fisher tensed. He'd heard what she could do but had never seen her do it. She looked unconscious, for all that she was still standing in the laundry with them. "There's a fire in the desert." Her voice had a dreamy quality that shivered down his spine. "It consumes everything in its path, even the rock below ground." Ardelle focused on him again. "How is it burning sandstone?"

"It's feeding off norrgel residue from the sacrifices the Exiles have made in recent years." He held his ground under her fierce stare but swallowed heavily. He knew Princess Ardelle saw things in the present, not the future or the past. The fire was still raging.

"Tell me what happened."

"Can you arrange for soldiers to search for survivors?"

"Survivors?" Ardelle's fist tightened around the hilt of her knife. "You didn't evacuate first?"

"We evacuated as many as we could," said Gaelan quietly. "Some doubled back, refusing to leave."

"Where are they?"

Gaelan moved as if to respond again but Fisher stepped forward. This was on him. "They didn't—" He shook his head. That sounded accusing, like it wasn't his fault. "The residue had seeped into the stone. I don't think anyone realized how flammable it is. I intended to destroy their cache so it couldn't be used but..."

He took a shuddering breath. "It was like liquid fire, bursting through the walls and floor, spraying molten rock everywhere, burning everything it touched. I don't know how far... Some will have survived. We need to look for them."

Ardelle glared at him. "Should I be worried about you setting Hawkesby on fire too?"

"No! Not unless you're stocking norrgel residue to be made into an elixir that you then try to convince people is good for healing."

Ardelle stilled. Not a twitch.

"No," gasped Fisher. "You can't."

"We've been approached," she said. "Tell me about this elixir."

"At first, it does everything they say it does. It reduces pain and swelling and speeds healing, but it's also highly addictive. The more the body has, the more it craves, and it builds up and they need more and then..." He swallowed against growing nausea.

"They get to a stage when they have too much and then it's just like being norrgel-struck. There's nothing left of them after that, except the usual norrgel residue."

"Wouldn't consuming the residue cause that immediately? The first time?"

"They mix it with other things to mitigate the effects. Fresh dead bodies for one." He looked at her sharply. "Have you had people go missing? Particularly people not likely to be missed?"

The silence stretched between them. Ardelle stepped back, her shoulders sagging. "That's why we're here. We thought there were only a few people—that's what was reported—but everyone we talk to tells us of someone else no one has reported."

It was on the tip of his tongue to offer to investigate for her, but a nudge from Gaelan stopped him. They could keep chipping away at the manufacturing, but they needed to find out who was providing the market. If they cut off the beast's head, they'd be able to rid themselves of the body. "Who has approached you?"

"Lord Zanderfeld, the Duke of the Lonely Isles. He has a potion he calls the Elixir that his healers have created to aid treatment of injuries and illnesses."

"The duke!" exclaimed Gaelan. "I thought it was the viscount pushing the Elixir." He glanced at Fisher. "Why would they say they're making it when it comes from Barthes? Could they have the recipe?"

"Ma Jeffries said she was the only one who had the complete recipe."

"She might have lied. We have to locate any Elixir production or storage plants and make sure we decapitate this beast." Gaelan strode toward the conveyor belt.

Fisher stared at the floor as they walked. He swallowed against his instinctive defense of his aunt as he remembered that she'd tried to kill him, and had probably tried to kill him when he was a child too. *She might have lied* somehow seemed a worse betrayal.

"How do we destroy this stuff when we find it?" Ardelle asked.

"Burn it," said Fisher. "Evacuate first."

"We have tens of thousands of people living here. I'm not burning it."

"If you find another way of destroying the Elixir, let us know," said Gaelan as he looked up at the belt carrying piles of linen.

The laundry was a series large high-ceilinged rooms with holes in the ceilings. Every now and then bundles of clothes would whoosh from a hole and drop onto one of the wide conveyor belts below to be sorted by workers on either side. Unerringly, the clothing landed on another conveyor belt and continued its journey toward cleanliness.

At one end of each belt was a large wheel laid flat on a stone pillar. A number of people, some of them children, gripped a handle at each of the spokes around the wheel to push it around.

From the bottom of the pillar, under the narrow boardwalk where the workers walked, was a system of levers and pulleys connected to the conveyor belt. With every circuit of the wheel, the belt moved about twenty feet.

The room was filled with steam. Some of it seeped and shot out around the conveyor belt, but there was a dense blanket of it sealing off part of the room. Fisher couldn't see what lay beyond, but knew wherever there was steam, there would be fire.

Everyone working in the laundries, even those he could see in other large rooms beyond this one, looked the same, for all they were different heights and builds. They wore blue-gray cotton trousers and tunics, and had a blue-gray scarf tied around their heads.

Everyone's head was tilted down at the same angle as they focused on their work. Apart from some of the uniforms looking slightly faded and worn, there were no distinguishing features. They still deserved saving.

Fisher ran to a conveyor belt and jumped on top, amidst cries of surprise. Someone pulled the clothes he landed on out from under his feet, nearly toppling him over. All around him people cried out, but the jumble of words was indiscernible. Those nearest to him reached for his legs, grasped at his trousers, but he pulled free and strode up the slope of the belt.

"Attention! There is an emergency and immediate evacuation is required." He kept walking along the conveyor belt as it traveled through the center of the laundry room, the upward slope getting steeper. About two-thirds along the length of the large room, shrouded in steam and the scent of caustic soda, a cry, louder than the others, made him pause.

"Get off the belt, you idiot!" Ardelle called as she rushed through the clouds of steam toward Fisher, like a ship emerging from fog. As she came closer, she dropped below him, her round face gleaming with sweat and terror.

The belt rose more steeply.

Fisher looked around but couldn't see anything through the thick whiteness. Beneath him, the belt moved steadily forward with regular little bumps. The air was hotter and thicker, and the steam denser.

Somewhere up ahead was the pop-pop-pop of bubbles bursting. The bumps under his feet became thumps and the belt jumped rhythmically. He widened his stance to maintain his balance and began to look for the best place to jump off. "Evacuate immediately."

Behind him, something large crashed to the ground, bounced, then another crash, all accompanied by a rise in screams and scurrying, more smaller crashes and cries of pain and panic, but Fisher's footing remained firm.

"Get him off!" Ardelle was frantic now, waving her arms and gesturing to other laundry workers as she disappeared beyond the thickening steam.

One of them rushed through the cloud and disappeared not far in front of him. The belt came to a sudden, jarring halt and he stumbled forward. There was a scream but it cut off as he stopped moving forward.

The panicked cries and running feet were a staccato counterpoint to the sudden cessation of the click-clack of the moving belts. He swayed, his body still wanting to move, but he forced a turn and take a few steps back the way he'd come. Below him a cacophony of voices flowed and ebbed, all of them frantic, some angry as well.

Fisher regained his balance. He looked uphill but could still see nothing through the thick billowing steam. Water dripped from his hair and trickled down his face and neck and into his shirt. When he peered over the edge of the belt, all he saw was bubbling, boiling water. He swayed, then steadied, staying perfectly still until he was sure he could turn around and walk back down.

The screams and scurrying behind him increased, quickly followed by the *whoosh, whoosh* he immediately recognized as Gaelan's wings. "*What* is he doing?" Shock snuffed his words as Gaelan's flight stirred the steam then blew it away.

Barely a dozen steps higher up, the conveyor belt stopped and curled under itself. Fisher judged the distance he'd already retreated and realized he had been about to fall off the edge directly into the boiling water below. He had no more time than that to catch his breath before Gaelan, huge and deep purple in the diffused light, swooped toward him and grabbed him around the waist.

Within seconds, the dragon lowered them to the floor, then dropped down beside them, changing back to his human form as he did. He dropped lightly to his feet and immediately turned his scowl to him. "Do you never think before you act? It's no wonder you need someone to protect you."

"Prot—! What?" Fisher stormed over to Gaelan, his fists indignantly jammed on his hips. "I don't need protection. I've been protecting myself for most of my life." He stopped, feeling the wrongness and unfairness of his claim. Gaelan had saved him countless times since he'd arrived in Linspar.

Gaelan stumbled back a few steps and tightness gripped Fisher's chest. He turned away and struggled to regain his equilibrium.

They still had a long way to go back to the Lonely Isles and he didn't want all of that time to be filled with resentful tension. Nor was he going to grovel and agree he needed protection. Most of the life-threatening things that had happened to him lately had happened because he was on this stupid quest to destroy the Elixir. Because of Gaelan.

Even as Fisher thought the words, he felt the unfairness of them. Parts of their quest had been instigated by Gaelan, but the Elixir and Barthes was all on him. His anger deflated.

For the first time since the dragon had brought them to the floor, Fisher looked around. Ardelle stood scowling, arms crossed defensively across her chest. Several others stood with her. Most of them looked scared. Around him the machinery that had been noisily clanging and spitting steam was still silent.

One section of the large room, where Gaelan had been before Fisher had jumped onto the conveyor belt, looked trashed. If he used his imagination, he could make out the shape of a dragon in flight in the debris. There'd be no work done in the laundry until that was cleared and repaired.

Fisher cleared his throat, not certain if he should offer to help them clean it up. From the increasingly angry scowls directed at him, perhaps not.

"You need to evacuate until the Elixir can be destroyed."

Ardelle moved to stand in front him. "I think you've caused enough chaos in Hawkesby. I will take whatever steps I deem necessary to ensure the safety of my people. One of those steps is that you and the *dragon*," she glared at Gaelan, "will be escorted from the city."

She turned to Gaelan. "It would have been courteous to announce yourself in the city, my lord, particularly as it seems you've been deceiving us for a number of years."

Gaelan inclined his head. "I will remember that for the next time, Highness." He made no other excuses or apologies.

Fisher was sure that if Ardelle had been a dragon, smoke would be streaming from her nostrils. He smiled at the thought of her breathing fire whenever someone angered her.

"Dawn, my dragon, has expressed an interest in speaking with you," she said to Gaelan after a steamed pause. Without giving any further information or waiting for a response, she gestured to three of her soldiers then strode from the room, her remaining soldiers trailing after her.

As she left, another soldier entered, followed by a motley group of men and women, all carrying tool boxes and ropes.

The soldiers left with them ushered them from the laundry and along the corridors until they reached the southern entrance to the city. One by one, they climbed the ladder to the opened trapdoors above. Once they were above ground again and a water skin dropped beside them, the soldiers retreated, the trapdoors were closed, and they were left alone and unprotected in the dying light.

A soft breeze drifted over them, making Fisher shiver. For the first time since they went underground, he remembered his injuries. He glanced at his burned arms. The blisters had burst and the burned skin was thick and beginning to flake.

"There's nothing more we can do here," said Gaelan.

Fisher humphed. "I don't know. I think there's still more of this city we could destroy." Hysterical laughter caught in his throat and he swallowed it back. If he gave into it, he'd probably laugh until he cried. "We didn't even find the duke. He's already left to return to Linspar." There'd be no "conquering hero" return for him: he hadn't achieved anything.

He checked the position of the sun then began walking south. "All we've managed to accomplish is to destroy two major communities and damage another. Not much of a quest." At least Ardelle took him seriously, even if she still thought him a traitor.

All was silent for half an hour.

"We could fly?" Gaelan kept pace with him.

"You can fly if you want." What he needed was to find a source of water to replenish what they'd drunk, and somewhere safe to spend the night. He didn't slow his pace.

"We could be home in an hour."

Fisher scowled. He didn't have a home but an hour flying with Gaelan seemed much more appealing than another night spent freezing in the desert—no matter how green they kept this section of it—followed by a day avoiding norrgel and sunstroke in even measure.

He shuddered at the memories of the first time he became a dragon. The burning so hot it felt icy cold. The pain so deep he couldn't feel it. He wasn't doing that again.

He walked another ten paces, watching the horizon shimmer in the distance, and imagined how long it would take him to walk to Grewin and then find the barge to Linspar.

Could Gaelan really accept him, knowing he was responsible for so many deaths? It hadn't seemed to be a problem so far, but he was sure Gaelan didn't fully understand all he'd done in the past. He didn't know how ruthless he could be. Fisher thought back to the way Gaelan's trust in his ability to do what was necessary, and wondered if Gaelan knew him afterall.

"Fine. You fly. I'll ride." He glared at Gaelan and narrowed his eyes when Gaelan's only response was a happy grin.

CHAPTER TWENTY-SEVEN

THEY LANDED NEAR THE pond in the cemetery with blue-tinged starlight glinting off the water and making mysterious shadows of the headstones. Fisher slid down to the ground. By the time he'd taken two steps away, Gaelan was human again and the blue glow was gone from the air.

"It's strange being back here," said Fisher quietly. The peacefulness of the pond jarred him. He stared at the glinting water, wondering how many people had surfaced there and never breathed again. "I hope Mistress Cray has made sure it never happens again."

Gaelan wrapped his fingers around Fisher's arm and led him toward the temple. They entered the empty gardens and wound their way between the vegetables and shrubs. The garden was empty, all the tools put away and the monks secure indoors.

When they reached the small side door, Fisher tried the handle but the door was barred from the inside. He placed a hand on the wall beside it and closed his eyes. Part of him wanted to reject what he could do, but he couldn't.

For whatever purpose, Fisher could read granite, could move through it.

"Can you get us through?" asked Gaelan.

Fisher nodded. "It's all granite as far as I can tell." His heart beat faster at the thought of getting caught in the stone again. Butting up against the sandstone lining had been more terrifying than anything else that had happened to him, including being engulfed in flames and tumbling off the mountain.

"Hold on tight." Once Gaelan's arms were securely around him and his face pressed against Fisher's hair, he stepped forward.

The rock washed over him like the ocean. Cool, rhythmic waves flowed and ebbed around him but like the current and pushed him inexorably forward, through the wall. Within seconds, he burst through, stumbling forward and gasping in air that didn't feel icy and thick.

In his ear, Gaelan sucked in a trembling breath then released a loud sigh as if savoring the fresh air in his lungs.

Fisher scowled at him. "The wall wasn't that thick. We were barely in there before we were out again. Nothing at all like the mountain." His face heated as he remembered what they had done while they were inside the mountain.

Gaelan grinned at him, his features relaxing. "Let's find Aunty Cray."

They walked down the corridor they'd arrived in. He gazed at Gaelan as he strode confidently along, his hand once again looped around Fisher's elbow. It was becoming oddly comfortable.

The castle was disturbingly easy to access. They found Mistress Cray in the throne room. Instead of thrones, there were padded, upright chairs around a large oval table. There were several groupings of chairs and low tables and along the wall, and two rows of less comfortable-looking seats between them and the door. Marks in the deep red carpet suggested the current furniture and arrangement was new.

Both fireplaces were lit but the flames were low; more for comfort than heat.

As they walked through the open doorway, Mistress Cray leaped to her feet. "There you are. After the tales the duke told, I wondered if you were still alive."

She grasped Gaelan's free hand in both of hers, then turned to Fisher. Her head did a quick back and forth between them and her grin widened. "That's marvelous. Congratulations." She reached out and touched each of their shoulders.

"No, you don't understand," said Fisher.

"Of course I do, dear." She patted his cheek. "You'll do arright."

That one mispronunciation quieted him. Mistress Cray had seemed like a completely different person without her country accent. With it, he thought he could trust her with anything.

"You seem to have accomplished a lot since we left you, Aunty Cray," said Gaelan. He slid his hand from Fisher's elbow and ran it through Fisher's hair and down his neck before he moved away. Fisher shivered and leaned into the touch so far that he stumbled.

Gaelan and Aunty Cray moved to one of the sitting areas, so he followed them.

"I have my people working on a financial audit. The viscount is under house arrest until that's completed.

"The duke returned last evening. I had him confined to his own quarters when he grabbed a sword from one of his guards and lunged at his son. The master healer is monitoring him, but he appears to be in the final stages of Elixir poisoning."

Gaelan's frown mirrored Fisher's thoughts on the duke. They'd travelled the length of the country looking for him, only to find he'd returned without them. Something was going and Fisher wanted to know what.

The master healer burst into the room, his face pale, eyes wide. "He... just like Brother Sand."

Mistress Cray rose smoothly and took the healer's hands. "Come and sit, master." She gestured to one of the guards who'd accompanied him. The man looked terrified and stood as far from the Healer as he could.

"Bring the master healer some wine. Then find someone to relieve you and the others who were with him at the time. Ask the sommelier for a small cask for you to share."

The guard regarded the healer solemnly then issued quiet orders to one of his men.

Once the healer was settled, Mistress Cray turned once again to Gaelan. "I've had the castle and temple searched and removed any Elixir we've found. I haven't destroyed it yet because I don't know the most effective way to do that and I can't dump it in the waterways."

"Burn it," said Fisher. "It's the only way to destroy it completely, but you can't do it on the island. Nothing will be left."

Mistress Cray frowned. "I'll find a barge to take it out to sea and dispose of it there."

"No one can be near the barge when the fire is lit. It explodes, and the oily flame will burn anything, even rock."

Mistress Cray scowled at him then turned to Gaelan for confirmation. Fisher bristled, but froze at the touch of Gaelan's fingers on his knee.

Gaelan patted his knee a couple of times as if to soothe his temper. "Fisher's right, Aunty Cray. We'll light the fire remotely and monitor the transfer of the Elixir. It's too dangerous to lose any to enterprising individuals."

"You've left me with a hell of a mess here, you know that?" Mistress Cray's scowl deepened. "Until a new leader can be elected, the duke and his son will remain here, and I have to stay and run the country while cleaning up the mess they've made of it.

"Do you have any idea how bad their finances are?" She didn't wait for a response. "The bookkeeper told me I owe him six bottles of pearl wine for the speed with which he got the information to me. Six! I haven't seen pearl wine for a decade. Where am I going to find six bottles?"

Gaelan mumbled something. Fisher snapped a surprised look at him to find the ever-confident dragon god blushing. "What is it?"

Gaelan turned a beseeching gaze to him before addressing Aunty Cray. "When did you say you would give him the wine?"

"I didn't. I promised him I'd look for some and get him whatever I could find." Her shoulders slumped. "He did such a golden thing for me and I don't even know where to look to find the wine for him. Even one bottle would be good." She eyed Gaelan speculatively. "If I remember right, my last bottle of pearl wine came from you."

He jumped to his feet, dragging Fisher up with him. "We have to get back to the island because..." He looked at Fisher as if he expected him to come up with a reason to leave so precipitously. Fisher raised his eyebrows and crossed his arms. "Um..."

"Um?" repeated Fisher. He pursed his lips to stop his smile breaking out. A flustered Gaelan was damned funny, but what was he flustered about?

"What's going on?" asked Aunty Cray. "Is it the wine? Shouldn't I have promised Jonathan I'd find some for him? I'll explain to him I couldn't find any. He knows how hard it is to come by."

"No, don't do that," Gaelan blurted out as he sidled toward the door. "I'll see what I can do." Resignation wilted him.

Fisher tugged him to a stop. "I don't know what's got you so hot and bothered, but we haven't finished arranging the destruction of the Elixir." He turned to Aunty Cray. "I know how to set the barge alight without risking anyone."

Something in the pit of his stomach told him it was important to allow Gaelan whatever secret he was trying to keep from Mistress Cray. That didn't mean he had to let him know he had just volunteered Gaelan to go all dragon and burn the barge for them. "If you can arrange for the barge to be towed out to sea west of the island at sunset, I'll ensure it's destroyed. Make sure it's towed a long way from land and the tow-craft returns to land immediately."

Mistress Cray dragged her gaze between them. "It'll be there tomorrow evening. I'll let you know where it is at supper."

Fisher looked at Gaelan, who looked about two seconds from bursting into smoke and slithering away. He tugged on Gaelan's arm, snorting when Gaelan jumped as if he was still trying to think of a reason to leave. He didn't seem to realize they didn't need to give anyone a reason unless they wanted to.

"We won't be here for supper. Don't worry, we'll find the barge. Just make sure it's there and everyone is back on land by sunset." He looked at Gaelan, hoping he hadn't misinterpreted anything but accepting even if he had, he'd be doing exactly this right now. "We're going home."

That made Gaelan jump, stumble and spin to look at him. His eyes were bright and his glowing smile wide. "You're really coming with me?"

"You told me you belong to me now." Fisher ignored Mistress Cray's joyful gasp. "It's time you showed me where you live so I can take the proper time to explain exactly what that means."

As they walked toward the door, Gaelan turned back to a stunned Mistress Cray. "Send a message to the village when the barge is in place and everyone's away."

They were through the door and halfway down the corridor to the front door when Mistress Cray recovered. "Gaelan!"

They stepped outside. As the door closed behind them, Fisher heard, "What about the wine?"

CHAPTER TWENTY-EIGHT

THEY WALKED THROUGH deserted streets and down narrow alleys that smelled of sweaty bodies and rotten food until they reached a secluded mooring with a small rowboat attached.

"This is me," said Gaelan quietly.

"We're not flying?"

Gaelan ducked his head as if he was shy or embarrassed. Fisher turned to face him directly, amazed that a dragon god who'd faced danger without a blink would be embarrassed about anything.

"Well," said Gaelan as he rubbed a hand across the back of his neck, "you're the only person here who knows I'm a dragon." His gaze was heavy and serious. "Everyone thinks I'm a traveling minstrel who lives on the island between seasons. Except maybe Aunty Cray."

"*No one* knows you're a dragon? Only me... and Checa and Heath and their dragons and the princess... and all those people in the laundry?"

"No one here."

"I know how to keep a secret." Fisher smirked as he imagined how long that would last with half the mainland already knowing about it. "Of course, I do have a tendency to do things that make you go all dragon to try to save me. You might want to rethink having me around." The tightness in his stomach belied his teasing tone.

"I have a feeling there won't be many secrets around you at all. I'll learn to live with it." Gaelan grinned but his gaze was firmly on his island.

Fisher crawled into the small boat that bobbed gently on the dark water. Gaelan cast off and joined him in the boat.

He rowed strongly, dipping the oars almost silently into the water. The boat angled against the current for the first half but then he changed the way he rowed, and they drifted across the water to the village on Gaelan's island.

The small marina was deserted when they pulled the boat up to a dock and tied it off. They jumped from the boat to the short pontoon, mostly feeling their way in the hushed night.

Gaelan took his hand. "We'll walk around to the other side of the island. It's better to begin from here so fewer people will see us."

Fisher shook his head but began walking along the crushed-shell beach. It was close to pitch black, only the flickering candles in house windows and the stars lighting a pale phosphorescence in the small wavelets that chased the beach.

After a short time, Gaelan released his hand and veered into the trees, climbing over roots and rocks and clumps of sharp grasses with ease. Fisher stubbed his toes on the rocks and sliced his hands on the grasses, but he kept going, his mind at once numb with fatigue and spinning with tension.

He kept trudging along, placing one foot in front of the other, ignoring the pain from the multiple small injuries he received with every step.

They stopped in a grove of trees that appeared to have multiple trunks and roots that grew from branches down to the ground. Gaelan wove his way between the strange roots and trunks of the largest tree. Following him was now automatic.

At the center of the tree, Gaelan stopped. "The entrance is here." He pointed to a triangular blackness at the base of the shadowed trunk/roots combination.

Fisher squinted but couldn't see anything other than a dark hole. "Are there steps?"

"No, it's a slope down. Go in backward so you don't hit your head."

He considered insisting that Gaelan go in first since he knew the way, but he was too tired. All he wanted to do was lay down and sleep for a week.

He turned and shuffled back into the hole regardless of what insects or snakes might be down there. He grabbed a root in each hand to lower himself down, surprised that they felt smooth. Gaelan must come this way often or had been doing it for a long time.

He slid backward and continued to slide until Gaelan said, "You should be able to stand up now. Turn around and you'll see where to go."

He stood, surprised that the tunnel was so light and warm. As Gaelan slid down to land softly beside him, he turned and blinked at a sudden flare of light that originated from around the corner.

As he traversed the short hallway, he noticed that the lower end of the sloped ceiling was compacted dirt and root ends from the tree above. At the other end it became sparkling dark rock that he was certain was crystal-embedded granite.

Beyond that, a room opened up. The walls were curved and sparkling, but as smooth as any temple or castle he'd ever seen. The floors were dark, sooty gray and appeared to be made of oval-shaped tiles with a pattern that looked like round burst bubbles. Each bubble hole glowed a brilliant blue-purple in the torchlight.

Across the other side of the room, a comfortable looking leather sofa and a couple of matching seats were arranged in a U-shape in front of a large stone fireplace. It was high enough a man taller than him would easily be able to walk through it.

The fire was already lit and blazing. That explained the source of the warmth; he was becoming almost too warm. He'd never need a jacket or scarf here.

Fisher walked toward the fireplace, trying to work out what was strange about the fire. Halfway across the room, he gasped. There was no back to it. The fireplace opened directly into the center of the mountain and the flaring volcanic flames.

"The fireplace is marble," said Gaelan quietly behind him. "It links directly to the center of the mountain. The view from the lip of the volcano is beautiful, although when it's more active the smell of the sulfur can be too strong to enjoy it properly."

It was only when Gaelan mentioned the odor that Fisher became aware of it.

"The mountain tries to make me comfortable here," said Gaelan.

He hadn't moved from behind him and Fisher didn't turn, not wanting to break the sense of intimacy that had built in the last few minutes.

"The floors are pumice stone embedded with tanzanites and the walls are granite, like the rest of the mountain." Gaelan touched Fisher's shoulder as he moved past, his fingers trailing away in a caress. "If you get lost, or think you can't get out of somewhere, you'll always be able to go through the rock."

Was that Gaelan's way of telling him he could leave any time he wanted? What if he didn't want to leave? What if he decided here, with Gaelan, was where he wanted to stay?

Gaelan continued past him and ducked through a narrow archway. Fisher followed, curious how far the living quarters went into the mountain and what else was in them.

The archway acted like a kind of funnel into other rooms and spaces carved out of the mountain in what appeared to be a haphazard way. One wall was covered floor to ceiling in wine racks.

He wandered over and looked at one of the bottles. Pearl wine. So was the next bottle, and the next. Fisher turned back to Gaelan who shrugged and blushed. "I'll make sure Aunty Cray gets a few bottles for Jonathan."

A chuckle escaped him. "That's why you were so weird? Why didn't you just tell her you had the wine and could give it to her?"

"That's every bottle there is. Once that's gone, there might never be another batch made."

"Why not?"

Gaelan's cheeks flushed dark red. "Pearl wine is only made when a dragon god is born, from grapes grown in the land of Diatera. It's blessed by all the dragon gods. There's no other wine like it."

There'd be no dragon god children if Gaelan was mated to him. "Oh." His stomach felt squidgy, but he wasn't sure if it was the thought that he'd never be able to give Gaelan children or if it was because he could so easily imagine the two of them raising children. He dropped onto one of the low seats in the middle of the room.

"Many of these rooms were formed naturally over a number of eruptions," said Gaelan. "There are a couple around the other side that I built so I'd be able to monitor things on that side of the mountain. There are several exits, in case it grumbles and we need to get out quickly."

"Is the volcano going to erupt?" He darted frantic looks around, mentally mapping his way out again. "Is that why it's so hot?" Sweat pooled at the base of his throat and trickled down his back. Was it hotter now than before?

"It's an active volcano. There's always going to be another eruption." Gaelan moved closer, cupping his hands over Fisher's shoulders. "It usually gives us plenty of warning. I'll teach you how to read it."

"You talk like it's alive."

"It might not be actively conscious like you and me, but it does have a pattern of behavior if you know how to read it. It takes a while to understand, but we have time."

"Do we?" That was what he really wanted to know. "How much time?"

Gaelan lifted his head. "It's quiet now. There's no danger. It's been like this for a few hundred years and hasn't shown any sign of significant change. I don't expect that to change soon. Your friend Ardelle will probably be able to give you a more accurate answer."

"She's not my friend. She threw us out of Hawkesby."

"She could have had you executed. I think that makes her at least a potential friend."

"That was probably because of you. After you went all dragon in her laundry, she probably just wanted us out of there."

"I might be a dragon god, but I'm not omnipotent. She's smart enough to know that, especially since she has a dragon of her own." Gaelan raised gleeful eyebrows as if anticipating an argument.

Arguing wouldn't change anything. Princess Ardelle would have executed him if he'd been alone. It was only Gaelan's presence that gave them the escape they needed. He couldn't even build any frustration at that fact. He should be grateful that Gaelan had been there and he was still alive.

"Come," said Gaelan. "I'll show you where we'll sleep."

He led Fisher into a large room on the other side of the corridor. The fireplace was rough-hewn granite, but still opened to the center of the volcano. Pink light glittered over the large round bed in the middle.

"Are you absolutely sure you want this, even knowing what I've done?"

Gaelan clasped his shoulders again. "I want you to listen carefully. I've explained this before, but I don't think you fully understand. You're my Concubine. You know now that a concubine isn't a whore; that's it's the chosen of royalty.

"Whatever you've done in the past is in the past. It's the person you've become that is the only person for me. You're my chosen. My mate. I'm the Dragon God and I will only ever have one Concubine. That's you. You're mine to protect and to cherish, mine to hold and to love.

"If you leave the mountain, I'll come with you. If you tell me you want to be alone, I'll stay nearby and make sure you're safe. If you tell me to go away and you never want to see me again..." Gaelan took a shuddering breath, "I'll respect your wishes and wait, watching for your return."

There was something wrong with Fisher's breathing. His chest was tight. "But I've killed people."

"I know. You did what you needed to do to survive, but you always tried to protect those who couldn't protect themselves. You gave the Exiles warning and time to evacuate."

"Not in Barthes."

"You didn't know the Elixir would burn like that."

"Before then."

"You were an Exile. Only the strong and ruthless survive there. You managed to not only survive but thrive while still maintaining your compassion." Gaelan drew him close so he could rest his head on his shoulder. "You aren't a ruthless killer, cutting down anyone who gets in your way. You protect those you love."

"You don't mind what I've done in the past and you want me to stay because I'm your Concubine." Everything Gaelan had said sounded wonderful, but Fisher couldn't forget it was only because he was some fated Concubine. It didn't mean Gaelan loved him for him.

"Yes."

Fisher deflated. This was more than he'd ever thought possible before. He didn't know why he wanted more.

"By the Blue Goddess," Gaelan said. "I love you."

Fisher gasped, still not quite able to believe it. Gaelan really loved him?

He looked around the room, finally locating the source of the pink glow. The walls here were granite, as were all the others, but they were heavily grained with rose quartz. It was romantic—a love den. And Gaelan wanted him there. It was time he stopped fighting it and started grabbing everything he wanted: Gaelan.

"Fisher?"

He grinned at the sudden uncertainty in Gaelan's voice.

"You've got five seconds to get naked and on that bed, husband, or you'll discover exactly what it's like to submit to your Concubine."

At Gaelan's silence Fisher turned to him. Gaelan stood, stunned, his hands on the buttons of his shirt. "I can't decide which I want more."

Fisher pointed to the bed. "Naked now."

And Gaelan was. His clothes disappeared in a flash and he dived onto the bed, twisting so he was on his back with his legs spread invitingly. "Take me, Concubine. I'm yours."

Always and forever.

Don't miss out!

Visit the website below and you can sign up to receive emails whenever E E Montgomery publishes a new book. There's no charge and no obligation.

https://books2read.com/r/B-A-ZBFJ-CFUBB

BOOKS 2 READ

Connecting independent readers to independent writers.